PRAISE FOR

WAR AND SPEECH

"Outrageous and uproariously funny."
—*Kirkus Reviews*

"The quick pace and hilarious dialogue will help
readers race to the end.... This book is the perfect
combination of *Bring It On* and *Mean Girls.*"
—*School Library Connection*

"Zolidis writes with humor and heart...and [with a]
flair for creating multifaceted characters with depth,
especially the bad guys."
—*Publishers Weekly*

BY DON ZOLIDIS

The Seven Torments of Amy and Craig (A Love Story)

War and Speech

WAR
AND
SPEECH

DON ZOLIDIS

LITTLE, BROWN AND COMPANY

New York   Boston

Copyright © 2020 by Don Zolidis
Excerpt from *The Seven Torments of Amy and Craig (A Love Story)* copyright © 2018 by Don Zolidis

Cover art copyright © by Jeff Östberg
Cover design by Tyler Nevins
Cover copyright © 2020 by Hachette Book Group, Inc.

Little, Brown and Company
Hachette Book Group
1290 Avenue of the Americas, New York, NY 10104
Visit us at LBYR.com

Originally published in hardcover and ebook by Hyperion, an imprint of Disney Book Group, in May 2020
First Trade Paperback Edition: April 2021

Little, Brown and Company is a division of Hachette Book Group, Inc.
The Little, Brown name and logo are trademarks of Hachette Book Group, Inc.

The publisher is not responsible for websites (or their content) that are not owned by the publisher.

The Library of Congress has cataloged the hardcover edition as follows:
Names: Zolidis, Don, author.
Title: War and speech / by Don Zolidis.
Description: First edition. | Los Angeles ; New York : Hyperion, 2020. | Audience: Ages 14–18. | Summary: Sydney is determined to sabotage the elitist speech team at her new school until she starts falling for the team's star member and sees she has a chance of shedding her "loser" status.
Identifiers: LCCN 2019054455 | ISBN 9781368010078 (hardcover)
Subjects: CYAC: Forensics (Public speaking)—Fiction. | High schools—Fiction. | Schools—Fiction. | Popularity—Fiction. | Prisoner's families—Fiction. | Moving, Household—Fiction.
Classification: LCC PZ7.1.Z65 War 2020 | DDC [Fic]
LC record available at https://lccn.loc.gov/2019054455

ISBNs: 978-0-7595-5617-1 (pbk.), 978-1-368-01481-6 (ebook)

Printed in the United States of America

LSC-C

PRINTING 1, 2021

For all the Speech and Debate kids

CHAPTER ONE

Eaganville

History had already started by the time I arrived.

I crept into the classroom, trying not to interrupt. It was a small class; Eaganville School for the Arts promised a student-to-teacher ratio that would be the envy of any high school in Minnesota. I scanned the room, looking for a friendly face. The faces that stared back at me were unlike anything at my previous school. I was in a room of *artists*. As one, their artistic heads swiveled to look at me. I was keenly aware that my clothes were from Target, my hair was only two colors, and I hadn't even pierced my septum. I felt like an untattooed, unpierced freak.

I mumbled a *sorry* and shuffled my boring sneakers to an open desk at the back of the room.

Eaganville was not a normal school in any sense of the word. First of all, it was housed in an old nunnery. Most of the classrooms were underground, and the corridors connecting them were a maze of twisting passages and narrow dead ends. Nothing made sense, nothing went in a straight line, and if you listened hard enough, you could hear the ghosts of dead nuns wandering the halls, searching in vain for a bathroom. Not only that, but the rooms didn't have numbers. They were named after famous artists. History was in the Klimt room, which had taken me twenty minutes to find. It was basically Hogwarts for bullshit.

"Take a seat, please," said the teacher, a sprightly sixty-year-old woman with short iron-gray hair. She wore a blazer and yoga pants and had about seven silvery bracelets on each wrist. She was probably big into astrology.

"My name is Ms. Banks," she said. "Or Miss B. Or Teach. I do not answer to 'Hey, Lady.'" The room buzzed with a little light laughter. Apparently, Miss B. was the shit. "You must be Sydney."

"That's what it says on my witness protection form," I said. Nobody laughed. Some people eyed me quizzically. "That was a joke. I make, um . . . jokes sometimes, you know, when I'm late."

"Ah," said Ms. Banks.

"No filter," I added.

"We get it."

It's astonishing how quickly you can become a social outcast in a new school. I seemed to have managed it in under thirty seconds. Cool, cool.

She put a foot on one of the empty desks at the front of the room and stretched like a lioness. "All right, let's get back into it. And remember, folks," she said, pointing to a large poster of Napoleon looking like a tiny badass in a very large hat, "history is written by the winners."

Huh. I guess I wouldn't be writing any history, then. I mentally crossed that off my career goals.

The closest I'd ever come to winning anything was the school geography bee in seventh grade. The final question had been "What controversial crop is a major export of Virginia?" and I'd strode confidently to the microphone, looked out at my parents, gave them a thumbs-up, and said, "Meth."

Real answer: tobacco. Sorry, Virginia. I didn't mean to do you like that.

Then there was the time in the championship soccer game in ninth grade when I managed to score two goals—against my own team. One goal, sure, that's a mistake. Anyone can do that. But two goals was an incredible accomplishment. I really should've won the MVP of the other team. In my defense, I was extremely horrible at passing the ball to our goalie, and no one should have let me have the ball. It was probably their fault, really.

My family were losers, too. But that's a whole different story.

"Why shouldn't the winners write history?" said a tiny blond girl wearing a gray shirt that said PEACE AND LOVE in chalky lettering. "Who else is going to write it? The losers?" The rest of the class chuckled in assent.

Ms. Banks tried to quell the uprising. "Well, Taryn, I can see why you would say that, but—"

Taryn cut her off. "If it had been a good idea, it would've won, right? And then we'd be learning about that. So, obviously, the winning idea was the best idea. Why is this controversial?"

"Maybe the other idea just wasn't sure of itself," I said, running my mouth.

Taryn turned to look at me. She had a pixie cut with pink highlights and the icy-blue eyes of a wolf. A hush fell over the rest of the class like I had just poked the mother of all bears.

"And if people would've just given it a second chance, it could've proved itself, but as soon as it made one mistake over and over again it was trashed by a whole bunch of judgmental people. And then it had to leave its previous environment and go to a new school. Or something to that effect."

Taryn blinked. "That's literally the dumbest thing I've ever heard."

"Well, I'm just saying that there are multiple perspectives—"

"And some of those perspectives are stupid and wrong."

I felt my face get hot. "Maybe *that* perspective is stupid and wrong."

Ms. Banks took a step back. I could feel the eyes of the class zero in on me. Taryn took a deep breath and tucked the pink ends of her hair behind her ears. "So you're super in favor of the gold standard, then?"

"I'm in favor of what now?"

"The gold standard. What we're talking about."

I noticed that everyone had a book open on their desk. "Ohhhh."

Ms. Banks gingerly lifted a syllabus and handed it to me. "This is actually a discussion about nineteenth-century monetary policy."

"Riiight," I said. "I withdraw my opinion, then. Carry on. Also does anyone have a copy of this book we're supposed to be reading?"

I kept my mouth shut for the rest of class, which was a personal record for me. I noticed pretty quickly that nobody disagreed with Taryn about ANYTHING—the gold standard, the moon landing, tectonic plates, anything. Not even the teacher. Taryn was out for blood. I decided not to make the class hate me any more and let her have at it.

"All right, hey, before we go," said Ms. Banks, right before class was over. "Any announcements for the week?"

I kept quiet. I felt it was best for me not to have announcements. Ever.

"Um . . . hey, I'm Lakshmi, if you don't remember," said a tall, brown-skinned girl with a long black ponytail. "We've got a really important basketball game coming up on Thursday, so we would really appreciate y'all cheering us on." She gave a slight thumbs-up as a current of amusement rippled through the class. "It would be really cool if we had like a big crowd showing a lot of school spirit just to like give us some moral support, 'cause we need it super bad."

A guy in the back of the room interrupted. "I'm sorry, are you inviting us to a sportsball game?" I took a closer look at him—he was deeply tan, had fluffy good hair, and wore a goddamn blazer with elbow patches.

"Not sportsball—I don't actually know what sportsball is—this is basketball."

"So you throw a round object through a hoop?"

Lakshmi blinked. "Yeah. That is a description of basketball, Milo."

Milo leaned back in his chair. "And you think this is a worthwhile use of your time? I mean, you're inviting us to this—don't you think this culture puts too much emphasis on sports and not enough emphasis on things that actually matter?"

Lakshmi stammered a bit. I looked at Ms. Banks, who was trying to ignore all of it.

Milo kept going. "Are you aware that studies have shown that there's no link between athletic achievement and success in college?"

"I don't think that's true—"

"So you just don't believe in peer-reviewed studies, then? Is that it? I'm sorry, do you have a background as a social scientist? I guess I missed that part of our education here."

"I'm just inviting people to a basketball game—"

"Why are you changing the subject?"

"I'm not changing the subject."

"The subject is do you believe in peer-reviewed studies? Are you a believer in science?" Milo chopped his hand in front of him like he was slicing her down with a mental katana. "Clearly there is research out there. That research shows no link between athletics and academic achievement, and yet you would bury your head in the sand and have us all *celebrate* you. For what? For your ability to throw a round object through a hoop? Can anyone think of a more useless waste of our time?"

Lakshmi twitched a bit, biting her lip.

God, what an asshole.

Sixteen heads swiveled toward me. Oh, had those words come out of my mouth?

Why yes. Yes they had. See, there *was* a way to make the class hate me more.

CHAPTER TWO

The Losers

"Just so you know," said Taryn, approaching my desk after class, her "Peace and Love" shirt shimmering malevolently, "if you have an opinion about something, you'd better be ready to defend it."

"Sorry I was just talking—"

"Right. You were *just* talking. Sounds were just coming out of your mouth with no connection to thoughts. I understand." She smiled sweetly. "But in this school, you'd better be ready to back it up. That's what we're about here."

People are not taking shit about the gold standard at Eaganville. Noted.

"Thanks for the pro tip," I said.

"Anytime."

"Hey, do you happen to know where the Arbus room is, 'cause that's where my math class is. I don't even know what time period Arbus is from."

"This is why they invented Google. To help people who don't know things." She tossed her head with the slightest twirl of her pink hair and headed out.

The Arbus room was located with the other photographers (who knew? I did, after I googled her), which only took me fifteen minutes to find. The hallways were madness, weird people rushing about, following their muses, scrambling underground like rats in tunnels. Luckily, after the bell "rang" (another piece of classical music that I didn't recognize, but I heard someone say, "Mahler! Good choice!") things were a lot emptier, so I was able to get lost in peace.

Wandering the halls gave me time to breathe. My old school, my old life, was gone. I absently checked my phone to see if any of my friends had messaged me. Nope. I couldn't really blame them after what went down, but it still stung. I was alone.

I passed by the guidance counselor's office, which was decorated with the pennants from the colleges and universities kids had been accepted to. It was a who's who of the best places in the country: Michigan, Northwestern, Boston College, Yale.

Earlier in the year I had been thinking I'd be putting up one of those pennants myself. Now? Probably not. When you fail half your classes the first semester of your junior year, your college dreams take a big hit. But that was probably the least of my worries.

Eaganville was small enough that everyone had the same lunch period. The cafeteria at least had been renovated since the days of the convent and had gleaming new tile and track lighting. That didn't seem to help the food, which was the same prison-caliber mush that I'd had at my last school. The sad little turkey-and-cheese sandwich I'd packed didn't seem so bad all of a sudden.

I held my sack lunch in front of me and scanned the boisterous, chaotic room. The tables were octagonal, surrounded by plastic benches, and they all seemed filled with people chatting, laughing, and completely unaware of my existence. I was used to people segregating by obvious cliques—the jocks, the preps, the band geeks—but the categories here were completely foreign.

People with piercings and blazers? Check.

Art students with partially shaved heads? Check, check, and check (there were three tables of these people).

People wearing ties? Why the hell not?

New Girl sits alone in the back, I guess.

"Hey bat girl!"

I guess there are worse nicknames. It was Lakshmi from first period, hustling over to collect me.

"Sydney, actually," I said.

"I just wanted you to know that was awesome this morning. You lit that motherfucker up. That was some badass shit."

I thought back to first period and didn't recall a nonstop stream of profanity coming out of this girl, and yet here she was. And I didn't recall lighting anyone up, either, seeing as how my confusion about the gold standard was eviscerated in front of a cheering audience.

"Who are you talking about?"

"Milo."

"Oh. Thanks," I said. "Yeah that guy was a total asshat. I thought the class needed to know."

"I love it. You got a place to sit?"

"No. I was figuring on sitting alone like a total outcast, but then I looked around the room and, um . . . looks like all the outcast roles are taken, so . . ."

She laughed and wrapped a strong arm around my shoulder, pulling me toward the back of the room.

"You can sit with us. We are some badass motherfuckers and we totally appreciate your take-no-shit attitude."

At the table were two of the least badass motherfuckers I'd ever seen.

"This is Elijah," she said, pointing to a gangly redhead with the physique of a scarecrow. He was so skinny it looked like he didn't have room for internal organs and was simply a collection of elbows and knees strung together with fishing line.

"Hey," he said, shaking my hand like an adult and looking me directly in the eyes with a kind of supernatural confidence. He had piercing blue eyes, deep and rich like undersea jewels, but not like I was paying attention to them or anything—

"And I'm Thomas," said a slightly husky Black kid in a sweater vest. Thomas had short-cropped hair, serious glasses, and a clipped way of speaking that strongly suggested he was a genius.

"This is the girl I was telling you about," said Lakshmi, settling in. "Right to Milo's face. 'Who is this asshole?'!"

They beamed at me.

"I believe I said, 'God, what an asshole,'" I said, taking a quick bow.

Elijah laughed. "That is amazing. You are my new hero. I mean, just to be clear, Lakshmi is my hero, but you're like second."

"Thanks. That means a lot."

"I'm sure it does."

Thomas shook his head in appreciation. "Do you know who Milo is?"

My smile died a little bit. "Apparently not. I'm new."

"Milo is Speech and Debate. Varsity."

"Ooooh," I said, making a big whoop gesture with my hand.

Thomas blinked. "Seriously."

Lakshmi cut in. "Yeah, I mean, next time you're gonna want to keep your mouth shut, but today was spectacular. Like, I love what you did today, but you also just made a serious enemy who will probably destroy your entire life. Just an FYI."

"Speech and Debate?"

"Yeah." Lakshmi's eyes went wide. "They are hard-core here."

"Like a gang?"

"No, like an after-school activity."

"Oh."

Lakshmi leaned over the table. "You're new, so you probably

got a pass today. But Eaganville has the number one Speech and Debate team in the country. They run the show, all right? They're like . . . worshipped. Taryn, that girl today?"

"Also Speech and Debate?"

"Yup. Even the teachers don't fuck with them. They're awesome."

Elijah put his hands up. "They're not that awesome. I was on the team."

"He was kicked off," said Thomas.

"I was not kicked off, I quit—"

"After they said, 'You're kicked off.' "

"Were you there? Were you in the tribunal? No."

"They have tribunals?" I said.

"The whole culture is fucked up," said Elijah. "I am a better person now. I am healthier; I'm able to actually sleep at night so that's a bonus. I'm living a normal life."

"Debatable," said Thomas.

"Anyway," said Lakshmi, with fiery glee in her brown eyes, "if you want to work out your rage, you should totally come out for the basketball team. We could use someone with raw, naked aggression and no fear of consequences."

"I would do that, but, um . . . I really suck on account of the fact that I'm the least coordinated person ever."

Lakshmi twisted her long black hair into a bun, and I noticed that she had actual muscles. "Don't even worry about it. You would fit right in. Sadly. You should see these bitches. They're like journaling during the games. The whole team is a disaster. No one gives a shit about sports at this school."

"You're making a really strong case for the basketball team right now," said Elijah.

"I'm just being real with her. It is a flaming shitstorm and you should definitely join."

"Or, barring that," cut in Elijah, "I do improv comedy, so . . ."

"Oh my God," said Thomas. "She's not doing improv."

"Anyone can do improv! *You* could do improv if you wanted. You wouldn't be very good, but you could still do it." Elijah turned to me. "Thomas is a theater snob. He doesn't actually perform in the shows, but he's an aficionado."

"I *choose* not to perform in the shows."

"Stage fright."

Thomas took off his glasses and rubbed his eyes. "It's not— Hmm. There are myriad reasons why one wouldn't want to be onstage—"

"I can't think of any."

"Besides, my talents are best used behind the scenes."

"Crying in the wings."

"Would you stop?"

"Sorry, guys," I said. "I don't have any talent, actually. That's not entirely true, I guess. I'm really good at being a loser. So, are there any activities here for losers?"

Thomas looked at his friends. "Improv comedy, theater, and basketball come to mind."

I laughed.

"We're all losers here," said Elijah.

"If you don't have any special talent," said Lakshmi, "why are you at a magnet school for the arts?"

"My mom and I moved into the district."

"There's a district?"

"There's like a small section of . . . um . . . apartments where this is the closest school and that's where you go if you don't have a car. I just ended up here; I didn't actually choose to be here."

Elijah whistled in surprise. "You're like the one normal kid in Xavier's school for mutants."

Thomas rolled his eyes powerfully. "Oh my God. First of all, there are other normal kids at Xavier's."

"Name five."

"Um, okay, no."

"You can't, then. You can't do it. My reference stands."

Lakshmi pulled me close to her. "Well, you're at a school for the arts now." She smiled wickedly. "Welcome to the Upside Down."

CHAPTER THREE

Tragic Home Life

The bus home was sparsely populated. Not a lot of kids took the bus from Eaganville; most drove their own cars, or stayed after school in one of the millions of after-school activities that didn't require sportsballs. It was early January, which was generally the worst time of the year in Minnesota. The sun sets at four in the afternoon, and when it is visible, it's like a pale, apologetic sun that's ashamed it's unable to melt the mounds of ice and snow.

I watched out the window as we passed through the over-developed McMansions on the western side of Minneapolis. My home, such as it was, was at the Crestview Arms, a crumbling apartment complex that had been grandfathered into the school district. Mom and I had landed here after my parents divorced and our life imploded.

And by imploded, I mean where one parent goes to prison and the other one declares bankruptcy. Next-level imploded.

We used to live in neighborhoods like that, I thought, passing the places that had hired people to take their Christmas decorations down. Of course, even when we were in the nice house, with actual things we owned, there were problems. But they seem small once you're forced to sell the car, sell the television, sell the jewelry, and hide the rest of the stuff in your cousin's basement so you don't have to declare it as an asset.

The bus stopped in front of the complex, a hive of eight three-story buildings that clustered together for warmth. I got out, pressed my little keycard to the gate that was designed either to keep people out or lock us in, and made my way through the snow to our apartment, keeping my chin down to my chest to brace against the cold.

My mom was already packing up our dinner when I walked through the front door. She was in the kitchenette area of the apartment, which was separated from the living room area by about nothing, really. It was all basically the same room. The carpet hadn't been cleaned from the previous tenants, so it was best to never look at it or contemplate what might have gone on here previously.

"How was your first day at the new school, sweetie?"

"Um . . . interesting, I guess." *Apparently I have made some mortal enemies, but no worries.*

Charlie, our bulldog, lumbered up to me, his giant tongue lolling sloppily out of the side of his cavernous mouth. I groaned under his weight as I picked him up, his stubby little legs pushing against me.

"Who's a good boy? Who's a good boy?! Charlie is! Yes he is!" Charlie's rubbery tongue washed my face with slobber.

Charlie was an illegal occupant of our apartment, since we didn't have the money to pay the pet deposit, which meant that I had to take him on very fast walks and occasionally pretend to enter different apartments with him if I spotted a Crestview employee.

"Does he need to go out?! Does Charlie need to go out?! Yes he does! Yes he does!" Charlie wiggled appreciatively as I went to get his sweater.

"Don't put him in the pink one," said Mom from the kitchen.

"I'm putting him in the pink one," I said, going to get the pink one.

"Luke's coming over later."

I stopped. "I'm putting him in the tutu, then."

I could sense my mom rolling her eyes from halfway across the room. "Sydney."

"Why are you trying to fit him into a conformist model of gender identity? Besides, we're all aware that you're the one responsible for his lack of testicles."

"Don't say testicles. It's gross. And he could've kept his testicles if he didn't hump the entire universe, which he did."

"Well...this is the glorious result, then. Behold him." I patted Charlie on the head. "Who doesn't have any testicles?! Charlie doesn't! No he doesn't! Charlie has no testicles!" Charlie vibrated with joy.

"Sydney. Please. Luke is coming over, and I don't want him to get confused about the dog's gender."

"Have you considered the fact that if your boyfriend is confused by your dog's gender, he might not be the guy for you?"

"Just do it."

"Fine." I scooped him up and headed for my closet-sized room. "I'll put him in the Wonder Woman outfit."

"We're going ice-skating tonight, remember."

I groaned.

Mom was having none of it. "Don't go all teenagery on me. You said you would come along."

"I hate ice-skating, and I don't really want to spend a romantic evening with you and Luke."

Luke had appeared like a malignant tumor sometime in October, after the divorce papers were fully signed. My mom decided to go on a health kick. She'd wake up each morning and go jogging—at first she tried to get me to go with, at which point I would moan, pull my hair over my face, and roll over like a majestic lion. (Seriously—have you been to a zoo? Those bastards sleep twenty hours a day and yet they also have time to be king of the jungle. #rolemodels)

Anyway, after the jogging didn't produce the intended results, my mom joined a CrossFit gym/cult, where she met Luke, lord of fitness.

"If you gave him a chance, you might like him," said my mom, following me into my tiny bedroom. "And I have tonight off and I want to spend some time with you."

"Why?"

"Because I love you and want to spend time with you. Jeez," she said, trying to smooth her auburn hair behind her ears. Her roots, which were a mixture of gray and brown, hadn't been done in two months, another result of our post-divorce collapse. "I know that things have been . . . crazy, and I thought it would be good for us to have some fun together, okay? With Luke. I know . . . he's sometimes very . . . *intense*, but can you please give him a chance?"

I put my head in my hands. "Yes, I will give him a chance, but I also want you to consider the possibility that he sucks. Will you do that? Objectively evaluate him and see if he sucks?"

"Fine," she said, wrapping me in a hug.

"Maybe we should come up with a rubric or something."

Luke looked like he had stepped out of a J.Crew catalog, except not quite as attractive. He stepped out of J.Crew's less attractive cousin's catalog. He was white, but he had spent most of his existence tanning, so his skin was best described as caramel, but not like tasty caramel, more like caramel that you find glued to the floor of a movie theater. His smile was a little messed up, he had one tooth that kind of jutted out, and there was something about his eyes that made you think he had been dropped on his head a lot.

The rest of Luke was muscle, and obviously, that's where his appeal lay. I get it. I'm not stupid. My mom was going through a midlife crisis. And here he was in all his snaggletoothed, tan, and meaty glory.

Even his knock was annoying. He rapped on our door too forcefully, as if to say, *Here I am, the gym biscuit of your dreams, blessed with an unfortunate amount of self-confidence.*

Mom had finished packing the dinner for our "picnic on ice," which sounded disturbingly romantic, and yet also extremely impractical.

"All right!" She tittered, opening the door for Luke.

"Hell yeah!" said Luke, embracing my mom and lifting her off the ground just to show off that he was good at lifting things. "We're gonna have trouble in this ice rink 'cause you're so hot you're gonna melt the ice." It was clear Luke had been practicing that on the car ride over.

"You remember Sydney," she said, gesturing in my direction.

"What's up, Syd?!" He put his hand up for a high five. "Don't leave me hanging."

I gave him a moderate five.

Charlie had his usual reaction to anyone coming over, which is to say that he lost his damn mind. He scrabbled over the faux hardwood floor, his little legs moving faster than his body could compensate for—he charged Luke, missed, and slid into the wall with a thump. He was not the most coordinated animal, but made up for it by being completely invulnerable. He shook off the collision and tried to jump on Luke's leg.

"All right, troops," said Luke, adjusting the Minnesota Wild jersey under his parka. "Let's rock and roll."

"Oh God," I muttered, not ready to rock or roll.

It's not that I didn't know how to skate. Obviously, I could skate. I grew up here, after all. I just didn't know how to skate *well*. And whenever I seemed to be getting better at it, I would backslide to the uncoordinated person I naturally was.

I remember the times when Dad would take me to the rink, and we'd manage a few circuits around the ice before stopping to warm up with hot cocoa. I always thought the best part of skating was when you weren't skating. My dad was a terrible skater, too, and we bonded over the fact that we always enjoyed stopping. There's a strange odor of frosty funk that permeates an ice rink—a combination of foot sweat barely masked by whatever deodorizer they've found, and the tears of a million bruised children that have hit the ice. It was basically a frosty hell.

We went to the Edina Ice Rink, which was far enough away from Eaganville that it was still affordable. Luke paid for himself; my mom paid for both of us.

It was a Monday night, so it wasn't crowded. There was a slow circuit of mediocre skaters wobbling their way around the rink in a clockwise fashion—my people. A gang of ten-year-old boys in hockey jerseys was sprinting over the ice like madmen, weaving in and out of the old people, about to die at any moment. Luke's people. Every so often they would get too close to a slow-moving adult, and the adult would collapse in a heap of pain while the boys would race away like evil icy leprechauns.

Luke, of course, was good at skating.

"He's so coordinated," marveled Mom, getting on the ice and joining the slow-motion clockwise parade.

I teetered next to her, trying to keep moving in a straight line. My ankles hurt immediately, which meant that I hadn't tied my skates tight enough, but I gritted my teeth and kept going. I didn't want Luke to see me flailing and think it was his role to offer me advice.

Too late. Luke veered close to us, sliding to a halt and sending a spray of icy mist into the air. "This is great for the quads," he said, patting his rock-hard thighs. "Yeah, just push into it. You feel it, right?"

"Oh man, this is great," said my mom, working her quads.

My quads were less appreciative of being roused from their slumber. I felt like a scarecrow, scraping my skates against the ground and trying to gather a bit of momentum. I managed a bit of speed, realized I was shit at turning, and rammed into the sidewall. I caught my gloves on the wall, slipped, and dropped on my butt.

Luke hovered near me, lent me a hand, and nearly lifted me in the air to get me back on my feet.

"The key to turning is in the glutes," he said, rapping his knuckles on his ass.

"Good to know," I said, resuming my awkward, lonely turn around the rink.

Luke did a spin, then skated backward near me.

"Have you ever thought about working out?"

"Um . . . that's not really my thing."

"Uh-huh, I hear what you're saying, but also—you know, the best time to start a journey is today."

"What about tomorrow?"

"Definitely not tomorrow. You doing any sports in school?"

"Nope."

He nodded sadly, then did another spin before returning to me with a new thought.

"You know what's awesome for brain activity? Exercise."

"My brain's fine, thanks."

"With your frame, you might want to try swimming. I think there's a lot of toning that could happen with your arms—"

"I'm thinking about carrying ropes," I said, trying to remember all of the ridiculous CrossFit exercises that my mom was always going on about. "That way, I could flap them up and down if there was ever a need for it, which I'm sure there will be."

Luke pouted his lips, lost in what I guess you could call thought. Was I making fun of him? You could almost see my comment working through the flowchart that stood in for his brain. Ultimately it landed on "suggest workout options," which is where his brain flowchart always landed. "I mean . . . you can start with the triceps if you want, but I'm thinking like a full-body regimen would be best, though. Just do some sculpting."

"Uh-huh," I said. "I'm gonna pass on the sculpting for now, but thanks for your advice."

"Anytime. High five!"

"Nope."

He looked momentarily sad, then fist-bumped me before skating off. Damn it.

I launched my way back into the sad stream of poor skaters, waving my arms to keep my balance like a toddler. I managed to turn the corner this time, using a series of spastic foot movements to navigate the curve. Success. I was getting better at this.

Too late I spotted the two letter jackets from Edina High School.

Shit.

The ice rink was awfully close to my old high school. I recognized the girls: Emily and Chandler. I barely knew Emily, but Chandler had been in my math class—we had hung out a few times. We were sort-of friends until ninth grade or so and then started drifting apart. My father's spectacular implosion, which led to local newspaper headlines, had been enough to push me from being merely unpopular to being full-blown outcast. Part of that was my own fault, though; I stopped going to class,

I stopped talking to people, even the ones who might've been sympathetic.

"Oh my God, Sydney!"

Crap.

"Chandler! Heyyyyy!"

Emily, who was a weaker skater than Chandler, snorted slightly as she kept waggling her arms to keep skating around the ring.

"How are you?" Chandler was a Minnesotan blonde, of common Norwegian stock, slightly ruddy in the face, but with long straight hair that never needed an iron. She wore an aqua-blue headband over her ears and generally looked amazing with no effort whatsoever.

"I'm good."

"Good." She drifted nearer to me, unsure of what to say. "Where are you going to school now?"

"Eaganville."

Chandler's eyes went wide. "I hear that's a freak show."

"Yeah, it's a little weird."

"Cool. But probably like filled with supersmart people."

"I guess."

Emily wobbled slightly on her skates. "How long is your dad in prison for?"

Chandler elbowed her. "Don't ask her that."

"Why not?"

"It's rude. Jesus."

"All right fine whatever," said Emily, raising her eyebrows in annoyance.

"No, it's cool," I said. "Um . . . it's fine. Two more years, if you want to get super personal."

Chandler tried to nod. "Cool."

Cool?

I guess it's not every day you learn how long somebody's dad is in prison, so most people aren't good at forming a proper reaction.

She looked like she was about to say something else, but a ten-year-old in hockey gear blitzed in between us, ducking under my arm, then swerving past a few old people. Three other little maniacs followed him like a biker gang, spreading havoc and ruin.

"I should go," I said. "Lots of skating to do, I guess. You don't have to pretend to care about shit if you don't." I tried to skate away without looking back, but unfortunately I was too slow to get away quickly. I made a slow, ungainly exit, leaving both of them openmouthed and exasperated.

Later, when it was time for the skating to be over, I sat on a bench on the outside of the rink, shivering in my coat, eating some cold meat loaf. Mom and Luke were still skating around the ice, and I watched through the Plexiglas shield, following them and the people with happy families around the ice. We had been a happy family once. It was hard to imagine ever being that happy again.

CHAPTER FOUR

God Speaks in Horrible Ways

By midweek, I was getting slightly better at finding my way through the maze of passages under the school. Most classrooms at Eaganville were underground—the assembly areas and offices were aboveground, but academics were largely banished to the basement. The twisting hallways were flanked by red lockers, which cut down on available space, and during passing periods clots of seniors moved as slow as possible to jam traffic to a standstill.

I rounded a corner, hustling for second period, when I was forced to navigate around a clump of theater kids singing a song from *Little Shop of Horrors*. There was a lot of singing in the hallways.

The song died as I edged by, and I could feel their eyes on me, like I was some kind of rare and curious animal. I held the strap of my backpack tightly, hoping that I was beneath notice, but I couldn't shut my ears.

"Oh shit," one of them whispered.

"Did you see this?" another one said, cradling a phone.

"No wonder she's a nightmare."

The news had gotten out.

One day, you're just a regularly hated new kid who has a problem with the gold standard and calls people on their shit, and the next day you're infamous. So much for starting over.

In math, a girl named Peace, who had one half of her head shaved and the other half dyed jet black, leaned over to me. She had a nose ring, and I could practically already see the inevitable neck tattoo that would complete her look. She probably had a trust fund.

"I heard your dad is in prison," she whispered.

I stared at my desk, and my mouth curled into a forced smile. I could feel the blood thumping in my ears. This was what happened. It would become a source of curiosity for some, amusement for others.

"What did he do?" asked Peace, leaning in farther.

"He created an animal-human hybrid," I said. "Some people think he's demented, but I think he's a visionary."

I went back to my homework.

Lakshmi was pretty cool with it, actually. We had been insep-arable since the first day of school; apparently she didn't really get along with the other girls on the basketball team and was a bit of an outcast herself. In any other school, she would've been a minor celebrity. She was the best player on the team, known for inflicting maximum pain on the opposing teams, and held the school record for both scoring and technical fouls. ("They're not technically fouls," she said.) But at Eaganville, skill in sports apparently counted for less than nothing.

"It's cool if you don't want to talk about it," she said as we scrambled to English class.

"Thanks."

"I mean it's bullshit anyway—why are people googling people? What the hell."

I managed a smile. "I'd rather just stay a mystery."

"Exactly. Learn to deal with uncertainty, assholes." She shook her head. "But if it were me, I would use it as an asset."

"It's not an asset."

"All these people here think they are championing whatever cause or some shit—you've actually seen it. You've lived it. You're like from the projects."

"I'm from Edina. That's not the projects, that's like moderate-income white suburbs."

"I say you embrace this identity." She spotted a mousy freshman with purple hair and glasses looking down nervously as we passed. "What?" said Lakshmi, jerking toward the frightened girl. "What?"

The freshman said nothing.

"Her dad's in prison. He's like a mob boss. Don't even fucking look at her."

The freshman let out a little squeak of fear, grabbed her bag, and hurried away.

"Um . . . Lakshmi," I said. "Maybe that's not the best way to go about this?"

"It's better to stand out than to fit in," she said. "Walt Disney said that."

"He didn't say that. He said your dreams will come true or some shit."

"The dude can say more than one fucking thing," Lakshmi said.

The quote "It's better to stand out than to fit in" was actually written in faux graffiti script on the walls of our English classroom. It was as if highly literate vandals had broken into the high school and written inspirational things all over the place.

"See," I whispered to Lakshmi, "James Thurber."

Our teacher Mr. Papadakis sat on the edge of his desk and put one corduroy-sheathed leg over the other. "Friends," he said, smoothing his hands over the ribs of his pants, "I love the creativity I'm seeing in this class. It's stunning."

Everything about the English class was designed to spark our creativity. Not only were there graffiti-like inspirational quotes everywhere, but there were posters of famous writers, looking gloriously iconoclastic. James Baldwin. Virginia Woolf. Aristotle. Walt Whitman looking like he lived out of a trash can.

"All right, though," Mr. Papadakis said, shifting into a fake tone where he was now pretending to be the "tough guy." He was twenty-six and had a liberal arts education, so he wasn't exactly intimidating. "I'm noticing that we didn't do all that great on our personal narratives. What's up with that?"

Was that a question? Did he expect an answer?

Mr. Papadakis strolled around the class. His shirtsleeves were rolled up to reveal his "Dream every day" tattoos, which, for some reason, he had on both forearms. Like it wasn't enough to dream every day once, you had to dream every day twice. They were written in a rather flowery, feminine script, which undermined their value as a symbol of badassery. His curly manbun rested majestically on the exact apex of his skull.

His eyes landed on Thomas. "Thomas," he said, putting his hands together like he was praying. "You're so brave. So brave." Mr. Papadakis closed his eyes in awe of Thomas's bravery. "Would you like to share your personal essay with us?"

"Not really," said Thomas.

A couple of kids in the class snickered.

"I mean, you're the author," said a tall Asian boy with spiky hair. "Shouldn't you want to share?"

Thomas folded into himself as the boy kept going. "I mean, I for one would love to hear it. I'm assuming it's about me."

"It's not about you, Andrew."

"Well, that's a change, then." He snickered.

"I'll share mine," I said, trying to make eye contact with Thomas, but he was looking down at his desk.

Mr. Papadakis turned toward me.

"Sydney, I'm not sure how inspiring your essay is."

"It's totally inspiring. I've been through a lot of adversity."

He bit his lower lip and casually sauntered over to my desk. "This wasn't a humor assignment."

"My life is not funny, Mr. Papadakis. I'm almost offended that you just said that."

"In your personal narrative you said you were raised by centaurs."

A murmur of laughter passed through the rest of the class.

"And I think that's pretty damn inspiring," I said.

"Uh-huh."

"But I was actually a member of a battle clan. That's a little different than being raised by them."

"I mean, I love . . ." He stopped, trying to think of something to love about me. It took him a second. "The originality of your idea, but the point of this assignment is to explore your identity. To find out who you are."

"I know who I am."

Little snippets of conversation were floating around me now. The rest of the class were talking about me—some were snickering. The assignment had been to write about an important moment in your life, but I figured perhaps baring my scars during the first week of class wasn't the wisest idea. Besides, centaurs were awesome.

"I know who I am," I repeated.

"Do you?" He locked eyes with me, like he was so deep.

"I do."

"Do you really?"

"I do, really."

He nodded, biting the bottom of his lip again as if he was about to say *Namaste*. And look, I know this dude was doing yoga. You don't get "Dream every day" tattooed on both arms without being big into yoga.

Andrew raised his hand again. "Mr. Papadakis."

"Andrew I've got this situation under control . . ."

Andrew didn't seem to think so. "I don't think it's acceptable that some people can write fictional narratives. That wasn't the content of the assignment."

"Thanks Andrew but I've—"

"I think we have to have standards. This is a class about challenging truth, right? What is the truth?"

Mr. Papadakis sighed. Andrew kept going. "If we allow Sydney to flout the rules of the assignment, then what's to stop someone else from flouting those rules? What's the point in having a personal narrative if she's not going to talk about her father?"

A hum of electricity went through the class. I could hear kids whispering to each other—"What's the deal with her father?"

Mr. Papadakis turned to me again.

"Sydney . . . I know about your actual background."

I felt the world get a little fuzzy at the edges. The sound escaped from the room as the snickering stopped. I could sense my own breathing. Had there been a memo to the teachers or something? Were we going to do this in front of everyone?

"This is a safe space," he said, just above a whisper, as seventeen other humans stared at me. Thomas still had his head down, but Andrew was looking directly at me.

He put both hands on the edge of my desk and leaned in.

"Let it out," he said.

"Mr. Papadakis—"

"Call me Emmanuel."

"Emmanuel? Please, please go fuck yourself."

So that's how I ended up in ISS.

CHAPTER FIVE

ISS or Something Like It

After school, Lakshmi was ecstatic. I found her in the gym, which was less of a gym and more of a large, empty room with terrible acoustics and poor lighting.

"You shoulda gone Wonder Woman on his ass. He's like, 'This is a safe space' and you're like, 'Not anymore, motherfucker! Pow!'"

She dropped her basketball and demonstrated a few punches.

"I'm not sure I'm going to be punching anyone."

Violence had never really been my problem. My mouth, as always, was my problem. Despite Lakshmi's enthusiasm for my outburst, I felt sick. I had come to Eaganville to get a new start, and three days in I was already failing.

"All right, try and guard me." Lakshmi dribbled between her legs, collided into me, then burst past me for a layup on a net that hadn't been replaced in years.

"That was a foul," she said. "You fouled me."

She drained a free throw, then tossed me the ball.

"I really suck at basketball," I protested.

"Don't get down on yourself; let's see what you got."

"I epically suck. I am the worst person ever at basketball."

"You haven't seen our team. Come on. I'm sure we can use you."

I dribbled robotically with my right hand, then threw up a shot that missed the hoop and landed two rows into the wooden stands.

"Yeah, you suck," she said, retrieving it. "So, you got one day of ISS, that's it?"

"Yup."

"That's not so bad."

Lakshmi took the ball, shimmied to the side, and launched a three-pointer that swished through the net. "That was terrible defense, by the way. You gotta get up on me."

"If I get up on you, you just dribble past me."

"Yeah, 'cause I'm so much better than you. You're basically fucked. But that's cool. No judgments. I still think you could start for our team. Let me see your vertical."

"I have a negative vertical."

"That's literally impossible."

I hopped and Lakshmi nodded, puffing out her cheeks.

"I can work with that."

"Can you?"

"It's not about physical skills. It's about aggression and belief."

"I think my physical skills are more suited to standing and talking. Maybe I should try out for Speech and Debate," I joked.

Lakshmi recoiled. "Don't even say that. They're evil. They're seriously like a cult."

"I thought they were like a gang."

"They're a gang cult. You don't want to go anywhere near them."

"All right," I said, throwing up my hands. "I'm just good at talking. I think it's my main skill."

"Are you good at being an asshole? 'Cause that's why they win."

I shrugged my shoulders. "Kinda, yeah."

At my previous school, in-school suspension was basically an exercise in staring at a wall for an entire day. I had actually perfected the art of falling asleep with my eyes open, which was a necessary survival skill in an atmosphere designed to bore you into submission. At Eaganville, we had peer counseling, which was worse.

After lunch I was marched to a room adjacent to the vice principal's office. It wasn't the standard punishment zone I was anticipating; it was aboveground, and instead of traditional desks there were two comfy armchairs. There was an ancient, unused fireplace on one side of the room, and it seemed like the kind of place where we could wear smoking jackets with elbow patches and drink snifters of brandy. The carpet was from the Cretaceous Period and there were several wooden bookshelves that held books no one had ever read. I was sitting cross-legged on one of the plushy armchairs when Logan entered.

He was about five-five, and even though I was told he was a senior, he had managed to completely avoid puberty up till this point. He was wearing a button-down and khaki pants and had more hair than was reasonable. Not that it was long, it was just thick, like an inky forest of curly blackness. I was pretty sure he had lost a comb or two in there at some point. He walked in like he had just downed three cups of coffee and was still trying to burn off the excess energy. He even sat quickly.

"All right," he said, settling into the comfy chair opposite me. He put one ankle on his knee, then thought better of it, switched knees, then decided to put both feet on the ground. One of them tapped spastically, like there was some current of electricity running through him that couldn't be turned off.

"My name's Logan. I'm going to be your peer counselor today." He squinted impressively.

"Sweet," I said.

"How does that make you feel?"

I eyed him. "Have you ever done this before, Logan?"

He scratched his nose. "I have, actually. One of my great loves is analyzing people's problems. I'm really looking forward to diving into yours."

"That must be really fun for you."

"Oh, sure. It's fascinating. Before we start," he continued, ankle still twitching, "I want you to think of me as essentially the same as a priest or a lawyer or a therapist." He looked me in the eyes. Logan had greenish eyes the color of fuzzy mold on cheddar cheese. "Anything you say here I will keep in utmost confidence. I am awesome at keeping things secret." He nodded and wiggled his eyebrows just a little bit.

I looked at the clock. Logan had been talking at me for four minutes. Fifty-six more minutes left to go. I hoped that an orbiting satellite would crash through the roof and obliterate both of us. Him first. Maybe I'd survive. Then I thought it would be better if a laser from space incinerated him. I could probably leap clear of the blast radius.

"So, let's get started, shall we? So . . . English class . . ." He opened a folder on his lap and put both his thumbs under his chin. "Words can hurt, Sydney. Just as much as fists."

"Can they?" I said.

"Yes, they can."

"Are you sure? 'Cause I've never been punched with a word before."

His mouth crinkled up. "If you're not going to cooperate with this process, I can always recommend that you get more peer counseling. Maybe tomorrow or the next day."

I swallowed my next quip.

"I find that sometimes people use humor to shield themselves from pain. Ergo, your essay about centaurs." He said *ergo*. He literally said *ergo*.

"Can I tell you something, Logan?"

"Please."

"The centaur thing was completely true. I'm a child of two worlds: horse and human." He blinked. "I can translate between English and horse language, which is basically just a series of whinnies." I neighed softly.

"Why would centaurs speak horse language? They have horse backsides and human faces. That makes no sense."

"You don't know us; don't make judgments."

He snorted. "More humor. I see. Why do you have these walls up, Sydney? Let's break them down together."

"My walls are fine, thanks."

"Are they?"

"Yes."

"Really? In your heart, is that what you want?"

The point of peer counseling was dawning on me: torture. Inflict as much psychological pain as possible. I would never yell at a teacher again, not if this was what was waiting for me on the other side.

"Yes, Logan," I repeated. "In my heart I do not want you breaking down my walls. Or scaling them. Or tunneling under them. I want you the fuck away from my walls because my walls are equipped with machine guns. And they will blow your ass away if you try to knock them down."

His smile cracked a bit. An evil silence settled between us.

"Okay," he said, recovering. "Let's talk about what you want to talk about. Why did you feel the need to use expletives with Mr. Papadakis?"

I didn't say anything.

"Is everything all right at home?" He looked over his notes.

"What does it say in your little notebook?" I asked.

"Don't worry about my notebook."

"I mean it probably says why, doesn't it? That's what was going on in class."

"I see." He nodded, jotting something down. "You want to tell me about your father?"

"Nope."

"I touched a nerve, I guess."

"Not really. I just have no interest in discussing my father with you."

He reached out, and

HIS HAND TOUCHED MY KNEE.

I focused on him. On his pasty face, the black hair that spiked up in a thicket—the mold-green eyes. A tiny bead of sweat on his forehead. The air in the room was suffocating—how many countless children had been peer-counseled to death in this very room?

I looked down at the offending hand.

"It's going to be okay," he said.

"It is not going to be okay if you don't remove your damn hand," I said.

He twitched a bit, and the hand moved away from my knee.

"Okay, um . . . just remember that this is a safe space."

"That's my trigger word," I said. "When I hear that, I explode."

He shifted in his armchair. "Maybe let's take a different tactic. Studies have shown that an increase in engagement might help you assimilate. Have you thought about joining a club or team?"

"Sure."

"Excellent—"

"I was thinking about Speech and Debate."

He coughed and looked away.

"What?" I said.

He turned back to look at me. "I'm actually varsity on the debate team, so I found your comment amusing."

"Amusing? How so?"

"I was just tickled by it."

"You were *tickled* by it? My comment *tickled* you?"

Logan vibrated ever so slightly, as if he was about to crack into a million pieces and shatter in front of me. "I'm sorry." He smiled, trying to hold it together. "Well . . . um . . . you should know that Speech and Debate is a lot of work. You can't just *pick it up* in the middle of your junior year. It requires discipline."

I raised an eyebrow. You could almost feel the waves of

testosterone-laden arrogance wafting off of him. "The centaurs taught me a lot of discipline," I said.

"Can I be honest with you?" he said. "I don't really think you would do well in forensics."

"What's forensics?"

He sputtered. "Speech and Debate. Sometimes it's called forensics. They're interchangeable terms."

"Forensics, like crime scene investigation?"

"If you don't even know what the term is, how do you expect to join the team? I mean you can't—you obviously can't join the team, so I don't even know why I'm entertaining this thought experiment right now."

"Why not?"

"There's a seriousness to it—"

"I'm totally serious."

"Are you? Are you, really? I know that you're simply trying to provoke me right now, that's what this is. You're erratic and violent, not exactly the qualities we're looking for."

"I think that will probably help me."

He laughed. "Perhaps you're not aware of the level of quality of our team. We're the number-one-ranked team in the country. Number. One. You don't just walk onto a team like that."

I shrugged. "Maybe you need some new blood."

"Maybe we don't."

"That was hostile," I said.

"It wasn't hostile, it was a statement of fact."

"Stated in a hostile way. See, I'm debating you right now and I'm winning."

He kicked at the legs of his chair. "You're not even close to winning."

"I'm kicking your ass at this, actually. Are you sure you're a debater, 'cause I'm not all that impressed with you right now."

"I went to Nationals last year; perhaps you've heard of it."

I shrugged again. "If you got to Nationals, the competition must not have been that tough," I said, switching to full troll mode to see if I could make Logan spontaneously combust.

"It's *Nationals*," he sputtered. "It's the National Championship! How do you think you can join a speech team if you're not even clear on basic concepts?!"

"Listen," I said, deciding to go all in. "You don't need to mansplain debate to me, all right? I was *on* the Speech and Debate team at my last school," I lied. "I was basically the LeBron James of Speech and Debate at my last school. That was my nickname: LeBron Speech."

"Bullshit. How do you not even know it's called forensics, then?"

"'Cause I'm messing with you. I wanted to see if you would condescend to me, which you did, thank you very much."

He squinted his eyes, trying to see through my obvious lies. He was turning a healthy red color now. Little beads of sweat were forming under his hairline. "That doesn't make any sense."

"I've been debating you for like five minutes and I've already flattened you, so—"

"You haven't flattened me!"

"You're totally flustered, you're reevaluating your life choices, you don't even know who you are anymore."

"Well, you can't join our team!"

"Maybe I will. Maybe I'll be there Monday. Maybe I'll take over your spot."

Let me add here that I had zero intention of joining his awful team—I just wanted to see if I could force him into an aneurysm.

He gritted his teeth. "You won't win. You aren't good enough. Besides," he added, "attractive girls tend to do better."

That comment sat there for a second. I looked at him, and the words slipped out of my head. The way he said it was as a statement of fact, a cruel fact, like it was complete in its own truth and couldn't be challenged. The barest glint of a smile crept across his face—you could tell that he felt he won—he just out-assholed me.

"I'm not attractive enough for Speech and Debate?" I said, trying to regain my footing.

"You might have been hot shit on your last team; you just wouldn't do well on ours." He shrugged. "We have standards, and the hot girls do better. It's been proven. There have been studies. I can send you links if you want."

My face tingled. I could tell that red blotches were forming on my cheeks, making me even less pretty, but I held myself still.

But when I look back on it, that was the beginning of The Plan. It started with this thought:

I'm going to wreck you.

CHAPTER SIX

Basketball–Slam Poetry in Motion

I was still stewing and bubbling with rage when I arrived at the girls' basketball game that night. There had been a lot of prodding by Lakshmi, and I finally relented. Staying after school was difficult, since I took the bus every day and would either have to beg for a ride home, or walk through subzero temperatures back to the apartment complex. I wasn't looking forward to either option.

Eaganville had spent all of zero dollars renovating the gym, and the wood floor was pocked and rutted with ancient wounds. The lighting was poor and the acoustics were awful, but the nine people sitting on our side of the audience didn't seem to mind.

The old wooden bleachers creaked and groaned as I settled into an empty section. We were squaring off against the Burnsville Blaze, which was a quintessential suburban team destined to kick all of our asses. The girls were tall, mostly white, and had deeply impressive ponytails. The visiting section of the stands, across the court, was filling up with a collection of heavy-coated Minnesotans; they had even brought cheerleaders.

As you might imagine, we had no cheerleaders. I wasn't sure if we actually had a cheer team or not, but I was certain they wouldn't be caught dead cheering at a sports event. The jazz band had assembled behind one of the baskets and was really going at it, though.

I picked out Lakshmi's dad almost immediately. His black hair was shot through with silver, and his attire could best be described as "asset manager." He wore a button-down light blue oxford shirt and black slacks and was probably going to be forced to giving me a ride home. He had the dead-eyed look of a parent who's attended too many losing games of his children.

"Go Lakshmi!" I yelled, pumping my fist in the air as the team came out for layup drills.

Lakshmi was wearing gray leggings under her basketball shorts and had her black hair pulled back behind a headband. Her gaze was steely as she swooped toward the basket, laying in shot after shot. She didn't smile, she didn't even talk to her teammates much. She looked like a programmable robot that was ready to slaughter humanity. I felt scared for the other team.

Then I spotted Elijah. He was wearing the kind of long black coat that a lot of geeks wore—the kind that signaled he sort of imagined himself as the Batman, hunched over the edge of a tall building and looking for crime.

"Hey," he said, tromping over to me. He put his hands in his pockets and rocked back and forth on his toes, causing the entire bleacher to squeak like a tortured mouse.

"What's up?" I said.

"Just here to watch." He jerked his head toward Lakshmi as if I didn't know who he was referring to. "Rooting. I'm here to root. Woo."

"Cool."

"I love watching her compete."

"I didn't know you guys were a thing."

He smiled, showing off his perfectly straight teeth. "We're not . . . actually a thing. There have been moments where we have been close to being a thing, but the thingness never truly materialized."

"Oh. So is this like a stalker situation?"

"No no no, it's not like that. I am a just a big fan of Lakshmi."

"Right."

Elijah waved at Lakshmi. She didn't see him. He waved again, a little more conspicuously. She still didn't see him.

"She's focused," he said. "Like death itself. I love it."

I laughed. "Are you sure it's not a stalker situation?"

He hunched his shoulders and sat down next to me. "I am here as a sports fan, nothing more. Even though I know absolutely nothing about sports."

"I think you're not alone in that."

"I figure the best way to be a fan is just to cheer for

everything." The teams were huddling up. "Huddle! Wooo! YES! GO LADY KNIGHTS! WOO!"

A mom sitting two rows in front of us turned around to give him the stink-eye. Her hair was colored in streaks and she had expensive earrings and was clearly a horrible person.

"I don't think you're supposed to cheer them when they huddle," I said.

"I am cheering all the damn time," he said. "I'm here for continuous support. Like a sports bra."

Elijah's bra-like functions were about to be tested. Lakshmi started out as a power forward, and it was clear from the outset that she was the only good player on our team. Unfortunately, the other team was filled with good players.

"Run, damn it!" I shouted, well aware of the fact that I would be no better if I were on the court. "Do the sports! DO IT! DO THE SPORTS!"

This time the mom in front of us swiveled entirely in her seat and glared at us. "Could you please cheer appropriately?" she hissed.

Elijah bugged his eyes out. "I'm sorry our exuberance is causing you stress."

"It might help if you were less stuck up," I said, and Elijah snickered. He was growing on me. She turned away from us. "They have pills for that sort of thing if you're interested," I said to the back of her head.

Halfway through the first quarter we were already down ten points. Our players were a bumbling mess, turning the ball over constantly, missing shots, and generally finding it difficult to move in a coordinated fashion. Lakshmi tried her best, driving through the lane, throwing up shots at the basket, and occasionally scoring, but it was hopeless.

"GOOD TRY!" shouted Elijah, clapping encouragingly, after one of our players missed the entire basket. He looked over at me, his blue eyes meeting mine just a second too long.

You could see the vein throbbing in Lakshmi's neck from space as she tried to contain her rage. She collided with another player, stole the ball, and sprinted to the three-point line, launching a high arcing shot that swished sweetly through the net. She high-fived the rest of the team so hard that they came away wincing.

"WOO!" I shouted.

"YES!" screamed Elijah over me, waving and failing to get her attention once again. "THAT'S MY PERSON! I mean . . . THAT WAS A GOOD THING YOU DID! I AM PROUD OF YOU AND I SUPPORT YOUR ENDEAVORS IN ATHLETICS!"

"You can stop now," I said, yanking him down by his arm, laughing.

"Sometimes the best thing to do is to keep going, even when other people are embarrassed by you. One of the rules of improv comedy."

"Is that your life philosophy? Just keep going even if you're being embarrassing?"

"I mean, what is being embarrassed, anyway?" he said. "It doesn't really exist, does it? These people"—he gestured vaguely at the mom sitting in front of us—"does their opinion of me matter? Does it matter what the other cheerleaders think of me?"

"They think you're a freak?"

"So? How does that hurt me?"

"Huh."

I thought back to English class—he had a point. Elijah stuffed his hands under his legs and vibrated with energy, once again shaking the bleacher.

I looked over at Lakshmi's dad. His expression hadn't changed too much, but he was clapping solemnly for his daughter. He had his phone out and was taking some blurry shots of the action. I felt a twinge of pain, thinking of my dad. Lakshmi's father might not have been a fountain of enthusiasm, but at least he showed up.

By halftime, the game was basically lost. Lakshmi had scored twelve points, which was half of our team's total.

"She's just awesome," Elijah said, smiling. "She's basically like an elf maiden, you know? Like a Lord of the Rings elf maiden? Basically super tall and immortal and really strong in combat."

"That wasn't exactly the first thing I thought of, but sure."

"Definitely." He rocked back and forth on his seat.

"Have you like told her how you feel?"

He tilted his head like a dog. "How I feel?"

"Your huge crush on her? Like . . . directly told her? Made a clear attempt at communication?"

"You think I have a huge crush on her?"

"Um . . . yes?"

"I can't just be here as a friend for another friend?"

"No."

"Like what you're doing?"

I blinked, a little flustered. "That's different."

"Oh, I see." He nodded, flashing his brilliant smile again. "You think that just because I enthusiastically support my friend—"

"Like a sports bra—your words—"

"Like a friendly sports bra, that I have some deep and unrequited love for her?"

"Pretty much." I smiled.

"That's interesting," he said, raising one finger. "That is really interesting. So let me pitch a scenario to you."

"Please. Pitch away," I joked.

"We've got the Snow Ball on Saturday—"

"What's the Snow Ball?"

"We don't have Homecoming or Prom, so the school basically ripped off Harry Potter and created a winter dance instead. It's this Saturday. There's a big assembly tomorrow for it—where my improv comedy troupe is going to perform ... AND"—he leaned in conspiratorially—"I could make a snow-posal."

I groaned. "Wait, the dance is Saturday and you're asking her *tomorrow*?"

"Well, she's ... maybe it's a last-minute decision. Big gesture, right? Maybe I needed to gather my courage."

I put my face in my hands. "Every part of this is a mess."

"All right, sure. But I could still rent a limo—"

I put my hand on his shoulder. "Just tell her how you feel. In private. I mean, you could go with the elf maiden thing. It's really dorky, but at least it's honest."

He nodded. "Yeah. I see that."

Lakshmi's three-pointer was the high point of the game. The second half was a miserable slog. The Burnsville players double- and triple-teamed Lakshmi when she got the ball on offense, forcing her to pass the ball to wide-open players who missed their shots terribly. By the time it was over, the highlight was our jazz band, which had moved on to improvisation, including an extremely impressive three-minute solo by our drummer.

"NICE EFFORT!" shouted Elijah, mustering up the energy for one last enthusiastic cheer.

When the game was finished, the mom in front of us stood angrily and stuffed her phone into her purse. "You know," she said, "there are times to cheer and there are times not to cheer, okay? And I think it's disgraceful that people like you can come to a game and ruin it for everyone. You should be ashamed of yourselves."

"I'm never ashamed of myself," said Elijah, continuing to grow on me. "It's a medical condition."

"If it helps," I said, "I'm ashamed for him."

She said nothing and stomped off. Elijah turned to me.

"I feel like we just had our own victory."

Lakshmi was full of joy after the game.

"Son of a bitch," she growled, kicking the bleacher with her shoe.

Elijah was about to high-five her and thought better of it. "I thought you were spectacular. You were just doing the basketball out there. You were out-basketballing everybody."

Lakshmi huffed and removed her headband, shaking out her black ponytail. "It's not fair," she said. "I'm busting my ass out there." She pulled her shoes off, wiggling her cramped toes. "How hard is it to pass the ball? Just pass the ball to someone who can shoot. Melinda's the absolute worst. She's out there, you can tell she's thinking about slam poetry, the whole game she's mumbling to herself. She's mumbling her *own* damn slam poetry to herself. I'm standing next to her, and she's like, 'The whoosh of the ball, the glare of the lights, sneakers squeaking.' What. The. Hell. Sneakers squeaking?"

"Slam poetry is a lot like improv actually," said Elijah, once again, unhelpfully. "I really respect it."

She blinked. "I don't know that that's helpful."

"He's supporting," I said. "Like a sports bra." I made a cupping motion with my hands.

She smiled weakly, then shook her head.

"I just want to win. One person can ruin a whole team, you know? I mean, granted, a lot of people on our team suck, but if you have one terrible person it doesn't matter how good everyone else is. You can bring the whole thing down."

Later that night, as I lay in bed, Lakshmi's words reverberated in my brain.

One person can ruin a whole team.

I saw Melinda toss up an airball, mouthing slam poetry the entire time.

I saw myself kicking not one, but two goals into my own goal.

You can bring the whole thing down.

Huh.

CHAPTER SEVEN

The Snow-Posal

The auditorium was located in the old chapel and was decked out as an advertisement for the Snow Ball at today's assembly. The art students had clearly been placed in charge of decorations, and they had gone all out with disturbing yet fancifully abstract depictions of frozen nightmares. There was a zombie Elsa, hanging streamers of white and blue, and carefully concealed sexually suggestive imagery. It was a gonzo art installation masquerading as a high school dance.

The entire school was there, crammed into the chapel, which echoed with the sound of eight hundred butts settling into the pews. Teachers prowled the aisles, imploring us to put away our phones. Assistant principals lurked near the back, headpieces on, listening to instructions from central command.

We were arranged by order of class year, so the seniors got to be up front, while the balcony section was reserved for the freshmen, who were busy shrieking like gibbons and climbing over pews in order to annoy people near them. But this was an art school, so it wasn't, you know, dangerous. It was what happens when you put eight hundred and sixty creative artistic teenagers in a room together: mass chaos.

Thomas and Lakshmi sat on either side of me. Elijah sat up front because he was a senior.

Principal Gustafson held a microphone and tried to get the crowd to settle down. One look at Mr. Gustafson and you knew he was in the wrong school; he belonged in a regular school. He was trying to rock his dad jeans and a sport coat, but it wasn't working for him, and just accentuated how goony he looked. He had glasses that went out of style in the nineties and had his white hair parted down the side.

"Okay now," he said in his Minnesota nice voice. "Okay then. Alrighty. All right, then. Let's settle down. We haven't got all day, people. Let's settle down. Well, we've got a great assembly for you today . . . okay, let's settle down, people. Okay. Alrighty."

The crowd's objective at this point was clearly to make Mr. Gustafson spend the rest of the day doing this, so we wouldn't have to go back for afternoon classes.

"So today we're going to talk about behavior at this weekend's dance. I just want to take a moment . . . Let's settle down . . . I just want to take a moment and appreciate the great job our art students did in decorating all this . . ." He gestured vaguely at the artistic monstrosity around him, and his eyes caught on something disturbing. "All this great art, which is almost entirely appropriate for a dance situation." His eyes returned to the clearly phallic streamers hanging overhead. "Okay then. Um . . . all right . . ."

Thomas leaned over to me. "It's times like this that I really love this school."

"Well, um . . . we have a treat for you because we are going to start today with a special performance by our amazing improv comedy troupe, the Knight Lights!"

Elijah got up from his seat in the front of the auditorium just as a tall blond kid dressed in a suit emerged from the wings, swiping his finger across his throat. The crowd buzzed like a famous guest artist had just arrived.

"Oh, wait, hold on!" said Principal Gustafson. Elijah was already scrambling over the lip of the stage. Principal Gustafson held his hand over the microphone as the new kid whispered something in his ear.

"Oh, fuck this," said Lakshmi.

"What's going on?" I asked.

Principal Gustafson put the microphone back to his lips. "Change of plans. We have an even more amazing treat for you. I know he needs no introduction, but I would like to welcome to the stage our returning National Champion in Humorous Interpretation, Hanson Bridges!" He clapped like a trained seal and handed over the mic to the tall kid.

Hanson looked like he was twenty-four, with a square jaw

and the dazzling smile and easy swagger of someone who had led a charmed life. Even the principal seemed small and ashen next to him, like Hanson was in color and everyone else was in black-and-white. The crowd went nuts. People were whistling.

Elijah remained frozen, mid-scramble, on the edge of the stage. He looked back at some other people in the front row with raised eyebrows.

"I want to give it up for our principal," said Hanson. "He's doing the best he can. Come on guys, give it up!" He clapped his hands together while still holding the microphone like a boss. The audience complied and gave him a smattering of applause. "Honestly," he said smoothly, like he was born to the spotlight, "we can't do what we do at this school without an administration that respects the arts. I honor that."

His eyes twinkled. "Now, I'm sure all of you want to hear about what the appropriate behavior at this weekend's dance is, but I'm going to spare you that and give you some information you might actually want." The crowd cheered. "Now, some of you may not be aware that our speech season is about to begin." He shook his head in mock sadness. "Someday, when you're old and in a retirement home, you'll look back on your life and you'll have regrets—*Man, I never did that thing I wanted to do, I never accomplished anything, I was not loved enough*—but there will be one moment, in high school, where you can say, *I saw the Eaganville Speech and Debate Team compete and by God, that was the high point of my life.*" He laughed for himself and sauntered around the stage with the mic. "I'm kidding, I'm kidding, I'm sure quite a few of you will have successful lives with no regrets and won't be complete losers like some other people."

He stood right over where Elijah was and casually shifted his eyes downward. The crowd erupted in laughter.

I felt my stomach twist into knots. I noticed Lakshmi was clutching the rail of the pew, the muscles in her forearms contracting.

"I think we've heard quite enough from the improv troupe, if you know what I mean. So I want to take the opportunity to bring out a team that actually deserves some applause: the returning varsity speech team!"

Thomas sighed next to me.

Lakshmi suddenly gripped my hand and made eye contact with me. "Now you'll see," she whispered in my ear.

The auditorium went instantly quiet as all the lights went out like the beginning of an NBA game. The speakers thrummed and crackled with noise.

What the hell is this nonsense?

AC/DC's "Back in Black" surged through the auditorium at a level of volume that would kill small birds. The bass waved through me like a roll of thunder.

Suddenly, the lights came on at full blast, blinding us, and then resolving to reveal a group of seven people standing onstage, posed with their arms across their chests like they were goddamn superheroes. The crowd gasped.

They were in business suits, and they looked like a commercial for angry personal-injury attorneys. Was it my imagination or was there was a slight breeze wafting their hair to make them look even more dramatic? It was like Goldman Sachs had just swooped in, kicked everyone in the balls, and taken command of the auditorium.

I spotted Logan, looking twitchy in a pin-striped number, standing back-to-back with Anesh, a kid I recognized from my math class. Anesh wore some kind of designer suit and had dark, flawless skin and poofy thick black hair. His cheeks sucked in, emphasizing his jagged cheekbones, and he looked like he'd been practicing a pouty lips look in the mirror for the past year. Taryn was there, too, the blond girl from history who was deeply invested in my wrongness about the gold standard. She looked amazing. Hot enough for Speech and Debate surely. Andrew from English class and the guy who'd debated Lakshmi the first day of school were there, too. Basically all the evil bastards I'd met so far.

That's when I saw Coach Joey Sparks.

My blood froze. I knew him.

He was about forty, with slicked-back black hair like a Mafia type. That was basically his entire look. While the kids behind him wore business suits, Joey Sparks wore a powder-blue windbreaker and sweatpants emblazoned with the Eaganville logo. He had a whistle around his neck for some inexplicable reason. I think he was wearing Keds.

"I want to introduce you to the greatest experience of your lives," he said, loping around the stage like a panther.

My eyes narrowed. I had seen him do this before.

"We have four returning national finalists!" he thundered, and the crowd erupted in applause. "More than any other team in this country." He waved his hand with grace, like a preacher. "More than anyone. And, my friends, I'd like to hear a better round of applause for Hanson, who is the returning National CHAMPION in Humorous Interpretation!" The crowd roared in approval, banging on the old wooden pews enough to cause the assistant principals to put a stop to it.

"What's humorous interpretation?" I asked Thomas, who shushed me.

Hanson raised his hands like he was cool. Apparently everyone agreed with his self-assessment.

Lakshmi leaned over to me. "Supposedly he already has an agent."

"For what?"

"For like acting and shit. Television."

Hanson took the microphone again. "Damn." Everyone laughed. Even the principal. He was laughing at a kid swearing onstage. "I gotta tell you guys. We are not gonna have just one champion this year. We might have two." He gave a beaming smile. "We might have ... three. And we might have ..." He waited expertly, then pointed two long perfect fingers at the audience. "You. You can join, even if you suck." He paused and the evil twinkle returned to his eyes. "Isn't that right, Elijah?"

Elijah had made it back to his seat by now and looked up as the crowd focused on him.

"I'm kidding!" Hanson laughed. He winked, and handed the microphone back to Coach Sparks.

"Thanks, guys—"

"Wait, wait, wait," interrupted Principal Gustafson. "This is the year Coach Sparks will be inducted into the National Forensics League Hall of Fame as a Triple Diamond coach. And we are proud of your legacy here at Eaganville, and we are ready for another championship season."

The crowd whooped and hollered and got to its feet, clapping like maniacs.

Everyone except me, Lakshmi, and Thomas.

Elijah found us after the assembly was over. He seemed to have shrunk; his usual exuberance had been replaced by a sad cloud of defeat.

"That was some bullshit," said Lakshmi as soon as she saw him.

"Thanks."

"I mean, I'm not gonna lie to you—I kinda hate improv comedy, but you were supposed to go on."

"I know," he said quietly.

I watched them. Was he going to ask her to the dance anyway? Was he going to let the chance slip away?

Why are you so interested, Sydney?

I didn't have a long history with boys. I had dated two guys named Chris at my last school, and by dated, I mean made out with at a party a few times. But there hadn't been anyone who had really *liked* me at my old school. And once the stink of family collapse and loserdom attached itself to me, no one really expressed that much interest. So I decided I didn't like anyone either, and that was that.

It didn't help that I wasn't good at anything, or that I wasn't hot enough for Speech and Debate. But those were minor problems, I guess.

I looked at Elijah. Was he really going to not say anything? He noticed me looking at him and returned the gaze; I tried to mentally communicate: *Ask her anyway.*

"So pretty cool about the dance," I said.

"This whole dance is bullshit," muttered Lakshmi. "Just a bunch of art kids acting out the patriarchy."

I waited for Elijah to say something, but his blue eyes were unfocused and strange, like he was still in shock.

"I was thinking of going," I blurted out. Lakshmi turned to me. "Not like with a date or anything, but just for, you know, fun."

She raised her eyebrows. "How would it be fun?"

"It could be fun," I said. "Besides, what else are you doing this weekend?"

She humphed. I caught Elijah's eyes, and he seemed to restart like he'd been jolted with electricity.

"I'd like to go," he said finally. "Maybe we could go together."

The briefest hint of a smile crossed Lakshmi's face.

"Sweet," said Thomas. "I'm all in."

CHAPTER EIGHT

My Dad

Visiting days at the Lakeville Correctional Institute were on Saturdays. Mom usually worked Saturdays, and she wasn't going to go anyway, so I took the bus alone to go see my dad.

It was always a little surreal and sad in the waiting area. It was one of those institutional places—charcoal-gray tile, cheap metal and plastic chairs that squeaked awkwardly whenever anyone moved. Yellowish, fluorescent lighting that flickered occasionally and made most of us look like zombies. It was almost entirely women—some had brought kids. A couple of toddlers climbed up on the chairs, legs dangling, kept in check by their mothers' phones.

Lakeville Correctional Institute was a minimum-security prison, mostly reserved for white-collar criminals or people determined not to be a flight risk. Since my father was about as dangerous as a blueberry muffin, he ended up here.

Unfortunately, he hadn't created any animal-human hybrids. His crimes were more in the tax-evasion family of felonies, which are both the least interesting and least understood crimes. He wasn't a mob boss, and I couldn't use his crimes to intimidate anyone. He was a thief. Who did he steal from? Everybody, I guess. Even me.

Especially me.

I'm not sure when exactly his financial advising business had started failing. I never thought we were rich growing up—we had a house with a yard and a pool (in Minnesota the pool was available to swim in about six hours out of the year, so I guess that was an extravagance). We had the kind of life where I had the luxury of not worrying about things; everything happened by magic. It didn't matter that my parents barely spoke to each other, or that we took vacations we couldn't afford. I just kept going, and I had no idea that he had resorted to shady tax maneuvers to keep the thing afloat and did ill-advised things like folding our mortgage into the black hole that was his company finances.

Our life became a slow-motion plane crash. We could look out the windows and see that the wings were on fire and there were weird gremlins eating the plane as we were going down. So the only logical thing was to pretend that the ground wasn't rushing up to meet us, keep spending money, and keep the throttle down. Maybe those gremlins would decide they were full and leave us alone.

At some point, my mom grabbed a parachute, ran for the back of the plane, and took a flying leap.

My dad crashed here.

I was still falling.

I got to the visiting room first. I hated getting there first.

It was almost unbearable to be in the room. My face burned, and I felt my chest tighten and constrict, like I had swallowed a rock and it had gotten lodged in my heart. I opened and closed my hands, feeling them tingle ever so slightly, like I was having a minor heart attack.

I usually tried not to feel sorry for myself. I mean, what was the point? No one gave a shit and it didn't help anyway. The key to surviving a disaster is keep your head down, not get too attached to anyone or anything, and gut your way through it with a sense of humor. That was the only way.

I had a flash of fear thinking about my dad—what was he going to look like this time? Had anything happened during the week?

Then I swallowed it, like I'd learned to do as a kid—you can make yourself stop crying if you get angry. And I had plenty to be angry about. Why had he done this? Why had he betrayed us?

The door opened and I heard his feet shuffle in. Slippers.

"Hey there, Squidney," he said. Then I was hugging him, and I could feel his thin, strong body under the scratchy jumpsuit they made him wear.

His hair, which had never been long, was cropped short, a silvery speckle over his entire head. He'd started wearing glasses, round, dusty things that never got cleaned. But otherwise he was still my dad.

"Hi," I managed, finally letting go.

He stretched out his pants and sat on the plastic chair.

"How ya doin?"

"Fine," I said.

"Yeah?"

"Started at a new school this week."

I watched the news filter through his brain. He had probably forgotten all about it. "Ohh. Oh that's right! Yeah, how's that?"

Well, let's see. I cussed out a teacher and everyone hates me and I'm not hot enough for Speech and Debate, apparently. Great first week, really.

"Um . . . it's okay."

"Good."

"How are things with you?"

He took a moment. It was always like this now. The awkward silences that would build up and threaten to swallow any conversation or connection we might have. So many things were painful. *How was it being in prison?* Did I just ask that?

"Uh . . . I'm getting by. There's a little library here, so I'm kind of working my way through that."

"Reading anything good?"

He shook his head. "You know, it's mostly self-help books and things, so—I guess maybe I could use some self-help, I don't know." He tried a smile.

I remembered him reading me bedtime stories as a kid, long past when I could've read them myself. He always had the greatest voices for the characters; sometimes he'd even make up his own stories. I don't know if he wrote them down during the day or not, but they had seemed fascinating, tales of a gorilla and a bunny, something like that. It was hard to remember them now. It was hard to remember how we used to be.

Another silence.

"So tell me something good," he said.

"I went to a basketball game this week."

He perked up. "Oh?"

"One of my new friends is a jock."

He coughed. "You could be a jock."

"I'm not a jock."

"You used to be really good at soccer—when you were like five."

"Nobody's good at soccer when they're five. If you can stand on your own, you're good at soccer when you're five."

"Well, you kept playing—not everyone keeps playing."

"Dad, I single-handedly beat my own team freshman year."

"That takes skill."

"No, it takes the opposite of skill."

"I still think you could be an athlete if you wanted to."

"Yeah, well, your judgment is suspect."

That stung. I didn't even mean it to sting, but I could see him recoil. For a moment I thought about saying something else to soften it, but the words got caught in my throat.

Silence gathered between us. This always happened, like both of us were raw nerve endings and any pressure applied to the wrong spot caused excruciating pain. Say one wrong word, and the conversation died.

I looked at the floor again, then at the side of the room. Anywhere that wasn't at him. Should I tell him about the dance tonight, or Mom and Luke, or the guy who was coaching the speech team?

No.

"Let me know if you need a shiv," I joked.

He laughed. At least I could give him that.

CHAPTER NINE

The Snow Ball

There were a number of problems with the Snow Ball situation:
One, we were going as a group. Two, I had nothing to wear, no
opportunity to go get something, and no money to buy a dress.
Lakshmi had offered to lend me one of hers, but seeing as how
she was built like a professional athlete and I was the shape of
a sushi roll, I politely declined. And three, my mother became
interested.

"A dance, huh?" said Mom, nosing into my room that afternoon as I was going through my entire wardrobe for the third
time, hoping to find some magic rats that could weave a new
dress for me.

"It's not really a dance," I said. "It's more like a gathering."

"The Snow Ball. I like it." She said *Snow Ball* in a vaguely dirty
way. "Well, I want to meet your friends when they come over."

It's not that I was hiding my mom. But if the apartment

complex wasn't embarrassing enough, my mom was already dressed for work in her cheddar-yellow SpongeBob SquarePants Roller Coaster outfit.

I suppose I should probably explain my mom's job. We have something called the Mall of America in the Minneapolis area, which was the first of the ginormous shopping destinations built in the United States at the end of the twentieth century in the vain hope of bringing about the apocalypse. Sadly, none of the giant supermalls actually ended life on Earth, so they still existed, pulsing with malevolence and shopping opportunities.

Once you start working for a place at the Mall of America, it's kind of like being trapped in a specific circle of Hell—you may bounce around a bit, but you are not leaving. In the past year, my mom had worked at the Rainforest Café, Ulta, the Buckle, and now at the Nickelodeon Fun Place Amusement Center and Roller Coaster of Doom.

Not its actual name. It had changed hands from one corporate master to another over the years, beginning life as SnoopyTime, and at some point it had morphed into the Nickelodeon center and was currently a writhing mass of screaming ten-year-olds eating cotton candy and getting themselves doused with green goop.

Every night Mom donned her pride-swallowing SpongeBob outfit and ran the rides for the overprivileged children of the Twin Cities. It was a job, it put food on the table, it supported us, and I worried that my new friends wouldn't understand it at all.

"Are you sure you want to meet my friends? They seem weird."

"Definitely." She absently poked through my tiny closet, sighing in displeasure. "I don't understand all this black. These are the clothes of a sad person, Sydney. You're not a sad person."

My lips tightened. *I'm not?*

"You need to celebrate yourself. You should enjoy yourself. You know, once I started working out, I felt so much better about—"

"Ugh. Mom."

She held up her hands. "I'm just saying! I decided I didn't need to be sad; I decided I didn't need to hide anymore. I could be out there, jogging, I could wear any color I want. Here I am. This is me. Deal with it." I leaned back on my bed, looking at the ceiling. "You know I'm right."

"I'm not really a colorful person."

"Lies," she said cheerily. "You used to be a colorful person, and then you decided that you were going to *wallow*."

"Oh, I *decided* I was going to wallow? Was that before or after Dad went to prison?"

She took a deep breath. "So you're just going to let that dictate how people see you? Walk around in black and look sad and have a sad story about your father? Is that what you want people to see when they look at you?"

"Can you just let me pick out an outfit and not psychoanalyze me right now?"

"I'm trying to help you."

"I'm fine. I don't need any help. At least I'm not throwing myself at the nearest guy with triceps."

She was about to say something and then stopped. "You don't need to be mean," she said quietly, and left my room.

I felt bad about my conversation with Mom, but her knack of looking on the bright side of things had the effect of always making me feel like shit. Somehow it always turned out that it was my fault that I wasn't being optimistic enough. Not only that, but it seemed like she was always regurgitating whatever self-help book she had been reading this week—all dictated by the gurus at the CrossFit cult. There was a book for everything. Exercise your way into your best life! Eat the right food! Wear bright colors! Tell your daughter what to do every day! Break your ex-husband out of prison with the power of positive thinking!

I finally chose something I didn't actively hate, a black-and-white dress that had survived the cataclysm—I think it was my eighth-grade graduation dress. It was a little tight, but if I decided not to breathe for the rest of the night, I'd be fine.

My friends managed to arrive exactly on time. Somehow Elijah had acquired a limo at the last minute, but he had skimped on the research for this one, and the result was that it was less of a limousine and more of a black Weinermobile.

Elijah had taken the whole thing seriously and was wearing a black tux. I'm not gonna lie—he looked great. His red hair was actually styled; it still looked unruly, but purposefully so now, and the cut of the tux accentuated his wide shoulders while hiding the fact that he probably weighed nineteen pounds. Lakshmi was killing it in a blue dress with just the right amount of sparkle— she had her hair done up and had found some earrings for the occasion. There were heels. She looked like a movie star slash basketball player.

The two of them together made me feel like I was a third wheel made out of cheese.

"Come in, come in," said my mom as Charlie bounded into view like a madman, slipped on the floor, and smashed into the wall. "You look wonderful. You are so pretty."

"Thanks," said Elijah, smoothing down his red hair.

Mom gurgled with laughter as Charlie slobbered all over Elijah's legs. Elijah patted him on the head, causing him to rise up and start humping his leg unfruitfully.

"Charlie, no!" I said, grabbing him by his collar and yanking his muscular little body backward, his tongue falling out of his mouth like a snake.

Thomas stepped in gingerly. He hadn't gone full tux like Elijah, which was a relief. He did wear a fanciful purple-striped sport coat and vest, though, which made him look like he'd just escaped from a poorly thought-out wedding designed by Tim Burton.

"You must be Sydney's date!" Mom cried, smothering him in a hug.

"Actually, we're more of a cluster," said Thomas. "Group date. It's not really a romantic event."

Elijah looked like he swallowed a frog.

"Well, maybe someone will get lucky," my mom added inappropriately.

"I'm gay, so I don't know that that's going to happen with this crew, but we'll see." Thomas smiled.

"I love gay people," said my mom.

"All right, Mom," I said, trying to force our way out the door.

"What?! Can I not say that? I love gay people, I really do."

"Great," said Thomas, giving her a thumbs-up.

"We gotta go," I said.

We started out at the Macaroni Grill in Burnsville.

Oddly enough, we had the only limo in the parking lot, but the place was packed.

The hostess sized us up and narrowed her eyes like she was expecting an invasion of high school students at any time. "I'll put you on the list," she said. "You're looking at probably thirty minutes."

"Sweet," said Elijah, making his way through the throng to our spot. I was sitting next to a six-year-old playing on a phone, smashing his thumbs over the screen and vehemently protesting every time he died. No one else in the Macaroni Grill was dressed up. We looked like refugees from a cocktail party gone horribly wrong. Thomas lingered nearby, proudly displaying his purple sport coat like he was a supervillain.

"You didn't make a reservation?" said Lakshmi once Elijah got back.

"Um . . . I had a lot going on."

"We're going to the Macaroni Grill on a Saturday night and you didn't make a reservation?"

Thomas sighed. "Why did you imagine you could plan anything?"

"No worries. I got this," Elijah said. He sidled back up to the hostess and I watched as he folded a five-dollar bill into his hand. He tried to slide it across the podium to her, and she looked at it like he was passing her a dead fish. Elijah nodded, then slyly opened his wallet to look for more cash. He took out two more one-dollar bills and tried to add them to the bribe.

He was back moments later.

"This place is bullshit," he said.

Thirty-nine minutes later we had a table. Our waiter, Tabb, wrote his name in purple crayon on the paper tablecloth and looked like he might break into song at any moment.

"I'll have a Chardonnay," said Thomas.

"Nope," said Tabb.

"Coke then."

"Cool." Tabb was so slick he didn't even need to write shit down. Tabb had this.

Lakshmi regarded him coolly. "I'll have a Chardonnay."

Tabb sized her up. With her hair up, in the dress, Lakshmi basically looked like a professional model slumming it with a few high school kids.

"I'm gonna need to see some ID," he said.

Lakshmi reached into her purse and pulled out an ID and handed it to Tabb. Tabb looked at it. Then he looked at Lakshmi. Then he looked at it again.

"Najima, huh?"

Lakshmi took one of the crayons and wrote *Najima* on the tablecloth. "I'm the babysitter."

"All right, then." Tabb bowed and retreated.

"Well-played." Elijah nodded approvingly.

"My sister let me borrow her ID. White people have a hard time telling the difference."

"Boom," I said, dropping my crayon on the table.

For the next few minutes we wordlessly drew pictures on the tablecloth in crayon, like anyone would do when presented with an expanse of white paper and a whole bunch of crayons. Lakshmi drew a pretty intricate flower pattern. Elijah drew a robot. Thomas concentrated on monsters. I had always been mediocre at drawing, so I drew a set of eyes looking back at me and wrote *I know what you did*. Just to lighten the mood.

Two glasses of Chardonnay (which our babysitter was sharing with us as covertly as possible) and a steaming plate of microwaved mushroom ravioli later, we were having a tremendous time. Elijah had made up a story about a previous girlfriend in Canada that we were all certain did not exist.

"I don't have pictures of her," he lied, trying to keep his phone facedown on the table.

Lakshmi had told us about her first childhood crush, who had turned out to be an asshole, and I was in the middle of telling my story.

"I've had two boyfriends, and they were both named Chris," I said. "And they were marginally attractive at best."

"Why did you go out with them then?" asked Elijah.

"Because I was dumb and I didn't know how to shoot people down. I figured if some loser liked you, you just had to say yes. But Chris number one dumped me because a friend of his thought I was ugly, and Chris number two bolted as soon as my dad's . . . criminal activity became known."

Lakshmi shook her head. "Boyfriends are supposed to stick by you when your family goes to prison. It's in the rules."

"I know! But I am now officially done with love. Done with it. I am planning on being a nun or a priest or a priestly nun—one of those. My mom has a new boyfriend—he's a piece of shit. So I have made a vow to myself to ban all lusty activity from my life."

Lakshmi raised her glass of wine. "I support you, sister."

"Well, I've never had a boyfriend," said Thomas.

Elijah guffawed. "Such a lie."

"It's not. Not a real boyfriend."

"What about Arjun?"

Thomas rocked in his seat. "I don't remember what happened there, only that a series of terrible mistakes were made. I was also young. And stupid. And naive. And stupid. And had terrible taste in men."

"He sounds dreamy," I teased.

Thomas blinked. "Arjun was a senior when I was a sophomore, and I only liked him because he could sing. That was the entire attraction. He had a great voice and the rest of him was only focused on the fact that he had a great voice. He literally sang to himself in the car with me. Not *to* me, mind you, *around* me."

"What about Andrew Chen?" asked Elijah, driving in another nail.

"Oh my God. Andrew Chen." Thomas seemed to quiver with rage. "Is it too much to ask of God to have him die in an octopus attack? If I could summon fish creatures, I would do it."

"What did he do?" I asked.

Thomas's head swiveled to look at me, then tilted to the side as if he had just lost a bolt keeping his neck upright. "What did he *do*?!"

"Here we go," said Elijah. "Andrew is Thomas's ex."

Thomas's eyes went wide. "Um . . . no. No, he is not. He's not gay. He's not bi. He's one hundred and thirty percent straight."

"I'm not even sure that's mathematically possible," I said.

"He manages. All right, so . . ." He stopped and gestured to

Lakshmi, who handed him her Chardonnay. Thomas took a big gulp, then handed it back. "You're the best babysitter I've ever had, by the way," he said.

"Thank you."

"All right so—he was basically my best friend last year, right? We were in *Singin' in the Rain* together. I taught that motherfucker how to tap-dance. And he was good. He had a lot of natural rhythm, which blinded me to the fact that he was a *serpent creature from hell.* The boy can move. And I had a huge crush on him, even though he totally confounded my gaydar."

"So you thought he was gay?" I asked.

"I didn't know, actually. I thought *maybe.* And I was too scared to ask him, so . . . after the musical we had student-written one-acts, right? And I wrote a very lovely, very trashy romantic play about a boy, who was possibly a little bit like me, coming out to his parents, and then falling in love with a guy who could dance. Right? And it was both beautiful and tragic and really, really poorly written."

"I liked it," said Elijah.

"Stop," said Thomas, waving him away.

"No, it was good! I mean not like good in the traditional sense, but more like frothy fun."

"*Frothy?* It was *frothy?* I have to remind you I've seen your improv comedy and half of your stuff is about proctologists, so your taste is suspect," said Thomas. "So—okay—I poured my heart out, misguided as it was, into this show. And I cast

Andrew, because I was sure this was the way into his heart. He would realize the play was about him, and his icy heart would melt, and then we would live happily ever after, and all that jazz, which of course, was also in the play because I'm into jazz.

"And all through rehearsals he'd drop these little hints, like, 'Oh, I'm so happy to be in this show, you're so talented, everyone else is a pile of shit, et cetera . . .' Little things to win my approval because everyone else in the show was a piece of shit, and the whole time he's screwing around with the stage manager, Megan, behind my back."

"No!" I said.

"Yes! Total betrayal. But that's like, chapter one, you know what I mean? In the book of what an amazing ass he is."

Lakshmi put a finger up and ordered another Chardonnay from Tabb. "What about his amazing ass?"

Thomas grimaced. "He does have an amazing ass. So get this—he joins the speech team this year, and I hear he is doing a piece *entirely about me*. Not only that, he is doing a piece about coming out to his disapproving parents. He's *pretending* to be gay in order to win tournaments. He's *stealing* my trauma, making it all about him, and slandering me in the process."

"Ugh. Don't get me started on the speech team," growled Elijah. "I want them all to contract diseases."

"They're the worst," said Lakshmi. "I want to fight all of them. I'd win, too. I would fight all of them and win."

"I'm thinking of joining," I said.

CHAPTER TEN

The Plan

Thomas leaned on the table and stared at me.

"You seem like a nice person," he said. "Why would you want to do that?"

"Well, I had a peer counseling session with Logan, and he said I wasn't hot enough for Speech and Debate, so—"

Lakshmi interrupted me. "Are you fucking kidding?!"

"Yeah, I know."

"You're so hot. I would totally do you."

"Thanks. That means a lot."

She laughed and raised her Chardonnay tipsily.

"I basically said I was the LeBron James of speech at my last school and that I was joining the team just to piss him off. I'm not gonna do it, guys. It was a joke. I have no idea what speech even is."

Elijah nodded. "Logan sucks. They all suck. And it's like—I

was on the team, all right, the whole culture is toxic. And Coach Sparks is the worst; he's like the boss demon in charge of it. He's practically satanic."

"Don't get me started on him," I said.

"You know him?"

Do I tell them? "I'm aware of his work. I've had encounters with him before."

"Yeah, well, he's the reason I quit. And he's the reason I can't . . ." He trailed off, biting his lip. "He ruins people, all right? I had a scholarship lined up with the U of M for next year—he called them up and they canceled it. He blackballed me."

"He can do that?" I said.

"He runs the school. He's more powerful than the principal. And if you cross him . . ."

Lakshmi set her glass down. "My little sister, Rani, is on the team."

"Shit."

"She's JV this year, but she's competitive, so she's gonna be varsity eventually. And then she's gonna like . . . turn into one of those sons-of-bitches."

"The varsity squad," said Elijah, "is the worst. They're like seven Voldemorts."

Thomas objected. "You can't have seven Voldemorts. That doesn't make any sense. They're Death Eaters, at most."

"They are fucking Voldemorts."

"The entire term 'Voldemorts' is nonsense."

"What about Andrew?"

"Okay, he's a Voldemort, and everyone else is a Death Eater."

"Fine, they're supervillains, then. Like the Legion of Doom or the Sinister Seven."

"The Sinister Seven isn't a thing," added Thomas.

Lakshmi slammed her fist on the table. "Can you two shut up and stop nerding out for a second? I don't give a shit who they are, someone needs to take them out."

Everyone was quiet for a moment.

"Like murder?" asked Elijah, hesitatingly.

"No!"

"'Cause Sydney's dad probably knows a guy."

"My dad's in prison for tax evasion, he definitely does not know a guy."

Lakshmi sighed. "No, I mean just—get him fired, destroy their grip on the school . . . something like that."

"Man," said Elijah. "I would pay good money to some other speech team to take them down. Just destroy them in open combat. Cheat if they have to. The whole varsity squad and Sparks."

Silence descended on the table.

I cocked an eyebrow.

One person can ruin a whole team.

"No one can beat them from the outside," I said. "But what if I could beat them from the inside?"

Lakshmi looked at me. "What are you talking about?"

"There's no way," said Elijah. "They're better than you. Plus, they all do different events. How could you beat all of them?"

"No no no," said Thomas. "I get it. You don't have to beat all of them. You could just be the bad apple that spoils the bunch. They wouldn't even know it was coming from you—the evil is inside the house."

Tabb arrived at the table. "What's up, peeps?" he said, and nodded his head ever so slightly. "Just wanted to let you know that I can give you the check at any time, and there's no rush, but if you guys are done then—"

"We're not done," said Lakshmi. "I'm gonna get a bottle of wine."

Tabb shook his head. "Look, guys, I know you think that you're cool as hell or whatever—"

Lakshmi narrowed her eyes. "Tabb, I like you. But what if I told you that I was really seventeen and you had mistakenly served me alcohol because you couldn't tell the difference between two Indian people? And furthermore, what if I went to your manager and said that you had served someone who was underage, even though you've been trained explicitly not to do that? How do you think that would reflect on you?"

Tabb's mouth disappeared into a tiny slit. "What are your demands?" he said.

"First, I'm gonna need you to clear these plates. Then, we need a fresh paper tablecloth and some sharpened crayons. Finally, a dessert menu for everyone and a bottle of your house white."

He locked eyes with her for a moment. "Very well, Najima."

We all leaned in with our crayons, looking at the paper tablecloth.

"First," said Lakshmi. "We write down what we want to happen, then we plan to make that a reality. But let me say this: What we do here tonight, no one breathes a word of it. This is officially a pact now. We are a secret organization dedicated to one thing and one thing only: the humiliation and destruction of the Eaganville Speech and Debate team."

We raised our glasses of cheap white wine, clinked them together, and drank.

"Can I just say right now," I said, "that we are probably doomed to failure."

"We're not doing this because it's easy," Elijah said. "We're doing this because it's hard. John F. Kennedy said that about mooning."

"He said that about going to the moon, not mooning," groaned Thomas.

"I'm pretty sure it was mooning, and I'm pretty sure mooning should be a part of our plan." He scrawled MOONING on the paper.

"This is about winning and losing," said Thomas. "These guys have been winning because they've been the biggest assholes on the block. We're the plucky underdogs. And the plucky underdogs always win."

"In the movies," said Lakshmi.

"They're the overdogs," said Thomas. "And they've been humping the shit out of everything for too long around here. And I say it's about time the humping ends."

"That was beautiful," I said.

"Thank you."

"All right," said Elijah. "We're going to use the principles of improv to make this reality. 'Yes, And.' We brainstorm. No idea is a bad idea, and then we decide on a plan."

An hour later, we had scrawled our basic principles in crayon.

WHAT WE WANT:
    JUSTICE (from Thomas)
    DEATH TO THE PATRIARCHY (Lakshmi, obviously)
    SAVE RANI FROM THE PATRIARCHY (Lakshmi again)
    COACH SPARKS FIRED (from Elijah)
    REVENGE (me)
WHAT THIS LOOKS LIKE:
    PUBLIC HUMILIATION
    COMPLETE DEFEAT OF ALL VARSITY MEMBERS
    PROBABLY SOMEBODY CRYING
    ANDREW CHEN LOSING COLLEGE SCHOLARSHIP
    MOONING

HOW DO WE DO IT:

STEP 1: Sydney joins the team as a secret agent, pretending to be good at speech.

STEP 2: Sydney infiltrates the Sinister Seven.

STEP 3: Somebody does Something.

STEP 4: Everyone on the team loses, publicly.

STEP 5: Coach Sparks is fired.

STEP 6: World peace and happiness.

"I know," said Thomas. "We Fleetwood Mac these sons-of-bitches."

"I don't know what that is," said Lakshmi.

"Fleetwood Mac was a band in the seventies or something. I think," said Thomas.

Elijah raised a hand. "Eighties."

"Maybe they were in the seventies and eighties."

"Pretty sure it was eighties."

"I'll google it," said Elijah, taking out his phone. You can probably see now why this was taking us hours. The wine was not helping us think or brainstorm any better.

"It doesn't matter when they were!" cried Thomas. "The point is: They were a band, and then everybody in the band started sleeping with everyone else in the band, and they all cheated on each other, and then the whole thing imploded."

"So you want me to hook up with everyone on the team?" I said. "'Cause I'm pretty sure I'm not gonna do that."

"Or you get all of them to hook up with each other. Love drugs," said Thomas. "That's how it works in *A Midsummer Night's Dream*."

"That's like the seventh Shakespeare reference you've made in the last hour," growled Lakshmi. "Can you stop it with that, please?"

Thomas gasped. "Shakespeare is helpful in all situations. I can't help it if you can't understand the language."

"I understand the language, it's just stupid to think that *Julius Caesar* has anything to do with this!"

"Um . . . wrong!"

"We are not stabbing anyone thirty-eight times!"

"Twenty-three times. Get it right."

Lakshmi put her hands on the table. "I've watched *The Bachelor*, so I know a shit-ton about personal conflict. All you need to do is lie to them, set up a situation where only one person wins, and let them start stabbing each other in the back. You're like a secret agent, you infiltrate them, and you just start talking shit behind everybody's back—"

"That's obvious," said Elijah. "And they'll see right through that. The only thing they respect is speech and debate skill. In order to get them to trust you, you have to be good."

"I'm really good at talking."

"I think you should start on the interp side, honestly. Debate requires you to actually do research and know facts."

"What's interp?" I asked.

Elijah went pale. "We're doomed."

"No, what is it?"

"Interpretation. Like competitive acting. With a whole bunch of specific rules. How the hell are you going to be on the team if you don't know anything?"

"Sorry; I had other things to do with my time in my last school, like not being weird."

He rubbed his head. "This is never going to work."

Lakshmi punched him in the shoulder. "Yes, it is. You can coach her. And besides, sending Sydney in as a sleeper agent is only part of the plan. The rest of us have to do our part."

"What is our part?" asked Thomas.

She tapped the *Somebody does something* step of the plan. "That's our part. And, Sydney, remember: Save my sister's brain."

"Got it."

Thomas chipped in. "If you can't beat 'em, join 'em. And then destroy them from the inside."

We clinked our glasses together again.

"I just want to say," said Lakshmi, folding up our table-cloth for safekeeping, "this has been my favorite high school dance ever."

CHAPTER ELEVEN

Nightmare at Applebee's

Unfortunately, my life was about to take a turn for the worse, which happened Sunday night at Applebee's, which I gather is a frequent site of disastrous life choices. My mom had wanted to get away from mall food, so we went out to Applebee's because she made no sense as a human being.

"So how was the Snow Ball?" she asked.

Oh, it was great, we never went to the dance, just stayed at the Macaroni Grill all night drinking wine and coming up with a conspiracy to ruin the speech team. Some memories will last forever.

"Fine," I said.

"Anything interesting happen?"

"Nope."

"Are you sure?"

"Mom."

"You should wear makeup sometimes," she said, finding a can of worms and opening it.

"What the hell? I just want a burger."

"You know what we should do? Like a mother-daughter makeover."

"Nope."

"It would be totes adorbs."

"Please don't say that."

"I mean it! Fine." She huffed. "So which boy were you on the date with?"

"It wasn't like a romantic thing, it was more like, um . . . talking."

"Talking is good. Did you like the red-haired boy?"

"Can we eat in silence please like the other families at Applebee's?" I tried to look at my phone.

"Sweetheart, you know the rule."

I put the phone back in my pocket. The Rule, which may be the only rule in my family, was that No Phones Were Allowed at the Table. It was instituted somewhere in the earlier battles of the War of the Parents, when there was a heated meeting of some sort or the other, and it was determined that the cause of all problems in our family was that phones were being used to block out emotions.

Unfortunately, without phones, those emotions broke free, careened around the room, and destroyed everything. Turned out both of my parents loved their phones more than each other.

Of course, lots of marriages survive people hating each other—it's a pretty common thing that happens when you live with someone for fifteen or twenty years, but when the money runs out, the FBI turns up, and someone is shredding documents, the dominoes fall pretty quickly after that.

"I just want to talk to you and have a conversation," said my mom. "Is that such a problem?"

"No," I muttered. "But having a conversation isn't the same thing as you criticizing my life choices."

"How am I criticizing your life choices?"

"Um, 'You should wear makeup it will be totes adorbs'?"

"It would be."

"Mom."

She raised her hands like she was being held up. "All right. Fine. You don't need to wear makeup; you are beautiful as you are."

"Thank you."

"You never need to take a shower or wash your hair or do anything else, either."

I rolled my eyes. "Not the same thing."

"I know, I'm kidding, have a sense of humor, jeez. Just tell me what's going on. I like that you're making friends—"

"You don't need to play matchmaker, though."

"All right, fine, I won't mention boys. Promise. Not even the cute red-haired one. I won't mention him at all."

I took a deep breath. "So school is not awesome and—"

"Hey, look at these two hot babes! You guys must be sisters."

I'd recognize that braying anywhere. Luke.

Mom got up and gave him a hug. His hand slid precariously toward her butt, and he kissed her with a slightly open mouth. He had come from the gym, which meant he was still wearing his action tights and his loose-fitting Under Armour tank top that showed off his impressive biceps and shaved armpits. (I should point out that it was about twenty degrees outside, but when you're a sexy CrossFit man, you become immune to all weather through the sheer force of your ego.) He sidled into the booth next to her.

"I thought you guys were sisters." He chuckled, as if the joke might become funny the second time around.

Mom giggled, patting his hand. "You are the worst."

"So how am I supposed to take that?" I said. "'Cause either way it's disgusting. You're either saying that my mom looks like a teenager, or I'm so decrepit that I look like I'm forty years old. Which is it, Luke? Am I super old or are you into teenagers?"

"O-kay," he said, his eyes wide in mock fear. "Lesson learned."

"I'm not comfortable with saying forty is 'super old,'" said my mom, using finger quotes like a boss.

"How about *seasoned*?" he said, bouncing up and down slightly.

"I don't like that, either." She smiled.

Luke pulled out the abnormally large Applebee's menu,

which was a brightly colored extravaganza of food products that bore no resemblance to what came out of the kitchen. "So what's good?"

The inoffensive rock-and-roll music wafted malevolently from the speakers as I realized he intended to have dinner with us. Not only that, but this rendezvous was in some way planned and sprung on me. I hoped a spontaneous black hole would form, sucking in all light and heat and energy from this universe and imploding on itself, utterly destroying Luke.

I'm not going to torture you with a transcription of the "conversation" that followed—here are the SparkNotes:

Minnesota Vikings. Injuries are bad. Evidence of a cruel God.

Minnesota Wolves. Lots of young guys. Exciting up-and-comers. Hope there are no injuries.

People at the gym who hurt themselves because they don't know what they are doing and they don't ask Luke for help.

Benefits of a paleo diet. Lean protein helps build muscle mass. Good to know.

Maybe Sydney would like to work out sometime.

Why bad attitudes are the real reason people are held back, especially Sydney.

Things came to a head over the question of dessert. Cavemen, who apparently were super healthy because they got a lot of aerobic exercise chasing after mammoths, never had dessert because they weren't exposed to refined sugars. Nice. Seeing as how I wasn't a caveman, I decided it would be cool to have a sundae lounging goopily on a bed of chocolate brownies.

"Sundae, huh? Wow."

"Yeah. But it's on top of a brownie, so that probably makes it healthier."

His eyes went blank, as if he were witnessing the death of all he believed in. "That's a lot of empty calories. I tell this to people at the gym all the time, eat for the person you want to be."

"The person I want to be is a person having a sundae on top of a brownie."

"All right," he said, "just know that you're making choices about yourself that have consequences. So, you gotta live with that."

"I think I'll manage," I said acidly. "I have amazing self-esteem, Luke. Amazing."

"Sweet." He put out a fist like he was going to fist-bump me. I eyed it.

"What are you doing right now?"

"I support amazing self-esteem, so I'm fist-bumping you."

"Uh-huh." I looked coolly at the fist still hanging over the center of the table. Then I looked at Luke. He looked back at me. Apparently we were going to stare down until I fist-bumped him.

I can do this all day, motherfucker.

Mom chuckled nervously and pulled Luke's hand back. "All right, all right."

"Mental fist bump," said Luke, smiling.

"Nope. I mentally blocked your mental fist bump."

Luke's snaggletoothed smile disintegrated as he realized I had outmatched him.

"We do actually have something to talk about *while* you eat your sundae," said my mom.

I felt cold all over. A chill wind of evil blew through the Applebee's, fluttering the unnecessary seasoning on the fries. I said nothing.

"Um . . ." she said. "So . . ." Her hand reached out toward Luke's and wrapped itself around it. "Luke and I have been talking, and . . . well . . . he's going to move in."

The sundae arrived but it was too late—life was over.

The fallout from the Luke-moving-in bombshell continued long after our bus ride home.

"Are you kidding me?! You've been dating that guy like two weeks!"

"Six months!"

"Who moves in after six months?!"

"Lots of people move in after six months; it's normal."

"Doesn't he have a place? Isn't his mom's basement available? Can't he live at the gym like the rest of the meatheads?"

She slapped her purse down on the kitchen counter. "His lease is up at the end of February, and we thought it would be a good idea to do this."

"Ugh." I flopped on the couch, and Charlie scrambled onto one of the cushions like a mobile cannonball. "This is nuts. You don't know anything about him."

"He's a very nice person."

"Have you *met* him? He's like an infomercial come to life! He's like a pamphlet, Mom. He's going to drop you as soon as he finds some other spray-tanned girl wearing tights that needs help on her quads."

"All right, that is enough."

"This is bullshit. Seriously. You don't know hardly anything about him, and you're *inviting* him into our home."

Charlie started barking.

"That is ENOUGH!"

"No, it's not! You don't get to make these decisions without me! You made decisions about Dad without me and now look at—"

"Oh, for God's sake, don't bring him into this! This has nothing to do with your father!"

"Well, he wouldn't just bring in someone dangerous—"

"Your father is in prison, Sydney! He's not winning dad of the year!"

Tears were brimming in my eyes now.

"Stop. Being. A. Spoiled. Brat. I can't afford the rent."

My face was hot with rage, but my breath caught in my throat.

"What do you mean, you can't afford the rent?"

"Exactly what it sounds like—I can't afford the rent."

"I thought—"

"You thought what? I still owe *lawyers* money for the divorce and the trial. I'm making practically nothing at the mall. I'm taking every shift I can, but my credit cards are maxed out and my credit is shit and I've got *nothing* for you, okay? I am worth negative money. I've been alive forty-four years and I'm worth less than zero dollars. All right?"

I sank into the couch.

"And all I can think about is that I wish I had *something* to send you to college after you graduate, but—"

"I don't think you have to worry about that, Mom," I said, swallowing the brick that was in my throat. "I think my fall semester grades took care of that."

Her jaw tightened. "Don't say that."

"Well?"

She sniffed. "You can explain it in your essay or something or—"

"I don't think they want to hear it."

"This is what I'm talking about. I want you to try. Give it a shot, see what happens. All people can say is no."

I let that sink in for a moment. Was she right? She settled in next to me.

"I know this is soon with Luke. But I wouldn't do this if I didn't think it was the right thing. And part of it is that we need the help. If he doesn't help us, then . . . then we might have two or three months before we have to move. And this time I don't know where we're moving to. Okay? If he pays half the rent, then I can start paying off my credit cards, I can build a little bit of money back. We have a chance, at least."

She patted my leg. "I don't know whether or not this thing with him is going to last, and I know, you have made me very aware, that you don't like him. And I understand that—you miss your father, I get it. There's just no other way I can do this."

"Okay," I said.

"I'm sorry."

"I'm sorry, too."

I leaned up and hugged her, feeling her tremble just the slightest bit.

CHAPTER TWELVE

Dawn of the Speech Team

I couldn't sleep.

There was a strange energy that overtook me once I had decided on The Plan. Like, finally I was doing something with my life. Finally I was striking back for the losers of the world. Every team I had ever been on had been pathetic, and I wasn't dense enough to think that I might not have been partly responsible. Whether it was the elementary school soccer team, or the middle school volleyball team, or my high school cross-country team, I had always been the weak link—the reason why we lost.

My family had always lost, too. My father had lost. My mother, clearly, was losing.

Was this going to change it? At long last, would there be an opportunity to use my ability to destroy the internal cohesion on any team to my advantage?

I thought about Mom and Luke, and I felt a pang of guilt.

There had to be some way to help out. How was I going to fit that in between my plans of secret revenge, infiltration, and conspiracy?

Elijah drilled me on the rules Monday at school.

"So it's like this," he said over lunch, munching his way through limp, greasy pizza. "There are two basic sides to speech. The debate side of things, which we're going to avoid like the plague, and the interp side of things."

I took notes.

"In interp, you generally have up to ten minutes to present a piece of literature. It's not reading out loud, it's *acting*, you're creating different characters, you're switching back and forth between them. There are different categories you can compete in: humorous, dramatic, duo, and original oratory. There are others, but let's not get overly complicated right now."

"What's original oratory?"

"That's where you make shit up. You basically create a speech on any topic. That's what Andrew Chen is doing when he's talking about Thomas."

"All right."

He slurped on his chocolate milk, then held me with his eyes. "You have to understand—these people, speech is their life, okay? All summer they go to speech camp. They have private coaches in the off-season. Once one season ends, they start prepping for the next season. They're obsessed and they're good, and they're going to see right through you if you suck."

"Have you been to speech camp?" I asked.

"I don't want to talk about speech camp."

"What happened at speech camp?"

"Focus, Sydney."

"Is that where you learned to repress your feelings and not ask out a girl you like?"

He dropped his crust onto his tray to mingle with the other crusts and hid his face in his hands. "I'm trying to get you to focus."

"You know, we should have put that into the plan: falling in love."

Elijah leaned forward. "You are *waay* too invested in this."

"You should've said something Saturday night. Like, just drawn something on the tablecloth with crayon. Maybe a cartoon heart or something."

"No thank you."

I elbowed him. "This is going to be my new mission."

"Your mission, should you choose to accept it, is to join the speech team."

"I can do two missions at once. I'm multidimensional."

"I think," he said, setting down his chocolate milk and fixing me with his blue eyes, "that you should focus on your plan and I'll focus on mine."

"Do you have a plan?" I asked, needling him.

"I have many plans."

I snorted. "Sure you do."

"Can we please talk about what you're going to do today? I want you to imagine yourself as a griffin. You need big griffin energy."

I stared at him.

"Do you know what a griffin is?"

"Yes. I've read Harry Potter, Elijah."

"All right, then—"

"I will have big griffin energy if you have big griffin energy."

He smiled just a bit. "Deal."

The speech team met in a large room on the first floor, with high windows that let you look out at the leafy trees that shielded the school from the rest of the world like the forest surrounding Narnia.

I had one of those moments where I saw myself walking as if from above, a determined look on my face, my backpack shouldered against the storm of unsuspecting humans around me. Everyone else was talking and laughing and preparing for their oh-so-amazing lives of special creativity—the piano lessons, the jazz band practice, the strange abstract art made from discarded rolls of toilet paper. I breezed through all of them, unnoticed: I was the spy. The ninja. The double agent. The ninja griffin double agent.

I had to convince them I knew my shit. That I was worthy of their attention.

I'm not here to ruin your life, I'm just a simple, not-so-hot junior looking to be awesome and make friends. Nothing to see here. No reason to be suspicious. By the way, do you mind giving me the passwords to all your phones because that would be super helpful.

They had built a special row of shelves above the windows, which went all the way around the top of the room, and sagged under the glorious weight of the enormous shiny trophies. Some of them were five feet tall at least, with four spires like they were cathedrals from the Middle Ages. You could practically hear the voices of previous speech teams, echoing down from the rafters.

We kicked ass once. Now it is your turn.

Someone had also painted CHAMPIONS ARE MADE HERE across the back wall, with a disturbing portrait of a steroid-infused knight practically bursting out of his ill-advised armor.

Logan was passing out little forms once we crossed the threshold. He stopped when he saw me.

"Sydney," he said, looking up at me. "I didn't expect to see you here. I didn't think this was your scene." He made air quotes around "scene" like a jackass.

I had prepared for this moment.

"Look, I am so sorry about what happened in peer counseling. I was being kind of awful to you, and I realize that you were just trying to help. I feel like you did an amazing job trying to penetrate my . . . walls." I brushed my hair behind my ears and shrugged just a little bit, overdoing it. I touched his elbow.

He huffed. "You can't just try out for the team on a lark."

"I did forensics at my last school," I said, dropping the vocab word I'd learned. "Maybe I wasn't the LeBron James of speech, but I was pretty good. I thought I could help."

"Help us do what?"

"Win a National Championship."

His eyes narrowed. "There's no National Championship."

"You know what I mean. Go to Nats. As a team. Get that third Diamond for Coach Sparks." I punched him playfully in the shoulder. "You know, I was thinking about getting a makeover, too, seeing if that would help, because of the . . . studies . . . showing that attractive girls do better. I googled it."

He nodded suspiciously. "It's good to live in a reality-based universe."

It was everything I could do not to crush his pasty skull between my not-attractive meat paws, but I managed it, rushing over to my seat before I killed him.

Hanson, the reigning champion in Humorous Interp, was clearly the leader of the group. He was sitting on top of one the chairbacks, with his feet on the seat of it, like it was some kind of throne, or he was so awesome that he couldn't sit like a mere human. He was hunched over with his elbows resting on his knees, ready for battle. You could tell that he practiced the superhero pose.

"New blood," he said, giving me a cool head nod.

I went over to him. "It's so awesome to meet you."

He closed his eyes and nodded. Yes, it was awesome.

"I'm new to Eaganville, but everybody is like in awe of you."

He smiled a dazzling white smile. "I'm just a guy like everybody else." He blinked. "I know that it might seem like I'm some kind of other species, but I'm really just a guy. With a loooot of talent."

I laughed in spite of myself.

"I'm kidding. I'm kidding. I work really hard. And also I have a loooot of talent."

"I get it," I said.

"Do you? I always think it's important to acknowledge that my gifts come from," he said, pointing silently to the ceiling. "The ghost people above. That's why after every speech I point up." He smiled again, his dimples flaring so deep you could plant crops in them.

I mean, he was funny. You had to give him that.

The other varsity members of the squad sat in the back of the room while the underclassmen huddled up front. I spotted a girl who looked like a smaller, tamer version of Lakshmi sitting front of center. She looked wide-eyed and innocent, which was strange, seeing as how she was related to Lakshmi. I settled in next to her.

"Hey," I said. "I'm Sydney."

"Rani," she said quietly.

"I know your sister."

"I'm sorry."

"No, no, she's cool." How was I going to save her brain? "Speech and Debate is fun, huh? Like a fun time. Like a fun leisure-type activity?"

"Yeah."

"Probably good not to get too wrapped up in it."

At that moment, Coach Sparks strode into the room.

All conversation stopped. Everyone sat completely still.

I noticed his Keds first, lightly squeaking on the hardwood floor. He had changed from his tracksuit to his regular teaching uniform: pleated khakis and a tucked-in burgundy polo shirt that stretched to show off his dad bod. His arms were thick and heavily covered in Italian hair, while the cords of his neck muscles seemed permanently flexed.

There was no way he remembered me, so I sat confidently in the front row.

When had I first seen him? Five years ago?

I smiled inwardly. He had no idea who I was. This was going to be fun.

I felt like Arya Stark, a cheerful young girl with a murder list. *Logan. Hanson. Taryn. Andrew. Coach Sparks.*

(Except I wasn't going to murder them, I was just going to crush their dreams and toss their broken, battered egos into a pit of gnashing wolf-beasts that I had trained for just such an occasion. I wasn't a monster, honestly.)

Coach Sparks stood in front of us, looking at the team, faintly disapproving. "This is what we've got?" he said quietly. "This is the team?" He looked sad.

You could hear the egos deflate. Nobody moved.

"All right," he said, putting his fists on his hips. He lifted one fist into the air and dropped his head, like he was about to launch into a prayer. I glanced around.

I've been here thirty seconds and this is already fucked up.

"You might not believe in God," he said. "But I want you to believe in yourself. And believe in this team. You come to me because you want to be winners. You think you know what winning means. But I am going to teach you that there is no winning, and there is no losing. There is only . . . domination. Because we don't win, we dominate. Dominate on three. ONE, TWO."

"DOMINATE," said everybody, and that wasn't disturbing at all.

"Domi . . . nate," I said, a half second too late because I wasn't sure whether he meant for us to say it after three or on three and I was never very good at chanting in unison because it always made me feel a little self-conscious and, frankly, cultish.

He looked us over. "I'm not sure I see people ready to dominate. I don't see people who are up to the challenge, to be honest with you. I see people who'd rather sit at home, watch television, text with their friends. Meanwhile, there's some kid in Saint Paul or Mankato or Burnsville and she's up before dawn and she's already in the library, and when you face her in a tournament, she's going to kick your ass. That's what I see. If you think you can't do it, you're right, you can't do it. If you think you can't work hard enough, you're right, you can't work hard enough. Is anyone here a loser?"

A gangly freshman boy in the back of the room laughed. Sparks zeroed in on him.

"You think that's funny? I just a made a funny statement?" The boy didn't say anything. "I asked you a question. You can't answer it. Half a second ago you were perfectly willing to INTERRUPT me, and now when I'm asking you a question, you don't have the decency to ANSWER IT? Do—you—think—that's—funny?"

". . . Yes?"

"Why?"

"Why is it funny?"

"Am I an idiot? Is that all you do? Repeat questions and waste my time? WHY."

"Why is it funny?"

Sparks kicked a chair.

"Um . . ." stammered the boy, "because it was a funny question."

"So—what you're saying—is that my question was funny BECAUSE it was a funny question. That's what you just said. This is a SPEECH team, Junior. We learn to TALK here. We learn to MAKE SENSE. I might have my work cut out for me with you. Don't I? Don't I have my work cut out for me?" He nodded, staring directly at the boy.

The freshman looked up at him, terrified, unsure of what to do.

"This is your chance, right now, to run. You hear me? There is an open door over there. If you can't mentally take it, if you aren't strong enough, I suggest you pick up your little pansy-ass backpack and skitter your cowardly rear end out that door. Because if you stay, sunshine, you better be ready to *work*."

Sparks locked eyes with him. Then, haltingly, the boy grabbed his backpack, took one look back at the rest of us, and raced out of the room. That might have been the bravest thing I've ever seen anyone do.

Sparks smiled in satisfaction. "Anyone else feeling like it's time to give up?" He waited. "We'll see. We shall see. Newbies, I want you to approach one by one. Veterans, you're gonna partner up and select a piece."

Coach Sparks sat on the edge of a long folding table and looked me over.

"I'm new to the team, but I'm not a newbie. I do dramatic interp," I said confidently as I approached.

"Where were you before?"

"Edina."

His gray eyes regarded me coolly. "I don't remember seeing you on that team."

"I got injured, so I missed a lot of meets," I said, trying to make shit up as fast as I could.

Injured? How do you get injured doing speech?!

"You got injured?"

"Like, um . . . I had a vocal cord injury. The piece I was doing was pretty intense, and it required a lot of um . . . vocal . . . like screams. So I kind of threw out my voice, so my doctor told me I needed to take some time off."

I'd like to point out here that being a secret agent is a lot harder than it initially appears. I made a mental note to myself that I needed to write down an entire fake history for myself and memorize it, which I probably should have done prior to actually meeting these people and inventing a monumental pile of bullshit that I needed to keep in order.

"Never heard of that. What piece were you doing?"

Oh, great, I need to make up more lies.

"It was like a German piece. In translation. I had kind of a bad experience with it, so I want to change to doing something else."

"Uh-huh. Did you go to State?"

"Uh . . . no, I didn't qualify for State."

He was not impressed.

"Show me what you've got."

Shit.

"I just want to start fresh this season."

"You don't have a piece selected already?"

"Um . . . I had one, and I think it was unworthy of me, so I'm going to find a new one."

He leaned back. "It's Sydney, right? Sydney. Look, I have a minimal tolerance for bullshit."

"Right."

"Right. So if you want to be on this team, you're gonna work. Maybe in *Edina* you could get away with coasting on the team, and getting hurt and being a whiny little girl, but on my team, you excel or you're gone. I only want people on this team who want to win."

"Okay," I said.

"There's no space for people who want to have an *experience* or *camaraderie* or a *good time*. This is not a good time. This is *work*."

"I got it."

"Are you gonna work?"

"Yes."

"Are you sure? 'Cause if you don't have the stones, you can chicken out now. I don't have time to waste."

"Right."

"And you will address me as Coach."

"Right, Coach."

I felt the wind sucked out of me, like I was in the presence of someone with so much gravity that he stole all the air out of a room. I was already sweating, and deep down, I felt the need to try to please him.

I'll show you. I'll impress you.

Then I swallowed it back down. That's not what I was here to do.

"You start on JV. Blaize does DI on varsity, so you can check in with her. And, Sydney? You do the work or you're gone. I'm not running a day care for losers."

"Yes, Coach," I said.

I found Blaize already practicing her piece in the hallway. She was less of a girl and more like a Valkyrie who had descended from Asgard and was blowing shit up down here on Earth. She was six feet tall, and had her blond hair braided in a complicated ropelike structure. She was clearly hot enough for debate and had probably parked her flying horse outside. She had a shiny Apple watch. She smelled like vanilla and joy and was going to be a major problem.

I felt like a sad, dull potato next to her.

I'd never actually seen someone perform a speech piece before, so I lingered at the hallway, spying on her. She stood facing the wall, pacing back and forth slightly, an imaginary cigarette in one hand and an imaginary glass of scotch in her other hand. Her face, when I could see it, was contorted into a sardonic smirk; her eyelids were heavy, and she even managed to quiver slightly, as if she was suffering from the tremors of alcoholism.

She was amazing. Her voice had a caramel throatiness to it, as if ravaged from years of smoking and hard living. She didn't seem like a high school girl anymore; she seemed like a washed-up golden age actress in her death throes. How the hell was I going to do this? How was I possibly going to get good enough to impress these people?

I clapped loudly when she finished.

"That was fantastic," I said, rushing up to her. "I was like, oh my God, you are like . . . who are you supposed to be?"

"Judy Garland."

"Dorothy? From *The Wizard of Oz*?"

"Yeah, this is post-career. After she got really screwed over by the studio and she got hooked on alcohol and drugs."

"Ohh. That makes more sense, then. I'm Sydney, by the way. Coach Sparks told me to check in with you 'cause I'm doing DI, too."

She smiled a perfect smile. "Awesome! I love DI—it's like my favorite thing in the whole world! You get to just like embody pain, you know? It's so cathartic. You're gonna be amazing, I can already tell!"

"Thanks. I'm pretty sure I'm amazing already, too."

Even her laugh was beautiful. "Do you have a piece yet?"

"No. I think maybe you're supposed to help me find something."

"Of course! We've got some pre-cut pieces in the script library, and if those don't work, I can help you find something else."

I was taken aback. I was expecting her to be a clone of Sparks, full of herself in the grand, pretentious manner of the other Sinister Seven. Shit. How am I going to be able to ruin someone so damn nice? Maybe it would involve holding one of her adorable stuffed animals hostage and then decapitating it. Maybe not, but I was open to all possibilities at this point.

"My theory is that DI is all about pain," she said as we headed back into the common speech room. The JV members of the team were pairing up, hunting through pamphlets and playscripts, reading material. I spied Rani working with a dark-haired girl in the corner. I resisted the urge to run up to her and tell her to run for her life.

"The best things are memoirs," Blaize continued. "You find someone who's been like tortured or kidnapped or homeless or something. The more your person has suffered, the better you'll do. Basically, if the audience cries, you win. Alcoholism is good. Diseases. If you can find something with cancer, that's great. Spina bifida. I haven't seen anybody doing spina bifida lately, so that's wide open. Depression is kind of played out, so I'd stay away from that. Plus it's low energy, too, no fun."

"Thanks."

She took out a half-dozen plays and spread them out on a folding table. "I don't really like to die at the end of my piece; some people love dying, but it's hard to do onstage and make it look decent. So if you're going for leukemia, make sure it's not all the way to the end of leukemia, know what I mean? What did you do at your last school?"

"Um . . . it was like about a girl who joined a gang. And it had um . . . like really harsh initiation stuff."

"That sounds amazing! What was it called?"

"'Girl . . . in a Gang.'" *Awesome, now I needed to go home tonight and write a fake ten-minute piece about a girl joining a gang and forced to eat a live cat or something.*

"Oh. Do you have a video of yourself doing it?"

"Why would I have one of those?"

She seemed concerned. "That way you can watch your performance. We record everything. You can even check it out on our YouTube channel."

"You guys are hard-core."

"I don't know that recording your performances is hard-core; I think it's pretty standard really—"

"But you know what I mean," I said. "Sparks."

She smiled sweetly. "He can be tough sometimes, but that's why we love him."

"Right."

"His favorite saying is that someone, somewhere, is rehearsing right now to beat you."

"I like that level of paranoia."

It was nearly six o'clock by the time practice was over. The sun had already set when we exited the building into the parking lot. Great mounds of dirty snow flanked the plowed area, and a freezing wind whipped in from the north, ruffling my hair and pricking my skin.

My mind buzzed with possibilities. I had done it. Step one: Infiltrate the team. Granted, I needed to go home and write a fake piece about being in a gang, possibly record it, and secretly upload it to the internet without anyone noticing, but that was minor. Then I needed to find a piece, cut it to ten minutes, secretly practice the hell out of it, and get good before I showed it to anyone on the team. I'd need Elijah for that. And then I needed to slowly excrete poison into the wellspring of the group creativity, fomenting conflict and driving them all mad.

I took a deep breath. This conspiracy was going to be a lot of work.

I smiled bitterly as I watched the other members of the team heading to their cars.

Anesh, Logan's debate partner, pulled his black leather jacket around him and headed for a Porsche SUV. I looked at the other cars: Saabs, BMWs, Mercedes. These people lived in a different world than I did. They were going to college, they were going places, they were going to win long after I was gone from the scene.

I spotted Logan striding across the parking lot, puffed up in his own arrogance, heading for a sleek silver BMW.

"You need a ride?" he said as his car beeped.

"Nope," I said, not relishing the amount of time I'd need to stand outside for the bus.

He stopped for a second. "You don't need to pretend like you can handle this, you know."

"I'm sorry?"

"I mean—I know why you're doing this."

I smirked, brushing the hair out of my face. "Wow, you're really perceptive, Logan."

"Sure. You want to prove a point to me. You want to say, 'I'll show you.' And that's fine, I guess. If that's your motivation. Michael Jordan basically did the same thing. Of course, he was blessed with natural talent."

"How do you know I'm not blessed with Michael Jordan–level talent?"

He chuckled. "Oh, I think it's pretty clear. But honestly: This is going to be too much for you. You're not going to be able to succeed under these circumstances. It takes a person with a special drive to compete in speech. Did you go to a speech camp this summer? I didn't see you there. Everyone who is anyone in speech goes. Because this isn't a regular extracurricular activity. If you want to win, this is your *life*."

I raised my eyebrows. "You got me there, Logan. I guess I'll never be good enough."

"Like, is it cool with you that you're just going to be sort of good? Is that a thing? Why do anything if you're just going to be okay? Why not be the best? What's the point of doing anything if you're not going to be the greatest ever?"

"Maybe I just enjoy the agony of defeat." I smiled.

"O-kay," he said, slipping into his car and pressing the button to start it.

I made like I was heading to a gray Lexus, then watched as he drove off. The parking lot grew silent, occasionally brightened by the passing headlights of a car. I tromped over the crusty snow to the bus stop, thrusting my hands in my pockets to protect them from the cold.

Life was unfair.

Did you expect it to be otherwise?

Instead of having to get a job, or having to help their families, these kids got to spend all summer working on their passion. They never had to worry about whether or not their parents could afford it; they had tutors, private coaches. They had a head start on everything, and did their best never to look back. No wonder they won and we lost. Their parents had won, and now they were making sure their kids won too. And that's how it would go until the end of time unless somebody stopped them.

I thought about my mom, working her ass off and still not making enough money to keep us safe. Not making enough money to send me to college or hire SAT tutors or put me in summer camps to fill out my résumé. Not having money for a therapist to see me through the worst of it.

Then I thought about me.

When the city bus came, I let it pass and called Lakshmi instead—I had something to go do.

CHAPTER THIRTEEN

Cookie Time

The manager, who was named Chad, was the shape of a Russian nesting doll (one of the larger ones) and the color of Elmer's Glue. His blond hair was stretched across his dome and his bulbous blue eyes bugged out of his head like he'd just seen a sexy cartoon lady. Chad settled in across from me, pursed his lips, and made them touch the bottom of his oblong nose.

"All right, then," he said. "Okay, now. Sydney."

"Yep."

"You know that's in Australia?"

"I've heard, yeah. That's amazing."

"Oh, sure. You betcha. Great city. Just, uh . . . just amazing."

"Have you ever been there?"

"Nope. But I watch videos. It's on my bucket list!" He chuckled, then shook his head as a wave of sadness washed over his face. "Oh, that bucket list. I got some things on there, let me tell ya. Yeah." Chad seemed lost in thought.

"You okay?"

"Gimme a minute." Chad took two. The interview was going well. "Soo . . ." he continued. "Why do you want to work at the Great American Cookie Factory?"

"'Cause I've heard it's better than the Pretty Good American Cookie Factory."

I kept my face completely straight. Chad blinked for a second, then burst out in a high-pitched giggle. "Hoo! That is funny. No seriously."

I leaned across the table and looked him dead in his enlarged eyes. "Because I would kick ass at this, Chad. I would kick fucking ass."

Thirty minutes later Chad offered me a starting position and ten to fifteen hours a week. It wasn't much, but it was something. I could work Sundays and pick up the occasional shift after speech practice was over without too much trouble. I'd be clearing just over a hundred dollars a week. All I really needed to do was humble myself and sell some unreasonably large cookies.

A strange feeling settled over me: pride. I could do this. I could find my way in the world. I took a deep breath and smelled the expansive mall air.

"You know, if you need money, I can always give you some," said Lakshmi, who had given me a ride to the Mall of America.

"That's really awesome of you, but I think I need to do this."

"We could say you're on the payroll. Raise funds. Hell, we could do a GoFundMe page for this and set you up. 'Secret Agent needs help taking down evil empire. Four thousand bucks.'"

I laughed. "Maybe we can save that for my special spy gadgets."

"Hell yeah. You could have like a pen that shoots fire. Logan's like, 'Attractive girls do better in—aaaaaaah, my face, my beautiful face!'" Lakshmi mimed her face being melted off with flames.

"That might be a little too hard-core."

"Then he could wear like a mask afterward. 'Don't debate me, I'm hideous!'"

Monday night was the quietest night at the Mall of America, but it was still packed with squads of suburbanites flitting from store to store. The buttery scent of popcorn hung in the air like a dream and the gleaming clothing stores beckoned to us. Kids stopped to gape at the tiny helicopter drones that hovered over our heads uselessly, dragging their annoyed parents toward the pop-up kiosks in the center of the halls.

We drifted too close to the center, and a chipper-looking man in a bow tie got in front of us, dubious-looking body lotion in hand.

"I bet you ladies would love to try this—"

"You don't know me," said Lakshmi, weaving around him and not breaking stride.

I snickered after we passed. "I want to be you when I grow up."

"All it takes is realizing that your time and space is important. Like, I'm walking here, and you're forcing yourself into my space. I don't need you in my space. I didn't ask you to get in my space. Do I have a look on my face that says I need to give you money for generic body lotion? No, I don't. Fuck right off, sir."

"That's amazing."

"If you want to really fit in on the speech team and be a winner, you need to have a take-no-shit attitude. That's what people respect. Don't ask for anything, demand everything. Imagine you have the confidence of a mediocre white man." She laughed.

"That's how I got a job!"

"See? Now you just need to figure out if you're being paid less than the boys."

"Huh."

"Maybe wait for your second shift before diving into their books, though. I don't know, I've never had a job, but I assume they frown on that sort of thing."

My mind drifted to Elijah. It had been doing that on occasion, like a default setting that summoned an image of him into my consciousness. Those blue eyes. That mischievous smile, like he was laughing all the time.

And totally in love with Lakshmi.

"How come you aren't like going out with anybody?"

She arched an eyebrow in my direction. "Um . . . 'cause we're in high school and the boys are stupid?"

"Right. But like . . . do you like anybody?"

"What are you getting at?"

"I'm not getting at anything."

"I don't like anybody right now," she said, absently readjusting her ponytail. "I mean, there are like some straight guys who aren't actively horrible, but they're not exactly blowing up my phone."

"Right. Never mind, then."

We made our way down a long, grinding escalator to the central section of the mall, arriving at its pulsating Nickelodeon heart. The SpongeBob roller coaster loomed over us like a monument to underwater fun and evil at the same time.

It cost about eighty dollars to get in, but the border guard was a kid named Lewis and he knew me.

"I'm just here to see my mom," I said.

"Word," said Lakshmi.

"I like seeing your mom," said Lewis.

"Shut the hell up," I said.

Lakshmi gave me a subtle thumbs-up.

Mom was stationed at the front of a long, twisting line of kids. They had replaced the original Snoopy figurines with plaster SpongeBobs and piped in chattering SpongeBob-type noises to drive the children into a screeching frenzy by the time they reached the actual ride.

On the weekends the lines were thick with rage and exhaustion, but on a Monday night it wasn't too bad. Still, Lakshmi moved past the kids with the kind of sweet decorum she used for everything in life—

"Official business," she said, pushing past a group of eight-year-old girls. "Official SpongeBob business. Hey. Move."

"You're cutting!" complained one middle-schooler.

Wrong move, buddy.

Lakshmi turned on him. "I will cut you. You know that? You want to feel what that's like? You see that girl over there?" She pointed at me. "Her dad's in prison. So step aside, son."

The kid stepped aside.

"You're kind of like a superhero," I said.

"I know."

We found Mom at the front of the line. She was wearing her bright yellow SpongeBob shirt and yanking the pull-bar down around squirming kids. She'd give a thumbs-up, and then the teenager running the controls would flip a switch and send ten thousand volts of electricity through the electrified rails, shooting the kids into a spinning maelstrom of nightmares and happy underwater songs.

"Hey there!" she called out when she saw us. "I thought you hated this roller coaster."

"I do hate this roller coaster. I was not lying."

Lakshmi raised her hand. "I'll take it for a spin."

Another middle school boy complained behind her, and she turned to glare at him.

"What's going on?" Mom said. "Is everything okay at school?"

"Yeah, um . . . I just wanted to let you know that I applied for a job."

"What?" She blinked, confused, and pressed a button after a new group of swarming children made their way to the roller coaster. The car jerked like it had stuck its finger into a socket, and lurched forward. After that car left, another coaster surged to a stop.

"Yeah, I got a job at the Great American Cookie Factory. Felt like I could marry my two great interests in life: money and cookies."

She was less than thrilled. "You just applied?"

"Like an hour ago. I got the job."

"It was badass," agreed Lakshmi. "I think she's got management potential written all over her."

"You didn't think about talking to me beforehand?" asked my mom.

"No. I thought it would be like a cool thing—I could help out with money around the apartment, I mean, not a lot of money, 'cause it's part-time, but this way Luke doesn't have to move in."

She opened her mouth to say something as the manager, a skinny white guy with gauged ears, hand tattoos, and a slightly more official SpongeBob uniform traipsed over. It was like he had an officer's uniform for *Star Trek*. He was probably all of nineteen years old and bursting with stupid authority.

"All right, then," he said, twisting his earlobes. "Let's keep things moving, Brandi."

"Absolutely," she said.

"You are a valuable member of the SpongeBob Team," he said, eyes squinting a bit. "But this is work time right now."

"This is actually important, so if you could take it down a notch, that would be sweet," said Lakshmi.

Mom cut in. "Sorry, sir, I'll get on it. Guys, I gotta get back to work. We'll talk about this at home."

"What the hell?" I asked.

"You've got school, you've got extracurriculars, that's what you should be focusing on right now."

My stomach sank.

"I did this because I thought it would help."

Skinny manager dude decided it was time to put the foot down. "Okay then, I'm going to say this a second time: If you're having a personal conversation, it needs to be on personal time. I didn't get to become assistant manager by letting things slide."

Lakshmi turned to him and read his name tag. "Let me ask you something, *Reggie*. Do you ever worry that you've become a tool of the man?"

Reggie twisted his long earlobes again. "I've made my peace with it."

"Guys," said my mom. "You need to go. I'll talk to you at home, Sydney."

"Fine," I growled, taking Lakshmi by the hand.

CHAPTER FOURTEEN

Debates

She didn't get home until after eleven, and by then I was lying in bed with Charlie and didn't feel like coming out. He blobbed on my bed, settling heavily onto my lower back.

Mom gingerly opened the door to my room and sighed.

"I can handle it," I said, facedown on the bed and unable to move.

"Charlie, get off of her."

"He's appreciating me right now. Charlie, don't move, please." Charlie looked back and forth at each of us, not understanding anything, his tongue dabbing happily.

"You don't need to do this, Sydney."

"What the hell, Mom? You said you weren't making enough money and—"

"That doesn't mean that I'm asking you to sacrifice yourself—"

"Holy shit, it's ten hours a week at the Great American Cookie Factory, it's not like I'm going to work in the mines! It's a little extra money for us. That's it. I'm tired of not having anything ever."

She was silent a moment. "Well, I'm sorry about that."

"I'm not blaming you. Okay? I'm helping. Let me help."

She sat on the edge of the bed. "I just want you to have the same life as the other kids at your school have."

"Well, I don't and I can't, so . . ."

"I want you to focus on school. You need to get good grades so—"

"I know."

"So you can get a scholarship. That's more important than a job."

She was just so hopeful for me. "They don't give you a scholarship when you have a two-point-two GPA, all right? They don't. It doesn't matter how good my grades are in the second half of my junior year, it's already done. So, you know, the sooner I just decide to have a job and stop having stupid dreams about college, the better."

It hurt as I said it. Of course it did. My parents had both gone to college; I had worked under the assumption that I was going to go practically from birth.

And, not gonna lie, I didn't have a specific desire to *do something* in college. I wasn't one of those people who had already mapped out their entire life—the kind of person with a very special passion who was going to get a feature written about them in the local paper. I had no idea what I was going to do, even if I went to college. I had always seen it as a glowing goal on the horizon, ivy-coated ancient buildings bursting with knowledge and importance and light. That's where people figured out who they were, and what they were going to do with their lives. How they fell in love. How they found their purpose. What kind of life could you have without it?

The mall, I guess.

But that's not fair, either. I'm sure there were plenty of people having amazing lives who didn't go to college, but in my mind there was so much pressure about it that not going felt like a death sentence. Your future would be slammed shut like a door. And then where would you be? In apartments like this, with boyfriends like Luke, for the rest of your life until you died.

"You're gonna be okay, Sydney," said my mom, noticing my death spiral.

"Sure," I lied.

"But if your grades don't stay up, you're quitting that job."

On Wednesday, speech practice turned into a bloodbath.

"Resolved," read out Coach Sparks. "A manned mission to Mars is a vital investment for the United States."

This was policy debate. Today two teams were practicing—Logan and Anesh on one side, with Rani and her partner, Sarah, on the other. Sarah was a tall, shy sophomore with long brown hair curtaining the side of her face, an oversized nose, and reams of eyeliner. She looked like a cautious deer that had wandered into our speech practice and was about to be slaughtered.

Rani was laying out the affirmative case, which was essentially a list of arguments in favor of a manned mission to Mars. She had a laptop in front of her, which she glanced at repeatedly as she fired off reason after reason why a Mars mission was important. As far as I understood it, after a certain amount of time, Logan would respond. Then Sarah would have a rebuttal, and then Anesh would rebut the rebuttal. There were a lot of butts.

"All right, stop," said Coach Sparks, cutting off Rani in the middle of her list. "You did a lot of work on this?"

"Yes?"

"Impressive." He walked a step away from her.

"Thanks."

"It's dogshit, but it's impressive."

The room went silent. Sparks turned back to Rani. "You think that's all it is? You find some sources on the internet, you make a list, you say them as fast as you can? You try to get all your 'research' out there? I don't care. The judges don't care. YOU ARE MAKING A CASE, YOU ARE NOT RECITING A LAUNDRY LIST. I thought you were gonna get up here and do something interesting! I don't want a list! It's not about 'work,' it's about how you present the work! Are you coherent? Are you persuasive? Are you clear? Does each piece of evidence follow up on the previous piece? I didn't hear any of that. Do better."

Rani's voice was broken and soft. "Yes, Coach."

I felt awful but managed to steal some glances at the other members of the team. The younger members, the JV kids, were watching in silent terror. Hanson was sitting in the back of the room, on top of a desk, smirking. *He was enjoying this.*

Sparks turned to Logan. "You think you can do better? Give me your first negative."

Logan consulted his own laptop, looked to the timer, and launched into a vigorous defense. He refuted Rani's points one by one, citing a litany of sources, and then sprayed a dozen more reasons why space travel was impossible, ruinously expensive, and unlikely to yield anything that would help us on Earth. He talked like a cheetah, running his words into each other, and gesticulated passionately. I didn't really understand a word he said because he was too fast, but it sure as hell seemed impressive.

"Time," called Sparks, cutting him off mid-sentence.

Logan sat back down in his chair.

"Why are you sitting down?"

"Because I'm finished?"

"You think you're finished?"

"My time is up."

"And you sat down because your time is up?"

Logan's confidence began to falter. He could sense the trap

coming, but he didn't know how it was about to be sprung. Tension filled the room like a membrane.

"Did you do a good enough job to sit down?"

"Yes, I did a good job?"

"You thought that was good? In your opinion of yourself, you thought what you just did was good?"

"Pretty good."

"Oh, it was just pretty good? A moment ago it was good and you were feeling pretty full of yourself and now all of a sudden you're not? Which is it, pretty good, or good? Or can't you tell the difference?"

Logan's smirk died on his face.

"What is the difference between pretty good and good?" said Sparks.

"Um . . ."

"*Um* is the difference? I missed that before. WHAT IS THE DIFFERENCE BETWEEN PRETTY GOOD AND GOOD?"

"I don't know."

"You better learn!"

"I mean, I had a lot of sources."

"And you didn't just hear me tell that girl that wasn't enough? Did you *not* just hear me explain that to Rani? And yet you come up here with your 'list of sources,' with NO FLOW, NO COHESION, NO ARGUMENT." He spun back to the room. "What are we doing here?" Nobody answered. I could hear people's hearts beating. "Somebody tell me what we're doing here."

I could feel my instinct—*just say something funny, Sydney, everyone will love you*—welling up inside of me. But everyone was so scared, so still, it seemed like suicide to say anything.

"Nobody can tell me what we're doing here? Not one of you, NOT ONE OF YOU IN THIS ROOM HAS ANY IDEA WHAT WE'RE DOING HERE?!" He spun back on Logan. "Do you know what you're doing?"

Logan's eyes opened in shock. He couldn't answer.

"DO YOU KNOW WHAT YOU'RE DOING?! ANSWER THE QUESTION. DO YOU KNOW WHAT YOU'RE DOING?!"

"I don't—I don't—"

"What?!"

"I don't understand—"

"You don't understand WHAT? You don't understand what?! What don't you understand?!"

Logan was like a beached fish gasping for water. His mouth was open, his eyes were wide, he had no idea what was going on. Coach Sparks got closer to him.

"You come in here, you're all confident that you can beat this freshman, and you don't bother to learn anything—you don't bother to put any effort into this, you think you can just cake-walk through an argument. What. Are. We. Doing. Here." He turned back to us. "ANYONE?"

I spoke before I could stop myself. "I mean, like, in a general sense, in life, we're here to procreate and continue our species, but in a specific sense, we're here to be fucking winners. Coach."

The whole room held their breath, waiting to see if I was to be executed or not. Sparks stared at me, blinked, then broke into a smile. "Sydney gets it."

The class exhaled. A lot of people probably started to hate me.

Sparks quietly turned back to Logan, who was red-faced and sweating. He spoke in a whisper, almost sweetly. "Go out into the hall. Get back to work. And next time, do something worthy of my attention."

Logan and Anesh collected their laptops and rushed into the hall. Sarah and Rani did likewise.

Coach Sparks paced in front of the room, then settled into a chair, straightening out his polo shirt. "Who else is ready to show me something?"

I shrank in my seat. *I am not ready to show you something.*

Nobody volunteered.

"Why are we having practice if you aren't working?" he asked casually.

"We'll go," said Milo from the back of the room.

I looked at him, remembering him in history class browbeating Lakshmi for mentioning her basketball game. Talking to her the same way Sparks talked to the team. Milo had wicked eyebrows; soft, puffy hair that he constantly ran his fingers through; and a deep non Minnesotan tan. Taryn, his partner, skittered to his side, looking tiny and gorgeous next to him.

They were doing duo, which was essentially a two-person acting piece with a ridiculous number of specific rules that made no sense. They couldn't make eye contact with each other, they couldn't physically touch each other, and there were no props or costumes allowed. All they had to work with was their bodies and their voices.

They were doing *The Hobbit*, which was impossibly complicated. Milo had seven different voices for dwarves. Taryn somehow acted out the roles for Gandalf, a goblin king, Gollum, and an elf, since there were essentially zero roles for girls in the entire book. The two of them together formed the neck of the dragon Smaug, speaking in unison in an otherworldly growl that froze the blood of the audience.

The highlight of the piece was when the two of them somehow *combined* to become a giant spider. Milo crouched behind Taryn, putting his arms out, moving them synchronously with her. They spoke in a doubled hiss, making the spider sound terrifying and unreal. Despite their awfulness as human beings, I was hugely impressed.

I did manage to steal another look at Hanson, though. He was watching them with a detached, slightly annoyed look on his face, as if the fact that they were *good* was a problem for him.

Sparks nodded when they were done. "You been working on that a lot?"

"Since summer," said Milo, fluffing his hair again.

"Taryn, what did you think of your performance?"

She squeezed Milo's hand. "Um . . . I think Smaug still needs work, but, um . . . I think we did okay."

They waited. The class waited. I spotted Hanson and Andrew, Thomas's nemesis, waiting in the back, uncertain whether they should attack or not.

Blaize raised her hand. "You guys are incredible. I mean, that was phenomenal."

Milo nodded and looked to Sparks. "What did you think, Coach?"

Sparks paused, then folded his hands in front of him. "It was solid. Good job!"

A ripple of relief went through the group, except for Hanson and Andrew, who seemed miffed.

Afterward, I found Taryn and Milo in the hall, working on their Smaug voice.

"That was so amazing, guys," I said.

Milo winked ever so slightly and you could tell he was thinking, *Yes, I am so amazing.*

"I mean, wow, the way you guys were in sync like that and the voices and everything—incredible. I like aspire to be like you guys." I was laying it on thick.

Taryn regarded me coolly. "I'm still waiting to see your piece."

"I'm not quite ready to show it yet."

"What are you doing?"

"Um . . . you'll see."

"Sure."

"You guys are so inspirational, maybe I should do a duo, too."

Milo's eyebrows flared. "Duo is all about empathy with your partner."

"Yeah, I see that."

"I don't know if you can have that, honestly, if you're self-centered."

I swallowed the wicked comeback that came to mind. "I don't think I have that problem."

"Lots of people don't think they have that problem."

I was going to have a hard time not killing her. They had survived the crucible of Sparks and were now top dogs in the group, apparently. I tried to get the conversation off the evil of my self-centered existence and onto what was most likely their favorite topic: their self-centered existence.

"So how do you guys, like . . . do all that stuff?"

Taryn was unimpressed. "Do all that 'stuff'?"

"Like, get in sync like that?"

Milo fluffed his hair and probably imagined himself being fanned by a warm Mediterranean breeze. "Some duo teams out there, they think it's about memorizing lines and creating characters. But what takes you to the next level"—he turned toward Taryn and mirrored her—"is the ability to feel what your partner is feeling: Two . . . become . . . one." He put his hands out and spread his fingers. Taryn slinked toward him, splaying her fingers but not touching. "In duo, you're not allowed to physically touch or make eye contact, so everything has to be instinctive, primal."

He turned to me, his eyes glinting wolfishly in the fluorescent light. "Taryn and I have a bond."

"A completely non-sexual bond," she added.

"That's right. Sometimes I don't know where I end and she begins."

"It's probably that actual physical space between you," I said.

"Sometimes," Milo nearly whispered, "there is no space between us. I can have my face right next to her butt, and I feel nothing. I mean, I am a heterosexual guy, don't get the wrong idea about me, but my eyes can be literal inches from her ass, and I am able to completely eliminate any sexual attraction to her."

"It's amazing," said Taryn. "Milo is so superior to regular guys. Most guys would look."

"I look. I just feel nothing," he said.

Taryn turned to him. "That's inspirational."

"Because I *choose* not to feel anything. I am greater than my hormones."

"If only other guys were like him."

"Other guys disappoint you." His eyes bored into her.

"They do." Taryn sighed, staring right back at Milo, reveling in her disappointment in the entire male gender.

"Maybe you're just asexual," I said. "That's cool."

"Oh no. I am very sexual." His eyes zeroed in on me, his

mouth open ever so slightly. "But my mind is my greatest sexual organ." He pointed to it and then casually brushed his fingers through his fluffy hair again.

In my mind, also my greatest sexual organ, I began to sketch out the path to their destruction.

CHAPTER FIFTEEN

Anesh

"This is useful information," said Lakshmi, draining a three-pointer, "but if we're gonna make some progress here, we need to go past the recon phase and into the ass-kicking phase. I mean, sucking up to them is a good first step and all, but you need to have them respect you. And in order to do that," she said, retrieving her ball and dribbling it behind her back, then tossing it to Thomas, "you need to kick ass."

I nodded. If there was anyone qualified to teach someone how to kick ass, it was Lakshmi.

We were meeting in the gym, since it was important for the conspiracy that we not be seen together. Elijah was well-known to the speech team, but we could meet here and be reasonably confident that nobody would bother us.

"Exactly," said Thomas. "Kicking. Ass." He heaved the ball

at the basket with both hands and missed terribly. "Not like that, though, that was a poor demonstration."

"Have you picked your piece yet?" asked Elijah. "That's pretty important."

"Yeah, Blaize has been explaining it to me. She's pretty nice, actually."

Elijah groaned. "It's a front, trust me. Underneath that very attractive exterior is a lion waiting to devour you."

"She totally shot him down when he asked her out," said Thomas.

"No," said Elijah. "No, that's not what happened."

"That's totally what happened. You were in love with her, which was kind of sad, because she is obviously like a different species than you and—"

Elijah threw up his hands in protest. "No. Absolutely not. I'm not even attracted to her. She is a fine person—"

"*Fi-ine.*"

"You don't know anything about it. We were friends. Before I left the team."

"Guys?" said Lakshmi. "I'm gonna suggest we table this bullshit for the moment. All right?" Elijah looked at her sheepishly. "What we need to do now is focus on getting Sydney into the inner circle."

At lunch the next day, I ignored my friends and looked for the other speech kids. I didn't spot any of the Sinister Seven, but I found the JV table easily enough.

Rani had her laptop out and was searching information on space exploration. She looked a little like Lakshmi, but softer, with blue-framed glasses tucked over her ears and her dark hair hanging loose behind her shoulders.

"Hey," I said, "can I sit here?"

"Sure," she said, not looking up from her computer.

I settled between her and Sarah, unveiling my sad sandwich with a flourish. "Um . . . so where are the other team members?"

"You mean varsity?" said Sarah, digging through a Tupperware of couscous and vegetables that looked suspiciously healthy. "They're in the varsity lounge."

"There's a varsity lounge?"

She nodded. "Where have you been?"

"At another school until this semester."

Sarah shrugged. "Right. Yeah, so, they hang out in the lounge at lunch. You have to be varsity to get in."

"How do you get to be varsity? Is there like a points system or something?"

"Nope. Sparks just tells you you're varsity."

"Well, I guess that's simple."

Sarah blinked like I had just said going to the moon was simple. "Sure."

I looked over at Rani. She had her head down and was scrawling notes on a notebook in her lap.

"Hey, I thought you did awesome the other day," I said.

"Thanks," she said quietly.

"I mean it, I thought you destroyed Logan and Anesh." She snorted, but didn't say anything. "Don't you think so?"

"I don't really want to talk about it."

"All right. But I think maybe the best way to think of it is that it's a process, right? Like you learn and you get better and it's probably best that you don't put too much stress on any one practice."

"I just have to do better, that's all. *We* have to do better." She looked up at Sarah.

"Don't look at me."

"Well?"

"Well, what? I had a solid round."

Rani shook her head and went back to writing in her notebook.

"I did!" protested Sarah. "Come on, Rani."

"Fine. You had a solid round. Whatever."

Sarah sighed heavily and scooped some more couscous into her mouth as I felt my stomach sink.

With a little more prodding, I was able to discover the location of the varsity lounge. I skipped out of lunch early, hoping to position myself near the door so that I could spot the Sinister Seven leaving. The more I became a fact for them, the more I would be able to break into their clique.

I checked my face in my phone as I hurried down the twisting hallway.

WWLD? What Would Lakshmi Do? I made my face look arrogant, but that didn't work. Confidence was key.

I arrived at the lounge, a frosted-glass paneled door that said FACULTY LOUNGE. They were eating in the faculty lounge? That couldn't be right, could it?

Anesh, Logan's debate partner, opened the door first, giving me a tantalizing glimpse of a room with actual tables and couches designed for adults.

Anesh was a bit of a mystery. I had seen him after practice in his ripped-from–*West Side Story* leather jacket and designer sun-glasses. He seemed completely unperturbed by the Minnesota weather, as if he were too awesome to be fully cold. When he got into his Porsche, he kept the windows down, even though it was barely above zero degrees.

I tried to act like I was just checking my phone and was just walking through, totally not spying on the varsity lounge or any-thing, but he spotted me almost immediately.

"Sydney, is it?" He drifted close, and I could feel myself enveloped in a wash of sweet-smelling cologne.

I looked up, feigning surprise. "Oh, hey . . . um . . ."

"Anesh."

"Oh, right yeah. I was just—looking for my English teacher and . . . I thought maybe he would be in the faculty lounge. . . ."

"Maybe. I don't really pay attention to the teachers in there."

"Oh, the teachers eat in there with you?"

He blinked. "Why wouldn't they?"

"Right. Sure. Of course. That makes sense."

His dark eyes burrowed into me, like a predator beast searching for weakness. "Walk with me."

"Sure. I guess what I was doing wasn't that important anyway," I said, trailing along in his wake.

Walking with Anesh was an experience. I could feel people's eyes on us, as if I was walking next to a celebrity or something. Of particular note was the effect Anesh seemed to have on girls and gay boys. He would catch someone's eye, and then nod ever-so-slightly as if to say, *I see you, and I see your desire, and I will address it at a later time.* He turned heads.

"So what's up with you?" he said, inclining his head just a bit toward me and sensuously raising an energy drink to his full lips.

"Um . . . nothing, just trying to finalize my piece."

"Sweet." He stopped and looked me directly in the eyes.

"Yup, so that's pretty much it," I said.

"I see."

"Just picking my piece."

He took a step forward, till he was hovering just a bit over me, invading my personal space. Once again his personal atmosphere of some Axe Body Spray variant enveloped my senses.

"If you ever need another set of eyes on it, let me know. I've got two."

"Sets of eyes?"

"No. Eyes."

"Oh. I thought you meant two sets of eyes, which is kind of weird."

"No, I just meant two eyes."

"Like, you've got one set of eyes on your face and another set of eyes on your feet or something."

Anesh pursed his lips, losing his bearing momentarily.

"Besides," I added. "I thought you did debate. I'm doing interp."

"Two different worlds," he said, regaining his player form. "Sometimes they come together."

"Yeah."

"So let me know." He tilted his head just to the side again and smiled ever so slightly. "I wish you wore better clothes. You could really be fantastic."

"Good to know. I'll take that into account when I'm getting dressed."

"You don't have to be hostile. It's just honesty. I'm a really honest person." He set a smooth hand on my shoulder and came close to my ear. "I can always let you know how honest in private."

I sensed another girl approaching us and recoiled from his touch. Her name was Andi, she was in my first-period history class.

"Anesh," she said in a brittle voice, trying to hold it together.

"What's up?"

"Did you get my text?"

"Yeah."

"And?"

He shrugged. "I'm not gonna respond to every text I get. I have a lot of demands on my time."

"Yeah, but—"

"Listen," he said, baring his teeth ever so slightly. "I'm not a person who apologizes, all right? That's for other people. And what does your need for an apology say about you? I want you to think about that."

She was about to say something, but he cut her off.

"This isn't a discussion that we're having right now. My life philosophy is not up for questioning, all right? So if you want to be with me, you're going to need to accept certain things."

She stared, openmouthed, completely unmoored.

"Good," he said. "I'll talk with you at another time. Now run along."

He turned his back on her, and she stayed a moment, then wandered away like she had a concussion.

"Chicks." Anesh smiled. "What can you do?"

Blaize found me in practice after school. "Just so you know, Anesh is well-known as a player."

"I'm shocked," I said.

"Anyone new to the team, he sees you as a conquest. He does this with all the new blood."

I thought about Rani. "Even the freshmen?"

"Especially the freshmen. He likes to tell people he's poly."

"Seriously?"

"Yeah. Last year he did DI. He did *The Game*."

"What's that?"

"Ugh." She turned to the stack of material in front of me, pulling out a dog-eared copy of *The Game: Penetrating the Secret Society of Pickup Artists*. "It's all about how to pick up women at parties by negging them and messing with their heads. It's awful."

"Ew."

"He did terribly with the judges, though," she said brightly. "That's why he switched to debate. Anyway, we need to find you a piece, right? If you're not ready for the first tournament . . ."

"If I'm not ready for the first tournament what?"

She looked at me. "You saw what happened the other day. Imagine that times fifty." There was fear in her eyes. "You don't want to get on Sparks's bad side."

"Have you ever been on his bad side?"

She chuckled nervously. "*Everyone* gets on his bad side at some point."

"Taryn and Milo did fine."

"Yesterday they did fine. Just because he praises you once doesn't mean you're getting praised again. You could do the exact same routine on two different days, and one day he would love it, and the next day he would tear it to pieces. You never know what he's going to like. You're never safe." She sorted through some of the pieces on the table. "No, no, overdone, no, no . . ."

I pressed her. "Why do you take it?"

"What do you mean, why do I take it?"

"If he's like erratic and vicious to people, why do you tolerate being treated like that?"

She shook her head and answered in almost robotic sentences. "Because he's a brilliant coach. Because we win. Because we're the best. We're the best because he's like that. That's how coaching works. Ugh, there's nothing here that's going to work for you. You need something with maximum pain and maximum shock. I gotta go."

She spun on her heel and walked away from me.

I finally found my piece later that day and showed it to Elijah and Thomas on Friday.

"You're doing what?" asked Elijah.

"*The Heroin Diaries,* by Nikki Sixx. She's fucking hard-core."

Thomas stared at me. "Nikki Sixx is not a woman."

"She's not?"

"No, she—he—was the bassist for Mötley Crüe."

"Drummer," said Elijah.

Thomas turned to him. "Can you not interrupt me with mistakes, please? He was the bassist. Google it."

Elijah got his phone out. "Damn it," he said, moments later.

"Huh," I said. "Well, this really changes my visualization of all the sex Nikki was having with groupies. I thought she was basically a queer icon."

"No."

"Ohhh . . . yeah, it's making more sense now. Blaize was telling me to pick out the most extreme thing possible for DI."

"The problem," said Elijah, "is that there's no way you can be good at *The Heroin Diaries*."

"Wait a minute," said Thomas. "This could be just the thing. She could stand out. Nikki Sixx is a rock icon—he's so far away from normal human experience that he might as well be an alien. Why not have a girl play him? The gender bending could help her rise above the crowd."

Elijah was not on board. "*The Heroin Diaries* finaled at Nats like two years ago."

"So?" I asked.

"So you don't want to do a piece that someone else has had success with. It's gauche."

"But she's a girl," argued Thomas. "It's a different twist on it. People won't compare her to the boys who've done well with it."

"And he doesn't die at the end," I added. "Which, I gather, is a significant bonus. It's all sex and drugs and rock and roll. Guys? Go big or go home. I'm ready to be the guitarist from Mötley Crüe."

Elijah was visibly pained. "Fine."

"Bassist," said Thomas.

"I'm not sure I understand the difference."

"We're screwed," said Elijah.

CHAPTER SIXTEEN

Work-Life-Love-Conspiracy Balance

There are about eight million videoclips of Nikki Sixx on YouTube. I watched him playing in the band, I watched interviews with him, I watched him drunkenly stumble around the stage and fall unconscious into a swarming audience of fans. He was larger than life, a primal force, a rock-and-roll icon reveling in constant, unrelenting debauchery.

I could relate.

Okay, so maybe I couldn't relate, but it gave me something to think about as I visited my dad in prison. Nikki Sixx had become supreme after dealing with childhood trauma. Maybe I could do the same? Maybe I could understand what he had gone through in some tiny way? Maybe I understood him in a way that ordinary speech kids couldn't?

Dad and I made our way, haltingly, through the small talk that usually composed half of our visits. I was doing fine; I was eating; school was okay; the weather was horrible. The usual things.

"We're supposed to get snow this week," he said.

"Yeah. I keep hoping climate change is going to make us more like Florida, but apparently that involves some type of global catastrophe, so I'm not supposed to root for it."

"I don't think it happens that fast."

"You're crushing my dreams, Dad."

He smiled a little bit. "How's your mom?"

Dating a model for Muscle & Fitness *magazine. The usual.*

"Uh . . . you know, working a lot."

"Can you say hi to her from me?"

"I will pass that along. I'm not guaranteeing a good reaction, but I'll let her know."

"Thanks." He pulled his arms behind him, stretching out his back.

"You okay?"

"Sure. It's just nice to stretch. We don't get a lot of chance to exercise, so . . ."

"I thought that's all you did in the joint. Pumped iron. Got swole. Put tattoos on your knuckles."

"You've been misinformed. Mostly it's a lot of doing nothing."

"Are you saying movies aren't accurate?"

He laughed. "You should be a stand-up comedian."

"I hear that's a stable and rewarding career, especially for women," I joked.

"Ouch."

"Um . . . by the way, I can't make it next week."

"Oh."

"I've got a speech tournament."

"Really?"

"Yeah, it's, um . . . yeah, I'm doing speech."

"Wow. I bet you're really good at that."

"The jury's still out. I guess we'll find out at the tournament."

"You'll do great. You could always talk. Not always . . . appropriately, but you could talk. I remember one time we were at the pet store getting your guinea pig and you launched into a whole argument that all the animals should be set free."

I laughed. "I don't remember this at all."

"You must've been five. Went right up to the girl working the counter: 'What have all these animals done wrong?! By what right are you holding them?!'"

"I'm one hundred percent sure I didn't say 'by what right.' What was I, like a five-year-old lawyer?"

"You were absolutely a five-year-old lawyer. You thought it was a travesty that the birds were locked in cages. Birds should be free."

"You are totally making this up," I joked.

"I'm not!" He reached across the table and took my hand. "You always believed in justice."

"Not all superheroes wear capes, I guess."

"Nope. But I think it's good you're doing speech. It's good for your college applications."

"Yeah."

"You need to have an extracurricular, right?"

I hadn't told my dad about the fall. What was there to tell him, anyway? That I faked being sick fourteen times? That I stopped turning in my homework? That I stopped talking to people? What good was that going to do him? Better to just lie and say everything's fine rather than pour the guilt on. He was hurt bad enough.

Was he?

Maybe he should've been protecting you instead of you protecting him.

I pushed those thoughts back down in my mind.

"You okay, Squidney?"

"Yeah. Yeah, it'll look good on my college applications. That's important."

He smiled. *Do I tell him?*

"And you'll never guess who the coach is."

He looked at me softly.

"Joey Sparks," I said.

The air darkened between us, like a curse had been spoken. "Oh." He swallowed. "Well, I'm sure that's . . . interesting."

"He's, uh . . . he's pretty tough."

"I bet he is."

"But the team is full of winners, so—"

My dad's eyes were far away.

"Just be careful," he said finally.

"I will."

"And I love you."

"Don't worry. I love you, too."

On Sunday, about thirty-five minutes into my first shift at the Great American Cookie Factory, I realized that eight hours was a long-ass time to do anything. How did anyone manage to be in a real factory? How could anyone stand on their feet that long? I could barely manage being in a Cookie Factory, and frankly, as far as factories go, the conditions might not have been that difficult.

I started out on the register, which seems like it ought to be fairly simple, but somehow managed to make me feel like an idiot because I couldn't navigate the control panels properly. It probably didn't help that I had loaded the cutting from *The Heroin Diaries* on my phone and practiced my lines in-between customers.

"I lay under the Christmas Tree, injecting two grams of Christmas Spirit directly into my veins," I muttered, then turned around to see a small child looking up at me with wide eyes. "Nah, it's cool, kid," I said. "I lived." His parents were also staring at me, openmouthed. "Don't do drugs, folks. Trust me. Died twice."

So I got moved to the back, where I could practice my lines as I decorated the enormous, wheel-sized cookies that formed the principal attraction of the place. My lettering, squeezed out through a frosting tube, was not terribly beautiful. Whoever normally decorated the cookies was some type of Cookie Monet. I was more of a Cookie Picasso (whose room I was in during fifth period—shit—I was actually learning things from the insane layout of the school). Picasso drew some cracked-out Cubist shit, which was definitely more in line with my aesthetic.

After my third pathetic attempt at HAPPY BIRTHDAY and HAPPY ANNIVERSARY, SWEETIE, I decided to mix in a CONGRATULATIONS YOU'RE NOT THE FATHER cookie to see what would happen. Rhonda, my only coworker aside from Chad, took the cookie in hand and slapped it into the front display case without so much as a snort.

Rhonda was a robust red-haired woman in her late forties who took smoke breaks every eight minutes or so, slipping out the back door, hustling down some godforsaken hidden passage in the Mall of America that led to a snowy break area where she could stand for five minutes, hunched against the cold, and suck down sweet nicotine from a cancer stick.

"I'm going for a break," she said for the ninetieth time in the three hours I'd been there.

"Cool, cool," I said. "What happens if someone wants to buy a cookie?"

She looked at me like roadkill. "You sell them a cookie."

"Cool, cool," I said, loading up my drug-addled nightmare narrative on my phone. Time to practice injecting heroin between my toes again.

I was interrupted by snickering at the display case, as a troupe of frat boys had spotted my artwork.

"Dude, we have to get this," said one dude to another dude.

"Dude, yes," said another one.

"Dude, fuck!" said one who was probably the poet of the group.

They handed over fourteen dollars and carried the cookie away like a trophy, saying *dude* some more.

From then on, I was unstoppable. I made a SMASH THE PATRIARCHY cookie, a HELL YES YOU'RE DIVORCED cookie, and an I KIND OF LIKE YOU cookie. They all sold within an hour. People were taking pictures on their phones and posting the cookies on Instagram.

Chad looked at one that read SORRY ABOUT YOUR ENDOMETRIOSIS and frowned. "Are you sure this cookie is going to have appeal?"

"Do you even know what endometriosis is, Chad?"

He bit his lip. He did not know.

"Do you know that one in ten women have it?"

He didn't know that, either.

"I want you to imagine if your uterus ripped its arms and legs off and then beat itself in the face with the stumps every month."

Chad imagined it.

"Yeah. The people who have it deserve cookies."

"Huh. Well, if you're sure . . ."

"Hey. I've been doing this for the better part of a morning, I'm pretty sure I'm an expert now."

"What a hoot."

"Indeed, what a hoot."

He smiled. "I like your spunk."

"Me too."

By the end of my shift, my feet ached and my neck was sore from leaning over the cookies. Even my hands hurt; I clenched and unclenched my fingers to try to bring feeling back to them. Not all of my cookies had sold, but the Great American Cookie Factory had done solid business. Even Rhonda had been impressed in between smoke breaks.

"Shit," she had said to me, which I translated as *I appreciate your creativity and the sense of artistry you bring to this retail hell-field.*

I felt that strange feeling again: pride. I had tried something new, something I had no experience in, and I had excelled at it. I mean, yes, the lettering on the cookies was god-awful, but they were funny, and that seemed to override the aesthetic concerns. Cool.

"Hey there."

I looked up. Elijah was standing at the counter, wearing his dark coat and a woolen hat. His coppery hair snuck out of the ridge of his cap, looking ever-so-slightly devilish.

"I thought I would swing by after your first day of work," he said, stuffing his hands in his pockets and shrugging his shoulders.

"You didn't have to do that."

"I wanted to see if you wanted to practice. If you want to get in with the cool kids, you're gonna have to do well in the first tourney."

"What does *do well* mean?"

"Probably final."

I nodded.

"You have no idea what finaling even means, do you?"

"I've been a little busy picking out my piece."

"Okay, so," he said as I folded my apron and dropped it in the bin. I turned back to Chad.

"Hey, do I get paid?"

He chuckled. "You are such a hoot."

"Do I get paid, though?"

"In two weeks."

"*Any*way," continued Elijah as we headed out into the mall proper, "every tournament is divided into rounds. There are more or less rounds depending on the size of the field—the Brooklyn Park Invitational is one of the bigger ones; there will probably be five rounds."

"Uh-huh."

"You perform your piece in groups of six. Then the judge rates all the performances and the top two people move on to the next round. You keep going, round after round, until you make the final stage. So if you're doing well, you might perform your piece three or four times on the same day."

"Got it."

"There's usually one judge in the preliminary rounds, and more judges once you get to the later rounds. When you reach finals, you'll have a decent-sized audience, but in the early rounds it's basically going to be you in a classroom with like five other people."

"Right. I got this."

"And you're gonna need like a competition outfit."

I thought about the assembly, the kids onstage in their business suits. I thought about my wardrobe.

"Just like a business suit," he said.

"I live in a tiny apartment with my mom and our dog; my dad is in prison; do you think I have a business suit? This is the nicest shit I own," I said, gesturing to my frosting-coated khaki pants that were the required uniform of the Cookie Factory.

"Does your mom have a blouse that might work?"

"I think so."

"And do you have like a pencil skirt? The judges like skirts."

"I don't wear skirts. And how the hell do you know these words?"

"My mom works in fashion—"

"Oh. And why should the judges care if you wear a skirt or not? Do the boys have to wear skirts?"

He smiled. "I'm just telling you how it is. Girls get marked down for not being ladylike."

"That is some bullshit right there," I said, vowing to make more SMASH THE PATRIARCHY cookies.

"You are correct."

"Ugh. Sexist asshattery."

"Sexist asshattery indeed."

"Can I wear my dress from the Snow Ball?"

He gritted his teeth. "That's probably too sexy." He caught himself. "I mean . . . not like . . . um, like I was paying attention to how sexy you looked in that dress, but in a general sense, as an objective principle, you don't want to wear something that . . . looks that good."

"Right," I said. "Feminine but not too feminine. Traditional double-standard bullshit."

He swallowed and nodded. "We should probably just get you a skirt."

"We?"

His cheeks turned pink. "Um . . . since we're here at the mall and, um . . . we're both members of a conspiracy, I thought we could . . . shop." He took off his hat and smiled, two dimples forming on his cheeks.

"Where's Thomas? I could use a gay best friend to do my makeover right now," I joked.

"I'm the only gay best friend you've got right now."

I looked him over. "You are a pretty sorry excuse for a gay best friend."

"That's what they tell me."

"I mean, thanks and all, but I don't really have, um . . . what's it called? Money for a skirt right now."

"You can pay me back."

I felt an alarm going off in the back of my head. He was going to buy me clothes? Take pity on the poor girl? What was this? Fear and shame spiraled inside of me; the fact that I couldn't afford it on my own and here was this guy, who seemed nice, offering to take care of things. How many times had that turned into a trap for my mom? Wasn't that exactly what was happening with Luke? Once they started buying things for you, you *owed* them.

There wasn't anything like that on Elijah's face, though. He seemed sincere, like he was trying to help out. But didn't he like Lakshmi anyway? Why was he spending so much time with me?

Ugh. *Stop overthinking this, Syd.*

I nodded, finally. "So let's *Pretty Woman* this bitch, then!"

"It's like one skirt. For under forty dollars."

"You don't have any idea how much skirts cost, do you?"

* * *

One skirt from Macy's and sixty-six dollars later, we were headed out to the frozen wasteland that constituted the Mall of America parking lot. *Lot* wasn't actually the proper word; it was more like a parking zip code. Light snow swirled around the yellow streetlamps, drifting down onto the icy mountains of gray plowed snow that clustered around the edges of the parking spots.

"So why did you quit the team, anyway?" I asked, hustling next to him. "I bet you were good."

"You wanna know?"

"No, I just asked the question because I'm making sounds with my mouth with no purpose or intention behind them—"

"All right, all right."

We got into his ten-year-old Dodge Caravan. Not what I expected.

"I thought your mom was in high fashion," I said.

"She's a buyer for JC Penney's."

"I'm not sure that's fashion."

"That's fashion."

I raised my hands. "All right."

"So, um . . . the story of me and Coach Sparks," he said, putting the minivan into drive and heading for the exit. He took a deep breath. "I was on varsity last year. Humor Interpretation was my specialty; I was really good at it. I had even gotten a couple of scholarships—decent places, too. I had an offer for a free ride at the University of Minnesota. I don't know if I was better than

Hanson or not, but I placed ahead of him a few times sophomore year. Obviously, he was the golden boy and I was the . . ."

"Silver boy."

"Yeah. But, um . . . in the middle of the season my cousin was in a car accident—she skidded out on an icy road and ran into a tree—like serious, Jaws of Life kind of shit, they medevacked her to Minneapolis, and um . . . I went to see her—this was the day before a huge tournament—I was supposed to be at practice, but I wasn't, and Sparks didn't really believe me that my cousin was in critical condition, so he was pissed when I showed up at the tournament on Saturday.

"He said he wasn't going to let me compete, to teach me a lesson about lying, but like—I competed anyway, and, uh . . . my head wasn't in it, and I dropped out at octofinals, which was like the second round. Afterward he came up to me and he was like, 'That's what you get when you don't try.'"

Elijah swallowed hard. He sniffed. "And I was blown away by that, you know? My cousin is in a freaking medical coma, she's probably not going to live, and I'm visiting her the day before the tournament because I'm a human being, you know, I have actual priorities. Speech is not the only thing in my life, right? And he tells me that? But I started arguing with him like an idiot, 'No, this is really important to me' and 'It's never going to happen again' and 'I'm gonna work twice as hard,' like I'm arguing with him that I'm never going to visit a dying relative again, you know?"

He shook his head and I saw his hands tense on the wheel. "It was fucked up. The whole culture is fucked up. Finally he's like—I remember exactly what he said—'You show up at this tournament and you do this to me? You embarrass me like this? I thought you were committed, I thought you cared, I thought this team meant something to you, but I guess I was wrong about you.'"

Elijah was looking straight ahead at the road, his hands trembling now. "Like he just tore out my heart in front of me, you know? And I'm like begging him to let me stay and he says he's gonna knock me out of varsity and I suddenly see myself from the outside, like, what is going on here? And I said it wasn't fair what was he doing and I blurted out that I was gonna quit. He looks at me, and he says, 'If you quit, you're gonna make me tell everybody who you really are. You're asking me to call up my friend at the U of M and tell him about you. At those other schools? They're gonna ask how Elijah's doing, and I'm gonna have to tell them the truth about you. How you lie to people. How you pretend to care. Who you really are.' And then he says, 'Of course I knew it all along.'"

Elijah wiped his nose with the back of his arm. "He did it, too. I walked away and all those scholarships disappeared, my friends stopped talking to me, I went from being an important person to a nobody. And I felt like it was all my fault, you know? If I hadn't made the decision to . . . see my cousin before she died, things would've been okay." He turned to me. "I mean, that's what Sparks does. You start thinking the whole universe rises and sets on that team. My cousin died four days later and I still questioned whether I should've gone to see her. Like I'd made a mistake."

"You didn't do anything wrong." I reached out and took hold of Elijah's hand.

"I complained to the principal afterward. He didn't believe me. Said nothing that Sparks did constituted a violation of any rules. He hadn't had any other complaints. And why was I trying to ruin the most successful program in the school? Maybe I was just jealous. My friends dropped me. Teachers started giving me lower grades. I lost my scholarships. Everything Sparks said he was going to do, he did."

"We're gonna get him. All of them."

He nodded, still sniffling. "Thank you."

"I just need to learn how to act like I'm on heroin."

He laughed in spite of himself, his eyes twinkling in the light of the dashboard. "You're gonna do great."

CHAPTER SEVENTEEN

The Brooklyn Park Invitational

The charter bus was waiting at six thirty in the morning. The sun was about thirty minutes from coming up; there was only a faint bruising on the horizon, and the temperature had dipped into the single digits overnight. The parking lot near the school was crusty with old ice and dirty snow, and my breath escaped in puffs. I hustled to the bus in my skirt, the frigid air biting through my panty hose. Goddamn sexism.

My stomach was flipping over and over again. I had managed to perform my routine a few times for other team members, getting encouragement from Blaize and subtle yet persistent denigration from Milo. I hadn't showed it to Sparks, which was contributing to my nervousness. He tended to focus only on his varsity team and let the rest of us fend for ourselves. You had to make him notice you before he would take an interest.

Why did I have to pick a plan that required me to succeed? Wasn't there a way to simply lower the average score of everybody and call it a day? Nope. Before every competition ever I had felt like this; felt my insides crawl around my ribs, looking for a way to escape. The unwholesome addition of gas might cause me to fart in the middle of a competition—I suppose that might help with the Mötley Crüe thing, but it wasn't exactly inspiring.

No, I was a loser. I had always been a loser. Secretly hoping to join the winners. And here I was.

The bus was largely quiet when I clambered into it—everyone was in their own rows, headphones on, leaning against the windows and deep in concentration. Except Taryn and Milo, of course. Taryn was sitting on Milo's lap. But they still had headphones on and were completely ignoring each other.

I spotted Hanson in the back. He had huge headphones on and was reading the Bible, which he carried around constantly. Not that he was religious or anything; he was doing the Bible for his piece. He had performed his HI once during the week, which was phenomenal, of course. He was doing Genesis, and everything about it was designed to be blasphemous. He had funny voices for God, Adam, Eve—he'd taken a black Sharpie and crossed out half the words of the Holy Word of God. Last year he had apparently won Nationals with *Hop on Pop*, by somehow turning Dr. Seuss's cute story into a drug-fueled hallucinogenic nightmare about attacking your father, and this year he was planning on outdoing himself. He was mouthing the words to himself silently—then screwing up his face, practicing his expressions.

I was nearly the last person on the bus. I spotted my own row just in front of Blaize, who had found an enormous and fancy coffee and was downing it like a champ. Her suit was burgundy and beautiful and amazing and probably cost a thousand dollars.

"Hi!" she said, reaching around the top of the seat like the walking dead. "How are you feeling?"

"All right," I lied.

"You're gonna be awesome," she said, rubbing my shoulders. "Just do your thing. Your piece is gonna kill."

"Thanks."

The next thing I knew, Sparks was sliding down the aisles, putting his meaty hands on the tops of the headrests. He had also dressed up for the affair. Instead of his usual polo and khakis, he had donned a sport coat and wore a tight black T-shirt. His constant stubble was gone, and his hair was slicked back and orderly. He had spent a lot of time on it.

He raised one finger and the team CLAPPED like a bunch of trained seals. "I need headphones off and eyes and ears up here."

It was amazing. The headphones were off in an instant and everyone's eyes were glued to him. Sparks should've sold instructional videos to parents on how to get teenagers to listen.

"It's okay to have some butterflies on the first meet, that's normal."

The bus released its brakes, and we pulled out of the parking lot.

"I want you to harness that energy. Take those butterflies, collect them, and grind them into butterfly paste. Then I want you to DEVOUR them." I looked around. Logan was nodding, and pantomiming catching, grinding, and eating butterflies. He had probably done this in real life.

"I want to talk a little bit about the teams at this meet. Yeah, Brooklyn Park is weak. Lakeville is weak. Burnsville . . . they got some talent. But I know one thing: You destroyed them last year. That's all they've been thinking about since: revenge. They want you to come in here and they want to TAKE YOU OUT. They want to see you humbled, beaten, defeated."

I cocked an eyebrow. I was pretty sure the Burnsville speech team had not been working their asses off to unseat us in a gory apocalypse of revenge. Then again, that's what I was doing.

The monster is inside the house. I smiled.

"Are we gonna let 'em?"

"No!" shouted the team in unison.

"I SAID, ARE WE GONNA LET 'EM?!"

"NO!"

The bus was on a major street now and lurched to a stop at a red light. The bus driver, a paunchy, middle-aged white guy with a cartoonish mustache, twisted in his seat. "I'm going to need you to sit down, sir."

Sparks raised one finger. "People are going to give you rules. People are gonna tell you to stop."

The bus driver turned around again. "Sir? Do you mind, please?"

"People are gonna tell you, 'Please stop, you are scaring me, you are too awesome.' I say you make your own rules."

"This is actually a law, sir."

"I say choose victory. On three—ONE TWO—"

The bus turned a corner, and Sparks fell to the side.

Brooklyn Park was a typical high school; a huge, blocky building with two stories and banks of windows and long, empty hallways. It was just after seven when we arrived. Our fans (that's right, we traveled with fans) were going to be flooding the scene a little after noon; no need to show up to see us cruise through the preliminary rounds.

We gathered in an open atrium to warm up.

This was my first team warm-up with the entire group, and it was enough to freeze my blood.

This is a cult.

Hanson stood in the center of all of us. We locked arms around one another's shoulders, ties swaying for the boys—I caught sight of Rani and Sarah and some of the other underclassmen who were being indoctrinated. The whole group moved as one, rocking back and forth like a basketball team, but without as strong a sense of rhythm.

Hanson chanted tongue twisters in the center of the scrum, twirling, worshipped like a demigod.

"UNIQUE NEW YORK, UNIQUE NEW YORK, UNIQUE NEW YORK!"

"UNIQUE NEW YORK, UNIQUE NEW YORK, UNIQUE NEW YORK!" we all shouted back at him like this was a completely normal thing.

"TOY BOAT, TOY BOAT, TOY BOAT, TOY BOAT!"

"TOY BOAT, TOY BOAT, TOY BOAT, TOY BOAT!" we yelled.

We yelled, we stretched our mouths, we chanted tongue twisters, and by the end of the display I was sweating, embarrassed, and chilled. If there had been any outside observers, they would have run for the hills.

ROUND ONE:

The first-round room was a science lab of some kind. There were no desks, only blacktopped workstations with stools next to them. A corridor led to a secret lab, which was blocked off with duct tape and a sign saying, YOU WILL BE DISQUALIFIED IF YOU PASS THIS SIGN. Nice. Clearly the science teacher loved having her lab used for speech on the weekends. She had perhaps also sabotaged the heating system, since it was barely fifty degrees. I could see my breath. I rubbed my legs together, using the friction to generate a semblance of warmth and trying to hide my envious glare at anyone who was wearing pants.

I sized up the rest of my competition. There were five of

them, and they twisted nervously around on the stools or doubled over their phones, trying to remember their scripts. One of the boys was pacing back and forth in the back of the room, gesturing to himself like a madman.

The judge, a short Indian kid who had probably graduated last year, sat in the middle of the room with a stack of yellow ballots. Elijah told me there usually was a desperate scramble to procure judges, so judges were plucked from unlucky community volunteers—some of them had done speech before, some of them were parents, and some, I assume, were simply kidnapped off the street. Our judge twirled a fountain pen between his fingers like he was cool, but then he dropped it, and it slid under one of the stools.

The first kid who went, a reed-thin blond freshman boy who didn't even have a proper suit, did a piece about getting cancer. He forgot his lines about two-thirds in and stood there, frozen for a good thirty seconds, right after his chemo, before he stumbled into the next part, shaking his head and silently cursing himself for being an idiot. The next kid also did a piece about getting cancer. He remembered his lines, though. Both of them survived, I guess.

My turn was coming up.

Adrenaline fizzed in my veins, and I felt light-headed. If I failed here, now, it could throw a serious wrench into our plans. What if it meant that I was always going to be a loser, no matter how hard I tried? That had been my experience with all competitions prior to this one. Why would now be any different?

But this was speaking. Just using your mouth. I had always been good at that. I thought about the pet store story my dad had told me.

By what right do you imprison these animals?

I smiled and focused on the whiteboard in the front of the room, concentrating on my name.

You can do this, Sydney Williams. You are a goddamn rock star. But not the kind that passes out in public; the kind that actually kicks ass before they pass out later in the privacy of their hotel room.

"Sydney Williams," said the judge, looking up from his notes.

Go time. I slapped my hands on the granite countertop.

"Ow."

You thought cancer was bad, motherfuckers? You have no idea how bad life can get.

I didn't actually say that out loud.

"Whenever you're ready," said the judge.

I was barely conscious during my routine, vaguely aware that I was acting like Nikki Sixx to a nearly empty room of over-dressed teenagers at eight in the morning. I hissed, I stomped around the stage, I felt the spirit of a heroin addict move through me—acting out the routine task of tying off my arm with a strip of cloth, holding it in my teeth and slapping my vein (my browsing history on YouTube was a parent's nightmare). I tried to capture his voice, snarling here and there with pleasure and pain, then launching into highly articulate riffs on the nature of addiction.

When it was over, I dropped my head, my chest heaving from the exertion of my second overdose in ten minutes. I caught a glimpse of the skinny blond freshman staring at me in openmouthed horror. *Yeah, little boy, you just grew up a hell of a lot, didn't you?* There was no applause. The judge silently scrawled some notes on the back of a notecard and said, somewhat shakily, "Thank you."

I sat back down.

If I thought my nervousness before the round started was bad, it was only because I hadn't yet experienced the joy of waiting for the results to be posted. Throngs of teenagers waited in the tiled hallways, shaking out their arms, warming up voices, and burning off energy. I paced back and forth, trying not to keep my eyes laser-focused on the scrap of wall where the advancers would be posted. Every time someone walked down the hall I analyzed them, trying to figure out if they would be the person to announce my fate.

Two strong arms wrapped around me from behind, and I smelled Lakshmi's shampoo.

"What's up?!" she said, spinning me around to face her.

"What are you doing here?"

"I'm fucking supporting you. Jesus." She winked. "I might

check out my sister's round, too, but she generally gets pissed off because I cheer loudly. Supposedly, you're not supposed to be like, 'FUCK YES!' after the first affirmative."

Several concerned underclassmen glanced toward her. Lakshmi stared back.

"What? I'm celebrating fucking language. Deal with it." She turned back to me. "How'd the first round go?"

"Um, I didn't puke, so that was good."

"You killed it."

"You weren't there."

"I sensed it. Like it came to me in the ether. I was thinking, Sydney is killing it right now." She slapped my shoulder, kind of hard. "You got this. Let's obliterate these sons-of-bitches."

"Now you sound like Sparks."

And just like that, the results were posted. I made it.

ROUND TWO:

An English classroom, still largely empty, but now the other competitors had gone through puberty. The suits fit; they looked more polished and secure. Juniors and seniors. Lakshmi settled loudly into the back to watch, giving me a thumbs-up and a snarl.

And then I saw Blaize.

"Oh my God, we're in the same room!" she said, enveloping me in a hug. "Sweet!"

Shit.

Two of the six competitors in this round would move on to the quarterfinals. I immediately started cataloging the other kids, seeing if there was anyone else I was likely to beat. I had seen Blaize's routine. She was phenomenal.

She was looking down at me with her perfect blue eyes; she was wearing heels, so she stood even taller than normal. *I am a sad little potato* reverberated through my mind.

"You're going to do so awwwwesommmme," she said, her words slowing down into an echoing, low-pitched jackhammer of noises. "I believvvve in yoooouuuu." Even her encouragement was perfect.

My energy dropped out through my feet, slipped to a drain in the center of the floor, and disappeared. I was going to lose.

The first guy went. Then the second. Then a girl who did a piece about a female Renaissance painter being tortured by the patriarchy. Then it was my turn.

I caught Lakshmi's dark eyes right before I headed to the front of the room.

She was mouthing something to me.

Fuck. Their. Shit. Up.

I took a deep breath. I started my intro, feeling the spirit of rock and roll take over my body. I had practiced this every spare moment I had—after school, on the bus, at night while holding Charlie; I knew what I was doing. I thought about who Nikki Sixx was, the trouble he'd had in his childhood, the way his life was different from the other kids around him. He was carrying a burden and the only way to ease that burden was through drugs. I went to that place inside me, remembering my father, when he lived with us, going straight to the time things were falling to shit. The screaming arguments my parents had. The times I hid in my room, headphones on, music blasting, trying to drown out the sound of my life collapsing.

"*The Heroin Diaries*, by Nikki Sixx," I said, my whole posture and voice changing. I was in the groove.

I made the slightest eye contact with Blaize. Her smile was fading. She looked . . . concerned. Was I actually going to be good?

It was like that moment in a boxing movie where the hero first makes the invincible opponent bleed.

She's human.

She can be beat.

It was on.

I killed the rest of my routine. Better than I had ever done it. My voice was smooth, powerful. I raced from side to side; I had my movements down, my lines memorized.

I was good. I was better than good.

When it was over, Lakshmi stood and clapped. No one else did.

"Um," said the judge. "If we can hold our applause, please, till after all the performers have gone?"

Lakshmi looked down at him. "I'm not going to do that." She looked at his name tag. "Steve."

Blaize whispered, "Good job," to me, and got up to do her turn as Judy Garland.

QUARTERFINALS:

Blaize scored the highest in the round, but I took second. Because of the nature of the tournament we were going to be paired up again from here on out. To the end.

This time Blaize went first. Her performance was flawless; devastating. People were crying afterward. Blaize had been to Nationals the year before, which meant she was in the top hundred or so performers in the country. She had won this tournament last year. At this rate, she was going to win it again.

"Dude," whispered Lakshmi after she was done. "She seems like she's been chain smoking for like forty years."

"I know."

"Like, did you see her hold those imaginary cigarettes? I'm like, holy shit."

"Yeah, I know."

She held my eyes again. "Listen, I'm going to tell you something I tell myself before every basketball game. You are a warrior queen bitch goddess."

"Wow."

"Yeah. Now you say it."

"I'm not sure I am a warrior queen bitch goddess."

"The hell you aren't," she growled. "Say it. *Say it.*"

I felt energy surging in me. "I am a warrior queen bitch goddess."

"Fuck yeah, you are." She slapped me on the butt as I headed to the front of the room.

SEMIFINALS

Blaize scored ahead of me again, but I was second again.

This time we were in the choir room, and there was an audience. There was a smattering of parents in the stands, but now there were other kids as well. People who had been knocked out in the earlier rounds had come to watch. I looked around for members of the varsity squad, but I didn't see anyone. They were still competing in their rounds.

Just before we were set to begin, Sparks walked into the room.

He stood in the back, but his presence was *felt*. People from other teams turned to look at him—you could hear his name being whispered on their lips. He was a legend. He stood like a statue, arms crossed over his chest, watching.

The judge this time was an older white man wearing a sweater over a button-down. He had a trimmed white beard and the air of someone who had been doing this a billion years.

The first boy who went, a tall, impossibly gorgeous Black kid with a lantern jaw, did a piece about testicular cancer that destroyed everyone in the room. Kids were weeping afterward for his balls. It was easily the best routine I'd seen all day, maybe even better than Blaize. Certainly better than me.

If that was the case, that meant only one of us was getting to the finals.

I swallowed hard. This was my moment. If I made it to finals, if I did well . . .

I turned to look back at Sparks. His eyes caught mine; his expression was like granite. I couldn't tell if he was impressed by me or not.

"Don't do it for him," whispered Lakshmi. "Do it for you."

"Thank you for being here," I said, holding on to her wrist. My mind flicked to my mom; she was working today and couldn't make it. I thought about my dad, who I was usually visiting at this time of the day. Neither of them was here. Unlike these other kids' parents, who had planned their whole day around this. These other kids who got camps paid for them during the summers, who didn't have to juggle jobs or other family bullshit around this. Who could afford their own clothes. Who had futures in front of them at expensive colleges. The winners.

I got to my feet and started my routine.

I did well, but I slipped up ever so slightly on a few of the moments. It wasn't my best routine of the day. Blaize had scored higher than me in every round so far—the scoring was cumulative, so all she needed to do was not come in last to beat me out for the finals.

I was doomed.

I hung my head, looking down at the scuffed tile. I couldn't look at Blaize as she performed, her caramel voice conveying the bitter disappointment of thirty years in Hollywood. I practically knew every word and every moment of her piece by this point.

"I wasn't a person," she crooned. "I was a property, something to be used and— "

She paused. She never paused here.

I looked up.

Blaize's eyes went the slightest bit blank.

She had forgotten her line. Everyone in the room knew she had forgotten her line.

The pause stretched from five seconds, to ten, to fifteen. A look of worry crossed her perfect face, replaced quite quickly with desperation.

She said her line again and managed to catch the thread of what she was saying, but the damage had been done: She had committed the inexcusable error of losing her momentum. Her perfectly executed veneer crumbled before us; she stammered a bit, lost her place again, and finally finished. She was the last one to go, so a smattering of applause followed her performance.

Lakshmi grinned.

When the results were posted twenty minutes later, it wasn't even a surprise.

I had beaten her.

I was going to the finals.

CHAPTER EIGHTEEN

Winning

I didn't fail. Not sure I triumphed, but it was close enough. The finals room was packed to the gills, and I even recognized a few other members of the team in the audience—they were coming to see me. I got up there, I did my thing, and I nailed it.

You don't find out the results right away. They hold those announcements until the final moment of the meet, where they hand out trophies the size of small European countries. But following my performance I felt lighter, like I was being filled up with helium. All the pressure and stress of the day evaporated—I needed a shower.

Sparks caught me in the hallway afterward.

"I saw something in you today," he said. It felt like a ray of sunshine.

Don't fall for it, Sydney. You know what this guy is. I pictured him cornering Elijah in the hallway.

"Thanks."

"You're gonna need to work on your transitions—your intro needs rewriting, and I want you to explore a more emphatic ending, but otherwise . . . impressive." His face cracked into a smile. "You're not gonna win this one, but you might win another one. Are you ready to join the big time?"

"I was born ready," I said, not able to stop my mouth from making the stupid comment.

"All right, then." His eyes bored into me. "I don't this do for just anyone, and you're the first person in a long time to get this on their first meet, so . . ." He stuck out a hand. "Welcome to varsity."

I was still floating when Lakshmi found me moments later. "We have just enough time to catch the original oratory final."

"Why are we doing that?" I hissed.

"Recon. Andrew Chen made it to finals."

"Right."

By this time of the day, I had basically memorized the layout of Brooklyn Park High School, so we barely needed to race to find the band hall. The place was already packed, mostly with Eaganville students, some of whom had painted their faces purple and gold like they were at a basketball game. Three bare-chested Eaganville boys were completely purple and sat in the front row, quivering with anticipation.

Lakshmi and I found a spot in the back of the hall and settled in. A few of the Eaganville students turned around to look—a girl waved. A boy caught my eye and smiled at me. A tall Asian girl swooped over to shake my hand.

"You were so awesome," she said.

"Thanks."

"Yes, she was," said Lakshmi.

"It was so inspiring the way you overcame your heroin addiction."

"Yes, it was," said Lakshmi.

"If I ever do heroin, I'm gonna do it like that." She nervously pulled her black hair behind her ears. "I mean I know—you didn't actually do heroin—but I *believed* it, you know? It was *so real.*" She leaned in close. "I would totally believe you were like a junkie."

"Thanks."

She rushed back to her spot, and I turned to Lakshmi. "What the hell."

"You're famous, boo. Enjoy it." She pulled out her phone to text Thomas. *About to see your boy Andrew perform.*

Original oratory is a mixed bag. Whereas dramatic interp is basically who-can-make-the-audience-cry-about-your-terrible-terrible-pain, the OO finalists were all over the map. One girl did a piece about feminist language, another boy did a piece about robots. The girl right before Andrew did an amazing, tearful piece about being homeless when she was in elementary school. The Eaganville fans shifted uncomfortably. If there was anything that would win OO, it was deep personal pain attached to a pressing social issue. It was like a highway to victory.

Andrew got up there.

"It wasn't love at first sight," he said. "And it wasn't like how they show it in the movies, the swooning, the gazing into each other's eyes, the little text messages in the middle of the night. Thomas was not what I was expecting when I fell in love."

A shiver ran through me. He was using Thomas's real name?

"Oh fuck this," muttered Lakshmi under her breath.

Andrew kept going, smooth as silk. "And I certainly wasn't expecting to star in a play that he wrote about us. And I certainly didn't plan on that play being the worst thing ever written in the English language."

The audience exploded in laughter. I gritted my teeth. Lakshmi squeezed my hand so hard it nearly crushed my bones. From there, Andrew launched into a hilarious and heartbreaking dismantling of Thomas, his playwriting ability, his grooming habits, his awkward texts, and his terrible family. It ended with a devastating scene where Andrew came out to his parents, who were furious with him for being gay and thought about sending him to conversion therapy. Everybody in the audience was crying.

I'm not going to lie—it was pretty great. Andrew was so slick and so smooth; when he turned into different characters, you believed it immediately. He slowed down in all the right spots so his bullshit lies about Thomas were devastatingly effective. I was impressed.

* * *

Thomas texted us later after Lakshmi recapped Andrew's performance.

Are you fucking KIDDING ME?!

Okay, number 1: HE IS STRAIGHT.

Number 2: I'VE MET HIS PARENTS. They're super chill.

They would have ZERO PROBLEM if he was gay.

Number 3: He quoted my play WRONG. I didn't even write half

that. I mean part of it was not good I admit but STILL.

Then came the series of gifs about dog explosions, nuclear war, and skeletons being incinerated.

Me

We'll bring him down.

Thomas

We need to bring him down NOW.

Lakshmi

Fuck yeah we will. I got ideas.

The auditorium was nearly full for the awards ceremony. People sat with their teams all over the audience. Most of the Eaganville fans had stuck around, so we took up a huge swath of rows in the center of the auditorium, like we were expecting to take all the trophies. Sparks was shaking hands with a few excited parents who had come to watch the action. He was so different with them, not the ball-busting tyrant we'd seen in practice; he was all smiles, joking and slapping backs. The rest of the team bubbled with excitement. I sat surrounded by the squad, which had turned into a well-dressed spasm of joy. Everyone seemed to have done well. People leaned across chairs, joking and laughing, taking photos of each other.

Blaize was taking it hard, though. She had her hair around the side of her face, hiding behind it like a curtain. I caught her eye for a second and she gave me a weak smile—her eyes were bloodshot. "You did so good," she said.

"Thanks."

I wasn't sure whether to go to her or not. Is that something a varsity member did for another varsity member? Consoled them? I didn't see a lot of consoling happening. I hesitated, then noticed Rani and Sarah sitting a few rows back, an empty seat between them.

They might need me more.

They had been entered in the novice debate side of things, where newcomers were sent to battle and bloody themselves before graduating to the death arena that was policy debate. I left Blaize and moved to a row right in front of them. They were both on their phones.

"How'd it go?" I asked, twisting around to look at them.

"Out in quarterfinals," said Sarah. "Pretty good."

"Cool."

Rani didn't say anything.

"That's good, right," I said, trying to be encouraging. "It's your first tournament."

"How did you do?" asked Rani.

"I, um . . . I finaled, but—"

The crowd hushed suddenly as the stage curtain parted to reveal tables sagging under the weight of enormous trophies. It looked like the entire budget of the Brooklyn Park School District had been spent on speech trophies.

"All right," said the MC. "ARE YOU READY FOR THE RESULTS?!"

The crowd roared like a sporting event. People lost their minds. Holy shit, were we ready.

As expected, Eaganville dominated. Anesh and Logan took second place for policy debate; Taryn and Milo took first in duo; Hanson won, Andrew won. And as for me . . .

"THIRD PLACE, *THE HEROIN DIARIES*, SYDNEY WILLIAMS."

My heart leaped into my throat. Chills ricocheted over my body as I scrambled to get out of the aisle and make my way to the stage. Third place. For me. Out of all the people who competed in DI.

Behind me, the speech team was whooping and applauding. Anesh blew me a kiss, the bastard. Even Blaize was on her feet, clapping as hard as she could. I felt like a part of the team. I felt like a winner. But most of all I noticed Sparks, standing up, pointing at me, and giving me a thumbs-up. Joy coursed through me like a drug.

I could get used to this.

But also I need to crush everyone's dreams, so let's put that on hold for the moment.

As we were heading to the bus, I saw Sparks pull Blaize aside into a classroom. The rest of the team kept going, but I circled back. Even though the door was closed, I could hear him.

"What was that?" He waited just a second. "No, don't say anything. You didn't say anything on the stage, why should you say something now? You think you can do this with being nice to people—you think a winning personality and a smile is going to get you to the top? You sit there, you spend all your time coaching Sydney, and she beat you. She. Beat. You. What does that say about you? A girl in her first meet took you down. And that's fine with you, isn't it? You don't care, do you? You don't have a killer instinct, so why am I wasting my time with you? Why am I wasting my time talking to you when I could be coaching someone who gives a shit? Are you going to Nationals this year? Do you think you're going to Nationals this year?"

Blaize said nothing.

"I asked you a question. Do you think you're going? There are a dozen Sydneys in a dozen schools—and that's in Minnesota. And you think you're going back to Nationals with an effort like that? No. Absolutely not. Do you know why?"

Blaize didn't answer that either.

"I asked you a question. Do you know why? Answer the question."

"... I don't know...."

"Because you think this is supposed to be fun. You want people to like you. PEOPLE LIKE WINNERS." I could hear him pacing around the room. "You were an embarrassment today. You ruined today for me. This could have been a great meet. But you, personally you, ruined it. How does that make you feel? That you ruined things for me? You don't care, do you? You're the type of person who doesn't care about people. You don't care about your teammates, you don't care about me—after all the time I spent coaching you, bringing you along, teaching you, you come in and you do this to me?"

I couldn't listen anymore. I slunk away, holding the third-place trophy in my arms like a child.

CHAPTER NINETEEN

Big Woman on Campus

On Monday, everything was different.

Word spread of my ascension to varsity—I don't know how people at Eaganville communicated, by owl perhaps, but the world had changed. Teachers smiled at me. People I didn't know came up to me to tell me how great I was. It was like I had acquired a golden glow that followed me everywhere I went.

Logan sidled up to me on the way to lunch. "Yeah, you feel that?"

"Feel what?"

"The rush of fame. The heady concoction of power and glory. Feel it." He actually clenched his fists.

"That's kinda weird, Logan."

He gave me a rakish glance. "This is just the beginning, Sydney. If you're varsity, the world is your oyster. And by world I actually mean this school, so not actually the world, to be completely clear. This school is your oyster."

"What does that even mean?"

"That means you get to crack it open, pour some hot sauce on it, and slurp it down." He thought about that for half a second. "Your stock just went up. Now, I don't have to tell you that higher status is more important for males than females as far as mating is concerned, so you won't just be able to snap your fingers and have any boy you like—unlike myself, who can claim any of the lower-status females. If I wanted to. Which I don't."

Man, even when this kid was being nice to you, he was obnoxious as hell.

"I think you're overstating the appeal of the speech team."

"Am I?" We walked right past the cafeteria, heading for the teachers' lounge. "Come on in."

He opened the door like a bellman, ushering me into the lounge. This place had apparently been an old study of some kind. There was wood paneling. Multiple couches. Tables with actual chairs. There was a goddamn coffeemaker. On one counter there were several hot dishes covered in tinfoil with the words *take some* and then a smiley face.

I noticed the actual teachers immediately, who were trying to ignore the kids in their midst like a group of lions trained to ignore antelope. They didn't even look in our direction.

Hanson and Andrew were already at the table the speech

team had claimed for their own. Hanson opened his arms in greeting, calling me over.

"There she is!"

"Here I am, I guess," I said, sitting down and opening my sack lunch.

"I heard you kicked some serious ass," he said, his lips forming a permanent charming smirk and his dimples flashing handsomely. Even his breath smelled sweet.

"Thanks."

He's evil, he's evil, he's evil reverberated through my mind. *But really cute. But evil but cute but evil.*

He looked over at me like a movie star. "I remember my first tournament. I was nervous as hell. So kudos." He said *kudos*. He was a person who said *kudos*.

"I will accept those kudos," I said, "and return them to you with additional kudos." I waved my hand like I was presenting a waterfowl to a king. "How was your performance?"

"It was awesome," he said. "Three people were so offended they got up and left during the middle of my speech. One of them was like, 'I didn't come here to watch God hump Satan in the garden!' That's not even what I was doing—God was sensuously massaging Satan, that was it. It got a little heated, of course, but there was no humping. They didn't even stick around for my Adam-and-Eve-and-all-the-animals bit."

I have to admit, Hanson's HI kind of appealed to me.

"What did your parents think of that? I'm kind of worried my mom will show up to mine and be like, 'I didn't raise you to do heroin like that!'"

"She prefers you to smoke it instead of mainlining?" he joked.

"Absolutely. My mom has strict standards of heroin usage. It was one of our first mother-daughter talks."

"I bet. Nah, my parents are cool. They don't give a shit. My grandma, though, crazy religious, like born-again, all that. Pretty sure if she saw my piece, she'd die of heart failure on the spot."

"Or kill you."

"I'd be in the middle of my piece and this old lady with a walker leaps from the stands to strangle me? I mean, that might happen anyway. Or she'd leave like really slowly."

I released my wilted turkey sandwich from its zip-locked prison. Talking with Hanson was actually kind of fun, even if he was the devil incarnate. Or the devil being given an inappropriate back rub by the Father.

He looked at my pathetic excuse for a meal. "If you don't want your lunch, I'm sure you can raid the food some of the parents brought for the teachers," he said, gesturing to the tinfoiled casseroles in the back. "Sometimes we order pizza, too."

"Nice. Who brought the wine?"

Hanson chuckled. "We're not allowed to do that anymore. It's a whole thing."

"It's bullshit, honestly," said Andrew, cutting in.

Taryn and Milo joined us a few minutes later, and Anesh swept in just after that, shutting the door on a girl mid-argument. I nearly gasped when Taryn took out actual silverware.

"Damn," I said.

"Yeah, that's nothing," she said, pointing to a door in the back. "There's even a faculty bathroom. You wouldn't believe how clean and peaceful that toilet is." She opened a notebook that said *Love* and set it next to her on the table, writing notes in loopy green ink.

"This is really great," I said, trying to calibrate my ass-kicking and ass-kissing.

I must become one of you. Act like I own the place. Stop the humility bullshit.

I made my way over to the casserole zone and scooped some onto a real plate. There was a little sign that said FOR TEACHERS ONLY that I casually ignored.

"Where's Blaize?" I asked when I got back to the table.

Logan shook his head. "Demoted."

"For only making semis at one meet?"

"Not our call," said Logan. "But only one person in each category gets to be varsity. So when you got promoted . . ." He made a whistling sound.

"And you're banished from the teachers' lounge? Harsh."

"It's motivational. At any point you could be dropped. At any point your star could fall. One day you're up"—he smiled wistfully, looking over at Taryn's notebook—"the next day you're down. The challenge is to stay up. Right, Milo?"

"What?" he said.

Even the teachers treated me differently. Mr. Papadakis approached me at the beginning of class and leaned over my desk, still reflexively flinching from me a little bit.

"Hey, I know you had a busy weekend, so take your time on that paper due tomorrow," he said.

"There's a paper due tomorrow?" I asked.

He chuckled. "Yeah, it's on the syllabus. We're examining symbolism in *The Scarlet Letter.*"

"Oh." I hadn't even cracked open *The Scarlet Letter.* We'd been talking about it for the last ten days, and I'd managed to keep afloat in class discussions by calling out the shitty sexism of the novel I hadn't read. "Um . . . things are really tough right now—with the team, and my home life and . . ."

"You know what?" He leaned in. "I don't normally do this, but . . . how about we just let this one slide? I know that you've been really invested in class discussions about *The Scarlet Letter,* so I deeply, deeply appreciate your contributions to class. So— you know what? I'm cool, you're cool, I don't need to see that paper." He winked.

The sunlit glory of the day ended right after school. "All right, troops," said Coach Sparks in practice. "I see you guys celebrating like you won Nationals. This was a pissant, tiny tournament with NONE of our serious competitors. There wasn't anybody at that meet that should have held a candle to any one of you. So I don't understand why you're whooping and hollering and carrying on like you just won State. You didn't win crap." He picked up the plaque we received for the highest-scoring team. "Here's what I think of this." He tossed it in the garbage.

Sparks pointed at Logan and Anesh. "You guys got smoked in the final round, so I'd wipe that grin off your face, if I were you. You lost to a team from Dundas. DUNDAS. There are about forty kids in that school, and half of them don't know how to read and you still LOST to them. You think that's good enough? You were garbage." He jabbed a finger at Taryn and Milo, who were canoodling. "You only won because the other team got DQ'd for propping."

I looked around, the question "What is propping?" dying on my lips, since apparently everyone else knew what he was talking about. (Later I learned that *propping* meant using a prop, which was illegal.)

"Your pops were off, your spider sucked, and Smaug sounded like a goat. NOT. GOOD. ENOUGH."

I noticed Blaize sitting near the back, head down. She looked like she hadn't slept all weekend. Sparks seemed like he didn't even notice her. Instead, he leveled his gaze at Hanson, the golden boy.

Oh shit, is he gonna criticize Hanson?

"Mediocre. I saw your performance: mediocre. You wanna

repeat as National Champion? Get your ass to work. That goes for all of you: Back to work."

The team exhaled as he released us from his steely gaze. We had taken home five trophies, and it wasn't anywhere near good enough. So much for reveling in victory.

From the hallway, I watched as Blaize stayed in the room after everyone else had cleared out. She tried to approach Sparks again, but he deliberately looked at his phone for a moment before saying in a low whisper, "I don't have anything to say to you until you prove you're worthy to be spoken to." Without waiting for a response, he walked out of the room right past me.

Gingerly, I crept back in. She was pacing in the back, underneath the shelves of trophies, going over her lines in double speed, like she was Judy Garland on amphetamines. (I mean, from what I gather, Judy Garland actually took amphetamines, but Blaize wasn't supposed to be on them during the routine.)

"You all right?"

She stopped and wiped her nose, turning away from me. "I'm fine."

"I thought you did a good job in the tournament, by the way." She scoffed. "Okay."

"I mean it. You were kicking ass until you forgot your line."

"It was so stupid. I never forget that line. I never forget any lines. And then . . . you know, you screw up one time, and then it's 'sorry Blaize you're out.'"

"I think that's bullshit."

She wiped her nose with the back of her hand again and laughed bitterly. "Three years. I've spent three years on this team—like every waking moment of my life has been spent doing this. I went to Nats, and I forget one line and it's like . . ."

"I know."

She looked down at me with bloodshot eyes. "And you come in, and you're the new golden child, so congratulations. Awesome. I mean it. Enjoy your time on the top."

"I don't know about that."

"No, it's true. This is what he does. He doesn't need two people specializing in DI, so why not just keep one?" She took a deep breath. "It's not your fault. I'm not mad at you, it's just the way things are. So now he wants me to fight like hell to get my varsity spot back. I'm gonna have to suck up to him even more."

"I didn't suck up to him," I said, trying to defend myself.

"No, I know you were good. Honestly. But . . . this whole team . . . it's so . . ." She searched for the word she wanted. "Toxic."

"Yeah."

"I should quit. I should walk away. If he's gonna throw me in the garbage like that plaque . . ."

"Don't quit," I said.

"Why not?"

"Because I have something to tell you."

CHAPTER TWENTY

Joining the Other Team

"No," said Thomas, rapping his knuckles on the pool table that formed the centerpiece of our new secret headquarters. "Absolutely not."

"She would be awesome," I said. "Think of it: *Two* people on the inside."

Elijah grumbled as he strode around Thomas's basement. "That's not how this works. You have *one* person on the inside. Once the conspiracy gets too big, you lose all hope of secrecy."

"She smells really nice."

"Don't you think I know that?! That doesn't matter."

"I'm all for it. Sisterhood, bitches," said Lakshmi, lounging in a black leather recliner pointed at the enormous flat-screen television that dominated one wall. "Besides, it gives us more options. They'll never suspect her since she's been on the team so long."

"Thank you," I said. "I trust her. Plus, she's outside waiting in her car."

"What?" gurgled Elijah.

It was nearly seven o'clock, and we had gathered in the basement of Thomas's perfectly manicured McMansion, which was a masculine paradise of epic proportions. Not only was there was a television that could be seen from outer space and a luscious pool table, but the walls were festooned with framed baseball jerseys. Baseball bats darkened with squiggly signatures were encased in crystalline cubes like we were in the goddamn Batcave. There was a couch the size of Mount Rushmore, matching La-Z-Boys, and a bar that had its own glowing Budweiser sign. It was like bro culture had been distilled and condensed into one subterranean realm, and we had been condemned to its depths.

"My dad played professional baseball for five years," Thomas had said, by way of explanation. "He was super excited to have a gay playwright for a son."

"I'm sorry for his loss," I joked.

"It's all good. There was an adjustment period," he added. "I think he was more concerned about my lack of athletic ability than my orientation, to be honest. He's cool with me being gay, he's not cool with me being unable to hit a curve ball."

Lakshmi twirled around. "This is like my Barbie dream house."

Blaize carefully made her way to the basement, eyes open in awe.

"This place is cool," she said. "It's like a sports bunker."

Thomas sighed and unrolled the paper tablecloth we'd taken from the Macaroni Grill. "This is basically our founding document. Like the Constitution." He gestured to the crayoned images of the Sinister Seven, where Blaize was drawn like a ginormous smiling blond devil. "Don't worry about that part," he said, taking a red crayon and X-ing out her face. "Not 'cause you're dead," he said, "because you're no longer part of the Sinister Seven."

I caught Elijah's eyes. There was a kind of delicacy about him now, as if he wasn't entirely comfortable in my presence. I kept imagining what had happened to him, and the vulnerability he'd shown to tell me about it. He smiled a bit and then looked down at the table.

Blaize looked over the plan. "You guys have put a lot of work into this conspiracy."

"Thanks," said Thomas.

"Before we go any further," said Elijah, "you need to swear to secrecy. What you have witnessed here tonight must never be spoken of, even on pain of torture or death."

"Torture, Elijah?" I said.

"It could happen."

"I'd do it," said Lakshmi. "I'd torture somebody."

"We're not looking for torture volunteers," said Elijah. "We're saying that—"

"I get it," said Lakshmi. "It was a joke."

Blaize set her jaw. "Sparks is a cancer on this school."

"And the other people on the team?" said Elijah. "Your friends?"

"They're not my friends."

"They sure seemed like your friends."

"I was nice to them, but I don't think they ever really liked me."

"You sure backed them up when I got kicked off the team."

I was about to intervene when Thomas grabbed my hand. "Let them do this," he said quietly.

"I'm sorry about that," she said.

"Are you?"

"Yes. What happened to you was totally unfair. And I didn't help, and I'm sorry about that. And he's done it to me, and he's gonna do it to more people after me."

Elijah considered it for a moment. "All right."

Lakshmi exhaled. "That was fucking intense. I thought you guys were gonna get out dueling swords or something."

"I could do that," said Elijah.

Lakshmi looked at Blaize's six-foot frame. "She would destroy you. By the way, you should totally come out for the basketball team."

Thomas looked over the tablecloth and changed it to *sinister six*. "All right, step one has essentially been completed. Sydney has been accepted into the clique," said Thomas. "Now we have to decide on the next step."

"How about we just videotape Sparks being a constant asshole?" I said.

"Is he any more of an asshole than a sports coach?" asked Lakshmi.

"Um . . . yes?" I said. "He is literally the devil incarnate."

Elijah shook his head. "Won't work. He's got too much power."

"We could mail a video to the school board or something."

"I'm telling you, he's driving enrollment at the school. He has friends in the legislature. The principal can't move against him while he's winning. He only goes down if the team goes down. Besides, it's not just about him, it's about the cult of personality he created."

"Then we need something public," said Lakshmi. "And huge. A failure."

"What if we get everybody disqualified?" I asked. "Like, okay, let's get everybody drunk or high or whatever and then we call the cops, the cops bust everybody—"

"And their rich parents get them out of trouble," interjected Thomas. "That's how it works. They know the judges, they know the cops. Nobody wants to have the pride of the town take the fall. Not for something simple like a party. We need to think bigger. Blaize, what would you do if you wanted everybody to lose?"

She stood there, silent for a moment.

"Even though people are in different events, everybody's really competitive with each other. Hanson wants to be the only champion. He doesn't want to share the spotlight with anybody. That kind of goes for everybody: They don't like each other. Nobody really roots for anyone to succeed. It's all like a gladiatorial arena."

"That's the way Sparks wants it," said Elijah. "He thinks competition makes people stronger. He switches his favorites randomly, just to keep people on their toes. You never know what he's going to say or who he's going to tear into."

"Right," I said, "but how do we exploit that?"

"We make them hate each other," said Lakshmi. "Instead of secretly wanting the other people to fail, we make them *actively* try to make everyone else fail."

"Poison the well," added Thomas. "Sexual frustration, jealousy, petty disputes, personality clashes."

"Let's turn this up to eleven," said Elijah in a British accent. He looked around. "Mine go to eleven. Everyone else's dials go to ten but mine go to eleven—has no one seen *Spinal Tap*?"

"Can we just do this without becoming British?" Thomas sighed.

"You've seen it," he said, turning to me. "You know what I'm talking about. They—"

Lakshmi cut him off. "I've got homework to do, so can we finish our evil plan, please?"

"So we're resolved," said Thomas, serious as hell. "We make them hate each other first. Then we move on Sparks. And what's the best way to make them hate each other?"

"Let's throw a party," I said.

CHAPTER TWENTY-ONE

Party Planning

When I got home from the meeting, Luke was installing a pull-up bar into the framework of our kitchen door. He drilled a few pilot holes with a cordless drill, and then drove the screws in, grunting manfully the whole time. I should add here that Luke was wearing leggings. I wish I was joking. Charlie scrabbled over to me on his little legs as soon as I walked in the door. I scooped him up like a wriggling goblin child and gazed at the pull-up bar in horror.

"Hola," said Luke, switching to Spanish for no apparent reason.

"Howdy," I said. "Hey, Mom?"

She emerged from her bedroom. "Hey, honey."

"What the hell."

Luke tested the bar with a grimace. "Check this out." He bent his knees and hung from the pull-up bar. The frame of the door groaned in protest, but the bar supported his weight. Luke executed a few perfect pull-ups because of course he did.

Mom was delighted. "Fantastic."

"Why is he installing things in the kitchen?"

"I put one in your mom's bedroom, too," he said, doing another pull-up. "If you want, I can put one in your room."

"Why would I want to do that?"

"Upper-body strength," he said. "Always important to maintain upper-body strength. This way, anytime you feel like it, you get on the bar, you do a pull-up. You're in the kitchen doing cooking stuff or whatever—hey, I got a down moment, I'm gonna do some pull-ups. You will be amazed by the transformation in your body."

"Greeeaaat."

He released the bar, his shoulders and chest heaving and a sheen of sweat forming on his forehead. "Fitness is not something you do in a one-hour period in gym class. Fitness is a lifestyle."

I turned to my mom. "Can I talk to you for a second?"

I pulled her into my room and shut the door.

"Okay, before you start," she said, "he's just helping out. He hasn't moved in—"

"But he's moving stuff in."

"Some things have been moved in, yes. Just some clothes and some equipment and things for his dietary needs."

"He has dietary needs now?"

"He needs a lot of whey protein. They're canisters. You won't even notice them."

I scrunched up my face in disgust. "I thought he wasn't going to be moving in."

"Why the hell did you think that?"

"The whole point of me getting a job was so we'd have enough money—"

She threw her hands up. "That's like a hundred dollars a week. *You* decided your job meant he wasn't moving in—you never asked me about that, you went ahead and did that without even bothering to talk to me about it beforehand."

"Do you want him to move in?"

"I enjoy his company, yes."

"For God's sake, why?!"

"Keep your voice down."

"He sucks, Mom. He's installing pull-up bars!"

"Which will come in handy. I can do pull-ups now."

"Well, let's throw you a fucking parade."

"Hey!" She flexed her jaw. "I LIKE him. I like spending time with him. And I LIKE that I actually wake up in the morning with energy and can go exercise and feel good about myself. It hasn't always been easy for me to feel good about myself. So I know you see that as some type of weird midlife crisis I'm in the middle of, but it's actually a choice on my part not to let myself fall apart after your father. I'm doing better than I've done in a long, long time. So shut your mouth for a second and be happy for me.

"You don't have to like him. You don't have to spend a lot of time with him. But you do have to be civil and not make constant snide little comments."

"That's basically my whole personality, so—"

"Goddamn it, Sydney, that's exactly what I'm talking about. You don't have to make everything a joke. I'm a human being, I'm moving on with my life, I deserve a little happiness."

"Do you know that there are female sea anemones that will switch gender if there aren't any decent males around?"

"I really don't see what sea anemones have to do with my dating life."

"I'm just saying—there are many possibilities."

She laughed in spite of herself. "Please be nice."

I sighed. "Fine. But can you seriously cut it out with my fitness journey shit? I don't like him criticizing my body, and I don't like you criticizing my body. I'm fine."

"Deal. And sorry about that."

"Okay."

"I think maybe he'll grow on you. Besides, Charlie really likes him."

"The fuck Charlie does."

Charlie, the traitor, was lying on Luke's lap when we came out of my room. He was rolled over on his back, exposing his pale white belly and his quivering little legs. Luke was rubbing his stomach. A long trail of slobber escaped the side of Charlie's mouth and was pooling on the ground.

"So," said my mom. "We need to celebrate Sydney's win at the speech tournament."

"Hell yes!" said Luke enthusiastically, revealing his snaggle-tooth. "Applebee's it is."

Yay.

There was no talk of my fitness journey at dinner, which was a huge improvement, and I will add that nobody batted an eye when I ordered a sundae. One important nugget of information presented itself, however. Luke was planning on attending the Central Minnesota CrossFit Jamboree and Gathering of Intense People, which was scheduled for the following weekend. It was going to be in Rochester, which was not exactly Central Minnesota, but I figured geography was low on their list of priorities, right after getting swole and getting even swoler.

"That sounds intense," I said.

"Oh yeah," said Luke.

"What exactly . . . um"—and I swallowed hard, because showing an interest in Luke was not exactly my bag, but whatever—"does one do at one of these things?"

Luke's face brightened. "There's a lot of events."

"Kind of like a speech tournament?"

"Yeah, except for like speech for your body. Your muscles do the talking." He chuckled. "And your will. It's mostly about will."

"Yeah, I figured."

"Luke is actually competing," said my mom.

"Wow." And then a tiny evil thought entered my mind. I turned to my mom. "Are you gonna compete?"

She blinked and brushed her hair behind her ears. "Oh, I'm not anywhere near good enough to compete in one of these things."

"They have to have like an over-the-hill division, right?"

"I don't think they call it that, but—"

"Why not? Why not go for it?"

"You should see these women," interjected Luke. "They're like superheroes of fitness. They're glorious. It's stunning what the human body can do when it's pushed to its limits."

"I can only imagine," I said. "But you should go, Mom."

"Honey, I can't win."

"Winning isn't the point. Competing is the point."

Luke pointed at me. "I like that. I like what you just said."

Mom looked down at her plate. "Well, I have to work this weekend anyway, so—"

"You can switch a shift, and maybe I can take a few extra hours to make up for the difference," I said. "Besides, I think the SpongeBob roller coaster will survive without you for two days. Maybe all the kids won't survive, but the roller coaster will be there when you get back."

"I don't know—I'm not . . ."

Luke took over. "You know what Wayne Gretzky said?" *Yes,*

Luke, tell us what Wayne Gretzky said. "You miss one hundred percent of the shots you don't take."

The tiniest flicker of a smile crept onto her face. "Why not? Sure. Yes, I'll do it. Sydney is competing in speech, why shouldn't I compete, too?" She let out a little squeal and reached her hand across the table to squeeze mine.

Moments later, I texted Lakshmi.

Party at my place.

CHAPTER TWENTY-TWO

Party-Apocalypse

The logistics of the party were fairly simple. Thomas and Elijah wouldn't be able to attend, as they were both well-known to members of the Sinister Six, but they said they had their own project to work on. Lakshmi, as a special guest, would be the only non-speech person there. Blaize, despite her recently demoted JV status, would arrive late for additional chaos.

With my newfound street cred in speech, I was able to secure the attendance of just about everybody. Basically, all I had to say was "exclusive for varsity" and "also I have a hot friend who would be there." That was all that was needed to get Logan and Andrew to commit.

Taryn was more suspicious. "Is Milo going to be there?"

"Milo is definitely coming," I lied. "I'm psyched about it—he's so hot."

"I don't really think of him that way," said Taryn.

"Oh, sure. But it doesn't hurt to have some eye candy at the party, you know what I mean?"

"All right. I'll be there."

I didn't even need to tell Anesh directly. He had some kind of extrasensory perception that alerted him to any party opportunities. He slid up to me, his leather jacket creaking slightly. "I hear you're throwing a party."

"Exclusive. Just for varsity. So none of your little groupies."

"Right."

"But my hot friend will be there."

His dense eyebrows lifted. "Is she a fan of debate?"

"She loves debate."

"And she's *actually* hot, right?"

"Unrealistically so."

"I'll be there."

"Yeah, you will."

Once I had Taryn, Milo was a given, so the only one noncommittal was Hanson.

"Oh man, I wish I could," he said, dimples flashing. "I've got dinner with Jeremy on Friday."

"Who's Jeremy?" I asked, intrigued. *Secret boyfriend?* Was I going to need to recalibrate my assessment of Hanson?

"Jeremy Jones. My agent."

"Oh."

Reassessment canceled.

"He's a pretty big deal. He actually reps Kevin Hart. We're on a first-name basis 'cause we're pretty tight."

Assessment doubling down.

"Well, maybe after your dinner with Jeremy, then," I said. "I'm sure we'll be going late."

"Yeah, well, Jeremy's getting me VIP passes to a concert in the city, so. I'll probably be hanging with some pretty important people."

"Wow. I guess make sure to remember us after you hit the big time."

"I'll try." He grinned. "But seriously," he said, leaning in, "I appreciate the offer. I just have so many things going on right now it's hard to juggle all of them. But if I get a chance, I'll stop by."

"I'll be waiting with bated breath."

"He's actually got an *agent*?" said Lakshmi as we hit Party City for decorations after school on Friday. "I thought that was just a rumor."

"The universe is unfair, so yes, he definitely has an agent."

"For what?"

"I don't know. His *memoirs*? Acting shit. Something."

Lakshmi groaned. "I love how he casually drops that in conversation. Sorry, I have to meet with my *agent*. My agent Jeremy, who is my bud. I could have dinner with you, but my *agent Jeremy Jones* says I need to watch my caloric intake. My *agent*

Jeremy Jones thinks it's a good idea that I be seen with *models*. Fuck that noise. I hope he does show up; I'll kick his ass."

"Focus. What color streamers do you think makes people hate each other the most?"

"All streamers make people hate each other."

"Blue and white it is, then. What kind of booze do you think we should get?"

"What do you have at your place?"

"I'm pretty sure my mom has some wine left over from the divorce—she never drinks it. We could get smashed on that."

"That is classy as fuck."

"I believe you've just given me the title of my memoir. *Classy as Fuck: The Sydney Williams Story*."

Lakshmi laughed and bounced into me, nearly knocking me into the Valentine's Day section of party favors. "Ooh," she said, examining them. "Maybe we should make it a love theme."

"Kill me."

"*Exactly*. What better way to drive people to hatred than with some enforced heterosexual corporatized bullshit? What if we made everybody write notes to the person they liked?"

"That's so middle school."

She touched her nose. "I say we go full middle school. Seven minutes in heaven, spin the bottle, Jell-O shots."

"You are an evil, evil person."

She bowed. "Thank you."

"Too bad Elijah won't be there," I joked.

She cocked her head. "Why?"

"'Cause he would be all over that spin the bottle. I think that would give him the courage he needs."

"To do what?"

"To . . . you know . . . summon his courage. To profess his undying love for you."

She snorted. "Whatever."

"He looks at you like you're Wonder Woman. Although, to be fair, you look a lot like Wonder Woman."

"Maybe he's just appreciating my kick-ass nature."

"Maybe he's desperately in love with you." I winced inwardly. *There I go again, saying things with my mouth before my brain thinks them.*

Lakshmi laughed it off. "I've known him for like three years, okay? He's not—we're friends."

"'Cause he's shy."

"Dude," said Lakshmi. "Have you *met* Elijah? He's in the improv comedy troupe. He gets up and makes a fool of himself in front of strangers. He is not shy. If he liked me, he'd tell me. You know what I think? I think *you* like him."

"What? No."

"And you're just like concocting this little fantasy romance between your two best friends because you're afraid of your massive lady boner for that ginger."

My mouth hung open. "I have no lady boner for him."

"Sure."

"I don't!"

Lakshmi pulled out a glittering garland of red hearts and shook it in my face.

"Okay, maybe I find him slightly appealing in a sort of anthropological sense," I said. "But he's super into you, so it doesn't matter."

"Okay, sport."

"If you were a guy, and you had the choice to like one of us, which would you pick?"

"What the fuck is that logic?"

"I mean," I said.

"What?"

"I mean look at you and look at me."

"What about it?"

I waved my hands at her. "Don't be stupid."

"I'm not being stupid, what are you talking about?"

"I mean, there's no, like, competition there."

"It's not a competition," she said. "And don't do that to yourself. If you like him, ask him out."

"He likes you!"

"Fuck. Sydney. You are worth it, okay?"

I laughed nervously and looked away.

"You are. Jesus. I don't know how it got into your mind that you're garbage, but you are an awesome person and that boy would lose his shit if you liked him."

I turned away, swallowing hard. *I don't think I'm garbage.*

But there was a little part of me that wondered . . . *maybe I do*. Lakshmi had struck a nerve. "Let's just get this shit and go," I said.

Of course we switched to red and white streamers, since it was more in keeping with our misplaced Valentine's Day theme. With the help of an old wad of packing tape, we slapped the streamers to the walls and ran them over the top of the living room. We had also picked up a few strings of red heart lights, which I arranged around the window (also with packing tape). These I had accentuated with a red-and-purple lava lamp that I had won in fourth grade from a Dave & Buster's. Combined with switching out the lamps with colored lightbulbs, it created quite a look.

"I think our theme has shifted from Valentine's Day to House of Ill Repute," said Lakshmi, observing the lava lamp.

"'Ill Repute'? You're such a dork."

"Whores. House of Whores, then."

"The word is *brothel*, thank you."

"Maybe we should make a sign," joked Lakshmi. "Just the word *brothel* and put it right over the door."

"I'm just imagining my mom coming home and seeing this. 'What did I tell you about starting brothels!'"

Lakshmi pretended to be me. "I did it for you, Mom! You said you wanted me to get a job and help out!"

"God, don't get me started. I took a ten-hour shift on Sunday."

"I think you'll be recovered by then. Pray for me, though, I have a basketball game tomorrow night."

"Oh shit."

"Yeah, it's our final game of the season."

"I'm totally coming, then."

"We're gonna get crushed."

"I'm still gonna be there. For moral support. To witness the crushing."

I rummaged through the pantry (it wasn't much of a pantry, it was more like a tiny closet stuffed with food) and emerged with four bottles of wine. "All right, you work on the Jell-O shots and I'll make sangria," I said, googling how to make sangria on my phone.

Opening the wine proved to be more difficult than I imagined. Mom didn't have a corkscrew; she had some kind of medieval torture contraption that had a spike and handles that had probably been used to stab out eyes during the Inquisition. I gave it a shot, but apparently it was more effective against eyes than corks, and all I managed to do was drill a tiny, pathetic divot out of the top of the cork.

"Here," said Lakshmi, taking the thing out of my puny hands. With impressive forearm strength she managed to break the cork in half, then extract both halves of the cork while only leaving a few chunks of it in the wine.

"Is that how you're supposed to do that?"

"Fuck if I know."

Sangria is basically fruit and wine punch (although, according to Google, it's supposed to steep overnight, but we didn't exactly have time for that), and I chopped up a bunch of apples and strawberries and tossed them into the bowl with two different kinds of red wine. The result was an abomination, but I hoped no one would really be able to tell the difference. Then again, with these kids, they'd probably been having the finest vintage wines since kindergarten, so who could say.

Anesh was the first one to arrive, exactly on time, and he looked at the Valentine's decorations like he had just stepped in dog shit. It was perhaps not helpful that Charlie launched himself at Anesh, ramming into his leg and colliding with the wall. I will add that Charlie looked resplendent in his pink tutu.

"Come on in. Woo," I said. "Party time."

He was wearing a floral shirt that was suspiciously open at the top, revealing two or three strands of meticulously combed chest hair. *Nice work, Anesh.* He also seemed to have taken a bath in Axe Body Spray before he arrived. Charlie immediately began humping his leg, showing both his dedication to the Valentine's Day theme and his poor taste in men. Anesh shook him off.

"He likes you," I said as Anesh tried to prevent Charlie's wriggly, muscular form from making love to his knee.

"Anybody else here yet?"

"Nope. Just you and me."

"And me!" called Lakshmi from the kitchen, where she was putting the Jell-O shots in the fridge.

"All right. All right, then." Charlie retreated back to his dog bed, satisfied. Anesh ran his eyes over the brothel décor. "I'm getting an interesting picture of your home life."

"I figured with it being so close to Valentine's Day that we'd do a Valentine's Day thing."

"I'm not big into romance," he said.

"Right."

"I'm more into the, uh . . . aftermath of romance." He winked.

"The bitter breakups?"

"No, prior to the breakups."

"The jealous rages?"

"No."

"The distant silences when someone spends more time on their phone than talking to you?" I loved talking to Anesh.

"What do you have to drink?" he said, giving up.

The "sangria" mutated over the course of the party. Every so often I'd add more fruit, and when the liquid began to get low, Lakshmi would open a different bottle of wine and dump it in. The sangria achieved consciousness about two hours in, and from there, began plotting to kill us, which it was doing very well.

Logan arrived next, dressed in his "party gear," which included a popped collar and ripped jeans, like he was trying to be in a music video from the eighties. Taryn and Milo showed up together, followed by Andrew, and that was the extent of our rager. By the time the third person arrived, Charlie was exhausted. It was a lot of work being a dog. Hanson was a no-show and Blaize was planning on joining us later, when we needed an extra boost of chaos. So it was me and Lakshmi and five of the Sinister Six.

Let the games begin.

It began like most parties, with us coagulating in the kitchen, clumped around the tiny island and trying to engage in conversation. It was not good. Andrew was clearly used to better parties, the kind of suburban keggers with swimming pools and hundreds of people you'd never seen before. You could feel the waves of disdain dropping off of him.

"So it's just you and your mom here, huh?" he asked languorously.

"Yup. Single mother and daughter." I high-fived Lakshmi for no reason.

"Well, I guess with your dad in prison this is what happens."

I plugged my mouth by sipping the bitter, evil sangria.

I struck Anesh first, leading him away from the kitchen to the couch. Despite his player reputation, he didn't have the highest tolerance for alcohol, and he was already slightly tipsy. *Weakened antelope*, I thought.

"You know, I have to just tell you—I saw you in the tournament the other day, and you were like killing it." I hadn't seen him in the tournament, of course, as I would rather disembowel myself than watch a policy debate round, but I hoped there were enough people in the audience that he wouldn't catch the lie.

He smoothed his hair a little bit and made unsettling eye contact with me. "That means a lot, Sydney."

"It's so impressive. I don't think that other team knew what the hell they were doing."

"Yeah, they show up and they haven't done any research and they just get destroyed."

"I know, right? I love how you like support your points." Inwardly, I started slapping myself in the face. *I love how you support your points?*

"I do a lot of supporting of *points*," he said, trying to insert a double entendre into the conversation and failing.

"It sucks so bad that you guys got second. That was a fucking robbery."

"It was one tournament."

"Oh yeah. Definitely." I touched his arm. "I shouldn't say this, but, um . . . I mean, it's pretty obvious."

"What's obvious?"

"You're the one with the talent. I shouldn't say it, I'm sure Logan is awesome or whatever, but . . . despite what he says, I think you are the one carrying that team."

If Anesh had been a cat, his little cat-ears would have just perked up. "What did he say?"

"Oh, you know how he is. He just talks shit. He probably doesn't mean anything by it."

"He talks shit?"

I waved my hand in the air. "No, I mean . . . I mean, you know, right?"

His thick eyebrows knotted and unknotted. "Know what?"

I looked around and leaned in. "He talks about you." Anesh's eyes started going back and forth. "But I don't believe any of it. And I don't think he's nearly as racist as he comes off with all that Bollywood shit. People just don't think about how they sound."

"What Bollywood shit?"

"It was a joke," I said. "He was just being funny. I don't even want to go into it." I patted him on the knee. "I need to check on the wine punch." I got up and left for the kitchen, glancing back ever so slightly to see the troubled look on his face. Bingo.

The key to ruining relationships, I've found, is that you can't do it all at once. You're just spreading seeds. You're like the Johnny Appleseed of evil, planting little ideas in people's heads, and you have to let them come to their stupid conclusions on their own. Of course, the idea that Logan was talking shit or doing some kind of racist impression of his partner was not really outside the bounds of possibility. He probably was. I was just bringing it to Anesh's attention.

Logan had glommed on to Lakshmi like a fungal infection. They were both in the kitchen when I got there.

"Do you mind not staring at my ass?" Lakshmi was saying.

"I'm about honesty," said Logan. "And I could tell you right now that I'm not gonna stare at your ass, but I think we both know that I'd be lying. So let's just be real with each other: I'm gonna stare at your ass 'cause it's inherently beautiful, and you can stare at my ass if you want." Lakshmi was about to say something when he put his hands up. "Of course I know, as a female, you are less visual than me. Males are extremely visual. And I am visualizing the hell out of that booty."

Lakshmi took a moment, pulling her hair back into a ponytail.

"Here's what I'm gonna say to that," she said in a measured voice. "Because I want to educate you right now, and I know that you don't have a lot of experience talking to other humans in a respectful way. But your ignorance right now is a choice, and this thing where you think that your little man handbook is telling you to be direct and abrasive to establish your alpha male cred isn't working. So you're not gonna look at me anymore, and I'm not gonna powerfully and completely wreck you in front of these nice people."

Logan nodded and a small voice came out of him. "Okay." He retreated out of the room.

I looked over at Lakshmi. "We're supposed to be encouraging conflict *between* them."

"Trust me," she said. "I know what I'm doing with that one."

* * *

Separating Taryn and Milo was almost impossible. Taryn was a wearing a midriff-exposing half-shirt despite the freezing weather, complete with tight pants and tall boots. She looked like a tiny evil pixie. Milo was in a shaggy sweater, and they intertwined with each other like vines. Eventually, though, Milo had to go to the bathroom, and I was able to insert myself into Taryn's sphere of attention.

"Can I talk to you in my bedroom for a second?" I asked her. She blinked.

"I really have to say something to you, and I don't feel comfortable saying it in front of everyone. Please. It would help me so much."

Reluctantly, she came, noticing the décor in my room like something was rotting. Charlie had retreated to my bed and lay on his back, his ruffly pink tutu rising and falling into the air with his raggedy snores. It really brought the room together.

"First of all," I said, "I feel like my understanding of things has really evolved since the start of school and I want to thank you for that."

She looked at me blankly.

"But that's not really what I wanted to talk to you about," I said, pulling the door closed and giggling just a bit. "Okay, so . . . this is really awkward . . . at first I thought you and Milo were a couple, and you guys are so amazing together—"

She was about to say something, and I cut her off. "I know, I know, you're not actually a couple. That's so inspirational that he's able to dominate his own feelings like that. I wish more guys would be like that, honestly. And I was like, he's so hot, you know, and maybe he would be into me, and I was kind of thinking about that."

"Milo has really exceptional taste," said Taryn. "So I don't know that he would go for you—"

"I know, I know, thank you for being so honest with me about my deficiencies. Because I know that Milo is waaay better than me and would never stoop to hook up with someone like me. I get that. Thank you for reminding me of that."

"I don't think he's even sending you signals," said Taryn. "That's not how he is."

"You're so right," I said, clutching her arm. "Besides, he's so into Blaize right now. Because I was like, 'Maybe he'd like me,' but then I saw him looking at her and I was like, 'Yes, I am here for this. I am here for this relationship.'"

Taryn's smile cracked just a bit.

"I ship them so hard. They could be like one of those couples where you combine their names? Blaizo. Milaize. Malaise. Needs some work."

"I don't really think that's a thing."

"But she is like—she's like an actual goddess, right? People are making statues of her. I'm pretty sure she's modeling for the art department."

"I don't think she's modeling for the art department. And besides, most of them do abstract art, so it doesn't really matter."

"She could be. She's amazing. And like a really good person, you know? That's the best part about Blaize. She's got this pure soul, you know? That's probably what's attracting Milo. And her body. I mean I don't want to body-shame anyone, but I'm not, I'm just body-appreciating her. I mean, I look at myself, or you, next to her—no contest, right? And I feel like Milo should be with someone really special."

"She's not even varsity anymore," she said.

"Right. Absolutely. Right. And that's another thing: Milo doesn't even care about that, right? But I need your help."

"To do what?"

"You know him so well," I said. "I want your help in hooking them up."

Taryn smirked. "Milo doesn't 'hook up.' He's not like that."

"Definitely," I said. "I really wish Blaize was here so I could see them in action. That would be like movie love."

"I honestly don't feel like he would like her."

"Don't you think they would be really cute together?"

"No. Blaize is superficial. And Milo is . . . he's deep, okay? I feel stupid saying it, but he's deep."

"Ohhh . . ." I said. "I think Blaize is deep, too. She's deeper than me. She thinks about all kinds of stuff."

"No offense, Sydney, but most people are deeper than you." She turned around, opened the door, then headed for the living room and sat on Milo's lap.

I texted Blaize: *Time for your entrance.*

* * *

When I got back to the living room, Lakshmi was trying not to tear Milo's fluffy head off.

"I'm sure there's shit that you like that I think is stupid," said Lakshmi.

"It's not actively ruining people's lives," said Milo.

"How am I ruining people's lives?"

"Oh, let's see, concussions, toxic culture, joint damage, inflated sense of self-worth. There's not a single study that shows the long-term effects of sports are positive."

"I'm gonna take your studies and shove them up your ass."

I intervened. "All right, all right, we don't need to debate right now. Besides, we know who would win." I managed to catch Anesh's eye. I surveyed the room. "But it's time for a special moment in tonight's party."

On cue, there was a rap on the door.

I opened it and Blaize burst in, holding a box. "Hey, guys! Who's up for Pictionary?!"

Andrew groaned.

"Hell yes!" I said.

A chilling mist swept through the party. I knew several of them were considering throwing themselves out the heart-lit window to escape.

Lakshmi pumped her fist. "Fuck yes. This is what I come to parties for."

Anesh yielded to the momentum, and by then it was too late to stop this train. They were doomed.

I had made certain not to consume too much of the sangria poison (it wasn't actually poison, but it probably tasted exactly like it) so I could concentrate on maximizing the relentless conflict inherent in Pictionary. I was an expert in this. My parents used to play Pictionary, and it was about 50 percent of the reason why they got a divorce. I mean, yes, there were the crimes, but those were secondary to the Pictionary slugfests.

The reason was that Pictionary required teamwork, the ability to draw, a competitive spirit, and a sense of fun, which were usually mutually exclusive. Plus, the game seemed to rely on your estimation of your teammates' intelligence, which drove everyone into clouds of murderous rage.

Child of divorce for the win! If there was one thing I understood, it was how even decent people could be driven to hate each other through continuous applied pressure. For a group of ravenous assholes, this would likely end with bodies on the floor.

I picked the teams to accentuate the conflict.

THE COMPETITIVE ASSHOLES: Andrew, Anesh, Logan, and Lakshmi (not that Lakshmi was an asshole, but she was the ringer).

THE MILO-IS-DEAD-SEXY TEAM: Me, Blaize, Taryn, and Milo.

It helped that Logan couldn't draw to save his life, Lakshmi intentionally shouted the wrong guesses at everything, and Andrew held everyone in contempt and considered guessing wrong answers to be beneath him. This sent Anesh into a catastrophic meltdown right from the start.

"What is that?" he yelled as Logan frantically drew what looked to be a fat baby with a nuclear missile.

"Look at it!" shouted Logan.

"I am looking at it! It's nothing! It looks like nothing!"

"Use your goddamn brain! What is wrong with you?!"

"A FLOWER!" shouted Lakshmi.

"Nothing is wrong with me! You can't fucking draw!" growled Anesh.

"I am awesome at this!"

"GLOBAL WARMING!" shouted Lakshmi again, cutting off Andrew.

"You are the worst! I have a four-year-old sister that's better than you!" seethed Anesh.

"Come on, guess something!"

"So I'm just supposed to shout random words now?! Is that your strategy?!"

"SUPERMAN!"

"And time," I said.

Logan turned his card, eyes red with pain. "It was the arms race."

Anesh gripped the sides of his head. "Draw an arm! Draw fucking arms! What is so hard about that?!"

"THIS IS AN ARM!" Logan scrawled maniacally on the paper again. "SEE?! SEE THE ARM?!"

"It doesn't really look like an arm." Andrew sighed.

Our side fared much better, which was even worse for everyone involved. I had tipped Blaize off to my strategy of sowing discord between Taryn and Milo, and her secret genius at Pictionary was the perfect strategy.

Milo was drawing a creature with three legs and a stick.

"I don't get it," said Taryn.

"What does it sound like?" I said.

"You can't say that," said Logan from the other side of the room. "I think she's disqualified. She's disqualified, right?"

"I'll allow it," said Lakshmi, who had appointed herself judge in these matters.

Milo drew action lines all around the creature.

"Is it moving?" asked Taryn.

"What does it sound like?" I repeated as Logan groaned again.

"Caterwauling!" shouted Blaize, and Milo lit up with joy.

"Yes! YES! Woo! High five!" He high-fived everyone, except Blaize, who jumped up to hug him. Taryn hugged him more.

"You guys are cheating!" yelled Logan, waggling a finger in our direction.

"We're not cheating," I said. "Blaize is just amazing at this. Isn't she amazing, Milo?"

Milo tried to nod, but he was underneath Taryn, so it was difficult.

"It's like you two can read each other's minds," I said. "It's so special."

The Pictionary was relentless, overly competitive, and awful. The sangria flowed and poison bubbled in the air. Logan and Anesh were barely on speaking terms. Andrew had had enough with his team and was checking his phone in annoyance. Taryn was guessing like a maniac now, trying to drown out Blaize. It was like the worst Thanksgiving ever. Logan had started getting a bit drunk, which only made him more Loganesque, and Taryn had resorted to downing enough sangria to drown a guinea pig.

There was a loud knock on the door, and my heart quivered. Hanson was there. "ARE YOU READY TO GET CRAZY?!" Everyone looked up. Eh. We weren't that ready.

Hanson's presence elevated things immediately. The music changed. The lights got more intense. People relaxed. He had a way of talking to people, leaning over one knee, looking them directly in the eye, like he was actually interested in what they were saying.

Things started improving. The sense of evil and dread that had descended with Pictionary began to alleviate. I watched it happen from my side of the room. Then I went to the kitchen to text Elijah.

CHAPTER TWENTY-THREE

Spinning the Bottle

ELIJAH

And you're sure you don't want me to send over a stripper?

ME

I am 1000% sure I do not want a stripper and I'm also
1000% sure you don't know where to find a stripper.

ELIJAH

I have Google.

ME

I am even more sure than ever I don't want a
googled-stripper.

ELIJAH

Well I wish I could be there. I want to see this.

ME

Maybe you could hide in my bedroom and peek out
through the door.

ELIJAH

                                           ME

                                         Not like that.

ELIJAH

                                           ME

                                         Stop it.

I looked up to see Hanson drifting into the kitchen.

"So, what happed to the VIP lounge?" I teased.

"I thought it might be more fun to come here."

"Seriously?"

"No, the lead singer was suffering from 'exhaustion,' so they canceled the gig."

"Oh. Why don't they just say he's in rehab?"

"Maintaining appearances, I guess." He smiled, loping around the tiny kitchen and taking a look at things. "Important to maintain appearances."

"It's probably not what you're used to," I said. "I think Andrew is spraying himself with disinfectant every time I turn my back."

"It's quaint."

"*Quaint?* That's a word I haven't heard used in relation to this place before."

"It's less boudoir-like than the living room. So that's a bonus."

"I believe the term you're looking for is *magical*."

He laughed. "Okay."

"So what did you and your *agent* talk about?"

He shook his head. "I could tell you, but then I'd have to kill you."

"Might be worth it."

"All right," he said, leaning over the little island and flexing his triceps. "I'm gonna do a couple of auditions as soon as speech season is over—Netflix has a new teen comedy and they're looking for an actual teenager. It's down to me and like three other guys."

"Wow."

"Yeah. I don't know if I'm gonna get it or not, but . . . I'm gonna get it."

"Oh."

"I always get what I want," he said, a wolfish gleam entering his eyes.

"That's good to know." I gulped.

"Some people just have it, you know."

"Like Milo," I said.

It was like I threw cold water all over him. "Milo?"

"Oh yeah. You've seen his duo, right? Most amazing thing I've ever seen. To be honest, he's probably the most talented person on the team."

Then I headed back to the living room before Hanson could say anything.

* * *

Lakshmi was holding court brilliantly when I returned. "You know what we should do?" Everyone waited. Logan swayed ever so slightly. Lakshmi turned and yanked the red streamers off the pull-up bar over the kitchen door. "Let's see which boy can do the most pull-ups."

Logan and Anesh recoiled as one.

"Oh, hell no," said Logan.

"What's the matter?" asked Lakshmi.

"Dude. No."

"I mean, if you don't think you can do one, I'm not going to force you."

He nearly swallowed his tongue. "I can do a pull-up."

"Can you do more than Anesh or Milo?"

Milo got up from the couch. "First of all, this is childish and stupid. I'm not going to subscribe to some kind of medieval masculinity contest with these people, especially since if you look at Anesh and Logan, they're clearly incapable of doing a single pull-up."

I clapped hard. "Woo!" I said a little prayer of thanks that Milo was such an incredible douche. It made things so much easier.

Milo gripped the pull-up bar with both hands.

"Do it!" I yelled.

He did one. Then another one. Then he kicked his legs and fought his way over the bar for a third time.

"The number to beat is three!" called out Lakshmi.

I filled everyone's drinks. "Whoever gets the most gets control of spin the bottle."

"What?" said Andrew, but I was already moving on.

Hanson did eight. Logan and Anesh tied with two each, although Logan swore up and down that Anesh was cheating and that he hadn't gone all the way down on his second pull-up, which meant he should have been disqualified. Anesh, for his part, was also convinced that Logan had cheated because he hadn't straightened out his elbows. It was amazing. Andrew declined to participate because it was obviously beneath him.

"I bet Taryn can do more than three," I said after the boys were done. She shook her head. "You weigh like eight pounds, I bet you can—I mean, seriously, if you can't reach the bar, I bet Blaize can lift you up."

"No thanks," said Taryn, narrowing her eyes and spitting venom at me. A kind of malicious silence descended on everyone. *That was pretty mean, Sydney.* A wave of regret passed through me. Was I going too far? Was it time to call it a night?

Then I overheard Anesh whisper to Andrew as soon as Lakshmi turned her back, "I'm so gonna hit that."

Game on, motherfuckers.

"I win, right?" said Hanson, winking at me. "Guess I always win."

Lakshmi spit on her hands and did ten pull-ups.

"I do believe we have a winner," I said, then added, "I know you weren't really trying, Milo; it's cool. How about we move on to the final game of the evening?"

"Ooh," said Blaize.

Lakshmi snatched an empty bottle of wine off the kitchen island. "All right, then."

Moments later, we had all gathered in a circle in the living room. The red light from the lava lamp and the colored lightbulb cast a hellish glow over our faces. I had brought out some candles and placed them strategically around the room, which unfortunately cast a slight cinnamon latte odor over the proceedings. Still, the flickering candlelight, the satanic heart lights, and the globular lava lamp were enough to turn my living room into a sordid nightmare. Some of the boys sat on the couch, but most of the girls were cross-legged on the ground. Charlie returned from the bedroom and lay in the center of us, panting happily and wanting to watch the darkness unfold.

"The game," said Lakshmi, her dark eyes flashing in the red light, "is seven minutes in heaven."

"Seven MINUTES?!" whined Logan from his perch on the arm of the couch. "It's supposed to be like sixty seconds!"

"I can basically do my whole speech in seven minutes," countered Andrew.

Hanson wasn't having any of it. "Are we like ten years old? What is this?"

Lakshmi eyed him. "You seem scared."

"I'm not scared, I'm just not into sleepovers anymore. Are we gonna get like a Ouija board out next?"

Damn, I wish I had thought of that.

"This'll be fun," said Lakshmi, turning her focus to the other boys in the room, her lips glistening ever so slightly. I watched as Logan, Anesh, and Andrew all seemed to quiver in anticipation.

"I'm game," said Anesh. "And, Logan, if you only need sixty seconds, that's okay. Some people don't take very long."

I couldn't tell if he turned red from the burn or the light.

Milo moved from the couch to the floor, extricating himself from Taryn. "I'm in."

"Sweet," said Blaize, tapping him on the knee.

"Let's do sixty seconds," I said to Lakshmi. "I think that will be enough."

She caught my eye and nodded. The air was thick with alcohol, volcanic hormones, and the heady scent of cinnamon-spiced latte. Perfect for terrible decisions.

"But here's the rule," said Lakshmi, putting a finger up. "I'm not here for heteronormative bullshit. That means, whoever the bottle points to, that's who you go in the closet with." A wave of discomfort and excitement passed through everyone. Most of the boys adjusted the way they were sitting. "I don't care if it's a boy, a girl, or Charlie."

Charlie laid his jowls on the floor and looked up.

"Okay, not Charlie. And since I did more pull-ups than all of you motherfuckers, I'm running this show." Lakshmi made eye contact with everyone in turn, and they all looked back, beaten.

We had them.

With a skilled spinner, it's never random. Lakshmi, with her overdeveloped sense of touch from years of basketball, was the perfect person to direct the ensuing madness. Add that to the fact that most of the people in the room were drunk, and our chances of success were high. I had scrawled out a list on a scrap of paper and given it to her to moments before.

ME–ANDREW

BLAIZE–MILO

LOGAN–ANESH

TARYN–HANSON

If we made it to round two, I had some other options available.

Lakshmi spun the empty bottle of pinot noir on the dingy carpet, subtly guiding it to our first marks. "Andrew . . . and . . . Sydney!"

I leaped up. Andrew was less enthusiastic.

The coat closet was less of a closet and more of a tiny cramped space that could barely fit four coats, much less Minnesota-grade enormous puffy winter coats. Andrew had to duck his head to avoid the ceiling, and both of us squished in. Lakshmi shut the door with a slam and everything went to darkness. I could hear

Blaize cheering from outside—I mentally made a note to thank the universe for delivering her into the conspiracy.

I turned my phone on, pointing it toward the floor to give us a little white light. He was very close to me; I could feel his breath on the top of my head.

"It's okay," I whispered, positioning myself near him. "I know you're gay. It's cool. I don't want to do anything anyway."

"Why do you think I'm gay?"

"I saw your piece."

He chuckled. "Oh, shit, really? Dude. That's fucking hilarious. No, I'm not gay. Jesus."

"Why do you say you're gay if you're not actually gay?"

"Are you serious right now? 'Cause it helps me win. I can get up there and be like, 'Oh, my dad wanted to send me to conversion camp, everybody cry for me!' What, I'm gonna be like, 'Yeah, I'm rich, and I'm tall, and I'm good-looking, and my parents are doctors. Tough life, right?' Nobody's gonna vote for me."

"So you're like lying with your piece?"

"Yeah, I make shit up. And the audience is so stupid they just fall for it."

Lakshmi flung open the door. "All right, quit making out!"

"Milo and . . . Blaize."

"Yes!" I pumped my fist and tried to make eye contact with Taryn. She wasn't looking anywhere near me.

"Do we have to do this?" said Taryn. "I mean, I just think

like . . . this is like so . . . childish and like hormonal and . . ."

"Don't worry; maybe you'll be next," goaded Lakshmi.

Taryn huffed, but it was too late. Milo was already on his feet. Blaize stepped over her and both of them climbed into the closet. I moved closer to Taryn.

"They are so cute," I whispered under my breath.

Lakshmi shut them in.

As usual, Anesh was my unwitting accomplice. "Dude, they are going so hard right now. So hard. He's got his tongue down her throat—"

"Would you shut up?" Taryn glared.

"You've got it all wrong, Anesh. I think it's more romantic," I countered. "He's probably just gracefully moving her hair out of her eyes, and they're just like staring at each other soulfully."

"In the dark?" said Anesh. "Nope. Hands are doing the talking."

Lakshmi joined in. "It can be both. It can be romantic and sensual at the same time. That's the best."

"You're so right," I said. "The eyes are staring, but the hands—"

"It's more like animal instinct," said Anesh.

"Is the sixty seconds up yet?" asked Taryn.

"Oh, whoops, I forgot to start the timer," said Lakshmi.

Two minutes and fourteen seconds later, Milo and Blaize came out of the closet, looking slightly flushed. Taryn was a tiny lump of pink-haired trembling anger by that point. I had cleared this particular combination with Blaize beforehand, and she was game (she wasn't interested in Milo at all, and she wasn't worried about him trying something).

"Nothing happened," whispered Milo to Taryn afterward. "I'm not like that. We just talked."

"About what?"

Blaize leaned over and touched Milo's knee. "Thank you," she said. "That was the most amazing . . . conversation of my life." Damn she was good.

Taryn twitched and was about to say something, but by then Lakshmi had spun the bottle again. "Logan . . . and . . . Anesh!"

Blaize roared lustily. Soon everyone else was joining in.

"What the hell?" said Logan.

"The bottle does not lie, my friend," said Lakshmi. "INTO THE CLOSET WITH YOU."

Anesh shook his head. "This is fucked up. And I'm way out of his league anyway."

Logan snorted. "In your dreams."

"You both deserve each other," snapped Lakshmi, yanking Logan to his feet and shoving him into the closet. Anesh turned to protest to the rest of the group.

Blaize pounded on the floor. "I want to see tongue!"

"You're not seeing anything," shrieked Anesh. "We're in the closet!"

"I want to hear tongue, then!"

Lakshmi took his hand and shut him in with Logan. She leaned on the door afterward, making sure they couldn't make a break for it. The rest of us were silent, trying to hear any noise from the inside.

Nothing. Lakshmi cautioned patience as we crept toward the door. I could hear Anesh faintly.

ANESH: Oh my God, your breathing is so annoying.

LOGAN: Oh, I'm sorry. I'll stop, then.

ANESH: Thank you.

LOGAN: You smell like you took a shower in pig intestines.

ANESH: Jealous much?

LOGAN: Of what?

ANESH: Dude, you just touched my knee.

LOGAN: I didn't touch your knee; there isn't any room in here.

ANESH: You totally touched my knee. You like approached me and touched my knee.

LOGAN: Why would I touch your knee? Your knees are the least sexy part of you.

ANESH: Oh, so you've made a list, then. What's number one?

LOGAN: I don't have a list.

ANESH: It's like a mental list, then? YOU DID IT AGAIN.

LOGAN: I didn't fucking touch you.

ANESH: WHY IS YOUR KNEE FONDLING
MY KNEE?

LOGAN: HOW CAN MY KNEE FONDLE
ANYTHING?

Whump.

LOGAN: OW!

ANESH: THAT'S WHAT YOU GET. OW!
FUCK YOU!

LOGAN: NO FUCK YOU!

Wham wham wham

Lakshmi looked at me, then flung open the door, allowing both of them to tumble out, red-faced and sweaty and spitting profanities. Anesh pulled his leg away from Logan and shoved him hard, knocking him into the wall. Hanson got up and rushed between them to prevent a fight.

"Whoa!" he said. "Guys, it's just for fun, all right?"

"Looks like you've really got that homophobia under control," said Lakshmi.

"I'm not homophobic," complained Logan, nursing his shoulder. "He's the one who's homophobic."

"Dude, whatever," said Anesh. "I'm the least homophobic person alive."

"My ass," said Logan. "I barely touched you with my knee and you freaked out."

"YOU WERE CARESSING ME WITH YOUR KNEE!"

"HOW IS THAT EVEN POSSIBLE?!"

"All right," I said, stopping them by raising my hands. "There's only one way to prove that you're both not homophobic . . . and that's by sending you back into the closet."

Ninety seconds later they were both sitting on opposite sides of the living room, no longer able to speak. Both of them were subdued, looking down at their feet. Taryn was glaring at Blaize and Milo. Andrew still seemed blissfully aloof.

"Taryn . . ." called out Lakshmi, deftly stopping the bottle on her. "And . . . Hanson!"

I kept my eyes glued to Milo. His veneer cracked ever so slightly.

"Woo!" I yelled. "Hell yes!"

"I still think this is immature and ridiculous," said Hanson.

"And yet we're still doing it," I said.

Afterward, it was pretty clear that Taryn and Hanson were the only couple who actually kissed during their time in the closet. When she came out, she had a shy smile on her face and pulled her blond-and-pink hair behind her ears. Hanson grinned goofily and rubbed the back of his neck. Milo fluffed his hair and stared out the window, deliberately avoiding looking at either of them. Taryn rubbed her mouth slightly, then settled into the couch, for the first time sitting somewhere that wasn't Milo's lap.

"I think we should keep playing," said Milo finally.

"Are you sure about that?" asked Taryn.

"Lakshmi hasn't even gone yet."

"The bottle hasn't pointed to me yet. I have no control over that."

"I thought you were a gentleman," said Taryn acidly. "Nothing happened when you were in the closet, right?"

"Nothing happened *before*. But maybe something will happen *now*."

But I wasn't about to risk additional combinations, or chance a spin that would pair Taryn and Milo together so they could kiss and make up. Best to let everyone sit with this for a while. The level of poison in the air was just right.

From there, the party continued to disintegrate until Ubers were called. One by one everyone filed out, barely able to look at, much less speak to, one another.

Mission accomplished.

Hanson lingered in the kitchen, filling his cup with the last of the sangria mutation. "I have to admit," he said as I cleaned up, "this was a pretty cool party. I had my doubts."

"Never doubt me," I said with a smile. "I'm good at planning."

Lakshmi was in the living room, patting Charlie on the head.

"You and Taryn," I wheedled. "That's pretty hot."

He smirked. "She's repulsive."

"And you still kissed her?"

"My lips are sealed. They weren't sealed in the closet, but they are sealed now."

"Oh, I see how it is. Do you kiss a lot of girls you find repulsive?"

"Depends."

"I guess I don't understand that."

"Just blowing off steam," he said, hopping onto the island and letting his long legs dangle over the side. He drained the dregs of the sangria from his cup. "If you can't act irresponsible every once in a while, what's the point of being a teenager?"

"I see. Can I ask you a question?" I said. "What do you think of Sparks?"

It threw him. He leaned back and looked at the ceiling. "Fuuuuck."

"No, seriously."

"I think he's a genius. I mean, all right, some people—they can't handle him. They aren't able to deal with that level of expectation. But like . . . he's an emperor of a tiny kingdom, right? Like, he is a very big fish in a very little pond right now. But the real world? That's how you succeed. You don't succeed by making friends or being nice to people. You succeed by being the best, letting everyone know you're the best.

"Let me let you in on a little secret. The key to winning . . . is not just trying harder than everyone else, it's believing—in your bones—like in your core—that you are *better* than the other people. You *deserve* to win because you're the greatest. People lose because they deserve to lose. He let me see that."

I looked at the floor. His words stung. "And if people get hurt along the way?" I asked "Like . . . Blaize?"

"If you're not a hundred percent, get the fuck out."

"Right."

He slid down off the island. "I've watched you in practice. And I heard what you did in that tournament. You could be really great at this, Sydney. You're a natural. And you're more than a natural, you're a killer."

He was close to me now, his blue eyes looking down at me. The fluorescent light above him lit the back of his head like a halo. He looked like an evil, smug angel.

"I could help you. If you want to be a winner."

I held my breath. "I don't know. . . ."

"Think about it. Going to Nats with me. Competing. I got an agent because I won last year—they saw the livestream. You could do the same thing. Get everything you want in life."

"I'm not sure I know what I want in life," I said, and that was the truth.

"I do." His hand was on my hip. My skin felt tingly all over.

Kiss him, Sydney. Use his hormones against him. It will allow you to break him later.

But I couldn't do it. That was the entirely ruthless part of my brain, the kind that didn't mind sacrificing everything for a goal, but that wasn't all of me, was it? I backed away, trying to laugh off the clear intent in Hanson's eyes.

"I'm pretty sure I won't make it to Nats, but I'll be happy cheering you guys on."

He straightened. "Sparks only takes the qualifiers to Nats. Everyone else stays home and watches the livestream with the rest of the school."

A cold shiver went through me. *Everyone else stays home?*

"What are you talking about? The whole team doesn't go?"

"Nah. Only the qualifiers. Fewer distractions. Sparks wants to make sure that only the best go—a perk for varsity, and people who don't succeed, they have to watch with everyone else. It also helps make sure nothing goes wrong. You know, if there's like jealousy or something."

"Oh."

And suddenly the path to the victory got a hell of a lot longer.

CHAPTER TWENTY-FOUR

Recalibration

"COME ON, LADY KNIGHTS!" yelled Elijah, stomping up and down on the risers, causing my head to hurt even worse. I had tried to steer as clear as I could of the sangria monster and Jell-O shots, but my head still felt like it was being jackhammered. It didn't help that Elijah was the loudest person of all the two dozen or so fans that were occasionally watching the basketball game.

Lakshmi had slept on the couch in my living room, beneath Charlie and an afghan that I found in the closet. Despite this, she was still a whirling demon on the basketball court, launching shot after shot. I could barely stand without help.

Thomas whistled appreciatively from the other side of me.

I had filled both of them in on the developments of the preceding night. We had succeeded beyond our wildest dreams, but a new roadblock loomed.

"The livestream is the key," said Elijah. "The whole school gets together and watches in the auditorium. It takes like an entire day."

"The whole school spends a day watching a speech tournament?"

Elijah nodded like this was a completely normal thing. "Only the final rounds are livestreamed, and the school only gets out to watch if we've got somebody competing. Last year we had finalists in four events, so it was pretty much the whole day."

"Eaganville is messed up."

"That's not even counting the charter buses that go to the meet. Last year it was in Denver, so it was like a four-day vacation."

I checked this year's location on my phone. "Kansas City."

"There will definitely be people going there."

"But the other speech kids aren't allowed to go?"

"I mean, you can go—you just can't stay in the hotel with the team or participate with the team."

"So that's our chance," I said. "We make sure everybody loses during the livestream in spectacular fashion and take out Sparks at the same time. That way the whole school will see it—"

"And their empire will fall," added Elijah. "The One Ring will be destroyed."

Thomas rolled his eyes. "This is more like tossing four rings into four Mount Dooms simultaneously."

"So we're all Frodo, then," said Elijah, nodding.

"Can we do this without nerd references, please?" I begged.

"One problem," said Elijah. "We need to get you into Mordor first."

"Guys? Please?"

Thomas agreed. "Before we even get in position to blow up the Death Star, you need to make it into the channel."

"English!"

Elijah put a hand on my shoulder. "You need to qualify for Nationals."

I heard Hanson's silky voice in my mind. *You can go to Nationals. I can help you.*

"Shit," I said.

"One thing, though," said Thomas. "There's no way we can let Andrew perform his piece on the livestream. Even if he loses. There's no way in hell he's getting up there in front of the entire school and talking shit about my playwriting ability."

"That's kind of strange that that's your last straw," I said.

"Well, that and everything else he does. He needs to go down before Nationals."

Blaize leaned over us from behind. "Don't worry. I've got a plan. Sydney, can you send me that recording you made of him in the closet?"

"Sure."

"I'll take care of him, then."

* * *

The jazz band tried its best to drive the team to victory, but the noodling piano solos and experimental drum sections weren't having the desired effect. Despite Lakshmi's best efforts, the team fell behind by ten points, then twenty. Lakshmi had her best game of the season, but it was hopeless. They were outclassed.

It didn't seem to matter to Elijah, who vigorously cheered her on at every turn, even when she got called for a flagrant foul for elbowing another girl in the chin.

"WOO. THAT IS SOME GOOD ATHLETIC ACTIVITY RIGHT NOW."

See, I thought, talking to an imaginary Lakshmi in my mind. *He's totally into you.* I did note, however, that after one particularly fierce basket, he leaped up and hugged me. I could feel the coarse fabric of his coat, and as I wrapped my arms around him, I felt the sensation of each individual rib poking through his skin. But that surely didn't mean anything. When he wasn't standing and cheering, he was bouncing up and down on the riser, annoying the weak collection of parents who were recording everything on their phones.

When the game was finally finished, we gave the players a standing ovation as they exited the court. Elijah's shoulder connected with mine, and he didn't pull away.

Lakshmi made her way up the bleachers.

"Next year," she said, "we're gonna get some actual fans here.

Hailey is going to finish her journaling before the season, and I'm gonna personally weed out any slam poets." Again she looked up at Blaize. "I know I've said this to you before, but I swear to God, I will kidnap a pony for you if you join the team next year."

"I'll think about it."

"Really?!"

"I'm not super coordinated—I did ten years of dance, but—"

Lakshmi's eyes widened. "Done." She rubbed her head. "Oh man, I slept like eight minutes last night."

"You did great," I said. "Seriously, it was like inspirational."

"Thanks for being here, guys."

"BIG HUG," said Elijah, wrapping his bony arms around me and Lakshmi. He strained fitfully and the five of us managed to huddle. Thomas lost his balance on a riser and nearly went tumbling down the side, but Blaize held him up.

"Lakshmi, we're going. Come on," said Rani, arriving like a ghost and impatiently tapping her foot. "Auntie is coming over for dinner tonight and Mom says it's time to go."

"You can chill," said Lakshmi, turning her back on Rani. "I'm not done celebrating."

"I don't know what you're celebrating for. You lost."

Lakshmi's head swiveled back toward her sister, *Exorcist*-style. "Excuse me?"

"You lost the game."

"Yeah, I'm aware of that."

"You had a failure for a season, so why are you acting like you're cool with that? I mean, I guess that's probably why you lost."

Lakshmi raised up her palm. "All right, hold up."

"What's the point of playing if not to win?"

"Well . . . it's a team sport, so—"

"So you're going to blame your teammates?"

Lakshmi held back from throttling the life out of her little sister but just barely. "I'm not blaming anyone. Okay, maybe I blamed some people earlier, but that's not the point—"

"The point isn't to win?"

"The point is to have fun."

"While winning."

"While competing."

"Right," Rani said sarcastically. "But I think if you're going to celebrate something, celebrate actually accomplishing something. You guys won like two games this season. And we have to come watch this crap. It sucks."

It's brutally awkward watching family members fighting in front of you, like you're paralyzed and your eyeballs have been forced open. Elijah tried to look away, hoping not to be recognized, Thomas was trying to find a reason to look at his phone, and Blaize was staring off into space. I kept wondering if I was going to need to leap in and prevent Lakshmi from tearing Rani's head off. I also wondered if it would be possible for me to prevent Lakshmi from tearing Rani's head off, considering that she could do ten pull-ups while I could do negative one.

Rani solved the situation by turning on her heel and heading back to her family.

Lakshmi stood there, shaking. "I thought you were supposed to stop Sparks from melting her brain."

CHAPTER TWENTY-FIVE

Back in the Cookie Mines

Mom did not triumph at the gathering of CrossFit Worshippers of Central Minnesota. Charlie was ecstatic at her arrival early on Sunday morning and rammed into her shins again and again. I imagined his little doggy voice saying, *I humped so many legs this weekend, Mama*. It was a good thing he couldn't talk.

"How was it?" I asked.

She moaned and flopped onto the couch. "I'm going to die."

"So that's good? You know what I've heard? Pain is just weakness leaving the body."

She propped herself up on her elbows and gave me the stink-eye. "Can I tell you how many tattoos of that I saw this weekend?" She dropped her head back on the couch cushion and groaned. "I have to work in an hour and my entire body is made out of Jell-O."

"See, you've already achieved my fitness goal." I ducked

as she threw a couch pillow at my head. "Come on, I have to work, too."

"Don't wanna," she whined, rolling facedown onto the couch. Then she looked up. "Why does it smell like cinnamon in here?"

On the bus ride to the Mall of America, we sat next to each other. She stretched out her legs continuously.

"So there was this one part—where I had to flip this tire? It was one of those tractor tires, you know?"

"Yeah, from all my farm experience," I said.

"Are you aware that there are things called tractors and they have tires?"

"Now I am."

"Anyway, you have to lift it and flip it over, and then lift it and flip it over again. And you have to keep doing that until you reach the finish line. So I thought: 'How am I gonna do this? This looks impossible.' And I see this other woman who's like five-one and pregnant and she's next to me, and she just like, GRUNTS, like a wild beast, and she just like HEAVES the thing over—I don't know if she was having crazy pregnancy strength—"

"Is this even recommended for pregnant women?"

"The body is an amazing thing. So I'm like, 'If she can do it, I can do it.' So I grabbed it, and I'm thinking, 'I own you, tire. I own you.' And I did it!" She laughed and looked up at the roof of the bus. "I didn't think it was possible, but I did it. Like four more times, too, before I really twisted something in my back."

"Are you okay?"

"Probably not, but the adrenaline got me through it." She patted my knee and turned to look at me. "So I want to thank you for pushing me to go."

"Oh."

"No seriously—if you hadn't pressured me, I wouldn't have done it, and I wouldn't have tried, and then I . . . wouldn't have known that I could flip a tractor tire."

"I can imagine that's going to come in super handy," I joked. "There's gonna be a farmer who has an emergency and like calls you—'By golly, all four of my tires fell off and I need someone to flip them back to the farmhouse. I don't want them to roll, gol darn it, I want them flipped in the most energy-intensive manner possible!'"

She laughed and looked down at her hands. "Look at this," she said, flexing and unflexing her fingers. Her palms were still red, and there were thick calluses on the pads just below her fingers. "When I was married to your father, I didn't ever want to break a goddamn nail. Part of the reason we didn't get divorced sooner is that I never thought I could make it on my own, you know? I figured I'd be lost without him." She sniffed, tears welling in her eyes. "I flipped a goddamn tire."

I leaned my head on her shoulder and wrapped my arms around her jellified, yet muscly core.

* * *

The Great American Cookie Factory was already in full melt-down mode when I arrived. Rhonda had called in sick on account of the fact that she was spending Sunday smoking (all right, that was conjecture on my part, but let's face it, Rhonda was not as invested in the Great American Cookie Factory as she could have been). Valentine's Day was on Thursday, and the pre-Valentine's rush is the busiest time of the year for cookie factories around the country. The week prior, Chad had given a brief presentation detailing the war between cookies and chocolates for the soul of lovers everywhere. This was serious.

"Oh, jeez, thank goodness you're here, we have a crisis," he said. He seemed to be coated in a thin layer of sugar, frosting, and unidentifiable goop.

"On it, boss," I said, saluting him.

The ovens in the back were working overtime and were completely stuffed with our signature oversized cookies. The counters were a riot of frosting tubes, sprinkles, and dirty dishes. I exhaled, dumped as many dirty dishes as I could fit into the sink, and tried to clear off a workspace.

Chad came back as soon as he had dispatched the latest customers. "So, um . . . we've been getting a lot of requests for, uh . . . funny cookies?"

"Oh."

"And I tried, but oh jeez they were, um . . ." I looked at one cookie that said BEE MINE, followed by a poorly dabbed honey-bee. "It's funny 'cause it's a bee. I thought of this one, too." He pointed to another one, which said HAPPY VALENTIME'S DAY with a clock next to it. "Some kids think it's Valentime's Day, not Valentine's Day, so."

I looked at them and frowned. "This is some bullshit, Chad."

He sighed sadly. "Yeah, I know. I need the special Sydney magic."

"It's dark magic."

"I know that."

"Like witch magic."

"Gotcha. Just give me some funny cookies."

I put up a finger as more people arrived at the counter. "I want full artistic autonomy. My cookies might not even have a Valentine's Day theme, they might scare the hell out of you, but I need you to trust me."

He nodded. "Done."

From there, it was ten straight hours of cookie baking, lettering, and decoration. I experimented with different fonts; I perfected the art of making little flowers. I was a human cookie machine. Some of the cookies scared Chad. He wasn't sure about THE TESTS CAME BACK NEGATIVE with little exclamation points around it (sold in twenty minutes to a group of sorority girls) or THIS HOLIDAY IS BULLSHIT, which also flew off the shelf. Even my HETERONORMATIVE LOVE IS FOR SQUARES found a happy home.

Word continued to spread, and soon there were people lining up to take photos of the cookies and post them on Instagram. In my spare time, I started an Instagram account of my own for the cookies and racked up five hundred followers by the end of the day. We ran out of dough just after three, which caused Chad to lose his mind calling other stores—it took about an hour to get an emergency resupply.

"Hoo!" he exhaled in a gap in the action near the end of my shift as I was putting the finishing touches on a YOUR BEST YEARS ARE BEHIND YOU cookie. "I never realized how bitter and sarcastic a lot of people are about love."

I smiled. My neck ached. It felt like I'd been flipping tractor tires for the past hour.

"Anytime you want more hours, you let me know."

"Well, I'm busy in school, so—"

"Oh sure, yah. I know. If you want to drop out of school and make cookies full-time, let me know!"

I tried to laugh it off, but it felt like he had just stuck a needle into my brain.

"Little joke," he said, noticing my discomfort. "I know that's not my thing. Jokes, that is."

"Yeah, I followed you," I said, shaking it off.

The call bell at the front dinged. It was Elijah. "Service!" he yelled, shaking his fist. "I demand service!"

"Hold your horses," called out Chad.

"No, it's cool, that's my friend," I said, dusting off my apron. Elijah was wrapped up in his heavy coat. He had taken off his hat, and it jutted out of the pocket. His cheeks were flushed, either from the cold or a mad dash through the Mall of America.

He was leaning over and reading the cookies in the display case.

"What are you doing here?" I asked.

"Just . . . examining your cookies," he said, trying to keep a straight face. "They're . . . surprisingly big." He broke into a shit-eating grin as he said it.

"Dude!"

"And . . . covered with frosting."

"Would you quit talking about my cookies?"

"I like this one. 'The Therapist Said I Should Give You Surprises.'"

"My cookies tell it like it is." I leaned over the counter. "So what are you really doing here?"

"Um . . . I thought you might want to practice or . . . I could give you a ride home."

Chad approached and handed me an envelope. In it was my meager paycheck and about fifty dollars in cash. "What's the cash for?" I asked.

"People started tipping. After I put out a jar."

"Damn."

"You earned it. All right, you crazy kids, get out of here."

I turned to Elijah. "I need to pay you back for that skirt."

"I've got a way you can do that," he said, motioning for me to follow him.

"Classy," I said, looking at the flora and fauna of the Rainforest Café. Every so often, the animatronic apes would lose their shit, shrieking and pounding their robotic fists in impotent fury. Toucans blared a cacophonous chorus, and even the robot elephant would extend his trunk and trumpet about the oncoming appetizers. Overhead, a starry sky winked down at us, punctuated by the occasional shooting star.

Elijah looked around. "This is exactly like being in the deep jungle."

"I'm sure," I said, laughing. "Have you spent a lot of time in the wild?"

"Definitely. You'd be surprised at how accurate this is." He pointed to a four-foot-tall plaster mushroom. "I mean, that is basically where I lived in my former life as an explorer. But there were actually fewer nachos in the jungle."

The lights of the Rainforest Café were on some kind of bizarre timer; every once in a while they would darken so much that it would be hard to read. "I think it's nighttime now," I said, using my phone to light the menu.

"This is when the beasts are most active," he joked. "The crazy part about this place is the people who bring their toddlers, and the toddlers like lose their minds. 'Mommy is taking me to the jungle to feed me to the animals.'"

"You could get a job here. Rock the khaki survival outfit look they got going on."

"Once again, highly accurate to jungle life."

I laughed. It was easy talking to Elijah, like a playful dance. He'd say something funny, then I'd say something funny back, and we'd try to keep it going like badminton, which had been the one athletic activity I enjoyed as a kid. Basically tennis except much less running and more staring at the sky.

Elijah smiled at me, and I caught the glint of his eyes in the dark restaurant. Lakshmi's words reverberated in my brain: *Lady Boner.* I felt a buzzing in my chest and took a deep breath.

"Can I ask you something?" he said.

Oh shit.

"Okay."

He took a deep breath. "The other day you said you knew Sparks from before? And that's been bugging me because I never asked you about that."

My face went red, but I'm sure he couldn't see it in the dim light. "Oh."

"What?"

"I thought you were gonna ask me something else."

No one said anything for a moment.

"I just thought," he said, "since I told you my story with him that maybe . . . he had done something similar to you. And I was going to add that to the reasons I wanted to destroy him. For you."

"No, it's not like that," I managed. "Um . . . He's basically the reason my dad is in prison."

Elijah snagged a cheese stick off the table and dipped it in the marinara sauce. "Holy shit, what happened? And if they killed somebody, you don't have to tell me."

So this is basically the story of How My Dad Goes to Prison.

"I don't know if this happened concurrently with his reign at Eaganville, but Joey Sparks was a motivational speaker. He used to do these bullshit self-help seminars—basically telling people that the reason they failed was because they didn't believe in themselves. Real basic stuff. But you know, he's magnetic, and with the right headset, lighting, and PowerPoint presentation, he's capable of bilking a bunch of midlife-crisis sufferers out of their money.

"My dad had a private financial consulting business. He used to work for a bank or something but then went into business for himself when I was real little. Which was great, because he worked out of the house, and I could hang out in his office. I used to read in there for hours; I would drag stacks of books onto the shaggy white rug on his floor. I lay on that rug for hours, imagining I had been shrunk to the size of an ant and was now on the surface of some huge furry dog. Or an explorer on an alien planet. He used to play his music on his computer loud when he wasn't on the phone—and when things were slow, he'd get down on the floor and read to me. And things were slow a lot. It was a really good life.

"I guess a good life for me meant bad business for him, though. I didn't know that, obviously, but it was one of the reasons my parents fought all the time. There was never enough money. Or my dad was always lying about the amount of money coming in. My dad was great at bullshit."

"The apple has not fallen far from the tree," said Elijah, munching on another cheese stick.

"Probably truth." I smiled. "So this goes on for years—things get worse and worse until Sparks comes along. Sparks is teaching this 'course' to professionals about maximizing their potential. Dad spends, I don't know, like three hundred dollars to do like six classes with Sparks, who knows jack shit about financial consulting, by the way."

"Shocking."

"My dad took me to one once. I think I must've been twelve. And it's like . . . just imagine Sparks and these like animated graphics on his PowerPoint talking nonsense about cultivating your winning aura, and receiving energy from the universe, and basically lying your ass off to get what you want. The ends justify the means. Winning isn't everything, it's the only thing. Fail, fail again, fail better, fail less. I mean—I was twelve and I basically wanted to stick my hand in a blender to get out of there.

"But my dad is *transfixed* by this bullshit. I mean, I'm watching him, he's staring at Sparks like Jesus himself has smashed through the roof and is giving a sermon about buying an expensive watch. It is fucked up. And afterward he changes everything he's doing. He moved his office out of the house—he got new clothes, he started acting like he had a ton of money. He had a money clip, got a Porsche. All smoke and mirrors shit to try to land high-flying clients. That was the plan, land a few rich clients by pretending you're a rich person, and then you pay off all the money. Of course he was lying to my mom during all of this; every time he bought something new, he was borrowing money from somewhere.

"Basically my dad's entire business was like Wile E. Coyote when he runs off the cliff. As long as he keeps running on air and not looking down, it works. He took out loans to pay his other loans. He did a whole bunch of shady shit; tax fraud, insurance fraud, forging documents—I mean, it was madness. Fake donations to fake charities; I don't know half of what he did. I just know that he got in deeper and deeper and kept digging."

Elijah nodded. "Seems like kind of a stretch to blame Sparks for that, though."

"Dad was a loser before Sparks. He was a criminal after."

"I guess."

"You know how he is. People *change* when they meet him. The kids on the team, everybody. He *ruins* people."

Elijah reached his hand across the table. I stretched to take it. "I'm sorry about that," he said, his eyes meeting mine.

"Thanks."

Our fingers stayed together a moment too long. A chill ran down the back of my neck. His index finger lightly brushed against the side of my index finger. Then it did it again.

Maybe it was time to figure out what the hell was going on?

"So," I said, letting my fingers slide back, "why are you really coming to hang out at the mall?"

He pulled his hands back, running them over the leopard-print table. "I didn't have anything else to do?"

"Oh, really? You don't seem like a let's-go-hang-out-at-the-mall kind of guy."

"A guy can't just drive to the mall for no reason? Maybe I'm a mystery."

I snorted. "Maybe you're a dork."

"That, too." He smiled and looked down again. "Um . . ." He looked up, his blue eyes looking black. I met his gaze.

"Yeah?" The air hummed between us.

OOH! OOH! OOH! The animatronic gorilla right behind me started roaring and pounding its chest, nearly knocking me out of my chair.

"This place is super romantic," he said.

"Are we supposed to be someplace romantic?" I asked.

"I don't know. We're just two friends—in a romantic jungle setting with . . . robot monkeys and cheese sticks . . . who are a part of a conspiracy. Nothing to see here."

"All right, look," I said. "Um . . . I mean . . . this is probably stupid and wrong, but Lakshmi and I were talking the other day, and she seems to think that you . . . like me in a certain non-friendly way, which is probably ridiculous because you are obviously in love with her, but this whole thing where you just come and hang out and be charming and cute or whatever is kind of messing with me right now, so if you could clarify that situation, that would be much appreciated."

Elijah looked like he'd been caught robbing a liquor store. "Uh . . ."

"Spit it out before some other animal starts yelling at us."

"Okay, I'm just really bad at this," he started. "I was never going to ask Lakshmi to the Snow Ball."

"What?"

"She's like my sister."

"You like worship her."

"She's like my really cool sister. I was gonna ask you. At the assembly. I wanted it to be a surprise. That's why I made it seem like I was going to ask Lakshmi—it was kind of a . . . misdirection. Then afterward you said you wanted to go and it became like a group thing. Then you said you had sworn off love and wanted to be a priestly nun. So I shut my mouth."

"Why didn't you say anything?"

"I guess I just didn't want to be the latest in a string of assholes. I was worried I would screw it up, and then I wouldn't be able to talk to you anymore. And I love talking to you." He stretched his hand across the table.

I slid my hand across the table and managed to touch his warm fingers.

"Jesus, this table is wide," I said.

"You know, in Europe couples sit side by side, not across from each other. That's what I've heard at least. If we were . . . you know . . . couple-inclined."

"Well, get your ass over here, then," I said.

The next thing I knew he was sitting by my side, and we were making out like a couple of Europeans.

CHAPTER TWENTY-SIX

Frodo Eats a Sweet-Ass Casserole

The plan was to strike again on Wednesday.

The bad feelings initiated by our brutal Valentine's Day Get-Together continued to metastasize over the week. Anesh and Logan were supposed to be preparing for the next tournament, but they spent most of their time alternating between awkwardly staring into space and squabbling over who was doing the most work. Anesh totally was, it wasn't even close, I kept telling him privately. Taryn and Milo were a twitchy mess, with Hanson volunteering to specially coach them, an offer that was not appreciated by anyone. After that rejection, Hanson offered to tutor me on my DI, but I told him that Milo was helping me since he was so talented. Only Andrew was unperturbed, blissfully practicing his cruel speech, unaware that his doom was nigh.

I spent most of my non-conspiracy time sending completely unironic kissy-face emojis to Elijah. We didn't have a lot of time together but managed to meet between the Rembrandt Room and the Monet Room for passing period make-out sessions. He wasn't necessarily the best kisser, but I was noticing improvement.

Lakshmi was smug about the whole thing. "Told you. I fucking told you," she said, pulling me aside when we met on Tuesday night in Thomas's basement.

"All right, you were right."

"You came together to destroy the speech team, but what you didn't expect . . . was to fall in love."

"Oh, shut up."

"Lust, then?"

Lakshmi laughed evilly as Thomas unrolled our murder plan on the pool table. "Gentleman," he said, looking at Elijah, "and three ladies, since we are now passing into the realm of illegality, I believe it's time we take code names."

"I'm not taking a code name," I grumbled.

"I'm gonna be the Scarlet Witch," said Elijah. We looked at him. "What?"

"As you're the only straight dude in this conspiracy, I find the fact that you're called a witch kind of confusing," said Thomas.

"I can't be a witch?" asked Elijah.

"Plus it's obvious."

"You just said I was the only straight guy! So the whole witch thing will throw people off."

"Scarlet. Your hair."

"Fine I'll be the White Witch, then."

Lakshmi grimaced. "Still."

Thomas threw up his hands. "If you're the Scarlet Witch, then I'm T'Challa."

"Oh, so we're all gonna be superheroes, then?" asked Lakshmi.

I rolled my eyes. "Jesus."

"I don't think you should be Jesus," said Blaize.

Thomas tried to steer things back to order. "All right, fine. I'm T'Challa, you're Scarlet Witch, no one is Jesus, and there's no superhero mandate. We'll get the other code names later. But first, this is how it's gonna go down . . ."

The Target? Taryn's evil "Love" notebook.

The Moment? Lunch. Wednesday.

Frodo (that's me) gets to the varsity/teachers' lounge early, joined by Sparkles the Unicorn (Blaize—I mean, come on, that's pretty obvious). Sparkles the Unicorn hides in the spotless faculty bathroom, enjoying the peace and clean toilet, waiting for a text from Frodo.

Frodo doesn't sit at the table yet, waiting for the moment when Taryn and the rest of the crew enter for lunch. Taryn, oblivious, tiny, pink-haired, sits as close to Milo as possible. Frodo takes the seat on her other side, unwraps unfortunate turkey sandwich.

Hanson expresses surprise and disgust that Frodo would eat a turkey sandwich when, check it out, dude, there are free parental casseroles for the taking. Frodo looks at them sadly, just as Taryn takes out "Love" notebook and sets it next to her on the table, writing down secret notes. (About what? We don't know. Poems about Milo? Possibly. We're about to find out.) Frodo gets up from the table, secretly texts Sparkles "Gamma-Omega" (which just spells *go* and is really dumb but the Scarlet/White Witch insisted on a special code in case the team is compromised or some stupid shit).

Sparkles the Unicorn emerges, refreshed, from the beautiful faculty bathroom, takes Frodo's seat at the table. Taryn is all outrage—how dare—how dare a JV person take a varsity person's spot?! Taryn stands up to her full height so she can look Sparkles the Unicorn, seated, chewing happily, in the eye.

Other speech members protest as Frodo returns and secretly brushes the "Love" notebook off the table and onto her foot, not making a sound. Sparkles says, "Fine! Fine! I'll go!" and emits tears, just as Frodo leans down to get something, then slides notebook along the floor just as the door to the faculty copy room opens, manned by T'Challa, until it ends up in the hands of the Scarlet/White Witch.

Scarlet/White Witch plops it onto the copy machine, punching in the copy code stolen from Mr. Papadakis's desk the day before.

Copies one page. Then another. Then another.

Taryn sits back down—is something missing? She can't place it yet, just as Sparkles the Unicorn collides with Sylvia.

(Lakshmi—when we pointed out that Sylvia was not a terribly fun or interesting code name, she pointed out that Sylvia was the best player in the history of the Minnesota Lynx, and if there was one thing people in this school wouldn't catch on to, it was the name of famous sports figures, especially female sports figures, because there was an inherent sexism regarding our lack of attention to them because fuck the patriarchy. So she was Sylvia.) So Sparkles bumps into Sylvia just outside the door to the lounge.

"Bitch," says Sylvia.

"Who are you calling a bitch?" says Sparkles the Unicorn.

"Oh shit, fight!" yells Frodo.

All boys scramble up from the table hoping to see two chicks duke it out in the hallway. Taryn attaches herself to Milo like a barnacle just as T'Challa swings open the door to the copy room again and the Scarlet/White Witch slides the notebook back to Frodo, who scoops it up and places it back on the table just as Sylvia says, "You know what? Feminism isn't about pitting women against women."

And Sparkles the Unicorn says, "Shit, you're right. We shouldn't be fighting. We should be sisters trying to destroy the patriarchy together."

At which point all the male onlookers grow sad that there will be no "chick fight" and return to the table, Taryn in tow, who discovers her notebook exactly where she thought she left it.

Mission accomplished.

And Frodo eats a sweet-ass casserole.

CHAPTER TWENTY-SEVEN

The End of Andrew Chen

Sparks was not in a good mood on the way to our next meet, the Minnetonka Masher. (Okay, it wasn't actually called the Minnetonka Masher, but that was what Blaize had dubbed it. This was going to be our first serious competition; most of the strong programs in the Twin Cities were going to be there.)

"I have to say," he said, standing in the aisle again, "that in all my years of coaching, this was one of the worst weeks of practice I've ever had." He looked down, biting his lip. Nobody said anything. "No cohesion. No effort. You want to whisper behind each other's backs, you want to spend your time complaining that life is unfair, DO IT SOMEWHERE ELSE. Not on my team. You got that? Not on my team." The last bit he said almost in a whisper, shaking his head.

We were disappointing him. We were letting him down.

He made his way down the aisle. The varsity members were in the front of the bus, while the junior varsity were clustered in the back for safety. "I could put any of these freshmen in your spots and they would do better. Because they care. And you don't." He turned to me, eyes blazing.

I thought I was ready, but his words blindsided me. I was so wrapped up in thinking about Elijah and how the day would unfold that I didn't see it coming.

"This is your first tournament as varsity, and how are you going to do?"

"Me?"

"Do you imagine I'm talking to somebody else?"

"How am I going to do?"

"Why are you repeating my question? Are you incapable of answering my question? YES OR NO."

My head swam. I couldn't even figure out what he was asking but I desperately wanted to come up with the right answer. *I had to.*

"Yes?"

"Yes, you are incapable of answering my question. YOU CANNOT ANSWER MY QUESTION."

"No!"

"No what?"

"I—"

"NO WHAT?!"

"No, I can—"

"Jesus, it's like talking to an idiot. Do you understand words, do you understand language, can you hear? Can you understand me?"

"Yes."

"Oh, you can?! 'Cause I was just asking you a perfectly clear question and you started stammering like a STROKE VICTIM! *HOW ARE YOU GOING TO DO TODAY*?!"

I started crying.

"You're crying. What the hell. You're crying now. That's your response to my question? You just start crying like a little girl? That's your solution here." He turned to the rest of the bus. "Does anyone have a pacifier? Sydney needs one."

I covered my face with my hands, tears streaming down my face. He leaned in close, hovering just over my head. "I don't think you're going to do well today," he whispered, then left.

Blaize found me afterward. The Sinister Six treated me like I was contaminated and stayed away. Fine with me.

"It's not about you," she whispered, wrapping me up in a warm hug. "That's what he does."

I could barely stand.

"You're all right," said Blaize, stroking my hair. "You're all right. You're gonna get him."

I wiped the tears out of my eyes. "I know. I know in my brain this is what he does but . . . shit . . ."

"Yeah."

"I don't know why I feel so bad; he's not even letting you compete in DI," I sniffled.

"Part of the plan," said Blaize. "I'm cross-entered today."

I looked up at her.

"I knew he was going to do that, so I entered in OO today, too. Didn't even tell him."

"You can do that?"

She winked at me. "You just concentrate on winning this tournament, all right? I've got my own part to play today."

In order to qualify for Nationals, you had to accumulate enough points over the season. Some tournaments held automatic bids, like winning the State Championship, but if you placed enough times in the tournaments throughout the season, you could qualify. My third-place finish at Brooklyn Park had garnered me a meager haul. I would need to do better this time.

As expected, the competition was rough. There were no bottom-feeders like at the last meet, kids who had joined speech on a lark and had stumbled into an event.

I tried to shut out what happened on the bus, but I couldn't. I barely made it through the first two rounds. My overdose wasn't as intense this time; my breathing wasn't as ragged as it could've been, the way I bugged out my eyes as the heroin flooded my system wasn't as persuasive. The shock of a girl doing Nikki Sixx had worn off.

And then it came. The list for the semifinals didn't include me. I had lost. Just like Sparks said I would.

Frodo, come to the OO Semis, texted Blaize. I shook off my disappointment and headed over.

The semis for original oratory were in a lecture hall. This school has lecture halls, I mused. The crowd that had gathered, about fifty of us (complete with our own Eaganville traveling cheering section), was mostly in the bottom rows of the stadium seating. There was a huge whiteboard behind a lectern with the names of the competitors scrawled in dry-erase marker.

Andrew Chen was going third. Blaize was fourth.

"How'd you manage that?" I whispered to Blaize when I found her contentedly sitting in the fourth row.

"Told the judge I was cross-entered. She let me pick the order." She smiled.

"I didn't even know you had a piece!"

"It's my piece from last year. It's about dying fruit bat populations in North America. It's pretty heartbreaking."

"Oh."

"Since you're here, you can help with the recording. Make sure to get Andrew's piece, and then my piece afterward."

We watched the first two competitors (Baby Boomers Are Ruining the World Because of Global Warming—Screw You, Old People, and Dating while Muslim) before Andrew got up.

Andrew stood silently in front of the whiteboard for a

moment, his head down and his hands clasped in front of him. His hair was spiked to perfection; his black suit fit him amazingly well. He looked like a winner. I started recording on my phone.

"It wasn't love at first sight," he began, making eye contact with the audience. "And it wasn't like they show it in the movies, the swooning, the gazing into each other's eyes, the little text messages in the middle of the night. Thomas was not what I was expecting when I fell in love."

Once again, a tremor ran through the audience. He had them in the palm of his hand.

His routine was even more polished this time around. Every joke was practiced, every line was smooth, even his little pauses for dramatic and emotional importance landed like a hammer blow. The audience loved him. It felt for him when he came out to his imaginary homophobic parents, it laughed along with him at the awfulness of Thomas's writing, it agonized with him when the imaginary Thomas broke his heart.

When he was done, the audience snapped into a standing ovation.

I turned to Blaize, who was still smiling.

The judge finished scrawling her notes on a little table in the center of the audience. "Blaize Rasmussen?"

Blaize didn't move. She kept smiling. I nudged her.

"Blaize Rasmussen?" the judge repeated.

And that's when Thomas walked into the room, dressed in a suit and bow tie.

"Blaize?" asked the judge, looking up.

"Yup," said Thomas. You could almost hear Andrew shitting himself.

"Whenever you're ready," said the judge.

Thomas gathered himself for a moment, then looked up at the audience. "The first thing you need to know about me is that my name isn't Blaize. It's Thomas." A wave of shock smashed through the audience. "And I'm *actually* gay.

"Everyone's experience coming out is different. My dad's a professional athlete and his one wish for me was that I would follow in his footsteps. There are actually videos of me at two years old holding a baseball bat taller than me. So my path has been challenging for him. My first experience coming out was when I was ten. I told my parents I was a pirate." The audience laughed. "In the school play. Mom, Dad . . . I need to tell you something: I'm a thespian."

The crowd gurgled with joy. "And I love other thespians. My dad didn't know what to do—he kept shoving more and more balls at me. Here, play with these. Here, play with these." Thomas stopped mischievously. "Dad, these are not the kind of balls I want to play with."

Laughter thundered in the room. He was good. He was *so* good. Thomas's routine was just as polished as anyone else's—he walked around the room, holding court like he was born on the stage. It was pretty obvious that he'd been practicing with Elijah since the night of the party.

"But I love my parents. And my parents love me. And when I did come out, my mom was ecstatic. 'I just thought you were uncoordinated!' But my dad . . . my dad cried. He didn't cry because he was sad I was gay, he cried because he was *proud*. He was proud because at fourteen years old I was strong enough to know who I was. And that's an amazing thing."

He kept going. He related the story of his writing; he even acted out little pieces from his play, which he put in context.

"I'm not gonna lie, it was not Shakespeare." The audience laughed with him.

Then finally, eight minutes in, he stopped. He took a deep breath, then looked directly at Andrew before turning back to the audience.

"Now, I could've stood up here and told you about Andrew Chen, but I didn't do that. I could've talked about the fact that he just talked about me using my real name. He assassinated my character for laughs; he lied about our relationship. We were never in love. Oh, sure, I liked him, and I did write that play, but he never liked me back. I don't feel bad about that, because, you see, Andrew Chen isn't gay."

The crowd murmured.

"But Andrew Chen's story *isn't* my story to tell. I don't have the right to tell his story. I only have the right to tell my story. So that's why . . ." He pulled out his phone; the audience gasped. This was propping—using a prop in competition—an automatic disqualification. "Blaize" would not be passing on to the next room. "I'll let him do it." Thomas hit play on his phone, and held it up to the microphone.

> ANDREW: Why do you think I'm gay?
> ME: I saw your piece.
> *ANDREW: Oh, shit, really? Dude. That's fucking*
> *hilarious. No, I'm not gay. Jesus.*

The crowd grumbled.

> ME: Why do you say you're gay if you're not
> actually gay?
> ANDREW: Are you serious right now? 'Cause
> it helps me win. I can get up there and be like,
> 'Oh, my dad wanted to send me to conversion
> camp, everybody cry for me!' What, I'm gonna
> be like, 'Yeah, I'm rich, and I'm tall, and I'm
> good-looking, and my parents are doctors.
> Tough life, right?' Nobody's gonna vote for me.
> ME: So you're like lying with your piece?
> *ANDREW: Yeah, I make shit up. And the*
> *audience is so stupid they just fall for it.*

Thomas stopped the playback. The audience roiled with anger. Thomas smiled serenely. "Thank you," he said, bowing and walking out the door.

I spotted Andrew in the second row, sitting entirely still like a statue, hoping that no one would see him. But they did. And they were angry.

He turned to shout at everyone. "Everybody lies!" Then he turned and bolted out of the room like a frightened deer before the mob descended on him.

CHAPTER TWENTY-EIGHT

Fallout

The fallout from the meet was immediate. Andrew didn't ride home with us. Neither did Blaize. She decided to go home with Thomas afterward. I hadn't realized it, but his parents had come to the performance. They were sitting in the back during his speech, crying.

I found Blaize before the finals rounds—she was outside in the cold, ready to escape.

"I'm quitting the team," she said to me. "There's no way I'm going back now. You're going to have to be the one to carry the torch to Nationals."

I held on to her. A cold wind stung my ears. "Why didn't you tell me you were doing this?"

"I thought it would be a big distraction. I didn't want it messing you up."

I bit my lip. *I messed up anyway.* "Thanks. But now what

am I going to do? You're the only person on the team who isn't a dick."

"It's not like I'm moving to Siberia, I'm just not gonna be on the team anymore. Sparks will find out I engineered the whole Thomas thing. He's going to try to burn down my future anyway. He'll put in calls to every college admissions officer he knows. We have to take him out at Nationals."

"You're still going to help?"

"Of course," she said. "You're going to need to keep fighting from the inside. But you can't be seen with me now. You still need to lead the resistance."

The bus ride home was ugly. We had another collection of trophies (Hanson had won HI, Taryn and Milo took first in duo, Anesh and Logan placed third), but there was nothing to show for two main events. Everyone had heard about what had happened to Andrew. I had the footage on my phone just in case and was prepared to upload it to YouTube in the event he resurfaced. But word of the live performance had spread, and he was nowhere to be found. Thomas had asked me not to upload it unless it was necessary. (Besides, since my voice was on that recording, it would've been pretty clear I was involved. I marveled at how smart Blaize was to take Andrew out before other varsity members might've been in the audience.)

A dark cloud loomed over Sparks in the front of the bus. He didn't say a word as we all took our seats. Even the junior varsity kids in the back were subdued. Everyone stared out the windows or checked their phones on the long, silent ride home.

Round One to the Good Guys, and no one seemed to think I was behind it.

Still, it felt awful to be on that bus.

Andrew didn't come back to the team. He barely came back to school. He was there for two or three days the next week and then vanished, perhaps returning to the public school in Ohio from whence he came, according to Thomas.

His place was taken by a girl named Chantal, who was a French foreign exchange student doing an OO about socialism and wind power and veganism. Chantal had shaved both sides of her head and kept the rest of her hair long and orange, like a loosely curled fluffy tail. She had a nose ring, a tattoo on her shoulder that said "The Yankee Clipper" for some reason, and gave no fucks about anything. Sparks announced that she was going to be elevated to varsity—doors would open, the faculty bathroom was now hers. I half expected to be dropped down to JV, but he ignored me for the moment.

I was pretty sure Chantal was going to be my new friend, until I talked to her.

"I've noticed your style," she said.

"Yeah, and I love what you're doing with all this," I said, gesturing to her homemade outfit.

"Right." She stared at me. "Why do you assume my comment was a positive comment?"

"Because . . . I thought it was?"

"Interesting."

"Wasn't it?"

"That's an interesting assumption to make, that's all. That says a lot about you."

"That I think . . . people are being nice to me?"

"Almost everything you say is a question."

I had the sinking suspicion I was losing this conversation. I didn't even know a person could lose a conversation until just now.

"So . . . um . . . what do you think of America?"

"Another question." She shook her head like she had just witnessed a burger being eaten by an American. "Sad."

I backed away slowly. The rest of the team had already split up to work on their pieces, but I found Rani in the back of the common room poring over her laptop with Anesh. Sarah was nowhere to be seen.

"Hey, what's up?" I said, sidling up to her.

Rani eyed me suspiciously. "Nothing."

"Can I talk to you for a second?"

Anesh looked concerned.

"Girl talk. You wouldn't understand. You probably don't want to understand. Ignorance is bliss. Just stay in your own little male bubble, it's cool."

Rani followed me into the hall, full of early-teenager attitude. "What."

"What's going on with Anesh?"

"He's just helping me with some research. Jesus."

"And what's going on with Sarah?"

"We hadn't finaled at any tournaments. None. Closest we came was semis, which is like basically losing. Coach suggested I get a new partner who matches my skills."

"Anesh?"

"No. He's with Logan. There's a junior named Olaf who is dropping his partner, too, so we're gonna team up. It's cool. This was a necessary thing. Sarah was like—I mean, she's fun and all, but that's not what debate is about. Olaf wants to win."

"Look, Rani, you can't ditch your friends just 'cause they're not good at speech."

Rani rolled her eyes like I was a parent. "Why not?"

"Because it's a dick move."

"That's something you complain about when you lose."

I tried to mentally squeeze my brain back into shape. *Oh my God, this child.* "It's better to be a decent person than a winner."

"Is it?"

I blinked. "Yes."

"Are we done? 'Cause Anesh is great at finding sources. Plus, he's super hot."

My heart shrank to the size of a grape and I gasped for air. "Ew. He's like a virus."

"An attractive virus."

"No."

"I'm not marrying him. I just like to look at something nice. *God.* You're not my mom." She headed back into the room.

It didn't help things that Luke spent the next two weeks moving in, one tiny carload at a time. For a single guy, he had an astonishing amount of stuff, most of it brightly colored and made out of some kind of neoprene plastic. There was an inexhaustible supply of protein powder tubs, which proliferated in our kitchen like toxic waste canisters. He owned a lot of spandex, and soon the entire place smelled like the lavender body wash that he scrubbed all over himself all the time, without ever pausing.

Luke owned eight yoga mats, which he stacked behind the television like rubbery firewood, and rotated between doing pull-ups in the kitchen and doing pull-ups in Mom's bedroom. I couldn't even bring myself to call it "their" bedroom. I retreated to my room most evenings and busied myself texting puppy gifs to Elijah to block out the sounds of exercise. At least I hoped they were the sounds of exercise.

None of that seemed to help me in the next two speech tournaments, where I lost in the quarterfinals in one, and in the semis in another. The rest of the team, despite the constant squabbling unleashed by my poisonous suggestions, was still chugging along toward an eventual National Championship. It was all falling apart. I hadn't been dropped from the varsity roster, but Sparks spent less and less time paying attention to me. My end was near.

I needed to win something, and I needed to win it soon.

I had one last chance before the State tournament, so I vowed to focus on nothing but making *The Heroin Diaries* brilliant. Nothing would distract me this time.

Still, the e-mail from my dad that just said *I miss you* nearly split my heart in half.

CHAPTER TWENTY-NINE

Visitation

I had missed three Saturdays in a row. Tournaments were on Saturdays, and they went all day—there was no time to visit my dad during the season. Since he had gone to prison, our weekly talks had been like oxygen to me. I felt a piercing pain in my stomach from missing the visiting sessions.

"I have to skip this tournament," I said to Sparks after school, swallowing my fear of him. *He's going to tear you apart now*, whispered the voice in my head.

His mouth was a slim line of disappointment. He didn't say anything.

"I have a family emergency, and I need to take care of it."

"You know if you miss this tournament the only chance you have of going to Nationals is to win the State Championship," he said calmly. I said a little prayer of thanks that he seemed calm.

"I know that."

"So you think you're going to win State."

"I mean, I could."

"You haven't finaled in a single tournament since the first one and you're going to win State." The very idea of it was preposterous.

"I hope so."

"Because you have a family emergency."

"Right."

"That you haven't mentioned before now."

"It's an emergency, like a sudden thing."

He lifted an eyebrow. "Right." He put both hands under his chin, thinking. "So I moved you up to varsity because I saw something special in you. After the very first meet I said, 'That girl *has* something.' I believed in you. I believed that maybe you had the drive to do this. I think I believed in you more than you believed in you."

My whole body tensed. I almost preferred it when he was screaming at me.

"So after all that, after all this time we spent counting on you, you're gonna come up with an 'emergency.' What is it, by the way?"

"I can't really tell you."

"You didn't have time to think of a lie?"

My face started buzzing.

"That's okay, you don't have to deny it," he said. "I just want to know where I stand with you. Whether you think it's okay to lie to me or not. Have I lied to you? I don't lie to you because I respect you, Sydney. Look at me." Involuntarily, I looked up into his gray eyes. "You could be so much better than what you are," he whispered. "But I guess we won't find out, will we?"

"I can't make it Saturday."

"Can't or *won't*?"

It felt like my skull was being crushed. Tears started springing to my eyes.

"I gotta go," I said, fleeing the scene.

Lakshmi didn't support my decision, either. "Dude. What are you doing?"

"I miss my dad," I said as she drove me home after practice. The weather had warmed to the point where some of the elephant-sized snowbanks, now gray with weeks of street dirt, were melting. Rivers of cold water splashed down the streets.

"Okay, but there's only two tournaments left—if you don't go to this one, you'll have to win State just to qualify."

"I know that."

"Yeah? And?"

"And I haven't seen my dad for almost a month, and it's killing me. Isn't that the whole point? What we're doing? That winning isn't the most important thing in your life? We're fighting that entire idea, right?"

"And how does not going to Nationals make your point? There's a ton of people counting on you. You're not the only one involved in this."

"Really? 'Cause right now it seems like it's just me, all right? I'm the person taking all the risks. I'm the person making all the sacrifices. And you guys, if this thing succeeds or not, you just go on living your lives and go to college, and I get to be assistant manager at the fucking Cookie Factory."

Lakshmi dropped her hands off the steering wheel. "First of all: Fuck that feeling sorry for yourself shit. You're better than that. Second: You think you're the only person risking something here? I gotta watch my little sister turn into a goddamn varsity clone for the past two months and you haven't done shit to stop that."

"I've tried—"

"Yeah, you've *talked* to her—"

"She doesn't listen to me—"

"Of course she doesn't listen to you; she's fourteen! And in case you missed it, that was the entire fucking point of taking down Sparks in the first place. So people like my little sister, who used to be decent, nice human beings, don't become overly competitive fuckwads. That's WHY we're taking him out, right? So we don't have to just rely on telling someone like Rani not to follow that ass clown, we get to SHOW what a toxic scrotal mess he is. Okay? Right? I believe I wrote that down?

"You know she's taking Adderall? I found it the other day.

She's taking Adderall so she can cram for tournaments. I hear her at night, all right? She barely sleeps. She's gonna have a fucking ulcer at fifteen if we don't do something to stop it. And I can't talk to her . . . I can't . . ." Lakshmi shook her head, fighting back tears. "I don't want to lose her."

"I hear what you're saying," I said. "But I gotta see my dad. And I promise you, I promise you, I will do everything I can to win State. All right?"

"I hope so."

Luke offered to give me a ride to the prison on Saturday morning. "I always figured white-collar criminals go to like a country club," he said as he hunched over the wheel in his Honda Fit.

"I mean, it's not like *Les Mis* or anything," I said, staring out the window.

"Yeah, I wouldn't say that it was. Like Lay Miz." I could almost hear the hamster wheel that powered Luke's brain activate and search for what "Lay Miz" was.

"It's a musical about the French Revolution. Based on a book about the French Revolution."

"Sweet."

"They basically dig trenches. It's probably like great cardio."

"You'd be surprised that physical labor isn't necessarily great for your body," opined Luke. "When done incorrectly, a repeated action can cause a lot of stress on joints and muscles."

"Yeah, that was probably the worst part of the French Revolution. The joint stress."

He laughed. "No doubt." We came to a stop in the parking lot. "You want me to wait while you're inside?"

"I'll catch the bus back, thanks."

"Sure thing." He rapped his knuckles on the steering wheel and scratched his scraggly beard. "You know, when I was six, my dad went to jail."

I turned to look at him. "No shit?"

"Yeah, he got in a bar fight. This was in Brainerd, so everybody knew everybody—somebody mouthed off, and my dad was kind of an angry drunk, so he ended up slashing the guy with a broken beer bottle. It was . . . really bad."

"Oh man."

"Yeah . . . he was kind of an awful piece of shit." Luke smiled. "I'm not saying your dad's a piece of shit, but I'm saying . . . I know what you're going through. If you ever want to talk about it."

I sat there for a moment, feeling the warm air blasting from the vent.

"No pressure or anything," he added.

"Thanks," I said quietly, opening the door.

Dad was paler than usual when he hugged me. He was essentially snow-colored.

"Hey there, Squidney!" He held on longer than he needed to. "Gosh, I was wondering what you were up to!"

"Conquering the world," I said, releasing him and sitting down.

He chortled and adjusted his glasses. "I bet you are." He sniffed, then scratched his knee. I smiled at him. What was there to say? What could I talk about that wasn't going to hurt?

"So, what are you up to?" he asked again.

"Um . . ." *A complicated revenge strategy against the motivational speaker that convinced you to take on too much debt, same old, same old.* "I've got a speech tournament coming up, so that's interesting."

"Oh, really?"

"Yeah, State finals."

"Wow. I wish I could be there."

Yeah, me too. But you're not going to be there.

"It's okay," I said. "Probably be kind of boring. It's like twelve hours of sitting down. For the parents. Like, people are recording it with their phones, but it's like, how often are you gonna watch that, right?"

"I think people watch them. I mean, if I had videos of you, I'd watch them."

I leaned back. "Sure."

"I would."

He was looking at me earnestly, believing what he said. Believing that lie. Did I believe the lies I was telling him, too? Something twinged inside of me.

"But you didn't take videos of me when you had the chance," I said. "So why would you watch them now?"

He seemed confused. "What are you talking about?"

"From like, age twelve on, you were barely there, so you don't have videos of me as a teenager—"

"You didn't want me to take videos of you then; you were embarrassed."

"No, don't turn this around on me. You weren't there—"

"I was working, honey—"

"Yeah, tax fraud takes a lot of time and effort, I guess."

He looked pained. He had shrunk into his chair; you could really tell that he had lost weight over the past few months. He had seemed enormous when I was a little kid, a larger-than-life personality from my vantage point on the floor of his office. And now here he was, a fragile thing. I could snap him in two with the right words.

"I'm sorry," he said, shakily. "I wish things had happened differently. I was trying to take care of you and your mother."

The urge to tell him the truth surged up in me. I pushed it down.

"I need to go," I said, not looking at him.

"Okay. I love you."

"I love you, too."

I thought about Thomas on the bus ride home. I thought about watching his speech.

I only have the right to tell my story.

When I got home, I started working on something new.

CHAPTER THIRTY

My Story

The State Speech Tournament was held at Chanhassen High School, which was located in a snazzy group of culs-de-sac that called itself a suburb. The weather had finally broken, and a clear bright sun rose on a day that was going to be nearly forty degrees. Everyone in Minnesota lost their minds when this happened, broke out their shorts and flip-flops, and deluded themselves into thinking it was warm.

With my vast Cookie Factory riches I had bought myself new shoes for the tournament. They were a slightly higher heel than I was used to, which was dumb; the last thing I needed to be doing was tottering around onstage like a robot with a low battery.

I sat alone on the bus.

Halfway there, Hanson dropped in next to me, looking like a *GQ* fashion plate in his new suit. "Hey."

I pulled out my headphones. "Hi."

"You ready for this? You in the shit now, son."

I stared at him blankly.

"That's from *Hamilton*," he said, which I knew. "Which I have seen twice. Basically means don't sweat it."

"I'll try, but when you're wearing panty hose, it sort of collects in your toes."

"Tell me about it."

"I just did."

He smiled wolfishly.

"I mean, I guess I could go into more detail if you wanted, but I don't think either of us would enjoy that conversation."

"You never know what people enjoy," he said, putting a foot up on the armrest of the seat in front of us, showing off his SpongeBob socks.

"SpongeBob," I said.

"My lucky socks."

"My mom actually works in the SpongeBob mines."

"I know." He smiled. "It's fate."

"What is?"

"You and me."

I tilted my head slightly.

This is your chance, Sydney. Lay the groundwork. Seduce the hell out of him. This was part of the plan, wasn't it? I could use this. I thought about Elijah. If only I could pause this conversation and text him right now.

"That frightens you, huh?" said Hanson, his blue eyes flashing in the sunlight.

"A little bit."

"That's natural. But I'm just human like anyone else."

"That's important," I said. "I only get involved with humans. Romantically."

"Species-ist."

"That's a lie," I said. "I love my dog. If my dog was a man, I would marry him. You know I sing to him in my spare time? Love songs."

"I sing love songs to my dog, too. She's amazing."

"My love songs are probably better. I make up a lot of songs apologizing for his lack of testicles."

"I'm pretty sure he still has testicles. They don't remove them when a dog gets neutered."

"You sure think you know a lot about balls, Hanson."

"I do indeed." He smirked. "I've been . . . learning about balls for a long time now."

We both cracked up. I knocked my shoulder into the side of him, then he pitched forward, shouldering me toward the window of the bus.

"Stop it," I said, still joking. "I'm going to get a run in my stockings."

He settled back into his seat. "I should've worn SpongeBob stockings."

"They make SpongeBob stockings?"

"They make SpongeBob *everything*." He waggled his eyebrows suggestively.

All right, I need an escape hatch from this conversation now.

But I was smiling in spite of myself. He was a jackass, and he was gross, and he was a raging egotistical fucknugget, but I had to admit, he was kind of funny. I lifted my headphones, the universal sign for *I am done with you now.*

"I gotta think about my piece," I said.

"Are you sure it's *your* piece you're thinking about?" he pushed, trying to keep the banter going.

"Yes, actually," I said. "I'm doing a new piece today, and I need to think about it."

"You're not doing heroin today?"

"Nope. All heroin-ed out."

"Ohhh, so did you invite your mom, then?"

I felt my face twinge. I hadn't. I had mentioned the State tournament of course, but in an "it's no big deal I'm just gonna keep speechifying and it's boring and you don't want to be there" kind of way. To be honest, the thought of her in the audience for this new piece terrified me. I figured she would be cool with me miming heroin injections, but maybe not with what I was planning on today.

"She's working today," I said. "SpongeBob mines."

"She's not coming to see you compete?"

"Some people have jobs." I tapped my headphones and turned away from him.

Hanson sat there, confused and irritated that I was dismissing him like a peasant. He tried to think of something to say, failed, and then headed back to his regular lair in the back of the bus.

Sparks had been less than enthused about my switching categories. Then again, he had been pretty clear that my refusal to put my life on hold for speech was a personal affront to him and he didn't need to bother talking to me again, so what was there to lose? I hadn't shown him the new piece I was doing anyway, which only confirmed his belief that I was cratering on purpose due to my low self-esteem. I was planning to fail.

Which was not my plan.

It wasn't until octofinals that I ended up in a round with Chantal. She was surprised and not all that thrilled to see me.

"I thought you were doing dramatic interpretation," she said after she entered the room.

"Why are you asking questions?" I replied, my eyes half-lidded.

"It's interesting that you think that was a question."

"Isn't it, though?"

Chantal raised an eyebrow, pulled her orange hair into a ponytail, and turned away from me. She was slated to go before me, and I could tell immediately that I'd be beating her this round. It's not that her program on veganism and wind power wasn't well-written, it was, but it wasn't as slick as some of the other ones. There was nothing special about it, and at State, you were either special or you were nothing.

I went last in the round, which was an advantage. We had written our titles in dry-erase marker on the whiteboard—Chantal's was a mouthful of pretension. Mine was simply My Dad.

I looked out at the room. We were in a room that was probably used for brainwashing of some kind. Whoever had been sentenced to teach in this room had clearly given up on providing a decent education years ago. The walls were white brick, barren of even the weakest piece of free art printed from the internet, like a sensory deprivation chamber. I couldn't even tell what subject was ostensibly taught here; maybe this was where they prepared people for a life of soul-crushing drone labor. The desks were arranged in six neat rows—five other competitors sat near the back, along with a handful of spectators and parents. No one I knew.

The judge was a retired teacher; at State they tended to get people who actually knew what they were doing. She had short white hair and perched a small pair of glasses on her nose.

"Whenever you're ready, Sydney," she said.

My fingers tingled and I closed my eyes, but I could still sense Chantal's vaguely superior, haughty gaze on me. I exhaled slowly, trying to suppress the nerves that were ready to spasm in my chest and shoulders.

"My Dad," I said finally. Then I went into it. "When people

find out your dad is in prison, they treat you differently. You can sense it almost immediately. It's like they think it's contagious. 'Oh, your dad's in prison for tax fraud, let me make sure to make it clear to you that there is *sales tax* on that gum you're purchasing there, young lady. Six point two-five percent. Deal with it.'

"It's not like my dad imparted that particular piece of wisdom to me, you know? He didn't sit down with me at night and read *The Little Engine That Could Because He Defrauded the Government.* I didn't learn that at his knee, you know? We didn't go out in the backyard to throw the ball around into offshore tax havens. 'Now, honey, when you're forging documents, make sure to come up with a fake name that sounds plausible.' That was not my childhood.

"No, we did normal things. We had a normal life. It *seemed* like a normal life. But then again, what did I have to compare it to? In middle school you don't really have a grip on what other kids are going through. You don't understand that not everyone's life revolves around hiding expensive things when people come over. Or not seeing your dad for three days because he has to go to Morocco, or the Cayman Islands, or hide from an investigator in a basement closet under a tarp. To be clear, he wasn't in that closet for three days. We let him out after two. That wasn't strange, that was just *life.*"

I could tell that I had the audience captivated, as small as they were. They laughed at every joke, and I knew they desperately, desperately *wanted* to laugh. They saw an awkward teenage girl telling a story about unbelievable pain, and they were so grateful I wasn't going to stab them in the heart immediately. That would come, of course. You couldn't win with just jokes. Not in any event. And not in life either, I guess.

I had practiced all week, every night after school when I got home. I had written down my routine, deleted everything, then rewrote it. I had been up till midnight every night, pacing around my tiny room, practicing every gesture, honing it until I knew every word I wanted to say. I knew when and where I was going to cry.

I went through my happy childhood, telling jokes, talking about the time I spent in my dad's office, lying on the floor, reading. Listening to his music. Singing songs. Before the crimes started. When I didn't realize we were poor.

"It really hits home when they repossess your car. It's all sort of abstract until you see the tow truck show up—they attach a hook to the bottom of the car—my dad had a Porsche at this point, cherry red, I mean, *maybe I should've seen the warning signs*." The audience laughed. "But these guys show up, and I don't know why every repo team has to have one fat guy and one skinny guy, but every time they took our things, it was the same general formulation. There's like a fat Batman and a skinny Robin, and they're like this dynamic duo of repo universe, you know? 'Come, Boy Wonder, let's get that car.' And they're always smokers. It's like moving men, but instead of moving it somewhere else, they're moving it to like an incinerator, I don't know."

I stopped and took a breath. The laughs were a little more unsure now, as if the audience didn't know it was supposed to be laughing at this.

"I use humor," I said, my voice shaking a bit. "I use humor. Someone once told me that people use humor as a *shield*. For me it's *armor*. It's the only thing they couldn't take." I bit my lip, stopping the tears in their tracks.

"They put a freeze on our bank account, because there was no money, you know? All the money that was supposedly in there was imaginary. It was all lies my father told us. My whole life, everything I could touch and see, the clothes I was wearing, all of them were *imaginary*.

"People ask me how is it possible to still love someone like that? My mom . . . I mean, she doesn't love my dad, right? She has the *luxury* of choosing not to love him anymore—oh, hey, this person lied to you for years and ruined your life, it's cool to cut that person out of your life, you know? Amputate them. Move on."

I wiped the tears off my face. "I see him every week. I go to the prison—there's visiting hours. There are so many people like me in the world, you know. I'll be there, in the waiting area before you're allowed in, and I just look around at all the other visitors—most of them are women—and I look around at them, and I want to shout, 'What are we all doing here?! Why are we loving these men who did these things? What the hell is wrong with us?'

"I love my dad. He's a criminal and I love him." I bit into the skin on the back of my hand. My whole body was shaking. There were tears rolling my down my cheeks now.

I exhaled one last time and lasered my eyes on the audience. "I don't get to *choose* not to love him. I remember the person he was—I remember lying on the floor of his office, I remember him tucking me in at night, the kind of person who would laugh at all my jokes and roll around on the floor and be kind—he was always kind—and I try not to think about . . . his life. It's better that way.

"He's not here. He can't come to these meets. I don't see him on holidays. I don't get to get annoyed that he's not paying attention to me. But he made me who I am."

I stood there, like a statue. Nobody in the audience was breathing.

I turned to the judge. "Thank you."

Then I got back to my seat, raw and open like a wound.

It was like setting yourself on fire every hour for ten minutes or so. I made it through round after round. Lakshmi arrived for the quarterfinals and hugged me after my performance, but she was the only one of my friends to make it. Obviously, Thomas and Elijah couldn't be there. Neither could Blaize. I had made sure my mom wouldn't be there, too.

When they told me I had won State, I was still crying.

CHAPTER THIRTY-ONE

The Dark Side

Sparks was floating so high that he might as well have been in orbit. Not only did I take the crown for OO, but Hanson defended his title in HI (only five people walked out) and Taryn and Milo won in duo. Three State Champions. Logan and Anesh had already qualified for Nationals, even though they didn't even final at State. All six of us were going on.

It was the most successful year in Sparks's illustrious career.

The story of my dad had only managed to bolster his legend. I felt sick.

Because of rules, Lakshmi wasn't allowed to give me a ride home. Everyone else's parents were there. Everyone else got a ride home. I had to take the bus back to the school. By the time the awards ceremony was over, it was nearly midnight, and I sat by myself, holding the huge trophy I'd won, staring out the window at the passing streetlights.

Sparks settled into the seat across the aisle from me.

"I caught your performance in the final round." He smoothed out his pants.

Luckily, the trophy took up the seat next to me on the bus, so he couldn't move too close. I didn't say anything.

"Nice work."

I suppressed the urge to tell him to go fuck himself.

"That's why I push you, you know. To get that out of you."

"I'm actually pretty tired," I said, trying to get him away from me.

"Mm-hm. Tough day."

"Yeah."

"I wish you would've shown that to me earlier. We could've cleaned some things up."

"Cleaned some things up?"

"You think it's perfect?"

"Well, I just won State, so."

"So you think that will win Nationals?"

I sighed and looked out the window. "I'm not really concerned about winning right now, honestly."

"Sure," he said, nodding. "But you should be."

"Man, you never stop."

"We've got two weeks until Nationals—you think there aren't other sob stories there? Kids who were homeless. Kids with terminal diseases. It's more than just crying and cracking a few jokes and telling a good story. You have to be exceptional."

"Can you just maybe give me a moment before starting in on this?"

"Why?"

"'Cause it's a decent, humane thing to do? Give me a minute."

"You think those other State Champions are resting? They're training right now."

"Oh my God, it's not *Hunger Games*, give me a second."

"No. Sydney. You have a chance to *win*. You were really good tonight, but you weren't great. I've never had someone win OO at Nats. Not once. I've only had one person final ever. You think this was tough? Imagine sixteen rounds. Over three days. Four hundred kids competing. You won't win if you don't push yourself."

"You keep telling me I can't win, and yet . . ." I held up the trophy, which was actually kind of difficult because it was so heavy.

"Your mom didn't come tonight, did she?"

I looked down at my hands.

"You didn't want her to see what you can do. I get it. It's painful. Sometimes it's easier to share pain with a roomful of strangers than the people we love."

"She had to work tonight."

"Right." He smoothed out his hair. "I want you to work with me on that piece."

I blinked away tears. The last thing I wanted to do was spend

325

hours opening my heart about my father to the guy who was responsible for him going to prison.

"I think I can do fine on my own, actually—"

"You think I give this opportunity to everyone? Give that much of my time? You could be the exception. You could *win*."

"That's all it's ever about with you, isn't it?"

"Why wouldn't it be? Do you know what you get for winning Nationals?"

"I don't know . . . I live, and all the other tributes are murdered?"

"It's a full-ride scholarship. Institution of your choice. You could write your ticket *anywhere*." I didn't say anything. "You know I looked at your grades from your last school. Edina?"

I focused on my reflection in the dark window.

"Pretty bad. Not the kind of thing a college is likely to overlook. But you know that. You would have to have a pretty exceptional accomplishment to get into a decent school with grades like that. Probably have to do more than just qualify for Nationals; you'd probably have to do really well there."

A little crack opened in my mind. A door I had already closed. Sure, there were careers you didn't need to go to college for, and maybe with a little luck and good grades my senior year I could apply to a community college. Maybe save up enough money to pay for a year, maybe take out a loan. Maybe it would turn out okay.

Maybe.

Or maybe something would go wrong; somebody would get sick, my mom could lose her job, I could fail a class, I could make a mistake somewhere along the way . . . and it would all fall apart. And I'd be struggling to keep my head above water every day of my life, and just like my mom I'd wake up at forty-four years old and be worth negative money. Maybe there was a better way.

What if I could get that scholarship? What if I could get into a good school? What if that would change my whole life?

"Work with me for two weeks. Let me help you. Let's try to win Nationals together."

He extended his hand.

I took it.

CHAPTER THIRTY-TWO

Servant of the Empire

The sun rose fitfully over our apartment the next morning. Mom, cheerfully oblivious, was doing her usual morning routine: making coffee and stretching on flat surfaces. Luke had thankfully gone for his morning run.

"How did it go yesterday?" called Mom as I trudged into the living room to pat Charlie on the head.

I didn't answer. My stomach felt like it had been hollowed out.

"How did it go?" she repeated. "I was hoping you would text an update or something."

"I did well."

"Really?! That's great!"

"I won," I said quietly, dropping on the couch.

"You won?!"

I nodded, trying not to look at her.

"That's so great!" She took a moment as the implications of

that rattled through her. "But you didn't . . . Why didn't you text me last night? Why didn't you tell me you were doing that well?"

"I knew you were working, so—"

"What? You could've texted. It's not like I can't check a text at work. Hell, I would've caught a bus to come up there and see you."

"You can't really get out of a shift—"

"I'm not like an ER doctor, sweetie, I run a roller coaster. I could've gotten someone to cover for me. I could've made it up there. You acted like it wasn't important—"

"It wasn't important."

"You won the State Championship!"

"But that was largely a surprise."

She was dumbfounded. "How much time did you have before you knew you were going to the finals?"

"Like an hour."

"And you didn't let me know?"

"Well, you haven't been to any of my other tournaments—"

She took a step into the living room. "But I would've . . . honey . . . I mean I can't take off every Saturday, but . . . I want to be there for you." She paused. "Do you *want* me to be there for you?"

"Of course."

"So why wouldn't you . . . Are you ashamed of me, is that what this is about?"

I gritted my teeth, fighting back tears. "No!"

"Then why?!"

Instead of answering I just fled to my room.

I beat myself up the next day at school. I should've told her. I should've let her know what I was doing. But the thought of her, sitting in the audience, hearing me talk about my pain, pain that she had a part in creating, it was too much. And maybe there was a part of me that thought if my dad couldn't be there to see it, then she shouldn't be there, either.

Ugh.

It didn't help that the school was treating us like conquering heroes returning from an overseas war. We had voyaged to the land of Chanhassen, slain the vile Chanhassenites, and returned with their heads on pikes. They had decorated the school for us on Sunday; there were purple and gold streamers everywhere (I recognized them from Party City), and banners were strung over the subterranean hallways. CONGRATULATIONS SPEECH TEAM! everywhere I looked.

A lot of kids had seen my final performance. More had heard about it. I felt their eyes on me in the hallway; I heard them whispering about me as I passed. Was it pity?

I kept my eyes on the floor; I couldn't even lift my head to look at anyone. I felt naked.

Even our first strategy meeting felt wrong. Lakshmi had lifted a bottle of champagne from her parents' fridge, and we struggled to get it open for a good ten minutes before giving up and watching an instructional video on YouTube.

"Woo!" she whooped, passing out red plastic cups to the members of the conspiracy and pouring the champagne. Thomas unrolled our mission statement/evil plan onto the pool table and crossed off another step.

Elijah hugged me and planted a kiss on my lips. "That was so amazing," he said. "I am just so in awe of you."

"Did you see it?" I asked.

"Lakshmi told me about it. But I imagine it will be up on the YouTube channel soon. I can't wait to see it."

That thought filled me with poison. The champagne tasted like a swarm of bees.

"You all right?" asked Blaize.

"Um . . ."

Elijah wrapped his skinny arm around my shoulder. "You're fine. You're great."

"It's just that, like, this was Sparks's best year as a coach. I'm making him look good." I set my cup down and stared at the green felt of the pool table.

"Right," said Lakshmi, "but now we get to destroy him. We get to destroy all of them in the most public manner possible."

". . . yeah."

"That was the plan we decided on. We get to the livestream. End it there."

"It's important," said Thomas. "The boss battle has to be the final moment."

"Right." I still felt ashen and drained.

"All right," said Lakshmi, "I've already rented a hotel room in Kansas City—the four of us will road-trip down there while Sydney goes on the charter bus."

"Road trip!" called Blaize, high-fiving Lakshmi with a slap.

Thomas passed out crayons. "I have some devious thoughts on how to disrupt everyone's chemistry and concentration in the finals. And I've been working with Taryn's notebook, and I have some seriously diabolical ideas."

"Question," asked Blaize. "Do we wait until they make the final round to strike? What if no one makes it to finals?"

"Hmm . . ." said Elijah. "I think the goal is to get a complete nervous breakdown on camera, possibly with police rushing to the scene and handcuffing them." Thomas looked at him. "I mean, granted, that's probably a difficult ask at this point. But I say we definitely wait for the livestream, which is only the final round."

"Yeah," said Lakshmi. "If they fail before that, they fail, but I have a feeling they'll get there. If everyone goes to Nats and craps out before the final round, that will be a disappointment but not a catastrophe."

"Regardless," said Elijah, "they'll put the Third Diamond ceremony on the livestream. No matter what happens, Sparks will be on camera. That will be the final moment."

It was like I was watching them from inside a cave. I could see my friends moving and talking, writing things down, arguing about stupid shit, but I couldn't rouse myself to take part in it. It all seemed hopeless.

"I'm out," I said finally.

Thomas turned to look at me. "What are you talking about?"

"I'm out. I'm not doing it."

"Doing what?"

"The Plan. The whole thing. I can't do this anymore. Look, I'm going to—I'm gonna try to win." I took a breath and shook my head. "I want to win. I don't want to be a secret agent anymore."

CHAPTER THIRTY-THREE

Training with the Enemy

It took about an hour of fighting before I fled Thomas's house. I didn't want a ride home, and I didn't have enough money for an Uber, so it took me forever to walk home. On the way, holding my coat to myself to keep warm, I wrote out a hundred texts to Elijah and deleted them all. What could I say? That everything he told me didn't matter? That what we'd been working on was a waste of time? That our entire relationship was based on something I was throwing away? How could he keep liking me if I did this?

But I had to, didn't I? This was the only path.

When I got home, my mom wasn't speaking to me either. Luke tried to offer some advice, but I ignored him and fled to my room, looking at the small third-place trophy I'd gotten at that first tournament, and then the enormous triple-decker one for the State Championship. These were my friends now. There was a knock at the door, then I could hear the television from my mom's bedroom. Everyone had retreated to their own camps.

Charlie snuggled up next to me, waggling his entire backside like an outboard motor. "Who's a good boy?" I asked, scratching the hard ridge of the back of his skull. He scrabbled up my body, his infinite tongue licking my face into oblivion. I tried singing. "He's the best boy in the worrrrrld, such a good doggggg with noooo balllsssss," but even that didn't cheer me up.

I tried to avoid everyone at the school the next day, but Elijah found me after second period.

"Sydney," he said, swimming through the throngs of people that crowded the narrow hallways. "Come on, talk to me."

I considered fleeing the scene as usual, but instead found myself face-to-face with him just past a display of Cubist art. He was wearing his most appealing flannel, which is to say it was a semi-appealing flannel.

"I can't really talk," I mustered. "Besides we can't be seen together in public; this is a secret affair."

"I don't care right now."

"Elijah—"

"Is it something I did?"

"No. Absolutely not. I just—I need to do this, okay? Just let me? I feel like shit already. I don't want to make things weird between us, too."

He looked physically pained, like I had jabbed a salad fork through his sternum. "All right," he said quietly. "If you think you have to do this, then I support that. I think it sucks and it's stupid, but I'm here to support all your sucky and stupid decisions." He managed a tiny sliver of a smile.

"I'm gonna support your sucky and stupid decisions, too," I said.

I hugged him, but he felt tense and broken—almost as broken as me.

I kept my head down the rest of the day until I got to rehearsal. Only the six National qualifiers were there. The room felt empty. No Rani. No Sarah. No Chantal. No Olaf. None of the other underclassmen whose names I hadn't learned. Just the Sinister Five.

Or Six. I guess we were six now, weren't we?

"All right, then," said Sparks, slapping his hands together. "Let's take a look at our work over the weekend and see where we messed up." He activated the projector and pulled up our YouTube channel.

I had seen Hanson's performance in practice, but I hadn't had the chance to see what happened in front of a live audience. The video came up on his intro—the twenty- or thirty-second opening that each competitor could write themselves before moving on to published material.

"When my uncle was struck by lightning," he began, "we were a little concerned." The audience immediately started laughing. "I mean, yes, there was the sizzled flesh and occasional spastic limb movements, but the real problem . . . was that he began to hear *voices*. 'Stu'—my uncle's name is Stu, in case you were wondering. 'Stu!' 'What?!' That's all the voices said. It's bad enough that you're hearing things, but how much worse is it if the voice is BORING? 'Stu!' 'What?!' 'Stu!' 'Shut up!' If only he had heard a voice that told him something *interesting*." Hanson smiled wickedly. "In this classic tale of violence, depravity, and the occasional reference to a severed foreskin, a homicidal madman orders his followers to kill, and kill again. The Bible. By God."

The audience lost their minds. From there, Hanson launched into a word-for-word interpretation of Genesis, creating a handsy, inappropriate God, an adorable Satan, and Minnesotan versions of Adam and Eve—with each character shift, he "popped," making a tiny noise with his mouth with a near instantaneous shift in posture, facial expression, and accent. He was amazing at it. His timing was perfect. He had performed this piece fifty times at least over the course of the season; every little nuance had been honed to a razor's edge. Every minute of it was pure blasphemous hilarity. You could almost hear the moments when someone's mind exploded in the audience and they walked out in rage.

When it was over, Sparks paused the video and looked out at us. "Thoughts?" he said. I sat on my hands. Sparks waited.

"Nobody has anything to say. Nobody has any *comments* they'd like to make on Hanson's performance. Nobody has any worthwhile observations about anything."

Milo raised his hand. "I kind of lost the distinction between Adam and Eve a little bit."

"Uh-huh," said Sparks. "Go on."

"And I didn't feel like it came together. At the end. There's not like a good button on it."

"It just sort of peters out," added Sparks.

"Right. It just sort of— The funniest part is the stuff with the Garden; when you get into the bit with Noah . . . you lose me."

Hanson twisted in his seat. "What do you mean, I lost you?"

"I didn't really find Noah fun."

"The audience seemed to find Noah fun. The audience was laughing."

"So?"

"So that's your opinion."

"Yeah, he asked for my opinion. I'm giving it. The Noah part kinda sucked. You should end on a high note."

"Oh, it sucked? At first I thought it wasn't fun and now it sucked?"

"Do you want honesty from me or not?" asked Milo.

"I guess I'd value your opinion more if you'd ever won anything."

Shots fired. Oh shit.

Hanson kept going. "No, I mean it's cool—thank you for

your misguided opinion. I'll take that into consideration when I win my next tournament."

"Whatever," said Milo.

Sparks paced in the front of the room. "Are you done? You want my opinion?" Both of them shut up. "Milo is right. What I see up there is a person afraid of taking risks, and—"

"I take risks," said Hanson.

The room froze. Sparks froze.

"Did you just interrupt me?"

"I'm just saying—"

"Did. You. Just. Interrupt. me." Sparks locked eyes with Hanson. "Answer the question. Did you interrupt me?"

Hanson stared forward, gritting his teeth. "Yes," he said.

"And you think you've earned the right to do that. You think, because you won some shit tournament, you can talk when I talk? That's what you think? IS IT?!"

"No, Coach."

"You go to Nationals on my say-so. I give the word, you go *nowhere*. This is my team, Hanson," he said, his voice taut like a bowstring. "*MY TEAM!*" He spun back to look at the projection. "You're coasting. You're sleepwalking. Because you haven't had any decent competition in this state. And when you get to Nats, it's not going to be enough to offend a couple of parents and force them out of the room. You're going to need to be tighter. I want you to revamp the entire Noah section—I want you to get something more original for your angel, and I want you to think about the fact that the goal is not to make people laugh, it is to win. And your first step is to admit your performance this week-end was a pile of shit."

He took a step toward the laptop that was running the pro-jector. "There is nothing sadder," he added, "than someone who wins their junior year and fails their senior year. It's the worst feeling in the world. You'll regret it your entire life. Let's take a look at Milo and Taryn."

And so it went. After we watched Milo and Taryn's duo, Hanson tore into them first, retaliating for the drubbing he'd taken. He found fault with everything, particularly with Milo's characters, whom he didn't find compelling, interesting, or fun. Sparks egged him on, drawing out the pain, then bringing in Anesh and Logan, who seemed to have a lot of critical thoughts as well.

Then he put my video on.

I couldn't watch it. I closed my eyes during the entire ten minutes, gritting my teeth and clutching the edges of my chair. It was nerve-racking listening to myself. In *The Heroin Diaries* I had the distance of doing a voice for the characters; I never spoke like myself. For this one, it was just me. I heard myself, the awkward, nasal, stupid way I had of talking. Why would anyone ever listen to me if I sounded like that?

"Thoughts," said Sparks, after it was over. I felt a gulf of pain open inside of me.

Taryn spoke first. "I didn't really believe it." It was like I was being stabbed.

Sparks nodded. "What didn't you believe?"

"I mean, I guess in OO you can just do whatever, but for me, I wanted there to be some kind of point to it."

"So you found it pointless. Say it. Say what you mean. Stop sugarcoating things."

"I mean, so what? You love your dad. Great. So does everybody. I don't get it."

I bit down on my tongue so hard I nearly blacked out.

"Sydney, you want to respond to that?" said Sparks.

"I mean, I didn't really care," added Taryn, even though nobody was asking her. "Sorry. That's just honesty."

Tensions were running high all throughout practice. "You feel that?" said Sparks, after we were done ripping each other to shreds. "That's what excellence asks of you. Complete commitment. That's what you're going to feel at Nationals. From everyone. You think your teammates were harsh on you today? You think I'm tough on you? Just wait."

Logan and Anesh had already retreated to the back of the room with their laptops flipped open. They were both working on the same document in real time, and it was probably going to cause them to murder each other.

"Would you stop changing shit in the Google Doc?" growled

Logan, highlighting a section of text and deleting it. "BuzzFeed is not an acceptable source!"

"Are you kidding me?" snarled Anesh, pasting the section back in.

"Dude."

"What?"

"I just deleted that."

"Yeah, and I just put it back in. Amazing how that works. If you don't like it, you don't have to use it, but I'll use it in my argument."

"I don't want either of us using evidence that's bullshit."

"It's on the internet."

"Are you intentionally trying to make us lose?!"

Sparks approached me. "You gonna do any work or are you just gonna watch them?"

"Sorry, Coach," I said, grabbing my things.

"Come over into the other room," he said, leading me out into the hall.

We sat down in another classroom. Sparks held the printed text of my OO in his hands, bouncing a red pen back and forth in his fingers. "All right, then," he said, scrunching up his face. "Let's take a look at this."

"I think it's probably okay."

"Well, you heard Taryn."

"Yeah, I mean—"

"What?"

"I don't really think she likes me, so." *And I despise her.*

"Why does that matter?"

"I think she was criticizing me just to criticize me. Just to be mean."

He leveled his gray eyes on me. "Lots of people are going to hate you. You know that, right? Because people fear excellence. It makes them jealous; every round you compete in there are going to be people in the audience wishing for you to fail. They're going to find anything, *anything*, to criticize in your performance."

I waited for the nugget of wisdom to come from that. "So what do I do with that?"

He shrugged. "Hate them first." He flipped the page. "You have to be willing to do anything to win. All right, let's punch this up. What Taryn said is true. You're not giving the audience enough of an emotional road map through your piece."

"Well, it's kind of how I experienced it."

"Nobody cares how you experienced it. Nobody's coming here for truth. What if we adjusted your dad's crime?"

"What do you mean 'adjusted'?"

"Tax fraud is pathetic and the audience isn't going to understand it. What if he was a drug addict?"

"He's not a drug addict."

"Let's say he's a heroin addict—you can use some of the stuff from your DI—he's a drug addict, he steals something, ends up in prison—I think you need to make the prison tougher, by the way, let's let the audience really feel what that's like."

"But, um . . ."

"He gets out of prison. He has an overdose. Dies. That way you can tie it into the opioid crisis. So you've got the health care system, you've got the judicial system, and you've got opioid addiction. You tie personal pain to a pressing social issue."

I just stared at him. "But none of that is true."

"It's called Original Oratory; it's not called Truth."

"But like the power of the piece is the—honesty—of it."

"The power of the piece is watching a cute girl cry about how much of a disaster her dad is."

I felt a shiver roll down my body.

Attractive girls do better at speech, there have been studies.

You take a pressing social issue and tie it to personal pain.

"Sydney," he said. "Everybody lies."

CHAPTER THIRTY-FOUR

Changes

Reluctantly, I made the changes Sparks suggested. My dad got hurt at his work (he was a blue-collar worker in this new version because that made me more sympathetic), he got prescribed painkillers for his recovery. He got hooked on those, then moved on to other drugs. He stole from the family. My parents broke up because of his addiction. He went to prison. He got out. He died. I was super sad about it.

It was garbage. And I felt like garbage even trying to fake the emotions that were supposed to come along with it. I guess it was like acting, in a way, but it felt more like lying.

Despite our hallway conversation, everything was off between Elijah and me, too. Since we didn't have any classes together, and we still weren't sure we could be seen together at school, we hardly saw each other. Mostly it was just awkward texts back and forth. I felt him pulling away from me.

Things weren't great at home, either. Mom was taking on extra shifts, and I barely saw her in the evenings. When she got home from work, I was usually ensconced in my room with the door shut, catching up on homework or practicing my piece. I stayed up long after she went to sleep, going over the new lines, trying to perfect every little moment. Even when I turned the lights out, I couldn't focus on anything other than my piece. It felt like a lead shadow was following me everywhere.

Luke had taken it on himself to start cooking the meals in the apartment when he wasn't ingesting high-protein shakes. Usually I got home and the whole place smelled like roasting vegetables and cooking meat. He had completely eliminated all processed food and saturated fats or whatever and I hated it. He also managed to do a lot of pull-ups while cooking, which was disturbing. Luke wore little wrist and ankle weights everywhere and did an unfortunate number of lunges.

Still, the food was better than anything my mom or I could cook. Instead of relying on the parent casseroles in the faculty lounge, I usually had leftovers in my lunch. They were good. I hate to admit it, but the improved diet actually made me feel better. One day I contemplated a pull-up, then decided against it.

When he offered me a ride to go see my dad on Saturday, I didn't turn him down.

"So . . . uh . . . I've been meaning to talk to you about something," he said on the ride.

"I don't really want to discuss my fitness journey with you at this point."

He laughed a bit. "That's not what I meant. But I have seen you eyeing that pull-up bar."

"Oh, God, stop it."

"All right, all right. But you'd be amazed at what upper-body strength can do for— Okay, I'll stop. Um . . . your mom is pretty upset."

"I know."

"And I don't really want to get in the middle of this, but it's a small apartment, and the vibe is seriously unharmonious right now."

"Unharmonious?"

"Or disharmonious, I don't know."

"I don't think either of those are words you should be using."

"Anyway. She's sad she didn't get to see you compete, and she's sad she's missed all your meets, but I guess she doesn't understand why you don't want her to come."

I didn't say anything.

"Here's what I'm thinking: Sometimes people do stuff because they're afraid that they're gonna hurt people. But when you do that you just end up hurting those people more. Right?"

I nodded.

"Like, if I got a client and he wants to do a four-hundred-pound dead lift, the longer he's afraid of that deadlift, the more he's gonna hurt himself. I mean, obviously, this scenario assumes that he's been working toward that goal and has done the preliminary work. I guess maybe it's a very good . . . um . . . word thingie."

"Analogy?"

"Yeah. Damn. I'm sure that's why you win. 'Cause you're good with words."

"It's not really a vocabulary contest."

"I don't know what it is; you won't let us go to the meets."

"The next one's in Kansas City, so I don't know that you're going to be able to make it, anyway."

He puffed out his cheeks. "Yeah, that's tough. Shit. But—all right—talk to your mom. Please. I mean, really, actually talk to each other. If you want her to listen to you, you need to listen to her."

I nodded. He was right. "Yeah," I said quietly. "Okay."

"You want me to wait here for you? Give you a ride home after?"

"Sure."

He smiled.

Dad looked slightly healthier than usual this time. His normally translucent skin had taken on the slightest sheen of brown.

"You got a tan!" I cried.

He examined his arms in surprise. "Once it's warm enough, they let us walk the yard."

"Ooh."

"Yeah, I was thrilled about it. Getting outside is pretty nice." He enveloped me in a hug. "Got some exercise."

"That seems to be catching. Exercise. Everybody's doing it these days."

"You look good, too."

"Except me." I cut him off. I had seen myself in the mirror. An entire week of not sleeping and constant caffeine consumption was not doing my skin any favors. "I'm just maintaining a constant level of continuous freak-out, which helps me burn calories."

"You still look nice," he said, ignoring the comment.

I didn't feel nice. I know I didn't look nice.

"You all right?" he asked, noticing my discomfort.

I took a deep breath. "Why did you say I looked nice?"

"Hm?"

"You said I still look nice, but I haven't slept the whole week, so it's pretty obviously a lie."

"I always think you look nice," he said, perplexed. "It's just a nice thing to say."

"Is it?"

"You want me to say you look tired?"

"Yes. Because I am tired. If you said I looked tired, we could talk about *why* I looked tired. When you say I look nice, we don't get to talk about why I'm tired."

He looked utterly befuddled. This was not the way we were supposed to talk to each other.

"I'm just trying to be nice," he said.

"But it's not the truth. That's what I'm getting at. We don't tell each other the truth. Like, I come in here, and we basically lie to each other and then . . . I don't know . . . maybe we should tell each other the truth about things."

"Are you all right?"

"No, Dad. No. I'm not all right. That's what I'm getting at. I've had a really crappy week and I'm not sleeping and I have no idea what I'm doing with my life, so . . . no."

"Oh, well, um . . . sorry about that."

"And?"

"And I don't know what you want from me."

I sighed. "I don't really know what I want from you, either. But I think I need you to just hear things. I need you to understand what's going on with me, because I can't be going around protecting you, that's not okay."

I took a deep breath.

Just dive in. Tell the truth.

"I am not okay. I know I come in here and pretend like everything's cool all the time, and put on a brave face and all, but . . . I am a fucking mess. I failed three classes in the fall. That's the main reason I'm at the new school, all right? It's not just 'cause Mom moved, it's because I wasn't really wanted there anymore. I'm gonna have to take a bunch of summer classes this year just to have enough credits to graduate on time. So this whole thing about college? I don't even know if I'm going.

"And—you need to hear this—some of that is my fault, but it is mostly your fault. And I'm done hiding things from you, I'm done shielding you from things, I'm done pretending that I'm the parent and you're the kid. You did all kinds of stupid, stupid shit that blew up our family, wrecked our lives, and is gonna result in me paying for a shit-ton of therapy in the event I ever get health insurance.

"I am *angry* with you. I push that down every time I walk into this room, and it goes all kinds of crazy directions sometimes— I yell at Mom, I yell at my friends, I told a teacher he could go fuck himself a couple weeks ago, that was maybe a poor idea, and ALL OF THAT is because I don't ever tell you to go fuck yourself."

He took off his glasses and wiped his forehead. "I see." He waited for a moment, waiting for another blow from me, but it didn't come. "Is that what you needed to say?"

"No. I think there's something else you need to hear."

I took out my phone and pulled up YouTube.

"What's this?" he asked.

"This is a piece I did . . . for speech."

My heart almost exploded watching him watch me. He held my phone in his hand like an unbearable light, his eyes glued to the screen, his mouth frozen open. He alternated from smiling like an idiot, to laughing his butt off during the funny parts, to watching in shock. By the end, he was pitched forward, resting his elbows on his knees and clutching my phone with both hands inches away from his eyes. His breath was ragged and shallow; tears were rolling down his face. I heard my voice. "My dad's a criminal, and I love him."

When it was over, he set my phone down and pressed his fingers into the bridge of his nose. His eyes were down. We both sat still for a long time, incapable of saying anything.

CHAPTER THIRTY-FIVE

Thomas Brings the Heat

When I got back to my apartment, Thomas was waiting in my living room. Charlie was sitting like a gremlin on his lap while my mom was asking him probing mom questions.

"And what does your mom do?"

"She's a lawyer."

"Ooh. Nice."

"She's a corporate attorney, actually."

"That's amazing."

Luke churned into the room, noticed Thomas, and stuck out his meat-paw to test Thomas's grip strength. (Thomas failed.) "What's up?" asked Luke.

"Hello, sir," said Thomas. I grimaced inwardly. Despite my growing acceptance of Luke, I still felt like no one should call him sir.

"What's going on, Thomas?" I asked.

"I thought we should talk."

"Ooh," said Luke. "*Talking*. Yes."

Mom slapped at his shoulder with her hand. "He's gay."

"Niiice," said Luke. "What? I love gay people. They're awesome. High five."

It took only two high fives before we made it to my room.

"First of all," I said, "what kind of monster drops over to someone's house without texting first?"

"Sorry." He surveyed the state of my room and gingerly brushed off the corner of my bed before sitting on it. "I didn't want you to say no. Or have a chance to clean up, apparently."

"Just so you know, I wouldn't have cleaned up, anyway."

"I really appreciate that honesty."

"Me too."

He took off his glasses and wiped them against his sweater. "Sydney? What the hell."

"Go on," I said, knocking the dirty clothes off the only chair I had in the room.

"This isn't like you."

"You've known me for like two months."

"And I respect you. And I think you're a wonderful person. And I'm your friend. And I think too much of you to let you do this without a fight."

"Nope. This is me now. I've joined the Dark Side. I'm a stormtrooper for Sauron now."

His mind broke a little. "You can't— That's not— Sauron is an entirely different universe from Star Wars—"

"They could be the same. What if one of the planets in the Federation was Middle Earth?"

He grunted as a shelf of his brain collapsed like an Antarctic glacier. "The Federation isn't . . . Look. I'm not going to let you destroy yourself."

"How am I destroying myself?"

"Please. You're taking advice from *Sparks* now? You're friends with the other varsity members of the speech team all of a sudden? It's painful to watch. And I have been watching you all week. You've let the thing you're pretending to be take over who you really are.

"And dear God Jesus, Elijah is killing me. You know what he did this week? He just sighs. LOUDLY. All the time. It's so annoying. It's like he's staring at the floor. 'Sydney walked on floors once. We walked on floors together. I thought we were gonna walk on floors together forever.' I can't even with that boy."

"I'm still walking on floors," I protested.

"Not with him, apparently. Or not enough. Or not in the magical way you did before, I don't know. But it's annoying and it's got to stop."

I laughed a little in spite of myself. Thomas was right, of course. Everything he was saying was true. Not just the stuff about Elijah, but the things about me. I thought about my dad, about how I had finally managed to tell him the truth.

"I don't know what to do," I said finally. "I feel like I'm letting everybody down, but I also feel like I need to do this. Everybody wants something from me, and I don't . . . I don't really know who I am anymore."

He nodded quietly. "Can I tell you a story? I . . . hid for a long time. A long time. So . . . when I was younger, my dad was more famous. People still recognize him sometimes, but it was constant when I was in elementary school. And I like worshipped him. I didn't worship him because he was famous, but it just sort of reinforced my idea of who he was.

"I mean, we would be at restaurants and people would come up to him, take pictures. Strangers, right? Can you imagine being at like Red Lobster, and every time somebody recognizes your dad they come up to get a picture with him? I became hyper-aware of it—all the signs. You see somebody stare for too long and then whisper to the person next to them. And then the whole table starts staring. And somebody probably takes out a phone and tries to zoom in on him. It was crazy. But I loved him so much. And I was so scared he'd find out who I really was.

"Because I had an idea—I thought I knew what he was going to do. Obviously he was gonna disown me and throw me out of the house and at the age of twelve I'd be living on the street reciting poetry for money. I had weird ideas of what street performers did in those days, I promise you. I mean, I had already written the poems. 'These are my living-on-the-street poems.' Like, specifically calibrated to get people to throw down quarters. Then

I figured, okay, I'll just wait until he's like eighty years old and then tell him when he's about to die or whisper it at his funeral, that makes total sense.

"But it's like—every day you're inside this shell, this gigantic robotic shell, and the real me is so deep inside this thing, hiding, running the controls, terrified that someone's gonna see in through the eyeholes and catch a glimpse of the tiny little person inside. And it is so *heavy* in that shell, it is so fucking exhausting hiding every second of every day—and you look around and you think, 'Is that what's going on inside everyone's head? Are we all like this? Or is it just me?'

"And I was finally like, 'Am I gonna do this the rest of my life?' There was a time, when I was little, when the shell didn't exist, you know? But I built it bit by bit, every time somebody teased me, every time a relative *corrected* how I was standing, or sitting, or looking, every day I built that shell. But finally—no more. We were at a barbecue, and my parents are there—this is the summer before my freshman year and I wanted to apply to Eaganville—and I finally said, 'I may not be entirely straight.' I was planning on saying, 'I'm gay,' but it came out like that. Maybe I was just hoping to confuse them a bit? And then I just had a bite of potato salad and I said, 'This is really good, by the way.'"

He stopped there.

"Well, and then what happened?!"

"Then my dad said, 'Your uncle Damion made the potato salad and that's why it's good.'" Thomas laughed. "No, um . . . it was so good, Sydney. It was *so* good. Not the potato salad but the coming out. I mean the potato salad was good, too, but—" He smiled. "I was afraid of something, *for years*, that was not as scary as I thought. And it took a little bit of adjustment but my mom said she loved me and my dad said he loved me and holy shit I felt a hundred pounds lighter."

"You shoulda had that in the play," I said.

"I did!"

"It was probably good, then."

"Maybe not as artfully. But what I'm saying is I know *you*. And whatever you think you can get from listening to Sparks, you're sacrificing too much to get it."

I nodded.

"It's so much better to be walking around without a shell. That means you get hurt a little more, but God, it's so much lighter."

He looked up at me, his dark eyes shining.

I knew what I had to do.

CHAPTER THIRTY-SIX

I'm Sorry I Was a Big Stupid Idiot

At work the next day, Rhonda was back. In my absence she had taken over the cookie lettering, but her spirit wasn't really in it. I saw a cookie that said HAPPY BIRTHDAY, JERK and another one that just said THIS IS A COOKIE. Shockingly, neither of them had sold.

Chad looked at me with desperate eyes. "We missed you. We missed you so hard."

I tried, but it was hard to have the spirit to make funny cookies when you feel like the world is collapsing. I had sent texts to all my friends the night before apologizing, asking to be let back in, wanting to rejoin the crew, but nobody had written back. Was that it? Had I missed my chance? And what did that mean for Elijah and me? My text to him was hanging out there, like a tiny little tree branch.

Hey. I'm really sorry about everything this week. Forgive me?

Being at work somehow made it hurt worse. I remembered the times he'd come to visit me as my shift was ending, our first time shopping, the dinner at the Rainforest Café—we'd barely had a chance to start a relationship before it looked like it was going to be over.

At four o'clock I looked up and he was there. Standing in his heavy coat even though it had warmed up outside. He had his hands in his pockets and was staring at the counter. He didn't approach. I made eye contact with him, but he was barely looking in my direction.

Fine. I went into the back and got my tube of icing. I wrote out I'M SORRY on a huge chocolate chip cookie and placed it in the display case. Elijah took a look at it, then stepped up to Rhonda.

"I'll take that one," he said, putting fourteen dollars down.

Rhonda handed him the cookie, and Elijah backed up about twenty feet, holding it in his hands, still staring at the counter, and still not really looking at me. I got out my icing again.

The second cookie said I MISSED YOU SO MUCH. He bought that one, too.

Then he bought one that said I'VE BEEN REALLY STUPID.

I put the fourth cookie in the display and stared at him. His arms were full now, like a pizza delivery guy. He looked at the newest cookie.

I THINK I LOVE YOU.

"I'll take that one, too," he said, his voice cracking, handing Rhonda the last of his money.

Chad came over and looked at the stack of cookies in Elijah's arms.

"You must really like her cookies," said Chad.

"You have no idea," said Elijah.

I reached over the counter and took his hand. "Come here," I said, pulling him back near the prep table. I took another blank cookie and got my icing ready.

KISS—no reaction—ME—he trembled—YOU—he stopped, curious—FOOL.

And then he was kissing me. His lips were soft and full and warm, and I felt the squish of his coat, and he pressed to the side of me.

Chad and Rhonda clapped.

"Woo!" called out Chad. "That was a hoot! That was—"

Then he saw that I'd written another cookie that simply said: LET'S DESTROY THESE MOTHERFUCKERS.

I didn't get a chance to see how fast that one sold, because we were already out the door.

CHAPTER THIRTY-SEVEN

Endgame

We arrived at the Kansas City Marriott Tuesday night. The tournament would take place Wednesday through Friday, with the finals rounds being broadcast during the day on the last day. My friends were staying at the Best Western across the street. Lakshmi had made a reservation under the name Najima. Elijah was bringing along a fake mustache.

There had been a cheerful reunion on Monday, many hugs were offered and accepted, and we had nailed down the complicated and glorious plan that would bring us ultimate victory. Now it was just up to us to execute it.

The first part of the plan was simple. As the only other girl on the trip, I would be rooming with Taryn. That would allow me to initiate Operation Break Milo's Brain at the earliest possible moment. Taryn wasn't especially inclined to talk to me or acknowledge my existence, busying herself taking up all available closet space by hanging up three separate power suits.

"It's so great that Blaize isn't here, right?" I said, plopping down on one of the twin beds once we checked into the hotel.

"Hmm," mumbled Taryn.

"You know her whole thing with Milo. Or I guess I should say Milo's whole thing with her."

"He never did anything with her."

"Oh, yeah, definitely. He's amazing like that. His self-control."

"Because he's a gentleman." Taryn was opening and filling the drawers to the dresser with her impossibly large selection of clothes, most of which said horrific things like LOVE EVERY DAY.

"You should've seen the outfit Blaize was wearing the other day . . . mm," I growled.

Taryn sneered. "She would."

"I know she would. And it looked *good*. Which is all the more amazing that Milo is able to resist, because, thanks to Logan, I know that males are extremely visual. That's just the way their brain works. Through the eyes. Involuntary, almost."

Taryn's hands paused just for a second as she was hanging up her last suit.

"I gotta tell you something else, though, since it's just us . . . when you were in the closet with Hanson . . . holy shit."

She turned to look at me. "What do you mean, holy shit?"

"Milo was like a dog—his ears were like whoop."

"I have no idea what that means. I don't really like dogs."

You fucking monster I will see you burn in hell. But I didn't say that.

"You've seen dogs before, though. When they're interested, their ears go up."

She squinted. "Not all dogs. I mean, like, basset hounds. Their ears don't do that."

"All right, not like a basset hound. But like another dog. He was *really* interested." It honestly wasn't that much of a lie.

The slightest glimmer of a smile crossed her face before she suppressed it. "So?"

"Shit. I'm just gonna come out and say this: He takes you for granted. He's like, it's great that I have this superhot chick who's like madly in love with me—"

"I'm not madly in love with him—"

"Of course, right, but I'm sure he *thinks* that. He thinks he can have you whenever he wants."

Taryn gritted her tiny perfect teeth. "What we have is totally beyond sexual."

"Definitely. One hundred percent yes." I nodded. "I'm just saying, *theoretically*, if you were to flirt with someone else, he might finally appreciate what's right in front of his face. Which is literally your butt during that spider scene in *The Hobbit*."

She squinted at me. "You have no idea what it means to be in a mature relationship."

* * *

She was probably right, but I did notice that Taryn wasn't sitting on Milo's lap in our first group meeting in the floor's minuscule lounge. She was nestled next to Hanson, who wasn't paying much attention to her, either. Milo's non-basset-hound ears were definitely up.

Sparks was in rare form. "The first rounds start at eight thirty tomorrow morning, so I want you to be in bed and ASLEEP by ten o'clock. Phones off. No running around in the hallways like the other squads. Every year I come to Nationals it's absolute madness—kids running around, people hooking up with other people—you are not going to find the love of your life in a hotel in Kansas City."

I looked at Milo, who was looking at Taryn, who was looking at Hanson.

"I leave other members home because I want complete concentration from you. I don't want to see any tweets about 'missed connections' about some girl in a pin-striped skirt from California, all right? This isn't *Love Connection*. Every other person here is trying to beat you. Understand that. Men, I want you showered and shaved by six thirty."

"Entirely shaved?" The words were out of my mouth before I could stop them. Logan suppressed a snort of laughter. Sparks leveled his fiery gaze on me. "I just thought maybe it was an aerodynamics thing," I said. "Like swimmers."

The rest of the group got quiet.

"Maybe you should've done HI," said Sparks, smiling like a normal human being. "That was funny."

The team exhaled.

"Ladies," he said to me and Taryn, "do whatever you need to do to look good. Remember that this is a business setting, not a dance floor. I don't want to see any four-inch heels."

No problem. Taryn frowned. I had seen her shoes—she was going to have to rethink some outfits.

"One last thing," he said. "You represent the entire team. You represent me. What you choose to do this week will define you for your entire life. Will you choose to be a loser? Or a winner? Some of you will make it. Some of you won't. That's all. It's only your life." He let that hang in the air for a moment, before adding, "All right, get out of here. Sydney, stick around."

I felt my stomach drop as everyone else filed out of the lounge. Sparks closed the door.

"You're making jokes now," he said flatly.

"I thought maybe it would be nice to add a moment of levity," I said, noticing that he now stood directly between me and the only exit.

"You thought that?"

"Yes."

"Because I wasn't doing enough as a coach, right?"

"Um . . ."

"You NEEDED to add a 'moment of levity' to help the morale

of the team. Right? Because I was doing a poor job as the coach of this team? Even though we have six National qualifiers."

"I'm sorry," I said.

"About what?"

"About making that joke."

"Just a second ago you told me that you felt it was necessary to make that joke. And now, moments later, you've changed your mind. I'm having a hard time understanding that."

Get out get out get out get out—

"I'm sorry, Coach," I said, again, trying to get to the side of him.

He didn't move. "Are you going to be a problem?"

"No, sir."

"No what?"

"No, Coach."

His mouth was slightly open. I could feel his warm breath on my face. "If you are trying to challenge my authority over my team, I will tear you apart. You understand me? I will throw you in the garbage. You say one more thing, you make one more little crappy joke, and I will slap the shit out of you."

My heart was pounding in my chest.

"You understand?"

"Yes, Coach."

I was still shaking when I made it into the hall. Logan was waiting for me like nothing was wrong.

"Hey, I just wanted to say thanks for breaking the tension in there."

A laugh escaped me. "What?"

"I mean sometimes Sparks can get a little intense."

I shook my head to clear my mind.

"The last couple weeks have been ridiculous," he said. "I don't even know where I am half the time."

I looked at him more carefully. He had deep bags under his eyes, just like everyone else on the team. Prepping for Nationals had nearly killed us.

Maybe Logan was just as much of a victim as the rest of us?

"By the way, you look like you've lost a little weight. Nice. I approve of that strategy."

My sympathy for Logan vanished as I pictured him being torn limb from limb by a pack of hyenas.

"How are things going with Anesh?" I said, hoping to open wounds.

Logan reacted like he had been whipsawed in the face. "Anesh is basically trying to ruin our entire team. He's such an ass."

"Tell me about it," I said, smiling ever so slightly as he fell into the trap.

"I'm getting a Coke if you want to join me."

"A Coke? At nine o'clock. Aren't you going to miss your bedtime?"

"Breaking the rules," he said, and laughed.

"Well, I guess I can have a *Diet* Coke," I said, imagining him being roasted over a spit.

We settled into the tiny refreshment closet, lit by the glowing light of the massive Coke vending machine. Logan slid to the ground on one side of it; I sat on the other.

"I can't go back to my room," he began. "Anesh is there and he's a nightmare. He plays his music at approximately a million decibels, so even though he's got headphones on, I can still very clearly hear the Kanye coming through."

"Well, Taryn is in my room, so I'm sure that will be continuous joy. And just so you know, and I've said this to you before, but I am one hundred percent on your side."

"Thank you."

"You are obviously the motor to the team."

"I'm aware of that. I've been aware of that since day one."

"It really sucks that you got paired with someone like Anesh."

"He keeps adding shit to the Google Doc. Stupid stuff. Somebody tweets something about space exploration, and he's fucking adding a source on our main document."

"I mean, that's like a crime in some countries."

Logan laughed and took a sip from his Coke, agitating him even further.

"I mean it." I kept going. "That is so wrong. You can't just add stuff without agreeing to it."

"The last meet," complained Logan, "I was doing second

affirmative and I'm in the middle of the round checking sources and he had added a whole new tweetstorm in there."

"That is bullshit. That is someone with a death wish."

"Ugh."

I let that sit for a second, then I pounced. "Have you ever thought about locking him out of the Google Doc?"

Logan shook his head. "I can't lock him out, because we need to be able to use it during the rounds."

"You're using one laptop, though, right? Just use your laptop."

Logan's eyes darkened.

"All you need to do," I said, "is change the password to access the file. Then Anesh can't screw it up. Use your laptop in the competition, and you're good to go."

He snickered just a bit. "What would I change the password to?"

"How about 'Anesh sucks'?"

It only took seven tries for us to guess the new password at the Best Western. "And the winner," said Elijah, "is AneshSucks69."

"How is that not the first thing you guessed?" Lakshmi asked.

Thomas rubbed his hands together. "Oh, we're gonna have some fun."

"This is my role," said Elijah. "Just get back to work on your story."

CHAPTER THIRTY-EIGHT

Advancing

At Nationals, everyone is assigned a number. I was #1616. When you advance a round, they post your number—that way nobody knows who they're going to be competing against in the next rounds, if they advance. You can only worry about yourself.

The first rounds are held in meeting rooms of the convention center, which get progressively bigger and more impressive until, for the final round, you compete on the stage of a massive auditorium with several thousand people in the audience, with a live video feed going out to thousands of other people on the web. The trophies, huge, skyscraper-sized monstrosities, are arrayed behind you like a wall of sentinels as you perform. We had watched videos of the finals performances over the course of the year to inspire us, but honestly, it was completely nerve-racking.

At the beginning it was like any other meet. Lakshmi gave

me a pep talk outside the bland, featureless meeting room before the first round.

"You're gonna do awesome. Don't worry about the plan right now. You just try to advance."

"Right." I nodded.

She looked me in the eyes and gripped my shoulders. "And hey . . . I get it. I know that the college thing is super important. And I know that I don't have that same . . . reality."

"Thanks," I said, looking down.

"And I just want to say that you're awesome and I'm cheering for you. You're gonna kick ass today."

"It's like eight o'clock in the morning and you're trying to ruin my makeup already. You are a terrible, terrible person," I joked, sniffling through it. "I'm glad you're my friend. You made this school bearable. Ever since the first day I didn't know what the hell was going on about the gold standard and I was pretty sure people thought I was the worst person alive."

She hugged me. "I wasn't paying any attention about the gold standard, either."

"I love you so much and I love that you don't give a shit about monetary policy from the nineteenth century."

We headed into the room. Lakshmi sat in the back and gave me a thumbs-up as I surveyed the competition. Kids from all over the country, dressed in suits. Some of them had their eyes closed and were silently mouthing their routines to themselves;

others were staring forward with nervous intensity, shaking out arms or legs.

We're all just kids, I thought.

Sucks that only one of us will live. I cracked myself up.

When it was my turn, I performed the routine Sparks and I had practiced. It felt a little gross, to be honest, but it was effective. I did a part where I walk in on my dad injecting himself with heroin and used the same movements I'd perfected as Nikki Sixx. It was gut-wrenching, still a little bit funny, and a complete lie. The audience was a little intimidated by me; they gave me a wide berth.

Afterward, Lakshmi raised one of her dark eyebrows. "I don't really want to talk about it," I said. With each passing round you could see the numbers that were garnering the highest marks. Number 1616 was advancing steadily. Other numbers were accumulating ones (the highest rating in the round) at a persistent clip as well. I started mentally clocking who my greatest challengers were going to be: #108, #525, #741. I couldn't help feeling like Katniss, scoping out the tributes who were posting the most kills.

Thomas was checking in with the other Eaganville squad members since he was least likely to be recognized. He kept texting things like *Hanson is the Antichrist and everyone loves him for it*, which I guess meant that he was advancing. Or *Dear God this Hobbit nonsense*, which could really mean anything.

On the second day, I kept cruising—but by octofinals I was getting twos and threes in rounds (each round started having more and more judges). I was falling behind and would soon be dropped. After a certain point, scores accumulated, which meant that you started each round with either an advantage or a deficit. When I made it to the semifinals, I started the round in second place. I'd need to win this round in order to have a chance to win finals.

The crowds were huge now, bursting with the hundreds of kids who had already been knocked out in previous rounds. I recognized a few of the numbers I was competing against—#108 (Being a Teenage Mom) and #525 (I Was a Refugee). The other leading competitor (#741) was on the other side of the bracket and I wouldn't know what their piece was until finals, if I even made it to finals.

I needed to get on that livestream. I needed to have a chance to speak. Our new plan depended on it.

Adrenaline and exhaustion rolled through me in waves. I'd performed the piece thirteen times in two days; my voice was sore, my body ached like I'd been through the tumble sequence of a dryer. Still, I had to admit, it was *easier* to lie up there than to tell the truth. I didn't have to suffer through the emotional trauma of repeating my life in front of strangers. Here I was *acting*. It was just like *The Heroin Diaries*. I didn't have to be myself.

Semis were in one of the ballrooms, and the audience poured in once they swung open the huge double doors. Competitors sat on the stage now, staring out at the sea of faces in the audience. The folding chairs spread out in thirty or forty rows, stretching all the way to the far back of the massive room. It was the largest audience I'd ever faced.

In the back, Mom stepped into the room, holding hands with Luke.

They had gotten here a little late; they took a seat about twenty-five rows back, squished among groups of brightly chattering teenagers. My heart pounded in my chest when I saw them. Suddenly the gigantic room was only the size of my mother's eyes.

The contest manager, a resolute Latinx woman with a highly sensible tan business suit, walked to the center of the stage.

"Number one-oh-eight, from James Bowie High School in Austin, Texas, Jasmine Wu."

The cheer that went up for her was thunderous. I shivered all over and tucked my hands under my thighs, trying desperately to keep it together. Jasmine, a tall girl in amazing shoes, strode up to the front of the stage with unflappable confidence.

"At first I didn't think it was true," she said, her voice clear and bright. "Then I thought about whether or not I could get on *Teen Mom*." The audience laughed. "Then I watched *Teen Mom*." The audience laughed harder.

I kept my head down during her performance, staring at the floor and listening to the sweep and power of her speech. It was the best thing I'd heard in any round, period. She was phenomenal.

And it's true, I thought, closing my eyes. It was obvious it was true.

And I'm gonna get up there and lie.

Jasmine finished and a thousand people erupted into applause.

"Number one-six-one-six, from Eaganville High School in Eaganville, Minnesota, Sydney Williams!"

The crowd roared for me, too. My mom lifted her hands over her head and clapped. Luke put two fingers in his mouth and whistled like a gym coach, because of course he had the loudest whistle of anyone in the room.

I exhaled, then walked to the front and stared out at the crowd. Mom had a smile on her face. I exhaled again.

You only have the right to tell your story.

Screw Sparks's stupid advice. I still remembered my original version.

"When people find out your dad is in prison, they treat you differently. You can sense it almost immediately. It's like they think it's contagious. 'Oh, your dad's in prison for tax fraud, let me make sure to make it clear to you that there is *sales tax* on that gum you're purchasing there, young lady. Six point two-five percent. Deal with it.'"

Afterward, it was a madhouse. My mom found me and hugged me—Luke gave me a serious high five.

"That was . . ." said my mom, losing the words and wiping tears away from her eyes. "I couldn't . . . you had . . ."

"Thanks," I said.

Luke nodded. "I was so stoked for you. So stoked. I woulda freaked out up there. All those people watching you? And you were like, I got this." His snaggletooth poked out in appreciation.

"I should've come to one of these sooner," Mom said, finally managing to make a coherent thought come out of her mouth.

"I'm glad you saw this one," I said.

"Me too."

We stood there a moment. "I'm so proud of you," she said.

"How did you get down here anyway?"

"I had Thursday off, so I asked Luke and—"

Luke took out his phone. "MapQuest said it was going to take seven hours to get here and I managed it in six fifteen. Woo. The Honda Fit has *balls*."

I looked at him. "If you're thinking of attaching truck balls to the back of your Honda Fit, I will hate you forever."

Luke contemplated this. "It would be pretty great if I put truck balls on the Honda Fit."

"Mom."

She put her hand on his shoulder. "He's just joking. I think. He'd better be joking."

"I swear to God, if I ever see them on there," I said, "I will neuter your car."

"Noted. I've always thought they should make truck ovaries, personally." He smiled. "Um . . . so are we sticking around for tomorrow? 'Cause if we're gonna make it back to the Twin Cities, we need to haul ass."

My mom wrapped her arm around me. "Do you want us to stay for the finals? I can call in sick tomorrow and—"

"Um . . . actually . . . please don't. I don't know that I made it and it's basically going to be the same thing."

"Are you sure?"

"Please. I mean it. Don't call in sick. You got to see me perform. I'm not going to do any better tomorrow." *And, possibly, I will be ending everything in a firestorm.*

"Okay, honey."

"Thank you for coming."

The conspiracy met in the Best Western right after the team dinner. The results had been announced for original oratory—I had received the three in the round, which meant I was the lowest qualifier for finals. Based on cumulative scoring, I was already mathematically eliminated from the championship. But at least I made it.

"Fuck yes!" growled Lakshmi, bouncing on one of the two queen beds in the room. The room looked just like you would imagine a hotel room inhabited by four teenagers for two days would look: a crime scene. The blinds had been drawn. The beds were unmade, dirty clothes were piling near the boys' side of the room, and multiple laptops had been set up. The paper tablecloth from the Macaroni Grill was tacked to the wall, complete with pushpins and string like a complex murder investigation.

Thomas was rather proud of the additions to the chart.

"Check it out; I printed out photos of each of the team members and posted them up here."

"This is some cracked-out shit," I said. "It looks like an FBI sting operation in here."

Blaize shook her head. "They won't let housekeeping in. It's a nightmare."

"How is housekeeping going to come in here?!" protested Elijah. "'Make the beds, but leave the conspiracy wall, please.'"

"Maybe just clean up your shit," said Lakshmi.

"Um, I did; it's Thomas's shit that's the problem."

Thomas gingerly lifted a crumpled pair of pants from the floor with his toe. "And what is this? This just magically arrived from the pants fairy?"

"Boys," complained Blaize.

Lakshmi moved over to where they had been charting Eaganville's progress through the tournament. "All right, then. Every member of the Sinister Six has made the finals. We've got our surprises prepared for duo and debate—I'm getting up at five in the morning, and, Blaize, are you ready?"

She lifted a homemade sign that said LET'S GO, HANSON in giant, glittery letters.

"That is evil as fuck and I love it," said Lakshmi.

It was gonna be a big day.

CHAPTER THIRTY-NINE

Order 66

Dawn rose on the Day of Reckoning. It would be nearly a full day off for the rest of the school; the final rounds of each event were scheduled back-to-back, all about to be on the livestream. I imagined Rani and the younger members of the team settling in to the auditorium. They were going to get quite the show today.

I double-checked everything: the speech I'd prepared, my makeup, my outfit, my steely plan for world domination. I wouldn't be winning today, but winning isn't everything, I told myself.

The finals rounds were all held in the main theater of the convention center, a double-balconied monster that could seat almost five thousand people. Everyone would be there. Except for the finalists for the other events. We were expected to be mentally preparing.

I'd be able to follow the carnage on my phone, though,

which buzzed with a group text just as the policy debate finals were beginning.

Scarlet Witch

Execute order 66.

T'Challa

Seriously?

Scarlet Witch

Yes.

T'Challa

We're going with this lame-ass prequel reference?

Scarlet Witch

The prequels are underrated.

T'Challa

I'm stopping this conspiracy right now so I can kick your ass.

Sylvia

Guys. FOCUS.

It started simply enough. Logan and Anesh were facing two girls from Florida, one of whom had a shaved head, an eyebrow ring, and a voice like a machine gun. They would have been formidable under any circumstance and might have won the round without our help. But for a true disaster, we provided a little aid.

I watched on my phone as Anesh took the First Affirmative. He did fine in the beginning, speaking from memory in rapid fire as he cruised through his opening, but eventually he had to glance at his laptop. His faced drained of color; his eyebrows knitted together in the briefest flicker of consternation. He kept speaking, paging down, trying to find the reference that he was looking for. Instead, I knew he was finding things written there like *I won't let you ruin this, Anesh* and *I am the only one doing anything on our team.* Anesh did his best, but his concentration was off—every time he needed a reference he glanced at the laptop only to come away angrier. He finished his argument as best he could, a mounting fury overtaking him as he returned to his seat. He glowered at Logan.

Scarlet Witch

Switching documents now . . .

Logan was unaware of the fact that Elijah, watching this live on his laptop, was inside the Google Doc. Just before Logan rose to provide the Second Affirmative, he merged the old Google Doc with a new one.

Logan rose and glanced at the laptop as he rattled off sources and statistics. Of course, when he looked at the file, he saw things like *I know what you're trying to do, Logan, and it won't work* and then *I can change passwords, too* and the words *Anesh Rules Anesh Rules Anesh Rules* followed by a reference to a BuzzFeed article.

Logan's brain was boiling inside his skull. Every time he looked at the document, he saw fresh evidence of Anesh's tampering. He tried to force a smile, he tried to keep soldiering on from his own memory, but without the digital references, he was even more sunk than Anesh, who was still staring at him with the white-hot heat of a thousand suns. The gloating, malicious additions leered at Logan from every corner of the Google Doc, causing him to twitch and foam at the mouth. Finally he got to the coup de grâce.

"You're quoting the *National Enquirer*?!" he shrieked, spinning on his partner and flipping over a chair.

At the exact moment the debate round was devolving into a professional wrestling match, I knew that Blaize was passing Milo in the hallway and handing him a thick envelope.

"Taryn wanted you to read this before you go onstage," she whispered.

She didn't turn around to watch him take three handwritten pages out of the envelope—if she did, she probably would have seen him begin to tremble, then spasm, then nearly collapse in a feverish sweat.

It had taken Thomas weeks, but he had fully mastered the looping, heart-laden script from Taryn's notebook. He had even found the exact same kind of pen, the forest-green ink that she used to write down her deepest thoughts.

And he had created an erotic masterpiece of epic proportions. All focused on Milo and all FILTHY as hell. I had read it the night before and nearly had a heart attack.

"The key is getting inside Taryn's brain," he'd confided

to me, showing me a poem that she had written about global warming that doubled as a metaphor for Milo's eyes. "It's a very dark place."

"That is messed up."

"She has a very limited but very effective vocabulary in smut. And her two-thousand-word erotic fanfiction on just what she wants to do to Milo in front of five thousand people is really exhaustively complete."

By the time Milo and Taryn stepped onto the stage for the duo finals, I could tell he had read and digested the letter. His eyes were a little wider than normal, like he had been freaked out to his core. He had the thousand-yard stare of a boy who had peered into the abyss of hobbit-based erotica and had emerged on the other side, a broken and terrified—yet still aroused—young man. Thomas had put his extensive nerd-knowledge to glorious, perverted madness. Taryn, oblivious, continued as normal. One of the rules of duo was that partners weren't allowed to make eye contact, which was probably helpful to Milo since he couldn't bear to look at her. He also couldn't touch her, which only served to heighten the erotic tension between them.

Milo was off the entire performance. When he was Bilbo Baggins and Taryn was Gandalf, you could tell he was lost in imagining Gandalf's sexy legs. When Taryn became a troll ready to eat the tiny hobbit, his mind was flashing back to Thomas's evocative descriptions of the bizarre sexual role-play she wanted to do about trolls and hobbits. That's not to even mention the deliciously wicked scenarios she had fantasized about as Gollum.

The moment when they formed the spider, when Milo crouched behind Taryn (who was wearing the tightest suit in her repertoire—encouraged, of course, by me), was the breaking point. Sweat poured down his forehead. His voice, a moment late, cracked, his movements were wrong, and finally he lost his balance, toppled backward, and fell on his ass.

Four members of the Sinister Six down. Two to go. The biggest fish, Hanson. The boy with no weaknesses. The returning National Champion, the person who'd won every tournament he'd entered this season.

The night before, Thomas had smiled as he laid out the plan. "It's perfect. Here's how it's gonna go down. . . ."

CHAPTER FORTY

Breaking Hanson Bridges

It began two weeks ago, but Hanson doesn't know that yet.

All he knows is that he sees Frodo during the duo finale. Frodo is preparing for her speech, saying her lines to herself, and she catches Hanson's eye.

"Dude, I'm so sorry," says Frodo.

"What?" says Hanson.

"They're looking for you."

"Who is?"

And at that moment, Hanson's phone buzzes. It's the contest organizers. They need to talk to him.

Back up thirty minutes and Sparkles the Unicorn, just after delivering three pages of mind-blowing hobbit erotica to Milo, has made a beeline for the registration desk to speak with the backup contest manager. Because, you see, Sparkles the Unicorn has heard some disturbing news:

It turns out Hanson Bridges has signed with an agent named Jeremy Jones. And it turns out Sparkles the Unicorn has a recording of a conversation about Hanson Bridges auditioning for a Netflix series.

And that's a problem. "Aren't we supposed to be amateurs?" complains Sparkles the Unicorn, using her very best and very sweet unicorn-like voice that is nothing like an aged Judy Garland. And the contest managers are about to let it slide because after all Hanson is a returning National Champion, but it just so happens that on the National Forensics League website there are official rules, and Sparkles the Unicorn just happens to have that website up on her phone and she just happens to casually slide that phone to the backup contest manager.

Who then texts the actual contest manager, who then gets in touch with Joey Sparks, who then gets in touch with Hanson Bridges.

Sparkles the Unicorn is very sad that this is happening and she wishes it didn't have to happen and then she says she has to go get ready to meet someone very special, and she leaves just as Hanson arrives to go into a private room with some Very Concerned Adults.

And Sparkles smiles as she walks away.

Just as Frodo prepares her own speech, moving into the room vacated by Hanson Bridges, going over the details of her speech the last time—it's a new speech and she's trying to learn it by heart and she needs a little bit of uninterrupted time before Hanson returns.

Because, as it turns out, Jeremy Jones does not, in fact, exist.

There was no Netflix audition, and Hanson is a big fat liar.

A fact that was discovered two weeks ago after some very involved internet searches.

Hanson, however, has been forced to admit this to the Very Concerned Adults for the better part of five minutes and is off his game when he comes back to the room he thought he was warming up in.

"You didn't happen to tell anyone about my agent, did you?" asks Hanson.

Frodo is very shocked that this would even be brought up. "No, I would never talk about your agent Jeremy Jones who also reps Kevin Hart who you are very tight with."

"Good." Hanson thinks about telling the Frodo the truth, but doesn't. "Um . . . right . . . 'cause I can't really go into details about that right now 'cause I have to stay an amateur until after this meet."

"Oh, definitely," says Frodo, getting the text that lets her know that Hanson has been distracted long enough to put Part B of the plan into motion.

Hanson checks his phone. "Oh shit, I gotta get ready for my performance!" And he rushes out the door, already flustered, and totally not thinking about what's going to happen to him next.

And Frodo smiles to herself and steps out into the hall—

And right into a guy wearing a badge that said, #941— Andrew Chen.

And that's when everything fell apart.

CHAPTER FORTY-ONE

Everything Goes Wrong

Andrew snarled, shoving me back into the practice room and slamming the door behind us. I stumbled backward, nearly falling over in my sensible heels.

"You fucking bitch," he said. "I've been waiting all week to find you."

He was wearing his competition suit; his name tag said he was from Cuyahoga Falls, Ohio.

"I know you're behind it. You and Blaize and all the losers you hang out with. Well, I'm not going to let you win. You think you're so fucking smart; you engineered that whole thing against me—I had to go back to live with my goddamn uncle in Ohio afterward, I couldn't even come back to school. Guess what, though? They have speech in Ohio, too."

"Yeah, I'm putting two and two together now," I said, backing farther into the room. "Just so you know, I recorded yours and Thomas's speeches. I didn't even upload it to YouTube since I figured I didn't need to destroy you on a viral level, but I guess now it's become appropriate."

"Thanks for letting me know." He smiled. "I'll be taking your phone, then."

I pulled it out, hitting a button. "Take one more step and I'll upload it right now."

He laughed. "Have you ever uploaded a video to YouTube? It takes like thirty years."

Shit.

"I'll scream."

"Everybody's in the theater. Besides, you don't want to hurt your voice, right?" He lunged for my phone, and I darted out of the way.

Andrew was thin, but he was tall and quick, and wasn't going to have much trouble cornering me and ripping my phone out of my hands. I backed up toward the far wall as he snatched an extension cord from an outlet. "I think I'm gonna tie you up and leave you here while I perform; I think that's poetic justice." He coiled the electrical cord like a rope, shifting back and forth in front of the door like a boxer. I kept my phone up.

"You're just going full villain now?" I said. "Monologuing?"

"As you know, I'm really good at monologues." He feinted forward—

Just as Thomas burst through the door.

Andrew backed up immediately, holding the electrical

cord like a wriggling snake. "You deserve everything you got. Writing a shitty play—you were so in love with me it was laughable, dude." Thomas clenched his fists. "What are you gonna do? What are you gonna do, you pussy? I thought you didn't believe in violence."

"You're right," said Thomas. "I don't solve my problems with violence."

"But I do," I said, punching Andrew in the face.

I wish I could say that I knocked him the hell out, but despite Lakshmi's five-second demonstration two months ago, it wasn't UFC quality. Andrew was more startled than injured, but he tripped backward over the cord and landed on his butt. Thomas was on him in a second, pinning his arms down. It only took us a few minutes to drag Andrew to a chair, tie him up, and stuff his tie in his mouth to shut him up.

"Wow, you're pretty good at that," I said afterward.

"My dad forced me to wrestle when I was younger. It was the only sport I was any good at."

Andrew struggled, but he lacked the upper-body strength to escape his bonds. Maybe he should've done more pull-ups.

"Thanks for coming to my rescue," I said.

"Starting the video chat was a nice touch."

"Technology for the win."

He smiled. "All right, you go out there and do your thing. I'll stay here with this guy. The hell if I'm gonna let him perform that speech on the livestream."

"Right." I nodded. "I have to admit, though—you actually do have worse taste in men than me. How are things going with Hanson?"

Thomas smirked. "Here's how it's going down . . ."

Two weeks ago there was a small disturbance right outside the main office of Eaganville School of the Arts—not a big deal, of course, just a minor thing when the secretary happened to be called away from her desk because a skinny red-haired boy tripped. That would not normally be a problem, but this boy was carrying an entire armful of papers, notebooks, books, and supplies for the latest improv comedy show, which went flying everywhere. The secretary rushed from her computer to help— some of these artsy kids are so clumsy—and failed to notice that the athletic Indian girl sitting in the office, waiting to see the nurse about a stomachache, had swiftly and silently repositioned herself in front of the secretary's computer. The red-haired boy could barely pick up all his papers—the secretary wondered why they didn't have lockers these days—and to make matters worse a blond girl and a husky Black boy just walked through the whole mess, scattering everything everywhere.

The secretary helped the boy gets his things together—he really was so clumsy—and was back at her desk within forty seconds, which, coincidentally, had been enough time for the other girl to open up the attendance file on a senior, find an emergency contact, and write down a phone number.

Which led to an elderly woman named Edith Bridges answering a phone call (because old people really do answer the phone) from a woman who sounded a lot like Judy Garland after she'd been used and thrown away by the studio.

"Congratulations! This is Mabel Thompson in the main office of Eaganville School of the Arts. We just wanted to let you know that your grandson has qualified to compete at the National Speech and Debate competition in Kansas City, Missouri."

"Oh, my goodness!" said Edith; she had no idea her grandson even competed in Speech and Debate. Too bad she lived in Iowa, which was too far away from Kansas City to make the trip.

"And good news! The school has decided to make sure that you can get a chance to see him compete, and we'll be sending you a driver to pick you up on the day of the performance. Just keep it a surprise!"

Which is why, at five thirty in the morning, on the day of the final competition, Sylvia/Lakshmi got into her SUV, drove 193 miles to Edith's home in Des Moines, Iowa, presented her identification as Najima, and drove Edith 193 miles back to Kansas City, Missouri, just in time for the final round of humorous interpretation.

Of course, the auditorium was packed to the gills at that point, so it was lucky that the Scarlet Witch had spent part of the morning securing a special VIP seating spot for Edith Bridges in the very first row, and it was also extra kind of Sparkles the Unicorn to give Edith a large, glittery sign that read

LET'S GO, HANSON, GRANDMA LOVES YOU for her to wave just as he stepped onto the stage.

And Hanson, as he stepped onto that stage, could not really see anything in the audience, except for the fact that the glitter in the sign caught the light just right, illuminating his grandmother's face, which also reflected off the very large and very conspicuous cross she wore as a necklace, and also perhaps—and this might have been his imagination—the control of the pacemaker his grandma kept in her purse, because his grandmother's heart condition was perhaps the only thing that Hanson Bridges hadn't lied his ass off about.

And at that moment, when the announcer said that "Hanson Bridges, from Eaganville, Minnesota, performing . . . The Bible," perhaps young Hanson caught sight of the joy in his frail grandmother's eyes that he was going to be performing the Word of the Lord for all these well-dressed young people in the audience.

And Frodo, watching on the livestream, saw Hanson Bridges stare in dumbstruck horror and terror, before fleeing without saying a word.

And Frodo said, "BOO-YA, MOTHERFUCKER."

And it was Good.

CHAPTER FORTY-TWO

One Last Speech

I took a deep breath.

The first thing you notice onstage is that the lights are blinding. You can barely see anything. You know there are a few thousand people out there—you can hear them shuffling and laughing and talking, but the most you can make out are the silhouetted outlines of heads. Otherwise it's just a presence; a massive, gravitational presence.

As the lowest qualifier, I was the first to go. All the finalists were waiting in the wings (well, except Andrew, but I wasn't letting on that I knew anything about his whereabouts) with our microphones attached. I caught Elijah's text just before I turned off my phone:

Elijah

In the audience now. Can't wait to see you.

Jasmine came up to me. "Good luck!"

"You too!"

The crowd was revved up.

I looked out at the blinding lights.

"From Eaganville High School for the Arts, Sydney Williams performing My Dad!"

The crowd roared in applause. The noise was deafening. Quite a lot of people in the audience had seen one iteration or another of my speech—some had seen the one where my dad died of a heroin overdose; others had seen the more honest version. None of them were going to see anything like that again.

I strode to the middle of the stage, looked out into the blinding lights, and spoke.

"Someone once said that Vince Lombardi said, 'Winning isn't everything—it's the only thing.'" I paused just a second. "The first problem with that statement is that it's a lie. Vince Lombardi never said that. It was actually said by the football coach at UCLA, Henry Sanders. He knew about winning, too. His football team won a lot of games. And when he was found dead in a hotel room with a sex worker named Ernestine Drake, she reported that his final words were, 'Football is a great game.'"

It was silent in the theater. The audience had no idea what to make of what I just said. You could tell half of them wanted to google Henry Sanders. The people who had seen my previous performance were stunned: This is not at all what I was talking about before.

"The man who followed Coach Sanders was named George Dickerson. He coached UCLA for three games before he had to be hospitalized with a nervous breakdown. His career record was one win, two losses, and two nervous breakdowns. He's in the UCLA Hall of Fame, by the way."

I paused again. I could feel the confusion rolling through the audience. No one knew what was going on.

"I'm not going to win this competition today. There are some really great performers coming after me, and one of them deserves to walk home with one of the trophies behind me. You see, I'm not trying to win today. That's going to make my coach, Joey Sparks, very angry. He cares about winning a lot. It's probably the only thing he truly cares about.

"And why shouldn't he care about winning, right? *Everyone* cares about winning. The principal at my school, who has been ignoring rumors for *years* about Joey Sparks, cares VERY MUCH about winning." A buzz went through the audience. "The parents who send their kids to my school care about winning. The parents who allow their kids to be on this team care about winning. They care SO MUCH that they don't care what happens to their kids because of it.

"Maybe it doesn't bother them that their kids stop sleeping. Maybe it doesn't bother them that somebody develops an ulcer from the stress. Maybe it doesn't bother them that kids on the team are forced to take drugs so they can push themselves past their limits. Maybe nobody cares if they feel like their lives are over forever if they don't win.

"I used to think that this was Joey Sparks's problem. It's not. I used to blame him for my father going to prison, but my father didn't go to prison because of Joey Sparks. He went to prison because there's a system that rewards people like Joey Sparks.

"And we love him, right? We love WINNERS. We even love cheaters who get away with it. The Supreme Court recently ruled that gerrymandering was legal. That's right. If you win, you get to cheat. You get to change the rules of the game so you can win easier next time. Fair? Fuck fair! Hell, if you cheat well enough you could be president of the United States."

The crowd roiled with surprise. Some people clapped. A current of nervousness was rumbling everywhere now.

"We love winners in this country and losers deserve to lose. That's what America is built on, and that's what my coach taught me. One of the other things he taught me is that everybody lies. And the other thing he taught me is that if you win, NOBODY CARES HOW YOU DID IT. If you're a winner, you can do anything. As a coach you can create an atmosphere where you pit your teammates against each other, right? That makes us stronger, doesn't it? That's being tough, yes? You can tell a girl on the team she's a personal disappointment and everything she's doing is trying to ruin your career. You can scream into a kid's face, you can insult them, you can terrorize them, you can emotionally torture them because that's all part of coaching, right? You BREAK someone down so you can build them up again, right? Haven't we all learned that? And if someone can't hack it, if someone gets depressed, quits, attempts suicide, WHO CARES? That person was a *loser.*

"And if anyone crosses you, you can get their scholarships revoked, you can shatter their self-confidence, get them to hate themselves, and no one will blame you. And if anyone has the audacity to complain about it, your principal will back you up. Hell, they'll probably BLAME the VICTIM for ruining the team!"

I paused, shaking. There was so much adrenaline in my neck that I could barely keep it together. The audience, all five thousand of them, was a thunderstorm now.

"And because he's a winner, Joey Sparks can tell me that he's gonna slap the shit out of me. And he's probably right, friends. He could probably do that. And two days later he could still get up on this stage and be inducted into the Hall of Fame."

I sensed him before I saw him. There was a flurry at the edge of my vision—someone climbing over the lip of the stage from the audience. It took my brain a second to register what was happening: Sparks was climbing out of the audience and charging right at me.

A couple of things happened at once: The audience roared in alarm, I nearly fell over as he got to his feet, and four other teenagers in suits, the other finalists, leaped from the wings to hold him back.

He was shouting something, spittle was flying from his angry mouth, but I couldn't hear it because of the noise of the crowd.

I turned to look at the audience as more people came to yank Sparks off the stage.

"That's pretty much it," I said.

Applause.

CHAPTER FORTY-THREE

The Aftermath

I moved into the Best Western with the rest of the conspiracy immediately following the performance, since I figured it would be a good idea to disappear, ghostlike, into the ether for a little bit. I didn't want to give Taryn the chance to choke me to death with her adorable mini-shirts.

I took fifth place in original oratory. Last in the round. Jasmine Wu was crowned the winner shortly after my speech. It was a madhouse afterward. I tried to make my way through the convention center, but kids kept coming up to me from other schools—people wanted my autograph. They wanted to tell me about their speech programs, how they were different, how if I was looking for a better program, I should totally join up. An admissions counselor from the University of Missouri found me and gave me her card, saying she'd look out for me.

Lakshmi had to give Grandma Bridges a ride back to

Des Moines, so by the time she reappeared it was close to midnight. She had the zombified look of a person who had driven eight hundred miles in a day, back and forth from the oh-so-exciting terrain of northern Missouri to the oh-so-exciting terrain of southern Iowa.

"Next time we do one of these conspiracies, one of you bastards is driving," she said, tossing her keys next to the television as she surveyed the room.

"I can't drive," I said.

"Neither can I," said Thomas.

"You don't want me to drive," said Elijah.

Lakshmi flopped on the hard mattress of the Best Western. "I talked to Rani on the way back. Apparently the school is burning down."

"Really?" I asked.

"I mean, not with actual flames. But I guess everyone was losing their minds that the team was crapping out, and then when you got up there"—she jabbed a finger at me—"all hell broke loose. I guess when Sparks charged the stage the principal tried to cut off the projector, but everyone had it on their phone at that point. Crazy shit. People started shouting. Somebody threw something. From what Rani heard, two other former speech members popped out of the woodwork to complain to the principal. People who graduated started talking."

I hadn't even thought to check my phone. I had twenty-nine text messages. Some from newspapers.

"Holy shit," I said. "I think we did it."

"Yeah, we did," said Lakshmi.

By the time we got back to Minnesota on Saturday I was moderately famous. (Okay, I had been interviewed by one newspaper, but I feel like that qualifies.) Word had spread over social media, though, and clips of Sparks trying to tackle me had made the local news. There were a lot of tweets about changing the culture.

When my mom came home from work, she was overjoyed to see me. She'd heard about what went down somehow, and enveloped me in a huge hug, her SpongeBob uniform clashing with everything else in existence. Charlie approached me like he approached everyone else—out of his mind with excitement.

"You did great, honey," my mom said. "So proud of you."

Luke came over, hands clasped behind his back. "I'm not even gonna high-five you right now, because you are beyond that. But I am mentally fist-bumping you."

I looked at him. "I am mentally fist-bumping you, too, Luke."

"Sweet." He nodded. "By the way, next time somebody tries to tackle you, I've got some killer moves I can show you. I used to teach aerobic kickboxing."

I thought about it. "I guess that's okay."

Mom took a look at me again. "Pretty badass, honey. Pretty badass."

"Yes, it was." I smiled.

* * *

Joey Sparks did not come back to Eaganville High School. He was placed on administrative leave without pay, indefinitely, while the school sorted through complaints about his behavior. Parents were calling up and wondering why the principal hadn't done anything about him sooner. His head was likely the next one on the chopping block. (Even though, let's be honest, this was Minnesota, so they were going to decapitate Principal Gustafson in the nicest possible manner while serving him a horrific fish dinner.)

At lunch, when we were back, I sat with my friends again. The surviving members of the varsity squad returned to the cafeteria, banished from the teachers' lounge and their inexhaustible supply of parent-made casserole. Hanson, who hadn't eaten a cafeteria lunch in more than two years, miserably trudged to a chair, holding a tray with a humiliated-looking slice of pepperoni pizza. I watched him take a bite, then set it down sadly, a single tear sliding down his cheek. (Okay, that was embellishment, but he had to eat cafeteria food and that was pretty harsh punishment, is what I'm saying.)

Taryn took the loss of the faculty bathroom particularly hard, and rumor had it she could be found wandering the halls during class time, looking for a place to pee in peace and quiet.

Rani approached our table.

"Can I sit here?" she asked quietly.

Thomas moved over. "Sure."

She settled in and took out her lunch, which was exactly the same as her sister's.

"So," she said, "I'm sorry I was being such a dick."

"Happens," said Lakshmi.

"Not to you. To Sydney."

"Um," said Lakshmi. "You were being a giant dick to me, too."

"You're my sister; of course I'm a dick to you. *God.*"

I cut in. "Apology accepted, Rani. And what did I tell you about Anesh?"

Rani looked wistful. "Mmm." Lakshmi smacked her shoulder. "I'm kidding, I'm kidding! He's such trash."

"Thank you," I said.

"He's good for a night or two and that's it."

Lakshmi's mouth opened in shock.

"God, I'm kidding again, you are so gullible! You think I'm a *child.*"

"You are a child," growled Lakshmi, looking up.

Sarah was standing there. "Hey. I was wondering if I could sit here."

"Please," said Rani.

As Sarah sat down, Lakshmi caught my eye and smiled.

On Wednesday, Taryn stopped me after history class. "I just want to say," she said, "that for most of this season I really hated you, but I'm over that, and now I don't think about you at all."

"That's wonderful to hear, I guess."

"I understand what you did. And I guess I . . ." The words hurt her coming out. "Slightly respect you for that. But also—me and Milo totally hooked up after that performance. It was hot. We're in love now."

I tried to escape.

"He showed me that *story*, and we *did* half of those things afterward."

"Okay, I'm leaving now."

"Just so you know. I'm currently writing a sequel and I would love it if you would read it."

"Nope," I said.

"Maybe I can do it for OO next year."

Logan, because he had thrown a punch at Anesh, did receive some punishment:

A day of ISS—with some peer counseling.

I smiled as I sat down opposite him. "Think of me like a priest. Or a therapist." I leaned in, holding a little notebook. "Tell me about your father."

As for my father, I told him all about it the next week. I even showed him the YouTube clip.

"Wow," he said. "Powerful stuff."

"Thank you."

"I told you that you were a good speaker. You know, they let some of those birds free after you talked to the pet store. You were that persuasive."

"They did not." I smiled.

"All right, fine, that was a lie. And I'm not gonna do that anymore. But you know what is the truth? You should be a motivational speaker."

"Not a chance in hell." I laughed.

EPILOGUE

I put the card for the admissions counselor at the University of Missouri on the library table and started my email.

Just wanted to let you know that I am super motivated and please ignore my grades from the fall because none of that was my fault basically everyone hated me for no reason, but it's all good . . .

I deleted it.

Just wanted to check in to see if you had a full ride available since I will be needing a mother lode of that sweet, sweet cash . . .

Deleted it.

I'll be in summer school this year, not because I have to, but because I love learning so much . . .

Deleted it.

I make a kick-ass sangria, so if that's something you're looking for in potential students . . .

Elijah wrapped me up from behind, his thin, strong arms pulling me backward. After the spectacle of Nationals, he had gotten the University of Minnesota to reconsider his scholarship. They'd reinstated it almost immediately.

"I like the sangria part," he said.

"What's the best way to explain nearly failing out to a college admissions officer?"

He kissed the side of my head.

"The truth."

I stared at the monitor. This was going to be hard, but it couldn't be harder than talking about it in front of a thousand strangers.

"And you're probably going to want to stress an extracurricular activity," he said. "Colleges love that."

I smiled, kissed him, then started writing.

The End

ACKNOWLEDGMENTS

Although the act of writing a book is a solitary one, it's impossible to do without help. A LOT of help.

First, I want to thank Marco Bazan and the entire speech and debate team at Bowie High School in Austin, Texas. Y'all took me in and made me part of the team.

As always, my superagent, John Cusick, remains a light in the darkness. Seriously.

Laura Schreiber deserves the lion's share of the credit for the many, many, many improvements she suggested. I also need to give a shout-out to Mary Mudd.

I need to thank the teams at both Disney-Hyperion and Little, Brown, who fought for this book and saw it through its final stages. I would also like to thank the following:

Mark O'Brien, Sangu Mandanna, and Holliana Bryan, who gave me lots of helpful notes.

All the speech and debate kids who have performed my plays over the years or have been forced to watch someone perform one of my pieces.

My sons, Michael and Eric, who keep me grounded, make me laugh so hard milk snorts out my nose, and are always up for a good round of Dungeons & Dragons.

And Anne Godfrey, who is there for me without question, whose thoughts and insights I treasure above all others, and who has taught me so much. I love you.

Turn the page for more from
Don Zolidis!

AVAILABLE NOW

PROLOGUE

I know it says *A Love Story* on the cover of this book. And it is a love story. But I want to mentally prepare you for it. The couple doesn't get together at the end. There is no happy ending. Spoiler alert.

I guess I probably should've said "spoiler alert" first instead of including it after I just revealed the spoiler, but what are you going to do? Not read the next sentence?

So, yeah. Prepare yourselves.

ONE

Breakup Number Three

January 22, 1994.
Janesville, Wisconsin.
Palmer Park.
11:54 p.m.

I didn't see this one coming either.

We were sitting in her car. She drove a 1980-something Subaru hatchback. Light silver. Spots of rust. The best thing about it was the four-wheel drive, which allowed Amy to navigate the icy roads of southern Wisconsin. It also had heat, which was a particular bonus. There was virtually no way to turn off the heat, however, so now it was emitting a blast of hot air reminiscent of the open mouth of hell.

I didn't really care about that, although it did make things more awkward and smelly than usual as we made out.

We were still wearing our winter coats. She had on a puffy

green fuzzy thing that I always thought looked like a field of moss, and I was wearing my black I'm-troubled-and-artistic woolen trench coat, which stretched down over my knees and got tangled in our legs.

There was also the matter of the gearshift—the Subaru was manual, so as we groped over six or seven layers of clothing, we'd occasionally get stabbed in the ribs.

Basically, it was awesome. Even though I wasn't exactly sure whether I had just felt her boob or a strange bunch in her sweater.

The windows had fogged up, and we separated, gasping for breath, a hot sticky, sweaty mess of raging hormones. If anyone was outside the car, it would be pretty obvious what was going on. Of course, seeing as how it was near midnight in late January in the most heavily forested part of Palmer Park, the only likely pedestrian would be the abominable snowman.

R.E.M. was on the radio. It was that song "Everybody Hurts," which was being played every hour by every radio station like some kind of horrible curse. It was about as romantic as a song about preventing suicide could possibly be.

"This song just pretends it's deep," I grumbled.

Amy pulled some of her blond hair out of her mouth, while I kept going.

"Everybody hurts sometimes? Wow. I never would have guessed. Thank you, Michael Stipe."

Amy didn't say anything, which was probably good because I was about to get on a roll. I have to say, though, that my thoughts about R.E.M. weren't entirely spontaneous—I had practiced this speech before in the shower. I was sure it was hilarious and would improve her mood if the kissing hadn't done the trick.

"Like, are there people out there who think this is a revelation? Like they're going through life, *Huh, I bet those people never hurt*, and then this song comes on and they're like, enlightened? *Oh, I guess everybody does hurt*. Please. The whole theme of the song is like, *Sometimes things are bad*. R.E.M. should be working as guest artists in a kindergarten." That was my favorite part of this bit. Imagining the quintessential college band of the '80s showing up and teaching five-year-olds about colors.

Amy wasn't laughing.

She was looking down at her hands. Her hair fell in a yellow curtain around the sides of her face.

My stomach started twisting up into knots. I broke into a cold sweat. These moments had been happening more frequently lately—Amy would stop, her eyes would glaze over, and you could tell that she was contemplating my utter destruction. At least that was my assumption.

"I've been thinking," she said finally.

"Shit."

"I think—"

"Wait. Hold on. I won't talk about R.E.M. anymore. I'm sure they're cool."

"That's not what—"

"Is it the coat? Is that the problem?"

"Craig." She said it like my sister said it. Like *Shut up, Craig*. I shut up. "I don't know that I can do this."

"Do what?"

But I knew what. Amy turned just a bit to look at me and I could see the tears forming in her eyes. Down came the knife into my heart. Stab. Stab. Stab.

"I don't think I can be your girlfriend." Her words hung in the air for a moment. R.E.M. continued to whine forlornly on the radio. I no longer noticed the heat pouring out of the vent.

I had tried two different approaches to the Amy-dumping-me problem previously. Those two approaches were

1. Cry and
2. Cry more, then hug her mom. (Don't ask.)

So it was time to try something new: arguing.

"Wait a minute. You said you weren't going to break up with me anymore!"

"I know. . . ." She fumbled for a Kleenex.

"But now you're breaking up with me?! This is not cool! You didn't want me to be clingy, so I'm not clingy, I did that—"

"Craig—"

"I'm wearing the hat! Look at this!" I yanked the hat she had given me off my head. "I'm not even a hat person, and I'm still wearing this! For you! I'm wearing this hat for you!"

(Okay, I admit, my arguing technique was not technically the best.)

"Can I say something?" she sputtered. "I don't care about the hat."

"Clearly," I fumed.

She looked up at the ceiling of the car, exasperated. "There are things going on that I can't tell you about. . . ."

"Oh, like before?"

The air froze between us. That was mean. I knew it was mean.

Amy disintegrated. She chewed on her bottom lip and I could see the tears running down her face now.

"Was this your plan?" I said. "Bring me out here into the middle of the woods like a mafia killing or something?"

"No . . ."

"No witnesses. No one will ever find my body."

"Craig—"

"Why were you making me out with me first if you were gonna dump me?"

"I'm not dumping you."

"We were going out earlier tonight, and now, apparently, we're not! That's a dumping."

"Okay, maybe a little," she conceded.

"I'm sorry I made the comments about R.E.M."

"I'm not dumping you because you don't like this song!"

"Well, I don't see why you're dumping me at all."

Amy pulled her hair behind her ears. "I just can't do this."

It felt like a dozen boa constrictors had slithered into the car and were crushing my chest. I reached for anything that could save me. "Like, think about how great we are. We don't ever fight, we don't—"

"We fight all the time."

"No we don't!"

"We're fighting right now!"

"This isn't a fight. This is a discussion. It's a thoughtful discussion. You're discussing doing something stupid, and I'm explaining to you why it's a bad idea."

"Craig," she said gently, "I don't want to hurt you." This is what she always said while she was hurting me. It was as if someone was taking an ice pick and stabbing it through my eye. *I don't want to hurt you. Stab. Stab. Stab. You're only making it worse by screaming and crying. Stab. Stab. Stab. This will feel much better when I do the other eye.*

"If you don't want to hurt me, *why are you hurting me*?!"

"I don't want to hurt you more. In the future." She stopped for a second. Her blue eyes looked silver in the dim light. "I'm sorry."

There was no arguing my way out of this. The snakes were breaking my ribs.

The reality of the situation sucked the air out of my lungs. We were breaking up. Again. For the third time. No more Amy. My senior year in high school had been utterly consumed by her and now it was evaporating. My plan for prom was gone; no more seeing her Monday morning at school, when I would look out at the sea of heavy jackets and try to spot her hair. No more talking about deeply philosophical things late at night. No more making out after we talked about the deeply philosophical things. No more deeply philosophical things at all. Goddamn it, R.E.M. We were over.

"Just . . . uggg . . ." I opened the door and stomped out into the snow.

The first thing you realize when you step outside in the middle of a January night in Wisconsin is that you're stupid. It was cold. Not cold in the sense that something in your freezer is cold but cold in the sense that there is no God. Negative-twenty-degree cold. It was snowing just a bit, drifting down in little flakes of death.

The upper part of Palmer Park was really just a forest with a parking lot. Oh, sure, there was a swing set in there somewhere, and if you fell down the hill you'd eventually end up in a frozen kiddie pool, but apparently the people of Janesville just gave up on this part. They probably had better things to do. Like fighting for their daily survival since they'd stupidly decided to settle in a frozen wasteland where the only food available was cheese curds.

We were up on the hill, and the dark trees around me were all bare. Their trunks were black in the night, in contrast to the foot of white snow that lay on the ground like a dream.

When it's below zero degrees, the air stings. It felt like a million little lumberjacks were chopping away at my exposed skin, probably because I was wearing a stupid coat that wasn't even all that warm, and had somehow abandoned the hat Amy had given me.

I stumbled away from the car, my tennis shoes punching through the upper crust of the snow and sinking into the loose freezing drift beneath.

Please follow me. Please follow me.

I should not have left the hat in the car. That was dumb. I am dumb.

I weighed the possible results of my action:

1. Death.
2. She runs after me and admits she was wrong, and we go back in the car and make out more and pretend this never happened.
3. She runs after me and admits she was wrong, and it is too late because I have already frozen to death.
4. She runs after me in order to admit she was wrong, and she ironically freezes to death before she can reach me.
5. Yetis eat me.

"Craig!" she yelled.

Bingo.

"Get back in the car! It's cold as hell as out here!"

"No!"

Stopping just long enough to put on her giant red mittens

that looked like feminine lobster claws, Amy got out of the car. Amy was dressed far more sensibly for the cold since she was far more sensible than me. She had her green fuzzy parka thing, her mittens, and a bluish hat that smelled like her hair and was probably the greatest thing in the universe. I had no hat, no gloves, and my jeans had holes in the knees.

"Goddamn it, it's cold!" she shrieked.

"I know! *What was wrong with the people who settled here?!*"

The other thing about cold this wretched is that it swallows sound, which was one of the many reasons I was shouting. Fun fact.

And then she was right next to me, hugging me like we were giant toddlers in snowsuits.

"I'm so sorry," she said. Her hair smelled like sunshine, and I let myself hug her back.

I have no girlfriend echoed through my mind. It was especially awful, since Amy was the only girlfriend I'd ever had, the only girl I'd ever kissed, and the only girl I'd ever fallen in love with.

And now we were apart again, even though we were standing as close as possible in the dark, freezing, bitter awfulness that is Wisconsin in January. I stayed there for two or three seconds, which is about the amount of time before frostbite sets in. My tears, if I'd had any, would have frozen on my face.

She pushed the hat back into my hands.

"I'm gonna need a ride home," I said.

TWO

An Incident from My Childhood That Explains This Nonsense

It was my ninth birthday party, which I shared with my sister, Kaitlyn, who also happened to have the same birthday.

We're twins, although, as you probably figured out, not identical ones. She definitely got the better deal in the genetic lottery. For most of my life I was scrawny, undersized, and had an unfortunate cowlick that looked as if some part of my brown hair had to jump for joy all the time. In middle school I took a pair of scissors to it in what has come to be known as *the hair incident*. I had a year-round tan and was all of five foot one until my sophomore year of high school. Kaitlyn, on the other hand, figured out the mysteries of hair care early on. Her auburn hair had a natural wave to it, like undulating sea-foam fanned by water nymphs. All of my friends thought she was hot. She was naturally athletic, like she had transplanted genes from an antelope or something—she was a star forward for the soccer team and ran track in the spring. She was also the devil.

It's kind of awful having a twin sister who's a hundred times cooler than you, and even worse is the period of time from age nine to fourteen or so when she's taller than you and can kick your ass. (Granted, even in high school, she could still kick my ass on account of her innate fierceness, but at least I was taller.)

The conflict between us probably started in utero (somehow I imagine her fetus forming a middle finger very early on), but it really began with our pets. Actually, it began with her pets.

I don't know who cursed our family, but from a very early stage it was clear that someone had stolen an unholy amulet from a sarcophagus or something and called doom upon us.

First, I killed her sea monkeys. Then I killed two or three jars of lightning bugs we'd collected in the summer (although that might have been the result of not putting air holes in the jars, but she never wasted an opportunity to blame me for the carnage). Even the pets I didn't directly slaughter met horrible ends. Things got bad when we got guinea pigs. Kaitlyn went through four of them: Muffin, Bo-Dag, Son of Bo-Dag, and Bo-Dag Three. Son of Bo-Dag escaped from his guinea-pig hutch and was not discovered until five days later when his corpse began to send off quite strong smells from our basement. He had gotten trapped behind our couch, which was unhappily situated on a hot air vent. Son of Bo-Dag had baked to death in furry terror. That was the worst pet death until I accidentally sat on Bo-Dag Three after a particularly brutal game of Sorry. I wasn't looking, and he had been let out of his home for a breath of fresh air only to find my butt descending on him, crushing him like a tiny, furry éclair.

She also had a hamster named Giggles that committed suicide. He put his little head in his hamster wheel and pushed.

And then there was Stephen.

We never should've got Stephen. My parents should've realized we were cursed and declared that no pet was safe.

But Kaitlyn was unstoppable when she wanted a pet. She made posters. She sang songs. She cut out pictures from magazines and made detailed presentations to Mom and Dad. And when I say she sang songs about getting a pet, I mean she continuously sang songs for three or four hours at a time. It was enough to make a hamster commit suicide.

Anyway, Stephen was a Persian cat we got from the Humane Society. He was a big white fluff ball. You could only see his little smashed-up face if you looked directly at him; otherwise, he looked like a snowball had grown little legs and was wandering around, pissed off.

If you've ever met a Persian cat, you know what I'm talking about. They're assholes.

Kaitlyn loved everything about Stephen. She loved the low growling sound he made whenever I came near him. She loved the way he'd let you pet him for three or four seconds before biting the crap out of your hand and trying to claw you apart.

She was also extremely protective of him—especially with me, as she blamed me for the slaughter of every animal she had ever loved, even the ones I didn't sit on or suffocate. (Although, to be fair, sea monkeys are not animals. They're shrimp, and they are also the lamest "pet" ever.)

Anyway, all of this is to set the scene for our ninth birthday party, which was fated to be the last birthday party we'd have together.

In previous years, our mom had managed to get us to agree to gender-neutral themes like "Muppets" or "balloon fun," but this year we were irreconcilable. I had chosen *The Hobbit* as my theme, which drove my mom into a worrying stress spiral, not least for the fact that I had demanded giant spider decorations. Kaitlyn, for her part, had chosen the exact opposite: Barbie.

As you can imagine, there was no universe in which Barbie and hobbits coexisted. (Either Barbie would be put on the front lines to be eaten by the giant spiders, or the hobbits would get new, snazzy outfits—either way it made no sense.) My parents had tried—well, actually, my mom had tried. My dad had thrown up his hands and offered "lions" as a possible solution, which was to say, he was going to take us to the zoo and feed us to lions if we couldn't compromise. His plan failed because we were at least half-sure he was joking. So there was a dividing line in our backyard—on one side, the denizens of Middle-earth, and the other side, totally unrealistic plastic women.

"They can't even stand," I said to her.

"Shut up," said Kaitlyn. "Go play with your dwarves."

"Hobbits. Dwarves are a different race."

"There is something wrong with you. Really wrong."

We had each invited the same number of people, but I had three acquaintances show up, and she had about thirty-seven girls there. From orbit, you could tell the difference between our parties. What's worse is that my friends, sensing that something like the plague was affecting my side of the yard, had gravitated over to the Barbie side because they were traitors.

"Let's put the parties together," offered my mom. "I feel like there's room for magic in the Barbie universe."

We both rolled our eyes at that.

Kaitlyn offered no concessions to my side of the yard, and went out of her way to show just how much more fun she was having than me. Equally horrible was the fact that each person at the party brought a present for one of us, all of which were now located on a "present table" that was 90 percent pink. It was all going horribly wrong.

This is where Stephen comes in.

All my life I have been afflicted by a lack of common sense, and it was particularly noticeable on this day. Here was my thought process:

I need to get girls to come over here. What do girls like? Cats. We have a cat. I'll bring him outside and carry him around. Then all will be well and we can play pin the scale on the dragon.

I found Stephen in his usual place, sitting under my parents' bed, pissed off and hating the world. I crawled on my stomach, fended off his claws, and managed to grab his back. He emitted the low, mournful growl that was his way of saying *Hello—please get the hell away from me.*

But I was undeterred, and managed to scramble out from under the bed and scoop Stephen into my arms like a white, puffy ball of evil.

Stephen was an indoor cat; my dad had long argued that he was an animal and needed to hunt, but he had been overruled by the fact that Stephen showed no inclination to ever go outside or do anything to acquire food for himself. He was pretty useless as a cat.

I brought him outside, feeling his furry body tremble in rage and panic.

"Look what I've got over here," I said in a singsong voice from my abandoned hobbit side of the yard.

Bringing something cute and fluffy into a group of thirty third-grade girls is a recipe for a stampede. Just as I imagined, they dropped their Barbie activities and rushed me.

Stephen's evil cat eyes went wide when he spotted the flood of girls. He braced his back claws against my sternum, tore through my shirt, and sprang away from me like he had been fired from one of my dad's guns. He shot to the ground and raced through the gaggle of girls like a thunderbolt. I had never seen him move that fast in his life.

He shot around the house and headed for the street.

I know what you're thinking. *A car ran him over, didn't it?*
Nope.

There was no car, but there was a giant German shepherd puppy that spotted a lightning-fast ball of white fur and thought it looked like a super-fun chew toy. By the time we reached the front yard, there was blood and fur and an adorable German shepherd being restrained by its horrified owner.

Death had come to our ninth birthday party. J. R. R. Tolkien would have been proud.

In my mind, I think of Stephen like the eternal pessimist. Every day I bet he thought, *I'm going to die today. I hate these people.* And at last, he was right.

Anyway, that was me in a nutshell. Trying to impress people the wrong way, only to have it end in horrible tragedy.

THREE

Breakup Number Five

April 15, 1994.
9:07 p.m.
My basement.

As I got older, I slowly conquered the entire basement of our house. At some point, it had been imagined as a family rec room, but the creeping tide of my nerdishness forced the rest of the family out due to sheer embarrassment. The fact that Kaitlyn and I had been largely at war for the past eight years had something to do with it as well. The faux-wood paneling my dad had installed in the late '70s was perfect for tacking up posters of dragons and aliens. I had transformed one of the old coffee tables into a diorama, which was complete with metal miniatures of wizards and dwarves. I had even found a couple of crappy old bookshelves and had filled them with an endless supply of fantasy novels. In short, it was a space designed to repulse females.

And yet I had brought Amy into it, and, miraculously, she hadn't run for the hills. She didn't mind sitting on the couch; she didn't mind the faint smell of death that still hung in the air from Son of Bo-Dag's immolation. She was cool with all of it.

We had set up an old television down there and spent much of the last month watching movies while buried beneath blankets. It was an exercise in escapism, of course, as both of our lives were in the process of falling apart. Hers was collapsing, while mine was merely deteriorating, and like good Wisconsin people we had both made the unspoken pledge not to talk about any of it and watch horror films instead.

Should we talk about our feelings regarding the ongoing tragedies in our lives? Oh look, Critters 3 *is on. I sure hope that will answer all the unresolved questions from both* Critters 1 *and* 2.

It wasn't a perfect system, and where there had once been long, deeply philosophical talks that lasted all night, there was now a sinister cloud of silence. It wasn't the best way to run a relationship, but it was a model that seemed to work for everyone's parents, so we were giving it a shot.

Anyway, we had just finished *Hellraiser II*, which was a lot worse than the original *Hellraiser*, so it was a lot more fun to watch. I had mastered the art of making funny voices during the entire movie (or at least, I thought I had mastered it; I probably annoyed the hell out of her, which might have been one of the reasons for the breakup, but who knows?), and I was on a particular roll that evening.

If you're not familiar with the Hellraiser series of movies, congratulations. Basically it's about a weird guy who wears black leather and has pins in his face. Like, three hundred pins in his face. He's named, surprisingly enough, Pinhead. Pinhead is summoned by demons every once in a while and sends people to hell, where they don't have a good time. Every once in a while he says, *We have such sights to show you.*

I had a great time imagining alternate employment options for Pinhead.

"What if he was, like, a tour guide?" and

"Wouldn't it be awesome if Disney bought the rights to this and put him in Disney World?" and

"Wouldn't it be great if he used the pins for storage? Like, hooked hot dogs to himself?"

So we were sitting there having a great time, and I had her hand in mine. She had fingers like a bird; they were pale and white and a little bony, but I loved them.

I suppose I haven't really described Amy. This is usually the point where the hero says that the heroine was beautiful and perfect and had eyes like moonbeams or whatever. And, yes, all that was true about her. She was way more attractive than me. I had no business being with this girl.

She also walked a little bit like a duck. Not in a stupid way. But she just ever so slightly shuffled a bit when she walked. She had a weird thing where her hips were double-jointed, which sounds totally awesome but kind of had no effect other than to make her capable of standing straight up and twisting her feet around to face about forty-five degrees behind her. Weird, right?

All that is to say she wasn't very athletic, and when she ran it was a bit awkward, which was just perfect for me, since I sucked at all things related to sports except for watching other people play them.

So, at this point in time, once *Hellraiser II* had finished, she let go of my hand and shuffled over to the backpack she had dropped at the foot of the stairs. She took a deep breath, like she was mentally preparing for something.

After having been dumped four times, I was especially sensitive to Amy's body language. If she sneezed, I felt my heart twinge. If she took too long to respond to a question like *How are you doing?* a feeling of cold, tingly terror would race up my spine. When she opened the backpack and took out a letter, I felt my stomach drop.

"What's that?" I asked.

"Um . . ." She looked down at her hands.

Shit.

"So I wrote you a letter."

"Great."

No response.

"Is it a nice letter?"

Silence. *It is not a nice letter. It is a letter of doom.*

"I've been thinking about things," she said finally.

"Nice things?"

Silence.

Then she started to pace. This was new. I hadn't been dumped with pacing before. She had the letter in her hands, was looking down at it, and was shuffling a bit back and forth. "I wrote down some things that I want to tell you . . . but every time we talk I can't seem to make them come out, so . . ." she said finally.

"What do you want to tell me?"

"That's why I wrote you the letter. To avoid actually having to say the things. . . ."

"What's the gist of it?"

She looked down at her hands and made a little noise like "Hurm." *Oh, that behavior I recognize. That's the universal sign for I must crush you now.*

I got up from the couch and started following her pacing. "You can talk to me," I said. "I know that I have been stupid in the past, and I am working on my own idiocy, and—"

"It's not about what you're doing," she said. "It's about what I'm doing."

"Are you breaking up with me again? Is that what you're doing?"

She looked down and made the terrifying "Hurm" noise again.

"You can't break up with me in a letter," I protested. "Letters are for good things. We've established this. We have a pattern!"

She tried a new tactic. "You're going to find somebody so much better than me."

"What? No, I'm not! Look at me! Are you insane?"

"You're a great guy; there are probably a lot of other girls you could be going out with, so I feel like I'm preventing you from finding them right now." Of all the lies Amy ever told me, this one was probably the most ridiculous.

"I don't like anybody else! I'm finding you! I found you! We found each other!"

"But I can't be found right now, Craig. That's what I'm trying to tell you."

"Why not?"

"I wrote it in the letter!" she said, her voice rising just a bit. She shook it back and forth in her hand.

"Tell me. Talk to me. What did I do wrong?"

"Ugh!" She looked at the ceiling. "You didn't do anything wrong! We do things wrong together."

Kaitlyn emerged from the stairwell with a bowl of potato chips. She crunched one into her mouth and stood there, watching us.

"Do you mind?" I yelled.

"You want one?" she asked, popping another potato chip in her mouth.

"We're in the middle of something here."

She turned to look at us, as if she hadn't heard the telltale sounds of Amy stomping my heart into dust yet again. "Oh crap," she gasped. "Are you dumping him again?"

"Can you leave, please?" I said.

"What is it this time?" she said. "Is it the commentary during movies, 'cause that's annoying as hell, right?"

"Would you get out of here?"

She put her hands up, starting to back her way up the stairs. "Don't blame me. I tried to adjust your personality and you didn't listen." She got about two steps up before she turned. "Hey, Amy, we should hang out sometime."

Amy twitched. "Uh . . ."

I picked up the nearest foam sword and threw it at her. Foam swords are not especially aerodynamic, so it glided harmlessly through the air and dropped to the ground about ten feet away from her.

"All right, whatever. I'll be upstairs if you need me."

Amy and I stood there for a moment, a few feet apart. I could hear my parents talking upstairs, as if everything was normal and I wasn't getting crushed once again. The air turned cold.

"Please read the letter, Craig." She shoved it into my hands, which were losing all feeling.

I tried a joke. "Does it say 'Just kidding'?"

But it didn't. She had put it in an envelope, and from the weight of it, it felt like half a novel.

"I think I preferred it when you dumped me in the middle of the woods."

Amy gave a halfhearted smile, like she appreciated my attempt at humor and was duly sorry that I was not terribly funny.

I tried to keep going, even though it felt like I was swimming through mud. "Actually, I prefer it when you don't dump me at all. Those are the best days. You know this isn't going to stick, right? You've already dumped me four times—"

"Three times."

"I think it's four."

"Three."

"I'm counting the thing two and a half weeks ago. Fine, three, whatever. You've dumped me three times and it hasn't stuck yet. So that's . . . that's just . . . you obviously are addicted to me like some kind of heroin addict . . . whatever it is I got"—I spread my arms out in a feeble show of bravado; I was highly conscious of the fact that I was in a dingy basement. With a crappy TV, faux-wood paneling, and an embarrassing collection of little monster figurines—"you can't get enough."

I paused. One eyelid stopped working. *This is a stroke. I think I'm having a stroke. Maybe if I die she'll change her mind. That's stupid, Craig. Why would she change her mind if you're dead? Then she can't go out with you at all.*

"Are you okay?" she asked.

"What?"

"You seem a little messed up."

"I'm getting dumped! And I'm probably having an aneurysm or something."

"I'm sorry."

"I would appreciate it in the future if you would stop breaking up with me." The words spilled out of my mouth like an avalanche of stupid. What did I think she was going to say to that?

Then she hugged me. The hug of death. The hug that meant *you're-such-a-great-guy-but-I'm-afraid-this-battle-station-will-be-fully-operational-by-the-time-your-friends-arrive.*

I held on. She patted my back like she was settling down an animal. I kept holding on.

"Craig."

"This sucks," I said.

"I know."

She let me go to arm's length and looked into my eyes. Her eyes were mostly blue, but not entirely blue; they faded to a kind of amber color near the edges. I used to think I would be looking into those eyes forever.

The world rocked a bit and went fuzzy at the edges. "Please read the letter," she said, and kissed me on the forehead.

Hours later, after she left, I took it out of the envelope. It was four pages long, on some kind of artisan paper that still contained tree bark and could only be found in specialty stationery shops in rural Maine. Her blue writing filled up the spaces like a long, spidery trail of doom. Amy was pretty seriously dyslexic, so misspellings abounded, but each one just reminded me how much I loved her. I read about two lines and then set it down as my world fell apart for the fifth time.

DON ZOLIDIS

grew up in Wisconsin, went to college in Minnesota, and is mostly known for being a really funny playwright. For the past five years, he's been the most-produced playwright in American schools. His more than one hundred published plays have been performed tens of thousands of times and have appeared in sixty-four different countries. He currently splits his time between New York and Texas, and has two adorable boys who will someday read this book and have a lot of questions. He aspires to owning a dog. He is the author of *War and Speech* and *The Seven Torments of Amy and Craig (A Love Story)*.